G. BERNARD SHAW

was born in Dublin in 1856, the product of an unhappy marriage which led his mother to follow a 'daringly original teacher of music', Vandeleur Lee, to London in 1873. Shaw followed three years later, a young man with two dominant characteristics: the passion of laughter, and a passion for reform.

Shaw's progress in London was dismayingly slow and he calculated that in the first nine years he earned less than ten pounds. This income was not contributed to by the five novels he wrote between 1879 and 1883 of which *An Unsocial Socialist* written last—in 1883—was published first. His other novels, in order of writing, were: *Immaturity, The Irrational Knot, Love Among The Artists,* and *Cashel Byron's Profession.*

In 1884 he joined the Fabian Society and with Sidney Webb formulated the political theories of this group. Shaw believed in the abolition of private property, the introduction of equality of income, the coupled vote and the de-mystification of relationships between men and women. He devoted a great deal of time to speaking at street corners, serving on committees and writing tracts, pamphlets and books, the most notable of which is *The Intelligent Woman's Guide To Socialism and Capitalism* (1928).

In 1885 Shaw began his celebrated career as critic and journalist. Seven years later his first play *Widower's Houses* was performed. Perhaps the most famous of over fifty plays that followed are *Arms and the Man* (1894); *Candida* (1894); *You Never Can Tell* (1895); *The Devil's Disciple* (1901); *Man and Superman* (1903); *The Doctor's Dilemma* (1906); *Pygmalion* (1913); and *St Joan* (1924).

In 1925 Shaw was awarded the Nobel Prize for literature. He refused a peerage and the Order of Merit from the first Labour Government.

Shaw married Charlotte Payne-Townsend, also Irish, and a Fabian, in 1898. They lived at Ayot St Lawrence in Hertfordshire until her death in 1943 and his in 1950.

VIRAGO
is a feminist publishing company:

"It is only when women start to organize
in large numbers that we become a
political force, and begin to move towards
the possibility of a truly democratic society
in which every human being can be brave,
responsible, thinking and diligent in the struggle
to live at once freely and unselfishly"

SHEILA ROWBOTHAM

VIRAGO
Advisory Group

AN UNSOCIAL SOCIALIST
BY BERNARD SHAW

A NOVEL

WITH AN INTRODUCTION BY
MICHAEL HOLROYD

Virago
London

Published by VIRAGO Limited 1980
5 Wardour Street, London W1V 3HE

First published 1884

An Unsocial Socialist © 1950 and new
Shaw text in Introduction © 1980, The
Bernard Shaw Estate, The Trustees of
the British Museum, The Governors and
Guardians of the National Gallery of Ireland
and Royal Academy of Dramatic Art.

Introduction Copyright © Michael Holroyd 1980

ISBN 0 86068 134 3

Printed at The Anchor Press Ltd
and bound by Wm Brendon & Son Ltd
both of Tiptree, Essex

INTRODUCTION

When Shaw came to London in 1876 at the age of almost twenty, he believed that he had turned his back on failure, poverty, obscurity, ostracism and contempt—which was "all that Dublin offered to the enormity of my unconscious ambition". Like most Irishmen he claimed to dislike most Irishmen, but he had not crossed the Channel for love of the English. He came to plunder the invader who had made Dublin useless to him. Armed with the English language he proposed to advance upon London as the capital of Literature, Art and Music, and set himself up as "a professional man of genius". Nine years later he calculated that he had made a little under ten pounds and produced, besides a mass of miscellaneous journalism, five long novels that had been turned down by almost every publisher in Britain and a number in America.

An Unsocial Socialist, originally called *The Heartless Man*, was the last and most ambitious of these novels. Shaw wrote it during 1883 in the Reading Room of the British Museum, first in shorthand and then transcribing it into longhand for the publishers. The plot revolves round Sidney Trefusis, the heartless socialist of both titles. At the beginning of the book, Trefusis shocks everyone by running away from his newly-married wife for the highly serious reason that he is in love with her and, even worse, she is beautiful and loves him. By society's standards it had been a brilliant match, full of money and romance. But society's standards have made women into a class of person fit only to be surrounded by children and flowers. With a man like Trefusis they can have no connection at all, except sex. Unfortunately the sexual attraction between Trefusis and his bemused wife Henrietta is strong—so strong, Trefusis gravely explains, that "our intercourse hinders our usefulness . . . the first condition of work with me is your absence. When you are with me I can do nothing but make love to you. You bewitch me."

Trefusis's work is the promotion of socialism. As Shaw's mouthpiece for neo-Marxism, he has a simple message that no one understands. The artificial inequality strangling the human spirit, and particularly the human spirit in women, will vanish, he declares, once "England is made the property of its inhabitants collectively". The choice was "Socialism or Smash".

To open people's eyes to socialism British socialists needed to study the romantic aspect of the movement, for it was women who, by giving a cause respectability, could make it grow. Shaw's women are sympathetically drawn but, as custodians of Society's standards, they embellish the Capitalist philosophy of Smash. Trefusis's aim, whether through sermonizing, flirtation or romantic insincerity, is to head them off from this course. He tries to nerve the instinctive part of them (their "souls") against their formal and affected selves. It is the old struggle to release natural vitality from a maimed and unnatural system of morality. The most attractive of these girls for whose socialist souls he wrestles is Gertrude Lindsay – Shaw's portrait of his girl friend Alice Lockett. Gertrude's father, Trefusis discovers, suffers from what country people call "the evil".

" 'Scrofulous ulcers!' he exclaimed, recoiling. 'The father of that beautiful girl!' He turned homeward, and trudged along with his head bent, muttering, 'All rotten to the bone. Oh, civilization! civilization! civilization!' "

From such disgust springs his passion for curing mankind. Prudently it is not Gertrude with her capitalist blight who becomes Trefusis's second wife, but Agatha Wylie—a girl who did not exist except in Shaw's imagination where she had been conceived from a glimpse of "a young lady with an attractive and arresting expression, bold, vivid, and very clever, working at one of the desks" in the British Museum Reading Room. Within the novel she has two advantages: she is not in love with Trefusis and she retains in her nature more of the uncorrupted child. Though as yet without substance, she is a herald of the New Woman.

But Trefusis is also affected by the society in which he lives. "He came out of me a liar, just as I came out of the womb of Nature what I am and not otherwise," Shaw wrote.

. . . Trefusis is only a liar as the novelist or the comedian is a liar. His bad side is the side on which he is an incorrigible mountebank; but his burlesques are burlesques of shams, unintentionally satirical and destructive—burlesque of the sham laborer and the sham lover of middle class romance. Have you noted, too, that it is always his terrible truth telling, and never his lying, that gets him into trouble.

By separating his socialist hero into two people, Shaw reflected the division he felt existed in his own character. Trefusis, the son of a millionaire, wishes to break all connection with his class and the society of exploitation that has made him rich. Some of the most entertaining pages of the novel are those where he becomes an insufferably talkative low comedian of a labourer—a Dickensian character called Smilash (a compound of the words smile and eyelash). In this partnership, Shaw the comedian and Shaw the reformer are brought together for the same ends. The character of Smilash appeals to the "vagabond impulse" in Trefusis, and the actor in Shaw.

Trefusis is Shaw's first socialist hero and Don Juan figure in whom he attempts to reconcile his sexual and political attitudes. The novel foreshadows *Man and Superman*, for Trefusis is a prototype of Tanner. Shaw was to speak of socialism as having given him a "religion". From the hour of his conversion, he wrote, "I became a man with some business in the world." He used this business like a magnet to shift his various contradictory impulses into new shapes, and line them up towards a political end. Within himself this achieved a harmony: but as a saviour of mankind Trefusis is largely unemployable. His ineffectiveness, like that of Tanner, is fixed in the futility of "Talking!" and the *"Universal laughter"* rather than action that it prompts.

Shaw had planned a novel of much greater length and larger scope "depicting capitalist society in dissolution, with its downfall as the final grand catastrophe". But having completed the first section, two monstrous chapters long, he found himself "too young for the job" and submitted the three hundred and thirty-six manuscript pages of *An Unsocial Socialist* as a complete novel.

It was an extraordinary book to have produced in the early 1880s—'the first English novel written under the influence of Karl Marx with a hero whose character and opinions forecast those of Lenin," Shaw later declared. He finished his revisions on 15 December 1883 and sent it five days later to Kegan Paul, Trench & Co. "It appears to us written in good style and language," they replied in their letter of rejection, "but it suffers, in our opinion, from the fatal effect on a novel, of not being interesting." Smith Elder & Co., the second publisher to read it, agreed: "We are afraid that the subscribers to the circulating libraries are not much interested in Socialism." David Douglas of Edinburgh and Chatto & Windus in London excused themselves from looking at it. For Macmillan, John Morley (who had previously advised Shaw to give up writing) reported that it was a Ruskinian "*jeu d'esprit*, or satire, with a good stroke of socialist meaning in it . . . The story is designedly paradoxical, absurd and impossible, as if it were one of Peacock's. But whoever he may be, the author knows how to write; he is pointed, rapid, forcible, sometimes witty, often powerful and occasionally eloquent." But, Morley concluded, the socialistic irony would not be attractive to many readers and it was "too clever" for the general public: "they would not know whether the writer was serious or was laughing at them." In refusing the book, Macmillan wrote that they would be glad to look at anything else he might write "of a more substantial kind" – a request that, Shaw replied, "takes my breath away". In his correspondence with Macmillan, he came as near making an exasperated appeal for sympathy as he could.

> All my readers, as far as I know them, like the book; but they tell me that although they relish it they don't think the general public would. Which is the more discouraging, as this tendency of each man to consider himself unique is one of the main themes of the novel. Surely out of thirty millions of copyright persons (so to speak) there must be a few thousand who would keep me in bread and cheese for the sake of my story-telling, if you would only let me get at them.

It was not the publisher but his new political friends who were to give Shaw his chance of getting at the public. What other novelist would allow his hero, pursued by an angry headmistress, two parsons and a posse of policemen, to stop and lecture his wife for some fifteen pages on Marx's theory of surplus value?

INTRODUCTION

It was too good a chance to miss. Instead of adding it to the pile of four other novels that the publishers had rejected, Shaw sent off his aborted *magnum opus* to J. L. Joynes, one of the editors of *To-Day*, a new "Monthly Magazine of Scientific Socialism". Joynes recommended serialisation of the novel to his fellow editor, the philosopher E. Belfort Bax, who replied: "Go on and prosper with Shaw . . ."

An Unsocial Socialist appeared in serial form between March and December 1884. Shaw was not paid, but for the first time he had an audience. "William Morris spotted it and made my acquaintance on account of it," he wrote. "That took me into print and started me."

Once his novels began to be printed, publishers finally woke up to them. America produced a number of enterprising piratical editions, while in Britain publication was handled more traditionally. "Your book has definitely been published some time," the firm of Swan Sonnenschein (nicknamed Moonschein) hazarded. In fact they had published *An Unsocial Socialist* in 1887, two years after acceptance and in an edition the early copies of which misspelt the publisher's own name and, on the title page, recommended Shaw as "Author of 'The Confessions of Byron Cashel's Profession,' etc., etc."—an excellent reason, Shaw warned collectors, "for pitching it into the fire." As for *Cashel Byron's Profession* itself, "I have never seen an advertisement," he informed the British publisher, "never met a human being who had ever seen one, never expect to meet one."

Shaw's political interests had devoured his ambitions as a novelist, but though he took only a remote interest in these works, claiming that they had sprung to life despite all his efforts to suppress them, he couldn't resist improving them a little and he extensively revised and augmented *An Unsocial Socialist* for its publication in book form. These revisions, amounting to several thousand words, were designed not to change its meaning but to make that meaning more clear.

By 1888 he had decided that his "book-writing days are over, unluckily . . . I should not know how to write a novel now." This disenchantment with writing novels is already apparent in *An Unsocial Socialist*. In the 1887 appendix to this book, which

INTRODUCTION

takes the form of a letter to the author from Trefusis, Shaw writes:

> I cannot help feeling that, in presenting the facts in the guise of fiction, you have, in spite of yourself, shown them in a false light. Actions described in novels are judged by a romantic system of morals as fictitious as the actions themselves.

Now that it was too late, publishers were urging him to go on. His books would work into a good circulation, Swan Sonnenschein told him, providing he "stick to novels, or go in for plays (which are even more suited to you, in my opinion) . . ." Shaw acknowledged that he might "descend as low as that one day", but five failures had been "enough to satisfy my appetite for enterprise in fiction" and it was not surprising that "I found nothing new for me to do in that direction". He was sick of the world of literature, fiction, publishers. The novelist was a "voluptuary in labor", he wrote in *An Unsocial Socialist*.

> Nine out of ten of them are diseased creatures, just sane enough to trade on their own neuroses. The only quality of theirs which exhorts my respect is a certain sublime selfishness which makes them willing to starve and let their families starve sooner than do any work they don't like.

Hesketh Pearson, adapting a remark of Oscar Wilde's, wrote that "there are two ways of disliking the works of Bernard Shaw: one way is to dislike them, the other is to like his novels"—the truth of which was to be demonstrated by George Orwell's attack on Shaw ("he has squandered what talents he may have had back in the '80s . . . Shaw's best work was one or two early novels . . . "). But his career as a novelist, as he himself said, "ended before it had begun". Although they carry many ideas that were to be developed in his plays, these novels seemed to Shaw to have been written by someone else—someone with his roots in Ireland who once upon a time dreamed of a grand literary conquest in London. That Shaw was almost dead, and the journalist who was about to be born in his place would write anonymously, under various pseudonyms, and finally as G.B.S.

Michael Holroyd, 1979

FOREWORD

THIS, the last of the Novels Of My Nonage, is, according to my original design, only the first chapter of a vast work depicting capitalist society in dissolution, with its downfall as the final grand catastrophe. But when I had finished my chapter I found I had emptied my sack and left myself no more to say for the moment, and had better defer completion until my education was considerably more advanced. Thirty-seven years having now been devoted to this process it is too late to resume the interrupted work; for events have outrun me. The contemplated fiction is now fact. My unsocial socialist has come to life as a Bolshevist; and my catastrophe has actually occurred in Communist Russia. The opinions of the fictitious Trefusis anticipated those of the real Lenin.

With the writing of this book my career as a novelist may be said to have ended before it had begun. As I have explained in the preface to Immaturity I employed myself in novel writing because nobody would employ me in any other sort of writing. It happened that just when I came to a standstill at the end of my first chapter as aforesaid my late friend William Archer pushed me into critical journalism by handing over to me certain jobs of his own for which he had little time and less inclination. I easily made good at criticism, which enabled me to make a living until, about ten years later, I discovered my main vocation in the profession of Shakespear and Molière, and thus returned to storytelling in its most highly specialized form.

I am not now likely to go back to novel writing. The novels of my nonage do not seem to me to call for a series of novels of my dotage. Their style seems quaintly oldfashioned nowadays; but fifty years hence my latest works will be indistinguishable from them in that respect. So, leaving them, with many apologies, to find what readers they can, I hasten on to the plays which succeeded them after that long interval during which I had left my novitiate behind and passed into middle age with its experiences and its freedom from the technical shyness of the beginner. In short, I had become, for better for worse, a different man.

G. B. S.

Ayot St Lawrence,
  18*th February* 1930.

AN UNSOCIAL SOCIALIST

CHAPTER I

In the dusk of an October evening, a sensible-looking woman of forty came out through an oaken door to a broad landing on the first floor of an old English country-house. A braid of her hair had fallen forward as if she had been stooping over book or pen; and she stood for a moment to smooth it, and to gaze contemplatively—not in the least sentimentally—through the tall, narrow window. The sun was setting, but its glories were at the other side of the house; for this window looked eastward, where the landscape of sheepwalks and pasture land was sobering at the approach of darkness.

The lady, like one to whom silence and quiet were luxuries, lingered on the landing for some time. Then she turned towards another door, on which was inscribed, in white letters, CLASS ROOM No. 6. Arrested by a whispering above, she paused in the doorway, and looked up the stairs along a broad smooth handrail that swept round in an unbroken curve at each landing, forming an inclined plane from the top to the bottom of the house.

A young voice, apparently mimicking some one, now came from above, saying:

"We will take the Études de la Vélocité next, if you please, ladies."

Immediately a girl in a holland dress shot down through space; whirled round the curve with a fearless centrifugal toss of her ankle; and vanished into the darkness beneath. She was followed by a stately girl in green, intently holding her breath as she flew; and also by a large young woman in black with her lower lip grasped between her teeth, and her fine brown eyes protruding with excitement. Her passage created a miniature tempest which disarranged anew the hair of the lady on the landing, who waited in breathless alarm until two light shocks and a thump announced that the aerial voyagers had landed safely in the hall.

"Oh law!" exclaimed the voice that had spoken before. "Here's Susan."

"It's a mercy your neck aint broken," replied some palpitating female. "I'll tell of you this time, Miss Wylie; indeed I will. And you, too, Miss Carpenter: I wonder at you not to have more sense at your age and with your size! Miss Wilson cant help hearing when you come down with a thump like that. You shake the whole house."

"Oh bother!" said Miss Wylie. "The Lady Abbess takes good care to shut out all the noise we make. Let us—"

"Girls," said the lady above, calling down quietly, but with ominous distinctness.

Silence and utter confusion ensued. Then came a reply, in a tone of honeyed sweetness, from Wylie:

"Did you call us, *dear* Miss Wilson?"

"Yes. Come up here, if you please, all three."

There was some hesitation among them, each offering the other precedence. At last, they went up slowly, in the order, though not at all in the manner, of their flying descent; followed Miss Wilson into the class-room; and stood in a row before her, illumined through three western windows with a glow of ruddy orange light.

Miss Carpenter, the largest of the three, was red and confused. Her arms hung by her sides, her fingers twisting the folds of her dress. Miss Gertrude Lindsay, in pale sea-green, had a small head, delicate complexion, and pearly teeth. She stood erect, with an expression of cold distaste for reproof of any sort. The holland dress of the third offender had changed from yellow to white as she passed from the grey eastern twilight on the staircase into the warm western glow in the room. Her face had a bright olive tone, and seemed to have a golden mica in its composition. Her eyes and hair were hazel-nut color; and her teeth, the upper row of which she displayed freely, were like fine Portland stone, and sloped outward enough to have spoilt her mouth, had they not been supported by a rich under lip, and a finely curved, impudent chin. Her half cajoling, half mocking air, and her ready smile, were difficult to confront with severity; and Miss Wilson knew it; for she would not look at her even when attracted by a convulsive start and an angry side glance from Miss Lindsay, who had just been indented between the ribs by a finger tip.

"You are aware that you have broken the rules," said Miss Wilson quietly.

"We didnt intend to. We really did not," said the girl in holland coaxingly.

"Pray what was your intention then, Miss Wylie?"

Miss Wylie unexpectedly treated this as a smart repartee instead of a rebuke. She sent up a strange little scream, which exploded in a cascade of laughter.

"Pray be silent, Agatha," said Miss Wilson severely. Agatha looked contrite. Miss Wilson turned hastily to the eldest of the three, and continued:

"I am especially surprised at you, Miss Carpenter. Since you have no desire to keep faith with me by upholding the rules, of which you are quite old enough to understand the necessity, I shall not trouble you with reproaches, or appeals to which I am now convinced that you would not respond" (here Miss Carpenter, with an inarticulate protest, burst into tears); "but you should at least think of the danger into which your juniors are led by your childishness. How should you feel if Agatha had broken her neck?"

"Oh!" exclaimed Agatha, putting her hand quickly to her neck.

"I didnt think there was any danger," said Miss Carpenter, struggling with her tears. "Agatha has done it so oft—oh dear! you have torn me." Miss Wylie had pulled at her schoolfellow's skirt, and pulled too hard.

"Miss Wylie," said Miss Wilson, flushing slightly, "I must ask you to leave the room."

"Oh, no," exclaimed Agatha, clasping her hands in distress. "Please dont, dear Miss Wilson. I am so sorry. I beg your pardon."

3

"Since you will not do what I ask, I must go myself," said Miss Wilson sternly. "Come with me to my study," she added to the two other girls. "If you attempt to follow, Miss Wylie, I shall regard it as an intrusion."

"But I will go away if you wish it. I didnt mean to diso—"

"I shall not trouble you now. Come, girls."

The three went out; and Miss Wylie, left behind in disgrace, made a surpassing grimace at Miss Lindsay, who glanced back at her. When she was alone, her vivacity subsided. She went slowly to the window, and gazed disparagingly at the landscape. Once, when a sound of voices above reached her, her eyes brightened, and her ready lip moved; but the next silent moment she relapsed into moody indifference, which was not relieved until her two companions, looking very serious, re-entered.

"Well," she said gaily, "has moral force been applied? Are you going to the Recording Angel?"

"Hush, Agatha," said Miss Carpenter. "You ought to be ashamed of yourself."

"No, but you ought, you goose. A nice row you have got me into!"

"It was your own fault. You tore my dress."

"Yes, when you were blurting out that I sometimes slide down the banisters."

"Oh!" said Miss Carpenter slowly, as if this reason had not occurred to her before. "Was that why you pulled me?"

"Dear me! It has actually dawned upon you. You are a most awfully silly girl, Jane. What did the Lady Abbess say?"

Miss Carpenter again gave her tears way, and could not reply.

"She is disgusted with us, and no wonder," said Miss Lindsay.

"She said it was all your fault," sobbed Miss Carpenter.

"Well, never mind, dear," said Agatha soothingly. "Put it in the Recording Angel."

"I wont write a word in the Recording Angel unless you do so first," said Miss Lindsay angrily. "You are more in fault than we are."

"Certainly, my dear," replied Agatha. "A whole page, if you

4

wish."

"I b-believe you *like* writing in the Recording Angel," said Miss Carpenter spitefully.

"Yes, Jane. It is the best fun the place affords."

"It may be fun to you," said Miss Lindsay sharply; "but it is not very creditable to me, as Miss Wilson said just now, to take a prize in moral science and then have to write down that I dont know how to behave myself. Besides, I do not like to be told that I am ill-bred!"

Agatha laughed. "What a deep old thing she is! She knows all our weaknesses, and stabs at us through them. Catch her telling me, or Jane there, that we are ill-bred!"

"I dont understand you," said Miss Lindsay haughtily.

"Of course not. That's because you dont know as much moral science as I, though I never took a prize in it."

"You never took a prize in anything," said Miss Carpenter.

"And I hope I never shall," said Agatha. "I would as soon scramble for hot pennies in the snow, like the street boys, as scramble to see who can answer most questions. Dr Watts is enough moral science for me. Now for the Recording Angel."

She went to a shelf and took down a heavy quarto, bound in black leather, and inscribed, in red letters, MY FAULTS. This she threw irreverently on a desk, and tossed its pages over until she came to one only partly covered with manuscript confessions.

"For a wonder," she said, "here are two entries that are not mine. Sarah Gerram! What has she been confessing?"

"Dont read it," said Miss Lindsay quickly. "You know that it is the most dishonorable thing any of us can do."

"Pooh! Our little sins are not worth making such a fuss about. I always like to have my entries read: it makes me feel like an author; and so in Christian duty I always read other people's. Listen to poor Sarah's tale of guilt. '1st October. I am very sorry that I slapped Miss Chambers in the lavatory this morning, and knocked out one of her teeth. This was very wicked; but it was coming out by itself; and she has forgiven me because a new one will come in its place; and she was only pretending when she said she swallowed it. Sarah Gerram.' "

"Little fool!" said Miss Lindsay. "The idea of our having to record in the same book with brats like that!"

"Here is a touching revelation. '4th October. Helen Plantagenet is deeply grieved to have to confess that I took the first place in algebra yesterday unfairly. Miss Lindsay prompted me; and—' "

"Oh!" exclaimed Miss Lindsay, reddening. "That is how she thanks me for prompting her, is it? How dare she confess *my* faults in the Recording Angel?"

"Serves you right for prompting her," said Miss Carpenter. "She was always a double-faced cat; and you ought to have known better."

"Oh, I assure you it was not for her sake that I did it," replied Miss Lindsay. "It was to prevent that Jackson girl from getting first place. I dont like Helen Plantagenet; but at least she is a lady."

"Stuff, Gertrude," said Agatha, with a touch of earnestness. "One would think, to hear you talk, that your grandmother was a cook. Dont be such a snob."

"Miss Wylie," said Gertrude, becoming scarlet: "you are very —oh! oh! Stop Ag—oh! I will tell Miss W—oh!" Agatha had inserted a steely finger between her ribs, and was tickling her unendurably.

"Sh-sh-sh," whispered Miss Carpenter anxiously. "The door is open."

"Am I Miss Wylie?" demanded Agatha, relentlessly continuing the torture. "Am I very—whatever you were going to say? Am I—? am I—? am I?"

"No, no," gasped Gertrude, shrinking into a chair, almost in hysterics. "You are very unkind, Agatha. You have hurt me."

"You deserve it. If you ever get sulky with me again, or call me Miss Wylie, I will *kill* you. I will tickle the soles of your feet with a feather" (Miss Lindsay shuddered, and hid her feet beneath the chair) "until your hair turns white. And now, if you are truly repentant, come and record."

"You must record first. It was all your fault."

"But I am the youngest," said Agatha.

"Well, then," said Gertrude, afraid to press the point, but determined not to record first, "let Jane Carpenter begin. She is the eldest."

"Oh, of course," said Jane, with whimpering irony. "Let Jane do all the nasty things first. I think it's very hard. You fancy that Jane is a fool; but she isnt."

"You are certainly not such a fool as you look, Jane," said Agatha gravely. "But I will record first, if you like."

"No, you shant," cried Jane, snatching the pen from her. "I am the eldest; and I wont be put out of my place."

She dipped the pen in the ink resolutely, and prepared to write. Then she paused; considered; looked bewildered; and at last appealed piteously to Agatha.

"*What* shall I write?" she said. "You know how to write things down; and I dont."

"First put the date," said Agatha.

"To be sure," said Jane, writing it quickly. "I forgot that. Well?"

"Now write, 'I am very sorry that Miss Wilson saw me when I slid down the banisters this evening. Jane Carpenter.' "

"Is that all?"

"Thats all: unless you wish to add something of your own composition."

"I hope it's all right," said Jane, looking suspiciously at Agatha. "However, there cant be any harm in it; for it's the simple truth. Anyhow, if you are playing one of your jokes on me, you are a nasty mean thing, and I dont care. Now, Gertrude, it's your turn. Please look at mine, and see whether the spelling is right."

"It is not my business to teach you to spell," said Gertrude, taking the pen. And, while Jane was murmuring at her churlishness, she wrote in a bold hand:

"I have broken the rules by sliding down the banisters to-day, with Miss Carpenter and Miss Wylie. Miss Wylie went first."

"You wretch!" exclaimed Agatha, reading over her shoulder. "And *your* father is an admiral!"

"I think it is only fair," said Miss Lindsay, quailing, but assuming the tone of a moralist. "It is perfectly true."

"All my money was made in trade," said Agatha; "but I should be ashamed to save myself by shifting blame to your aristocratic shoulders. You pitiful thing! Here: give me the pen."

"I will strike it out if you wish; but I think—"

"No: it shall stay there to witness against you. Now see how I confess my faults." And she wrote, in a fine, rapid hand:

"This evening Gertrude Lindsay and Jane Carpenter met me at the top of the stairs, and said they wanted to slide down the banisters and would do so if I went first. I told them that it was against the rules, but they said that did not matter; and as they are older than I am, I allowed myself to be persuaded, and slid."

"What do you think of that?" said Agatha, displaying the page. They read it, and protested clamorously.

"It is perfectly true," said Agatha solemnly.

"It's beastly mean," said Jane energetically. "The idea of your finding fault with Gertrude, and then going and being twice as bad yourself! I never heard of such a thing in my life."

" 'Thus bad begins; but worse remains behind,' as the Standard Elocutionist says," said Agatha, adding another sentence to her confession.

"But it was all my fault. Also I was rude to Miss Wilson, and refused to leave the room when she bade me. I was not wilfully wrong except in sliding down the banisters. I am so fond of a slide that I could not resist the temptation."

"Be warned by me, Agatha," said Jane impressively. "If you write cheeky things in that book you will be expelled."

"Indeed!" replied Agatha significantly. "Wait until Miss Wilson sees what *you* have written."

"Gertrude," cried Jane, with sudden misgiving, "has she made me write anything improper? Agatha, *do* tell me if—"

Here a gong sounded; and the three girls simultaneously exclaimed "Grub!" and rushed from the room.

CHAPTER II

ONE sunny afternoon, a hansom drove at great speed along Belsize Avenue, St John's Wood, and stopped before a large mansion. A young lady sprang out; ran up the steps; and rang the bell impatiently. She was of the olive complexion, with a sharp profile: dark eyes with long lashes; narrow mouth with delicately sensuous lips; small head, feet, and hands, with long taper fingers; lithe and very slender figure moving with serpent-like grace. Oriental taste was displayed in the colors of her costume, which consisted of a white dress, close-fitting, and printed with an elaborate china blue pattern; a yellow straw hat covered with artificial hawthorn and scarlet berries; and tan-colored gloves reaching beyond the elbow, and decorated with a profusion of gold bangles.

The door not being opened immediately, she rang again, violently, and was presently admitted by a maid, who seemed surprised to see her. Without making any inquiry, she darted upstairs into a drawing room, where a matron of good presence, with features of the finest Jewish type, sat reading. With her was a handsome boy in black velvet, who said:

"Mamma, heres Henrietta!"

"Arthur," said the young lady excitedly, "leave the room this instant; and dont dare to come back until you get leave."

The boy's countenance fell, and he sulkily went out without a word.

"Is anything wrong?" said the matron, putting away her book with the unconcerned resignation of an experienced person who foresees a storm in a tea-cup. "Where is Sidney?"

"Gone! Gone! Deserted me! I—" The young lady's utterance failed, and she threw herself upon an ottoman, sobbing with passionate spite.

"Nonsense! I thought Sidney had more sense. There, Henrietta, dont be silly. I suppose you have quarrelled."

"No! No!! No!!!" cried Henrietta, stamping on the carpet.

9

"We had not a word. I have not lost my temper since we were married, mamma; I solemnly swear I have not. I will kill myself; there is no other way. Theres a curse on me. I am marked out to be miserable. He——"

"Tut, tut! What has happened, Henrietta? As you have been married now nearly six weeks, you can hardly be surprised at a little tiff arising. You are so excitable! You cannot expect the sky to be always cloudless. Most likely you are to blame; for Sidney is far more reasonable than you. Stop crying, and behave like a woman of sense, and I will go to Sidney and make everything right."

"But he's gone, and I cant find out where. Oh, what shall I do?"

"What has happened?"

Henrietta writhed with impatience. Then, forcing herself to tell her story, she answered:

"We arranged on Monday that I should spend two days with Aunt Judith instead of going with him to Birmingham to that horrid Trade Congress. We parted on the best of terms. He c—couldnt have been more affectionate. I will kill myself; I dont care about anything or anybody. And when I came back on Wednesday he was gone, and there was this lett—" She produced a letter, and wept more bitterly than before.

"Let me see it."

Henrietta hesitated, but her mother took the letter from her, sat down near the window, and composed herself to read without the least regard to her daughter's vehement distress. The letter ran thus:

"*Monday night.*

"My Dearest—I am off—surfeited with endearment—to live my own life and do my own work. I could only have prepared you for this by coldness or neglect, which are wholly impossible to me when the spell of your presence is upon me. I find that I must fly if I am to save myself.

"I am afraid that I cannot give you satisfactory and intelligible reasons for this step. You are a beautiful and luxurious creature:

life is to you full and complete only when it is a carnival of love. My case is just the reverse. Before three soft speeches have escaped me I rebuke myself for folly and insincerity. Before a caress has had time to cool, a strenuous revulsion seizes me: I long to return to my old lonely ascetic hermit life; to my dry books; my Socialist propagandism; my voyage of discovery through the wilderness of thought. I married in an insane fit of belief that I had a share of the natural affection which carries other men through lifetimes of matrimony. Already I am undeceived. You are to me the loveliest woman in the world. Well, for five weeks I have walked and talked and dallied with the loveliest woman in the world, and the upshot is that I am flying from her, and am for a hermit's cave until I die. Love cannot keep possession of me: all my strongest powers rise up against it and will not endure it. Forgive me for writing nonsense that you wont understand, and do not think too hardly of me. I have been as good to you as my selfish nature allowed. Do not seek to disturb me in the obscurity which I desire and deserve. My solicitor will call on your father to arrange business matters, and you shall be as happy as wealth and liberty can make you. We shall meet again—some day. Adieu, my last love,

"SIDNEY TREFUSIS."

"Well?" cried Mrs Trefusis, observing through her tears that her mother had read the letter and was contemplating it in a daze.

"Well, certainly!" said Mrs Jansenius, with emphasis. "Do you think he is quite sane, Henrietta? Or have you been plaguing him for too much attention? Men are not willing to give up their whole existence to their wives, even during the honeymoon."

"He pretended that he was never happy out of my presence," sobbed Henrietta. "There never was anything so cruel. I often wanted to be by myself for a change, but I was afraid to hurt his feelings by saying so. And now he has no feelings. But he *must* come back to me. Mustnt he, mamma?"

"He ought to. I suppose he has not gone away with any one?"

Henrietta sprang up, her cheeks vivid scarlet. "If I thought that I would pursue him to the end of the earth, and murder her. But no; he is not like anybody else. He hates me. Everybody hates me. You dont care whether I am deserted or not, nor papa, nor any one in this house."

Mrs Jansenius, still indifferent to her daughter's agitation, considered a moment, and then said placidly:

"You can do nothing until we hear from the solicitor. In the meantime you may stay with us, if you wish. I did not expect a visit from you so soon; but your room has not been used since you went away."

Mrs Trefusis ceased crying, chilled by this first intimation that her father's house was no longer her home. A more real sense of desolation came upon her. Under its cold influence she began to collect herself, and to feel her pride rising like a barrier between her and her mother.

"I wont stay long," she said. "If his solicitor will not tell me where he is, I will hunt through England for him. I am sorry to trouble you."

"Oh, you will be no greater trouble than you have always been," said Mrs Jansenius calmly, not displeased to see that her daughter had taken the hint. "You had better go and wash your face. People may call, and I presume you dont wish to receive them in that plight. If you meet Arthur on the stairs, please tell him he may come in."

Henrietta screwed her lips into a curious pout and withdrew. Arthur then came in and stood at the window in sullen silence, brooding over his recent expulsion. Suddenly he exclaimed: "Heres papa, and it's not five o'clock yet!" whereupon his mother sent him away again.

Mr Jansenius was a man of imposing presence, not yet in his fiftieth year, but not far from it. He moved with dignity, bearing himself as if the contents of his massive brow were precious. His handsome aquiline nose and keen dark eyes proclaimed his Jewish origin, of which he was ashamed. Those who did not know this naturally believed that he was proud of it, and were at a loss to account for his permitting his children to be educated as Christians. Well instructed in business, and subject to no emotion outside the love of family, respectability, comfort, and money, he had maintained the capital inherited from his father, and made it breed new capital in the usual way. He was a banker, and his object as such was to intercept and appropriate the immense saving which the banking system effects, and so, as far as possible, to leave the rest of the world working just as hard as before banking was introduced. But as the world would not on these terms have banked at all, he had to give them some of the saving as an inducement. So they profited by the saving as well as he, and he had the satisfaction of being at once a wealthy citizen and a public benefactor, rich in comforts and easy in conscience.

He entered the room quickly, and his wife saw that something had vexed him.

"Do you know what has happened, Ruth?" he said.

"Yes. She is upstairs."

Mr Jansenius stared. "Do you mean to say that she has left already?" he said. "What business has she to come here?"

"It is natural enough. Where else should she have gone?"

Mr Jansenius, who mistrusted his own judgment when it differed from that of his wife, replied slowly, "Why did she not go to her mother?"

Mrs Jansenius, puzzled in her turn, looked at him with cool wonder, and remarked, "I am her mother, am I not?"

"I was not aware of it. I am surprised to hear it, Ruth. Have you had a letter too?"

"I have seen the letter. But what do you mean by telling me that you do not know I am Henrietta's mother? Are you trying to be funny?"

"Henrietta! Is _she_ here? Is this some fresh trouble?"

"I dont know. What are you talking about?"

"I am talking about Agatha Wylie."

"Oh! I was talking about Henrietta."

"Well, what about Henrietta?"

"What about Agatha Wylie?"

At this Mr Jansenius became exasperated, and she deemed it best to relate what Henrietta had told her. When she gave him Trefusis's letter, he said, more calmly: "Misfortunes never come singly. Read that," and handed her another letter, so that they both began reading at the same time.

Mrs Jansenius read as follows:

"ALTON COLLEGE, LYVERN.

"*To Mrs Wylie, Acacia Lodge, Chiswick.*

"Dear Madam—I write with great regret to request that you will at once withdraw Miss Wylie from Alton College. In an establishment like this, where restraint upon the liberty of the students is reduced to a minimum, it is necessary that the small degree of subordination which is absolutely indispensable be acquiesced in by all without complaint or delay. Miss Wylie has failed to comply with this condition. She has declared her wish to leave, and has assumed an attitude towards myself and my colleagues which we cannot, consistently with our duty to ourselves and her fellow-students, pass over. If Miss Wylie has any cause to complain of her treatment here, or of the step which she has compelled us to take, she will doubtless make it known to you.

"Perhaps you will be so good as to communicate with Miss Wylie's guardian, Mr Jansenius, with whom I shall be happy to make an equitable arrangement respecting the fees which have been paid in advance for the current term.

"I am, dear madam, yours faithfully,

"MARIA WILSON."

"A nice young lady, that!" said Mrs Jansenius.

"I do not understand this," said Mr Jansenius, reddening as he took in the purport of his son-in-law's letter. "I will not submit to it. What does it mean, Ruth?"

"I dont know. Sidney is mad, I think; and his honeymoon has brought his madness out. But you must not let him throw Henrietta on my hands again."

"Mad! Does he think he can shirk his responsibility to his wife because she is my daughter? Does he think, because his mother's father was a baronet, that he can put Henrietta aside the moment her society palls on him?"

"Oh, it's nothing of that sort. He never thought of us."

"But I will make him think of us," said Mr Jansenius, raising his voice in great agitation. "He shall answer for it."

Just then Henrietta returned, and saw her father moving excitedly to and fro, repeating, "He shall answer to me for this. He shall answer for it."

Mrs Jansenius frowned at her daughter to remain silent, and said soothingly, "Dont lose your temper, John."

"But I will lose my temper. Insolent hound! Damned scoundrel!"

"He is *not*," whimpered Henrietta, sitting down and taking out her handkerchief.

"Oh, come, come!" said Mrs Jansenius peremptorily, "we have had enough crying. Let us have no more of it."

Henrietta sprang up in a passion. "I will say and do as I please," she exclaimed. "I am a married woman, and I will receive no orders. And I will have my husband back again, no matter what he does to hide himself. Papa, wont you make him come back to me? I am dying. Promise that you will make him come back."

And, throwing herself upon her father's bosom, she postponed further discussion by going into hysterics, and startling the household by her screams.

CHAPTER III

ONE of the professors at Alton College was a Mrs Miller, an old-fashioned schoolmistress who did not believe in Miss Wilson's system of government by moral force, and carried it out under protest. Though not ill-natured, she was narrow-minded enough to be in some degree contemptible, and was consequently prone to suspect others of despising her. She suspected Agatha in particular, and treated her with disdainful curtness in such intercourse as they had—it was fortunately little. Agatha was not hurt by this, for Mrs Miller was an unsympathetic woman, who made no friends among the girls, and satisfied her affectionate impulses by petting a large cat named Gracchus, but generally called Bacchus by an endearing modification of the harsh initial consonant.

One evening Mrs Miller, seated with Miss Wilson in the study, correcting examination papers, heard in the distance a cry like that of a cat in distress. She ran to the door and listened. Presently there arose a prolonged wail, slurring up through two octaves and subsiding again. It was a true feline screech, impossible to localize; but it was interrupted by a sob, a snarl, a fierce spitting, and a scuffling, coming unmistakably from a room on the floor beneath, in which, at that hour, the older girls assembled for study.

"My poor Gracchy!" exclaimed Mrs Miller, running downstairs as fast as she could. She found the room unusually quiet. Every girl was deep in study except Miss Carpenter, who, pretending to pick up a fallen book, was purple with suppressed laughter and the congestion caused by stooping.

"Where is Miss Ward?" demanded Mrs Miller.

"Miss Ward has gone for some astronomical diagrams in which we are interested," said Agatha, looking up gravely. Just then Miss Ward, diagrams in hand, entered.

"Has that cat been in here?" she said, not seeing Mrs Miller, and speaking in a tone expressive of antipathy to Gracchus.

Agatha started and drew up her ankles, as if fearful of having them bitten. Then, looking apprehensively under the desk, she replied, "There is no cat here, Miss Ward."

"There is one somewhere; I heard it," said Miss Ward carelessly, unrolling her diagrams, which she began to explain without further parley. Mrs Miller, anxious for her pet, hastened to seek it elsewhere. In the hall she met one of the housemaids.

"Susan," she said, "have you seen Gracchus?"

"He's asleep on the hearthrug in your room, maam."

"But I heard him crying down here a moment ago. I feel sure that another cat has got in, and that they are fighting."

Susan smiled compassionately. "Lor bless you, maam," she said, "that was Miss Wylie. It's a sort of play-acting that she goes through. There is the bee on the window-pane, and the soldier up the chimley, and the cat under the dresser. She does them all like life."

"The soldier in the chimney!" repeated Mrs Miller, shocked.

"Yes, maam. Like as it were a follower that had hid there when he heard the mistress coming."

Mrs Miller's face set determinedly. She returned to the study and related what had just occurred, adding some sarcastic comments on the efficacy of moral force in maintaining collegiate discipline. Miss Wilson looked grave; considered for some time; and at last said: "I must think this over. Would you mind leaving it in my hands for the present?"

Mrs Miller said that she did not care in whose hands it remained provided her own were washed of it, and resumed her work at the papers. Miss Wilson then, wishing to be alone, went into the empty class-room at the other side of the landing. She took the Fault Book from its shelf and sat down before it. Its record closed with the announcement, in Agatha's handwriting:

"Miss Wilson has called me impertinent, and has written to my uncle that I have refused to obey the rules. I was not impertinent; and I never refused to obey the rules. So much for Moral Force!"

Miss Wilson rose vigorously, exclaiming: "I will soon let her know whether——" She checked herself, and looked round hastily, superstitiously fancying that Agatha might have stolen into the room unobserved. Reassured that she was alone, she examined her conscience as to whether she had done wrong in calling Agatha impertinent, justifying herself by the reflection that Agatha had, in fact, been impertinent. Yet she recollected that she had refused to admit this plea on a recent occasion when Jane Carpenter had advanced it in extenuation of having called a fellow-student a liar. Had she then been unjust to Jane, or inconsiderate to Agatha?

Her casuistry was interrupted by some one softly whistling a theme from the overture to Masaniello, popular at the college in the form of an arrangement for six pianofortes and twelve hands. There was only one student unladylike and musical enough to whistle; and Miss Wilson was ashamed to find herself growing nervous at the prospect of an encounter with Agatha, who entered whistling sweetly, but with a lugubrious countenance. When she saw in whose presence she stood, she begged pardon politely, and was about to withdraw, when Miss Wilson, summoning all her judgment and tact, and hoping that they would—contrary to their custom in emergencies—respond to the summons, said:

"Agatha, come here. I want to speak to you."

Agatha closed her lips, drew in a long breath through her nostrils, and marched to within a few feet of Miss Wilson, where she halted with her hands clasped before her.

"Sit down."

Agatha sat down with a single movement, like a doll.

"I dont understand that, Agatha," said Miss Wilson, pointing to the entry in the Recording Angel. "What does it mean?"

"I am unfairly treated," said Agatha, with signs of agitation.

"In what way?"

"In *every* way. I am expected to be something more than mortal. Every one else is encouraged to complain, and to be weak and silly. But I must have no feeling. I must be always in the right. Every one else may be home-sick, or huffed, or in low spirits. I must have no nerves, and must keep others laughing all day long. Every one else may sulk when a word of reproach is addressed to them, and may make the professors afraid to find fault with them. I have to bear with the insults of teachers who have less self-control than I, a girl of seventeen! and must coax them out of the difficulties they make for themselves by their own ill-temper."

"But, Agatha—"

"Oh, I know I am talking nonsense, Miss Wilson; but can you expect me to be always sensible—to be infallible?"

"Yes, Agatha; I do not think it is too much to expect you to be always sensible; and—"

"Then you have neither sense nor sympathy yourself," said Agatha.

There was an awful pause. Neither could have told how long it lasted. Then Agatha, feeling that she must do or say something desperate, or else fly, made a distracted gesture and ran out of the room.

She rejoined her companions in the great hall of the mansion, where they were assembled after study for "recreation," a noisy process which always set in spontaneously when the professors withdrew. She usually sat with her two favorite associates on a high window seat near the hearth. That place was now occupied by a little girl with flaxen hair, whom Agatha, regardless of moral force, lifted by the shoulders and deposited on the floor. Then she sat down and said:

"Oh, *such* a piece of news!"

Miss Carpenter opened her eyes eagerly. Gertrude Lindsay affected indifference.

"Some one is going to be expelled," said Agatha.

"Expelled! Who?"

"You will know soon enough, Jane," replied Agatha, suddenly grave. "It is some one who made an impudent entry in the Recording Angel."

Fear stole upon Jane, and she became very red. "Agatha," she said, "it was you who told me what to write. You know you did, and you cant deny it."

"I cant deny it, cant I? I am ready to *swear* that I never dictated a word to you in my life."

"Gertrude knows you did," exclaimed Jane, appalled, and almost in tears.

"There," said Agatha, petting her as if she were a vast baby. "It shall not be expelled, so it shant. Have you seen the Recording Angel lately, either of you?"

"Not since our last entry," said Gertrude.

"Chips," said Agatha, calling to the flaxen-haired child, "go upstairs to No. 6, and, if Miss Wilson isnt there, fetch me the Recording Angel."

The little girl grumbled inarticulately and did not stir.

"Chips," resumed Agatha, "did you ever wish that you had never been born?"

"Why dont you go yourself?" said the child pettishly, but evidently alarmed.

"Because," continued Agatha, ignoring the question, "you shall wish yourself dead and buried under the blackest flag in the coal cellar if you dont bring me the book before I count sixteen. One—two—"

"Go at once and do as you are told, you disagreeable little thing," said Gertrude sharply. "How dare you be so disobliging?"

"—nine—ten—eleven—" pursued Agatha.

The child quailed, went out, and presently returned, hugging the Recording Angel in her arms.

"You are a good little darling—when your better qualities are brought out by a judicious application of moral force," said Agatha good-humoredly. "Remind me to save the raisins out of my pudding for you tomorrow. Now, Jane, you shall see the entry for which the best-hearted girl in the college is to be expelled. *Voilà!*"

The two girls read and were awestruck; Jane opening her mouth and gasping, Gertrude closing hers and looking very serious.

"Do you mean to say that you had the dreadful cheek to let

the Lady Abbess see that?" said Jane.

"Pooh! she would have forgiven that. You should have heard what I said to her! She fainted three times."

"Thats a story," said Gertrude gravely.

"I beg your pardon," said Agatha, swiftly grasping Gertrude's knee.

"Nothing," cried Gertrude, flinching hysterically. "Dont, Agatha."

"How many times did Miss Wilson faint?"

"Three times. I will scream, Agatha; I will, indeed."

"Three times, as you say. And I wonder that a girl brought up as you have been, by moral force, should be capable of repeating such a falsehood. But we had an awful row, really and truly. She lost her temper. Fortunately, I never lose mine."

"Well, I'm blowed!" exclaimed Jane incredulously. "I like that."

"For a girl of county family, you are inexcusably vulgar, Jane. I dont know what I said; but she will never forgive me for profaning her pet book. I shall be expelled as certainly as I am sitting here."

"And do you mean to say that you are going away?" said Jane, faltering as she began to realize the consequences.

"I do. And what is to become of you when I am not here to get you out of your scrapes, or of Gertrude without me to check her inveterate snobbishness, is more than I can foresee."

"I am not snobbish," said Gertrude, "although I do not choose to make friends with every one. But I never objected to you, Agatha."

"No; I should like to catch you at it. Hallo, Jane!" (who had suddenly burst into tears) "what's the matter? I trust you are not permitting yourself to take the liberty of crying for me."

"Indeed," sobbed Jane indignantly, "I know that I am a f—fool for my pains. You have no heart."

"You certainly are a f—fool, as you aptly express it," said Agatha, passing her arm round Jane, and disregarding an angry attempt to shake it off; "but if I had any heart it would be touched by this proof of your attachment."

"I never said you had no heart," protested Jane; "but I hate when you speak like a book."

"You hate when I speak like a book, do you? My dear, silly old Jane! I shall miss you greatly."

"Yes, I dare say," said Jane, with tearful sarcasm. "At least, my snoring will never keep you awake again."

"You dont snore, Jane. We have been in a conspiracy to make you believe that you do, thats all. Isnt it good of me to tell you?"

Jane was overcome by this revelation. After a long pause, she said with deep conviction, "I always *knew* that I didnt. Oh, the way you kept it up! I solemnly declare that from this time forth I will believe nobody."

"Well, and what do you think of it all?" said Agatha, transferring her attention to Gertrude, who was very grave.

"I think—I am now speaking seriously, Agatha—I think you are in the wrong."

"Why do you think that, pray?" demanded Agatha, a little roused.

"You must be, or Miss Wilson would not be angry with you. Of course, according to your own account, you are always in the right, and every one else is always wrong; but you shouldnt have written that in the book. You know I speak as your friend."

"And pray what does your wretched little soul know of my motives and feelings?"

"It is easy enough to understand you," retorted Gertrude, nettled. "Self-conceit is not so uncommon that one need be at a loss to recognize it. And mind, Agatha Wylie," she continued, as if goaded by some unbearable reminiscence, "if you are really going, I dont care whether we part friends or not. I have not forgotten the day when you called me a spiteful cat."

"I have repented," said Agatha, unmoved. "One day I sat down and watched Bacchus seated on the hearthrug, with his moony eyes looking into space so thoughtfully and patiently that I apologized for comparing you to him. If I were to call him a spiteful cat he would only not believe me."

"Because he *is* a cat," said Jane, with the giggle which was seldom far behind her tears.

"No; but because he is not spiteful. Gertrude keeps a recording angel inside her little head, and it is so full of other people's faults, written in large hand and read through a magnifying glass, that there is no room to enter her own."

"You are very poetic," said Gertrude; "but I understand what you mean, and shall not forget it."

"You ungrateful wretch," exclaimed Agatha, turning upon her so suddenly and imperiously that she involuntarily shrank aside: "how often, when you have tried to be insolent and false with me, have I not driven away your bad angel—by tickling you? Had you a friend in the college, except half-a-dozen toadies, until I came? And now, because I have sometimes, for your own good, shown you your faults, you bear malice against me, and say that you dont care whether we part friends or not!"

"I didnt say so."

"Oh, Gertrude, you know you did," said Jane.

"You seem to think that I have no conscience," said Gertrude querulously.

"I wish you hadnt," said Agatha. "Look at me! I have no conscience, and see how much pleasanter I am!"

"You care for no one but yourself," said Gertrude. "You never think that other people have feelings too. No one ever considers me."

"Oh, I like to hear you talk," cried Jane ironically. "You are considered a great deal more than is good for you; and the more you are considered the more you want to be considered."

"As if," declaimed Agatha theatrically, "increase of appetite did grow by what it fed on. Shakespear!"

"Bother Shakespear," said Jane impetuously; "—old fool that expects credit for saying things that everybody knows! But if *you* complain of not being considered, Gertrude, how would you like to be *me*, whom everybody sets down as a fool? But

I am not such a fool as—"

"As you look," interposed Agatha. "I have told you so scores of times, Jane; and I am glad that you have adopted my opinion at last. Which would you rather *be*, a greater fool than y—"

"Oh, shut up," said Jane impatiently; "you have asked me that twice this week already."

The three were silent for some seconds after this: Agatha meditating, Gertrude moody, Jane vacant and restless. At last Agatha said:

"And are you two also smarting under a sense of the inconsiderateness and selfishness of the rest of the world—both misunderstood—everything expected from you, and no allowances made for you?"

"I dont know what you mean by *both* of us," said Gertrude coldly.

"Neither do I," said Jane angrily. "That is just the way people treat me. You may laugh, Agatha; and she may turn up her nose as much as she likes; you know it's true. But the idea of Gertrude wanting to make out that she isnt considered is nothing but sentimentality, and vanity, and nonsense."

"You are exceedingly rude, Miss Carpenter," said Gertrude.

"My manners are as good as yours, and perhaps better," retorted Jane. "My family is as good, anyhow."

"Children, children," said Agatha admonitorily, "do not forget that you are sworn friends."

"We didnt swear," said Jane. "We were to have been three sworn friends, and Gertrude and I were willing, but you wouldnt swear, and so the bargain was cried off."

"Just so," said Agatha; "and the result is that I spend all my time in keeping peace between you. And now, to go back to our subject, may I ask whether it has ever occurred to you that no one ever considers *me*?"

"I suppose you think that very funny. You take good care to make yourself considered," sneered Jane.

"You cannot say that *I* do not consider you," said Gertrude reproachfully.

24

"Not when I tickle you, dear."

"I consider you, and I am not ticklesome," said Jane tenderly.

"Indeed! Let me try," said Agatha, slipping her arm about Jane's ample waist, and eliciting a piercing combination of laugh and scream from her.

"Sh—sh," whispered Gertrude quickly. "Dont you see the Lady Abbess?"

Miss Wilson had just entered the room. Agatha, without appearing to be aware of her presence, stealthily withdrew her arm, and said aloud:

"How *can* you make such a noise, Jane? You will disturb the whole house."

Jane reddened with indignation, but had to remain silent, for the eyes of the principal were upon her. Miss Wilson had her bonnet on. She announced that she was going to walk to Lyvern, the nearest village. Did any of the sixth form young ladies wish to accompany her?

Agatha jumped from her seat at once, and Jane smothered a laugh.

"Miss Wilson said the *sixth* form, Miss Wylie," said Miss Ward, who had entered also. "You are not in the sixth form."

"No," said Agatha sweetly, "but I want to go, if I may."

Miss Wilson looked round. The sixth form consisted of four studious young ladies, whose goal in life for the present was an examination by one of the Universities, or, as the college phrase was, the "Cambridge Local." None of them responded.

"Fifth form, then," said Miss Wilson.

Jane, Gertrude, and four others rose and stood with Agatha.

"Very well," said Miss Wilson. "Do not be long dressing."

They left the room quietly, and dashed at the staircase the moment they were out of sight. Agatha, though void of emulation for the Cambridge Local, always competed with ardour for the honor of being first up or down stairs.

They soon returned, clad for walking, and left the college in procession, two by two: Jane and Agatha leading, Gertrude and Miss Wilson coming last. The road to Lyvern lay through acres of pasture land, formerly arable, now abandoned to cattle, which made more money for the landlord than the men whom they had displaced. Miss Wilson's young ladies, being instructed in economics, knew that this proved that the land was being used to produce what was most wanted from it; and if all the advantage went to the landlord, that was but natural, as he was the chief gentleman in the neighborhood. Still the arrangement had its disagreeable side; for it involved a great many cows, which made them afraid to cross the fields; a great many tramps, who made them afraid to walk the roads; and a scarcity of gentleman subjects for the maiden art of fascination.

The sky was cloudy. Agatha, reckless of dusty stockings, waded through the heaps of fallen leaves with the delight of a child paddling in the sea; Gertrude picked her steps carefully, and the rest tramped along, chatting subduedly, occasionally making some scientific or philosophical remark in a louder tone, in order that Miss Wilson might overhear and give them due credit. Save a herdsman, who seemed to have caught something of the nature and expression of the beasts he tended, they met no one until they approached the village, where, on the brow of an acclivity, masculine humanity appeared in the shape of two curates; one tall, thin, close shaven, with a book under his arm, and his neck craned forward; the other middle-sized, robust, upright, and aggressive, with short black whiskers, and an air of protest against such notions as that of a clergyman may not marry, hunt, play cricket, or share the sports of honest laymen. The shaven one was Mr Josephs, his companion Mr Fairholme. Obvious scriptural perversions of this brace of names had been introduced by Agatha.

"Here come Pharaoh and Joseph," she said to Jane. "Joseph will blush when you look at him. Pharaoh wont blush until he passes Gertrude, so we shall lose that."

"Josephs, indeed!" said Jane scornfully.

"He loves you, Jane. Thin persons like a fine armful of a woman. Pharaoh, who is a cad, likes blue blood on the same principle of the attraction of opposites. That is why he is captivated by Gertrude's aristocratic air."

"If he only knew how she despises him!"

"He is too vain to suspect it. Besides, Gertrude despises every one, even us. Or, rather, she doesnt despise any one in particular, but is contemptuous by nature, just as you are stout."

"Mf! I had rather be stout than stuck-up. Ought we to bow?"

"I will, certainly. I want to make Pharaoh blush, if I can."

The two parsons had been simulating an interest in the cloudy firmament as an excuse for not looking at the girls until close at hand. Jane sent an eyeflash at Josephs with a skill which proved her favorite assertion that she was not so stupid as people thought. He blushed and took off his soft, low-crowned felt hat. Fairholme saluted very solemnly, for Agatha bowed to him with marked seriousness. But when his gravity and his stiff silk hat were at their highest point she darted a mocking smile at him, and he too blushed, all the deeper because he was enraged with himself for doing so.

"Did you ever see such a pair of fools?" whispered Jane, giggling.

"They cannot help their sex. They say women are fools, and so they are; but thank Heaven they are not quite so bad as men! I should like to look back and see Pharaoh passing Gertrude; but if he saw me he would think I was admiring him; and he is conceited enough already without that."

The two curates became redder and redder as they passed the column of young ladies. Miss Lindsay would not look to their side of the road, and Miss Wilson's nod and smile were not quite sincere. She never spoke to curates, and kept up no more intercourse with the vicar than she could avoid. He suspected her of being an infidel, though neither he nor any other mortal in Lyvern had ever heard a word from her on the subject of her religious opinions. But he knew that "moral science" was taught secularly at the college; and he felt that where morals were made a department of science the demand for religion must fall off proportionately.

"What a life to lead and what a place to live in!" exclaimed

Agatha. "We meet two creatures, more like suits of black than men; and that is an incident—a startling incident—in our existence!"

"I think theyre awful fun," said Jane, "except that Josephs has such large ears."

The girls now came to a place where the road dipped through a plantation of sombre sycamore and horse-chestnut trees. As they passed down into it, a little wind sprang up, the fallen leaves stirred, and the branches heaved a long, rustling sigh.

"I hate this bit of road," said Jane, hurrying on. "It's just the sort of place that people get robbed and murdered in."

"It is not such a bad place to shelter in if we get caught in the rain, as I expect we shall before we get back," said Agatha, feeling the fitful breeze strike ominously on her cheek. "A nice pickle I shall be in with these light shoes on! I wish I had put on my strong boots. If it rains much I will go into the old chalet."

"Miss Wilson wont let you. It's trespassing."

"What matter! Nobody lives in it, and the gate is off its hinges. I only want to stand under the veranda—not to break into the wretched place. Besides, the landlord knows Miss Wilson; he wont mind. Theres a drop."

Miss Carpenter looked up, and immediately received a heavy raindrop in her eye.

"Oh!" she cried. "It's pouring! We shall be drenched."

Agatha stopped, and the column broke into a group about her.

"Miss Wilson," she said, "it is going to rain in torrents, and Jane and I have only our shoes on."

Miss Wilson paused to consider the situation. Some one suggested that if they hurried on they might reach Lyvern before the rain came down.

"More than a mile," said Agatha scornfully, "and the rain coming down already!"

Some one else suggested returning to the college.

"More than two miles," said Agatha. "We should be drowned."

"There is nothing for it but to wait here under the trees,"

said Miss Wilson.

"The branches are very bare," said Gertrude anxiously. "If it should come down heavily they will drip worse than the rain itself."

"Much worse," said Agatha. "I think we had better get under the veranda of the old chalet. It is not half a minute's walk from here."

"But we have no right—" Here the sky darkened threateningly. Miss Wilson checked herself and said, "I suppose it is still empty."

"Of course," replied Agatha, impatient to be moving. "It is almost a ruin."

"Then let us go there, by all means," said Miss Wilson, not disposed to stand on trifles at the risk of a bad cold.

They hurried on, and came presently to a green hill by the wayside. On the slope was a dilapidated Swiss cottage, surrounded by a veranda on slender wooden pillars, about which hung a few tendrils of withered creeper, their stray ends still swinging from the recent wind, now momentarily hushed as if listening for the coming of the rain. Access from the roadway was by a rough wooden gate in the hedge. To the surprise of Agatha, who had last seen this gate off its hinges and only attached to the post by a rusty chain and padlock, it was now rehung and fastened by a new hasp. The weather admitting of no delay to consider these repairs, she opened the gate and hastened up the slope, followed by the troop of girls. Their ascent ended with a rush, for the rain suddenly came down in torrents.

When they were safe under the veranda, panting, laughing, grumbling, or congratulating themselves on having been so close to a place of shelter, Miss Wilson observed, with some uneasiness, a spade—new, like the hasp of the gate—sticking upright in a patch of ground that some one had evidently been digging lately. She was about to comment on this sign of habitation, when the door of the chalet was flung open, and Jane screamed as a man darted out to the spade, which he was about to carry in out of the wet, when he perceived the company under the veranda, and stood still in amazement. He was a young laborer with a reddish-brown beard of a week's growth. He wore corduroy trousers and a linen-sleeved corduroy vest; both, like the hasp and spade, new. A coarse blue shirt, with a vulgar red-and-orange neckerchief, also new, completed his dress; and, to shield himself from the rain, he held up a silk umbrella with a silver-mounted ebony handle, which he seemed unlikely to have come by honestly. Miss Wilson felt like a boy caught robbing an orchard, but she put a bold face on the matter and said:

"Will you allow us to take shelter here until the rain is over?"

"For certain, your ladyship," he replied, respectfully applying the spade handle to his hair, which was combed down to his eyebrows. "Your ladyship does me proud to take refuge from the onclemency of the yallowments beneath my 'umble rooftree." His accent was barbarous; and he, like a low comedian, seemed to relish its vulgarity. As he spoke he came in among them for shelter, and propped his spade against the wall of the chalet, kicking the soil from his hobnailed blucher boots, which were new.

"I came out, honored lady," he resumed, much at his ease, "to house my spade, whereby I earn my living. What the pen is to the poet, such is the spade to the working-man." He took the kerchief from his neck, wiped his temples as if the sweat of honest toil were there, and calmly tied it on again.

"If youll 'scuse a remark from a common man," he observed, "your ladyship has a fine family of daughters."

"They are not my daughters," said Miss Wilson, rather shortly.

"Sisters, mebbe?"

"No."

"I thought they mout be, acause I have a sister myself. Not that I would make bold for to dror comparisons, even in my own mind, for she's only a common woman—as common a one as ever you see. But few women rise above the common. Last Sunday, in yon village church, I heard the minister read out that one man in a thousand had he found, 'but one woman in all these,' he says, 'have I not found,' and I thinks to myself, 'Right you are!' But I warrant he never met your ladyship."

A laugh, thinly disguised as a cough, escaped from Miss Carpenter.

"Young lady a-ketchin cold, I'm afeerd," he said, with respectful solicitude.

"Do you think the rain will last long?" said Agatha politely.

The man examined the sky with a weather-wise air for some moments. Then he turned to Agatha, and replied humbly: "The Lord only knows, Miss. It is not for a common man like me to say."

Silence ensued, during which Agatha, furtively scrutinizing the tenant of the chalet, noticed that his face and neck were cleaner and less sunburnt than those of the ordinary toilers of Lyvern. His hands were hidden by large gardening gloves stained with coal dust. Lyvern laborers, as a rule, had little objection to soil their hands; they never wore gloves. Still, she thought, there was no reason why an eccentric workman, insufferably talkative, and capable of an allusion to the pen of the poet, should not indulge himself with cheap gloves. But then the silk, silver-mounted umbrella—

"The young lady's hi," he said suddenly, holding out the umbrella, "is fixed on this here. I am well aware that it is not for the lowest of the low to carry a gentleman's brolly, and I ask your ladyship's pardon for the liberty. I come by it accidental-like, and should be glad of a reasonable offer from any gentleman in want of an honest article."

As he spoke two gentlemen, much in want of the article, as their clinging wet coats shewed, ran through the gateway and made for the chalet. Fairholme arrived first, exclaiming: "Fearful shower!" and briskly turned his back to the ladies in order to stand at the edge of the veranda and shake the water out of his hat. Josephs came next, shrinking from the damp contact of his own garments. He cringed to Miss Wilson, and hoped that she had escaped a wetting.

"So far I have," she replied. "The question is, how are we

31

to get home?"

"Oh, it's only a shower," said Josephs, looking up cheerfully at the unbroken curtain of cloud. "It will clear up presently."

"It aint for a common man to set up his opinion again' a gentleman wot have profeshnal knowledge of the heavens, as one may say," said the man, "but I would 'umbly offer to bet my umbrellar to his wide-awake that it dont cease raining this side of seven o'clock."

"That man lives here," whispered Miss Wilson, "and I suppose he wants to get rid of us."

"Hm!" said Fairholme. Then, turning to the strange laborer with the air of a person not to be trifled with, he raised his voice, and said: "You live here, do you, my man?"

"I do, sir, by your good leave, if I may make so bold."

"Whats your name?"

"Jeff Smilash, sir, at your service."

"Where do you come from?"

"Brixtonbury, sir."

"Brixtonbury! Wheres that?"

"Well, sir, I dont rightly know. If a gentleman like you, knowing jography and such, cant tell, how can I?"

"You ought to know where you were born, man. Havent you got common sense?"

"Where could such a one as me get common sense, sir? Besides, I was only a foundling. Mebbe I warnt born at all."

"Did I see you at church last Sunday?"

"No, sir. I only come o' Wensday."

"Well, let me see you there next Sunday," said Fairholme shortly, turning away from him.

Miss Wilson looked at the weather, at Josephs, who was conversing with Jane, and finally at Smilash, who knuckled his forehead without waiting to be addressed.

"Have you a boy whom you can send to Lyvern to get us a conveyance—a carriage? I will give him a shilling for his trouble."

"A shilling!" said Smilash joyfully. "Your ladyship is a noble lady. Two four-wheeled cabs. Theres eight on you."

"There is only one cab in Lyvern," said Miss Wilson. "Take this card to Mr Marsh, the jobmaster, and tell him the predicament we are in. He will send vehicles."

Smilash took the card and read it at a glance. He then went into the chalet. Reappearing presently in a sou'wester and oilskins, he ran off through the rain and vaulted over the gate with ridiculous elegance. No sooner had he vanished than, as often happens to remarkable men, he became the subject of conversation.

"A decent workman," said Josephs. "A well-mannered man, considering his class."

"A born fool, though," said Fairholme.

"Or a rogue," said Agatha, emphasizing the suggestion by a glitter of her eyes and teeth, whilst her schoolfellows, rather disapproving of her freedom, stood stiffly dumb. "He told Miss Wilson that he had a sister, and that he had been to church last Sunday, and he has just told you that he is a foundling, and that he only came last Wednesday. His accent is put on, and he can read, and I dont believe he is a workman at all. Perhaps he is a burglar, come down to steal the college plate."

"Agatha," said Miss Wilson gravely, "you must be very careful how you say things of that kind."

"But it is so obvious. His explanation about the umbrella was made up to disarm suspicion. He handled it and leaned on it in a way that showed how much more familiar it was to him than that new spade he was so anxious about. And all his clothes are new."

"True," said Fairholme, "but there is not much in all that. Workmen nowadays ape gentlemen in everything. However, I will keep an eye on him."

"Oh, thank you so much," said Agatha.

Fairholme, suspecting mockery, frowned, and Miss Wilson looked severely at the mocker. Little more was said, except as to the chances—manifestly small—of the rain ceasing, until the tops of a cab, a decayed mourning-coach, and three dripping

33

hats were seen over the hedge. Smilash sat on the box of the coach, beside the driver. When it stopped, he alighted, re-entered the chalet without speaking, came out with the umbrella, spread it above Miss Wilson's head, and said:

"Now, if your ladyship will come with me, I will see you dry into the shay, and then I'll bring your honored nieces one by one."

"I shall come last," said Miss Wilson, irritated by his assumption that the party was a family one. "Gertrude, you had better go first."

"Allow me," said Fairholme, stepping forward, and attempting to take the umbrella.

"Thank you, I shall not trouble you," she said frostily, and tripped away over the oozing field with Smilash, who held the umbrella over her with ostentatious solicitude. In the same manner he led the rest to the vehicles, in which they packed themselves with some difficulty. Agatha, who came last but one, gave him threepence.

"You have a noble 'art and expressive hi, Miss," he said, apparently much moved. "Blessings on both! Blessings on both!"

He went back for Jane, who slipped on the wet grass and fell. He had to put forth his strength as he helped her to rise.

"Hope you aint sopped up much of the rainfall, Miss," he said. "You are a fine young lady for your age. Nigh on twelve stone, I should think."

She reddened and hurried to the cab, where Agatha was. But it was full; and Jane, much against her will, had to get into the coach, considerably diminishing the space left for Miss Wilson, to whom Smilash had returned.

"Now, dear lady," he said, "take care you dont slip. Come along."

Miss Wilson, ignoring the invitation, took a shilling from her purse.

"No, lady," said Smilash with a virtuous air. "I am an honest man and have never seen the inside of a jail except four times, and only twice for stealing. Your youngest daughter—her with the expressive hi—have paid me far beyond what is proper."

"I have told you that these young ladies are not my daughters," said Miss Wilson sharply. "Why do you not listen to what is said to you?"

"Dont be too hard on a common man, lady," said Smilash submissively. "The young lady have just given me three arf-crowns."

"Three half-crowns!" exclaimed Miss Wilson, angered at such extravagance.

"Bless her innocence, she dont know what is proper to give to a low sort like me! But I will not rob the young lady. Arf-a-crown is no more nor is fair for the job, and arf-a-crown will I keep, if agreeable to your noble ladyship. But I give you back the five bob in trust for her. Have you ever noticed her expressive hi?"

"Nonsense, sir. You had better keep the money now that you have got it."

"Wot! Sell for five bob the high opinion your ladyship has of me! No, dear lady; not likely. My father's very last words to me was—"

"You said just now that you were a foundling," said Fairholme. "What are we to believe? Eh?"

"So I were, sir; but by mother's side alone. Her ladyship will please to take back the money, for keep it I will not. I am of the lower orders, and therefore not a man of my word; but when I do stick to it, I stick like wax."

"Take it," said Fairholme to Miss Wilson. "Take it, of course. Seven and sixpence is a ridiculous sum to give him for what he has done. It would only set him drinking."

"His reverence says true, lady. The one arf-crown will keep me comfortably tight until Sunday morning; and more I do not desire."

"Just a little less of your tongue, my man," said Fairholme, taking the two coins from him and handing them to Miss Wilson, who bade the clergymen good afternoon, and went to the coach under the umbrella.

"If your ladyship should want a handy man to do an odd job up at the college, I hope you will remember me," Smilash said as they went down the slope.

"Oh, you know who I am, do you?" said Miss Wilson dryly.

"All the country knows you, Miss, and worships you. I have few equals as a coiner, and if you should require a medal struck to give away for good behavior or the like, I think I could strike one to your satisfaction. And if your ladyship should want a trifle of smuggled lace—"

"You had better be careful or you will get into trouble, I think," said Miss Wilson sternly. "Tell him to drive on."

The vehicles started, and Smilash took the liberty of waving his hat after them. Then he returned to the chalet, left the umbrella within, came out again, locked the door, put the key in his pocket, and walked off through the rain across the hill without taking the least notice of the astonished parsons.

In the meantime Miss Wilson, unable to contain her annoyance at Agatha's extravagance, spoke of it to the girls who shared the coach with her. But Jane declared that Agatha only possessed threepence in the world, and therefore could not possibly have given the man thirty times that sum. When they reached the college, Agatha, confronted with Miss Wilson, opened her eyes in wonder, and exclaimed, laughing: "I only gave him threepence. He has sent me a present of four and ninepence!"

CHAPTER IV

Saturday at Alton College, nominally a half holiday, was really a whole one. Classes in gymnastics, dancing, elocution, and drawing were held in the morning. The afternoon was spent at lawn tennis, to which lady guests resident in the neighborhood were allowed to bring their husbands, brothers, and fathers—Miss Wilson being anxious to send her pupils forth into the world free from the uncouth stiffness of schoolgirls unaccustomed to society.

Late in October came a Saturday which proved anything but a holiday for Miss Wilson. At half-past one, luncheon being over, she went out of doors to a lawn that lay between the southern side of the college and a shrubbery. Here she found a group of girls watching Agatha and Jane, who were dragging a roller over the grass. One of them, tossing a ball about with her racket, happened to drive it into the shrubbery, whence, to the surprise of the company, Smilash presently emerged, carrying the ball, blinking, and proclaiming that, though a common man, he had his feelings like another, and that his eye was neither a stick nor a stone. He was dressed as before, but his garments, soiled with clay and lime, no longer looked new.

"What brings you here, pray?" demanded Miss Wilson.

"I was led into the belief that you sent for me, lady," he replied. "The baker's lad told me so as he passed my 'umble cot this morning. I thought he were incapable of deceit."

"That is quite right; I did send for you. But why did you not go round to the servants' hall?"

"I am at present in search of it, lady. I were looking for it when this ball cotch me here" (touching his eye). "A cruel blow on the hi nat'rally spiles its vision and expression and makes a honest man look like a thief."

"Agatha," said Miss Wilson, "come here."

"My dooty to you, Miss," said Smilash, pulling his forelock.

"This is the man from whom I had the five shillings, which

37

he said you had just given him. Did you do so?"

"Certainly not. I only gave him threepence."

"But I shewed the money to your ladyship," said Smilash, twisting his hat agitatedly. "I gev it you. Where would the like of me get five shillings except by the bounty of the rich and noble? If the young lady thinks I hadnt ort to have kep the tother arf-crown, I would not object to its bein stopped from my wages if I were given a job of work here. But—"

"But it's nonsense," said Agatha. "I never gave you three half-crowns."

"Perhaps you mout 'a made a mistake. Pence is summat similar to arf-crowns, and the day were very dark."

"I couldnt have," said Agatha. "Jane had my purse all the earlier part of the week, Miss Wilson, and she can tell you that there was only threepence in it. You know that I get my money on the first of every month. It never lasts longer than a week. The idea of my having seven and sixpence on the sixteenth is ridiculous."

"But I put it to you, Miss, aint it twice as ridiculous for me, a poor laborer, to give up money wot I never got?"

Vague alarm crept upon Agatha as the testimony of her senses was contradicted. "All I know is," she protested, "that I did not give it to you; so my pennies must have turned into half-crowns in your pocket."

"Mebbe so," said Smilash gravely. "Ive heard, and I know it for a fact, that money grows in the pockets of the rich. Why not in the pockets of the poor as well? Why should you be su'prised at wot appens every day?"

"Had you any money of your own about you at the time?"

"Where could the like of me get money?—asking pardon for making so bold as to catechize your ladyship."

"I dont know where you could get it," said Miss Wilson testily; "I ask you, had you any?"

"Well, lady, I disremember. I will not impose upon you. I disremember."

"Then youve made a mistake," said Miss Wilson, handing

38

him back his money. "Here. If it is not yours, it is not ours; so you had better keep it."

"Keep it! Oh, lady, but this is the heighth of nobility! And what shall I do to earn your bounty, lady?"

"It is not my bounty: I give it to you because it does not belong to me, and, I suppose, must belong to you. You seem to be a very simple man."

"I thank your ladyship; I hope I am. Respecting the day's work, now, lady; was you thinking of employing a poor man at all?"

"No, thank you; I have no occasion for your services. I have also to give you the shilling I promised you for getting the cabs. Here it is."

"Another shillin!" cried Smilash, stupefied.

"Yes," said Miss Wilson, beginning to feel very angry. "Let me hear no more about it, please. Dont you understand that you have earned it?"

"I am a common man, and understand next to nothing," he replied reverently. "But if your ladyship would give me a day's work to keep me goin, I could put up all this money in a little wooden savings bank I have at home, and keep it to spend when sickness or old age shall, in a manner of speaking, lay their 'ands upon me. I could smooth that grass beautiful; them young ladies'll strain themselves with that heavy roller. If tennis is the word, I can put up nets fit to catch birds of paradise in. If the courts is to be chalked out in white, I can draw a line so straight that you could hardly keep yourself from erectin an equilateral triangle on it. I am honest when well watched, and I can wait at table equal to the Lord Mayor o' London's butler."

"I cannot employ you without a character," said Miss Wilson, amused by his scrap of Euclid, and wondering where he had picked it up.

"I bear the best of characters, lady. The reverend rector has known me from a boy."

"I was speaking to him about you yesterday," said Miss Wilson, looking hard at him, "and he says you are a perfect stranger to him."

"Gentlemen is so forgetful," said Smilash sadly. "But I alluded to my native rector—meaning the rector of my native village, Auburn. 'Sweet Auburn, loveliest village of the plain,' as the gentleman called it."

"That was not the name you mentioned to Mr Fairholme. I do not recollect what name you gave, but it was not Auburn, nor have I ever heard of any such place."

"Never read of sweet Auburn!"

"Not in any geography or gazetteer. Do you recollect telling me that you have been in prison?"

"Only six times," pleaded Smilash, his features working convulsively. "Dont bear too hard on a common man. Only six times, and all through drink. But I have took the pledge, and kep it faithful for eighteen months past."

Miss Wilson now set down the man as one of those keen, half-witted country fellows, contemptuously styled originals, who unintentionally make themselves popular by flattering the sense of sanity in those whose faculties are better adapted to circumstances.

"You have a bad memory, Mr Smilash," she said good-humoredly. "You never give the same account of yourself twice."

"I am well aware that I do not express myself with exact-ability. Ladies and gentlemen have that power over words that they can always say what they mean, but a common man like me cant. Words dont come natural to him. He has more thoughts than words, and what words he has dont fit his thoughts. Might I take a turn with the roller, and make myself useful about the place until nightfall, for ninepence?"

Miss Wilson, who was expecting more than her usual Satur-day visitors, considered the proposition and assented. "And re-member," she said, "that as you are a stranger here, your character in Lyvern depends upon the use you make of this opportunity."

"I am grateful to your noble ladyship. May your ladyship's goodness sew up the hole which is in the pocket where I carry my character, and which has caused me to lose it so frequent. It's a bad place for men to keep their characters in; but such is the fashion. And so hurray for the glorious nineteenth century!"

He took off his coat, seized the roller, and began to pull it with an energy foreign to the measured mill-horse manner of the accustomed laborer. Miss Wilson looked doubtfully at him, but, being in haste, went indoors without further comment. The girls, mistrusting his eccentricity, kept aloof. Agatha determined to have another and better look at him. Racket in hand, she walked slowly across the grass and came close to him just as he, unaware of her approach, uttered a groan of exhaustion and sat down to rest.

"Tired already, Mr Smilash?" she said mockingly.

He looked up deliberately, took off one of his wash-leather gloves, fanned himself with it, displaying a white and fine hand, and at last replied, in the tone and with the accent of a gentleman: "Very."

Agatha recoiled. He fanned himself without the least concern.

"You—you are not a laborer," she said at last.

"Obviously not."

"I thought not."

He nodded.

"Suppose I tell on you," she said, growing bolder as she recollected that she was not alone with him.

"If you do I shall get out of it just as I got out of the half-crowns, and Miss Wilson will begin to think that you are mad."

"Then I really did not give you the seven and sixpence," she said, relieved.

"What is your own opinion?" he answered, taking three pennies from his pocket, jingling them in his palm. "What is your name?"

"I shall not tell you," said Agatha with dignity.

He shrugged his shoulders. "Perhaps you are right," he said. "I would not tell you mine if you asked me."

"I have not the slightest intention of asking you."

"No? Then Smilash shall do for you, and Agatha will do for

me."

"You had better take care."

"Of what?"

"Of what you say, and—are you not afraid of being found out?"

"I am found out already—by you, and I am none the worse."

"Suppose the police find you out!"

"Not they. Besides, I am not hiding from the police. I have a right to wear corduroy if I prefer it to broadcloth. Consider the advantages of it! It has procured me admission to Alton College, and the pleasure of your acquaintance. Will you excuse me if I go on with my rolling, just to keep up appearances? I can talk as I roll."

"You may, if you are fond of soliloquizing," she said, turning away as he rose.

"Seriously, Agatha, you must not tell the others about me."

"Do not call me Agatha," she said impetuously.

"What shall I call you, then?"

"You need not address me at all."

"I need, and will. Dont be ill-natured."

"But I dont know you. I wonder at your—" she hesitated at the word which occurred to her, but, being unable to think of a better one, used it—"at your cheek."

He laughed, and she watched him take a couple of turns with the roller. Presently, refreshing himself by a look at her, he caught her looking at him, and smiled. His smile was commonplace in comparison with the one she gave him in return, in which her eyes, her teeth, and the golden grain in her complexion seemed to flash simultaneously. He stopped rolling immediately, and rested his chin on the handle of the roller.

"If you neglect your work," said she maliciously, "you wont have the grass ready when the people come."

"What people?" he said, taken aback.

"Oh, lots of people. Most likely some who know you. There are visitors coming from London: my guardian, my guardianess, their daughter, my mother, and about a hundred more."

"Four in all. What are they coming for? To see you?"

"To take me away," she replied, watching for signs of disappointment on his part.

They were at once forthcoming. "What the deuce are they going to take you away for?" he said. "Is your education finished?"

"No. I have behaved badly, and I am going to be expelled."

He laughed again. "Come!" he said, "you are beginning to invent in the Smilash manner. What have you done?"

"I dont see why I should tell you. What have *you* done?"

"I! Oh, I have done nothing. I am only an unromantic gentleman, hiding from a romantic lady who is in love with me."

"Poor thing," said Agatha sarcastically. "Of course, she has proposed to you, and you have refused."

"On the contrary, I proposed, and she accepted. That is why I have to hide."

"You tell stories charmingly," said Agatha. "Goodbye. Here is Miss Carpenter coming to hear what we are talking about."

"Goodbye. That story of your being expelled beats—Might a common man make so bold as to inquire where the whitening machine is, Miss?"

This was addressed to Jane, who had come up with some of the others. Agatha expected to see Smilash presently discovered, for his disguise now seemed transparent; she wondered how the rest could be imposed on by it. Two o'clock, striking just then, reminded her of the impending interview with her guardian. A tremor shook her, and she felt a craving for some solitary hiding-place in which to await the summons. But it was a point of honor with her to appear perfectly indifferent to her trouble, so she stayed with the girls, laughing and chatting as they watched Smilash intently marking out the courts and setting up the nets. She made the others laugh too, for her hidden excitement, sharpened by irrepressible shootings of dread, stimulated her, and the romance of Smilash's disguise gave her a sensation of dreaming. Her imagination was already busy upon a drama, of which she was the heroine and Smilash the hero, though, with

43

the real man before her, she could not indulge herself by attributing to him quite as much gloomy grandeur of character as to a wholly ideal personage. The plot was simple, and an old favorite with her. One of them was to love the other and to die broken-hearted because the loved one would not requite the passion. For Agatha, prompt to ridicule sentimentality in her companions, and gifted with an infectious spirit of farce, secretly turned for imaginative luxury to visions of despair and death; and often endured the mortification of the successful clown who believes, whilst the public roar with laughter at him, that he was born a tragedian. There was much in her nature, she felt, that did not find expression in her popular representation of the soldier in the chimney.

By three o'clock the local visitors had arrived, and tennis was proceeding in four courts, rolled and prepared by Smilash. The two curates were there, with a few lay gentlemen. Mrs Miller, the vicar, and some mothers and other chaperons looked on and consumed light refreshments, which were brought out upon trays by Smilash, who had borrowed and put on a large white apron, and was making himself officiously busy.

At a quarter past the hour a message came from Miss Wilson, requesting Miss Wylie's attendance. The visitors were at a loss to account for the sudden distraction of the young ladies' attention which ensued. Jane almost burst into tears, and answered Josephs rudely when he innocently asked what the matter was. Agatha went away apparently unconcerned, though her hand shook as she put aside her racket.

In a spacious drawing room at the north side of the college she found her mother, a slight woman in widow's weeds, with faded brown hair, and tearful eyes. With her were Mrs Jansenius and her daughter. The two elder ladies kept severely silent whilst Agatha kissed them, and Mrs Wylie sniffed. Henrietta embraced Agatha effusively.

"Wheres Uncle John?" said Agatha. "Hasnt he come?"

"He is in the next room with Miss Wilson," said Mrs Jansenius coldly. "They want you in there."

44

"I thought somebody was dead," said Agatha, "you all look so funereal. Now, mamma, put your handkerchief back again. If you cry I will give Miss Wilson a piece of my mind for worrying you."

"No, no," said Mrs Wylie, alarmed. "She has been so nice!"

"So good!" said Henrietta.

"She has been perfectly reasonable and kind," said Mrs Jansenius.

"She always is," said Agatha complacently. "You didnt expect to find her in hysterics, did you?"

"Agatha," pleaded Mrs Wylie, "dont be headstrong and foolish."

"Oh, she wont; I know she wont," said Henrietta coaxingly. "Will you, dear Agatha?"

"You may do as you like, as far as I am concerned," said Mrs Jansenius. "But I hope you have more sense than to throw away your education for nothing."

"Your aunt is quite right," said Mrs Wylie. "And your Uncle John is very angry with you. He will never speak to you again if you quarrel with Miss Wilson."

"He is not angry," said Henrietta, "but he is so anxious that you should get on well."

"He will naturally be disappointed if you persist in making a fool of yourself," said Mrs Jansenius.

"All Miss Wilson wants is an apology for the dreadful things you wrote in her book," said Mrs Wylie. "Youll apologize, dear, wont you?"

"Of course she will," said Henrietta.

"I think you had better," said Mrs Jansenius.

"Perhaps I will," said Agatha.

"Thats my own darling," said Mrs Wylie, catching her hand.

"And perhaps, again, I wont."

"You will, dear," urged Mrs Wylie, trying to draw Agatha, who passively resisted, closer to her. "For my sake. To oblige your mother, Agatha. You wont refuse me, dearest?"

Agatha laughed indulgently at her parent, who had long ago

45

worn out this form of appeal. Then she turned to Henrietta, and said, "How is your *caro sposo*? I think it was hard that I was not a bridesmaid."

The red in Henrietta's cheeks brightened. Mrs Jansenius hastened to interpose a dry reminder that Miss Wilson was waiting.

"Oh, she does not mind waiting," said Agatha, "because she thinks you are all at work getting me into a proper frame of mind. That was the arrangement she made with you before she left the room. Mamma knows that I have a little bird that tells me these things. I must say that you have not made me feel any goody-goodier so far. However, as poor Uncle John must be dreadfully frightened and uncomfortable, it is only kind to put an end to his suspense. Goodbye!" And she went out leisurely. But she looked in again to say in a low voice: "Prepare for something thrilling. I feel just in the humor to say the most awful things." She vanished, and immediately they heard her tapping at the door of the next room.

Mr Jansenius was indeed awaiting her with misgiving. Having discovered early in his career that his dignified person and fine voice caused people to stand in some awe of him, and to move him into the chair at public meetings, he had grown so accustomed to deference that any approach to familiarity or irreverence disconcerted him exceedingly. Agatha, on the other hand, having from her childhood heard Uncle John quoted as wisdom and authority incarnate, had begun in her tender years to scoff at him as a pompous and purse-proud city merchant, whose sordid mind was unable to cope with her transcendental affairs. She had habitually terrified her mother by ridiculing him with an absolute contempt of which only childhood and extreme ignorance are capable. She had felt humiliated by his kindness to her (he was a generous giver of presents), and, with the instinct of an anarchist, had taken disparagement of his advice and defiance of his authority as the signs wherefrom she might infer surely that her face was turned to the light. The result was that he was a little afraid of her without being quite conscious of it; and she not at all afraid of him, and a little too conscious of it.

When she entered with her brightest smile in full play, Miss Wilson and Mr Jansenius, seated at the table, looked somewhat like two culprits about to be indicted. Miss Wilson waited for him to speak, deferring to his imposing presence. But he was not ready, so she invited Agatha to sit down.

"Thank you," said Agatha sweetly. "Well, Uncle John, dont you know me?"

"I have heard with regret from Miss Wilson that you have been very troublesome here," he said, ignoring her remark, though secretly put out by it.

"Yes," said Agatha contritely. "I am so very sorry."

Mr Jansenius, who had been led by Miss Wilson to expect the utmost contumacy, looked to her in surprise.

"You seem to think," said Miss Wilson, conscious of Mr Jansenius's movement, and annoyed by it, "that you may transgress over and over again, and then set yourself right with us" (Miss Wilson never spoke of offences as against her individual authority, but as against the school community) "by saying that you are sorry. You spoke in a very different tone at our last meeting."

"I was angry then, Miss Wilson. And I thought I had a grievance—everybody thinks they have the same one. Besides, we were quarrelling—at least I was; and I always behave badly when I quarrel. I am so *very* sorry."

"The book was a serious matter," said Miss Wilson gravely. "You do not seem to think so."

"I understand Agatha to say that she is now sensible of the folly of her conduct with regard to the book, and that she is sorry for it," said Mr Jansenius, instinctively inclining to Agatha's party as the stronger one and the least dependent on him in a pecuniary sense.

"Have you seen the book?" said Agatha eagerly.

"No. Miss Wilson has described what has occurred."

"Oh, *do* let me get it," she cried, rising. "It will make Uncle John scream with laughing. May I, Miss Wilson?"

"There!" said Miss Wilson indignantly. "It is this incorrigible flippancy of which I have to complain. Miss Wylie only varies it by downright insubordination."

Mr Jansenius too was scandalized. His fine color mounted at the idea of his screaming. "Tut, tut!" he said, "you must be serious, and more respectful to Miss Wilson. You are old enough to know better now, Agatha—quite old enough."

Agatha's mirth vanished. "What have I said? What have I done?" she asked, a faint purple spot appearing in her cheeks.

"You have spoken triflingly of—of the volume by which Miss Wilson sets great store, and properly so."

"If properly so, then why do you find fault with me?"

"Come, come," roared Mr Jansenius, deliberately losing his temper as a last expedient to subdue her, "dont be impertinent, Miss."

Agatha's eyes dilated; evanescent flushes played upon her cheeks and neck; she stamped with her heel. "Uncle John," she cried, "if you *dare* to address me like that, I will never look at you, never speak to you, nor ever enter your house again. What do you know about good manners, that you should call me impertinent? I will not submit to intentional rudeness; that was the beginning of my quarrel with Miss Wilson. She told me I was impertinent, and I went away and told her that she was wrong by writing it in the fault book. She has been wrong all through, and I would have said so before but that I wanted to be reconciled to her and to let bygones be bygones. But if she insists on quarrelling, I cannot help it."

"I have already explained to you, Mr Jansenius," said Miss Wilson, concentrating her resentment by an effort to suppress it, "that Miss Wylie has ignored all the opportunities that have been made for her to reinstate herself here. Mrs Miller and I have waived merely personal considerations, and I have only required a simple acknowledgment of this offence against the college and its rules."

"I do not care *that* for Mrs Miller," said Agatha, snapping her fingers. "And you are not half so good as I thought."

"Agatha," said Mr Jansenius, "I desire you to hold your

tongue."

Agatha drew a deep breath, sat down resignedly, and said: "There! I have done. I have lost my temper; so now we have all lost our tempers."

"You have no right to lose your temper, Miss," said Mr Jansenius, following up a fancied advantage.

"I am the youngest, and the least to blame," she replied.

"There is nothing further to be said, Mr Jansenius," said Miss Wilson determinedly. "I am sorry that Miss Wylie has chosen to break with us."

"But I have not chosen to break with you, and I think it very hard that I am to be sent away. Nobody here has the least quarrel with me except you and Mrs Miller. Mrs Miller is annoyed because she mistook me for her cat, as if that was my fault! And really, Miss Wilson, I dont know why you are so angry. All the girls will think I have done something infamous if I am expelled. I ought to be let stay until the end of the term; and as to the Rec —the fault book, you told me most particularly when I first came that I might write in it or not, just as I pleased, and that you never dictated or interfered with what was written. And yet the very first time I write a word you disapprove of, you expel me. Nobody will ever believe now that the entries are voluntary."

Miss Wilson's conscience, already smitten by the coarseness and absence of moral force in the echo of her own "You are impertinent" from the mouth of Mr Jansenius, took fresh alarm. "The fault book," she said, "is for the purpose of recording self-reproach alone, and is not a vehicle for accusations against others."

"I am quite sure that neither Jane nor Gertrude nor I reproached ourselves in the least for going downstairs as we did, and yet you did not blame us for entering that. Besides, the book represented moral force—at least you always said so; and when you gave up moral force, I thought an entry should be made of that. Of course, I was in a rage at the time, but when I came to myself I thought I had done right, and I think so still, though it would perhaps have been better to have passed it over."

"Why do you say that I gave up moral force?"

"Telling people to leave the room is not moral force. Calling them impertinent is not moral force."

"You think then that I am bound to listen patiently to whatever you choose to say to me, however unbecoming it may be from one in your position to one in mine?"

"But I said nothing unbecoming," said Agatha. Then, breaking off restlessly, and smiling again, she said: "Oh, dont let us argue. I am very sorry, and very troublesome, and very fond of you and of the college; and I wont come back next term unless you like."

"Agatha," said Miss Wilson, shaken, "these expressions of regard cost you so little, and when they have effected their purpose are so soon forgotten *by you*, that they have ceased to satisfy me. I am very reluctant to insist on your leaving us at once. But, as your uncle has told you, you are old and sensible enough to know the difference between order and disorder. Hitherto you have been on the side of disorder, an element which was hardly known here until you came, as Mrs Trefusis can tell you. Nevertheless, if you will promise to be more careful in future, I will waive all past cause of complaint, and at the end of the term I shall be able to judge as to your continuing among us."

Agatha rose, beaming. "Dear Miss Wilson," she said, "you are *so* good! I promise, of course. I will go and tell mamma."

Before they could add a word she had turned with a pirouette to the door, and fled, presenting herself a moment later in the drawing room to the three ladies, whom she surveyed with a whimsical smile in silence.

"Well?" said Mrs Jansenius peremptorily.

"Well, dear?" said Mrs Trefusis caressingly.

Mrs Wylie stifled a sob and looked imploringly at her daughter.

"I had no end of trouble in bringing them to reason," said Agatha, after a provoking pause. "They behaved like children, and I was like an angel. I am to stay, of course."

"Blessings on you, my darling," faltered Mrs Wylie, attempting a kiss, which Agatha dexterously evaded.

"I have promised to be very good, and studious, and quiet,

and decorous in future. Do you remember my castanet song, Hetty?

      " 'Tra! lalala, la! la! la!
        Tra! lalala, la! la! la!
        Tra! lalalalalalalalalalala!' "

And she danced about the room, snapping her fingers instead of castanets.

"Dont be so reckless and wicked, my love," said Mrs Wylie. "You will break your poor mother's heart."

Miss Wilson and Mr Jansenius entered just then, and Agatha became motionless and gazed abstractedly at a vase of flowers. Miss Wilson invited her visitors to join the tennis players. Mr Jansenius looked sternly and disappointedly at Agatha, who elevated her left eyebrow and depressed her right simultaneously; but he, shaking his head to signify that he was not to be conciliated by facial feats, however difficult or contrary to nature, went out with Miss Wilson, followed by Mrs Jansenius and Mrs Wylie.

"How is your hubby?" said Agatha then, brusquely, to Henrietta.

Mrs Trefusis's eyes filled with tears so quickly that, as she bent her head to hide them, they fell, sprinkling Agatha's hand.

"This is such a dear old place," she began. "The associations of my girlhood—"

"What is the matter between you and hubby?" demanded Agatha, interrupting her. "You had better tell me, or I will ask him when I meet him."

"I was about to tell you, only you did not give me time."

"That is a most awful cram," said Agatha. "But no matter. Go on."

Henrietta hesitated. Her dignity as a married woman, and the reality of her grief, revolted against the shallow acuteness of the schoolgirl. But she found herself no better able to resist Agatha's domineering than she had been in her childhood, and much more desirous of obtaining her sympathy. Besides, she had already learnt to tell the story herself rather than leave its narration to others, whose accounts did not, she felt, put her case in the proper light. So she told Agatha of her marriage, her wild love for her husband, his wild love for her, and his mysterious disappearance without leaving word or sign behind him. She did not mention the letter.

"Have you had him searched for?" said Agatha, repressing an inclination to laugh.

"But where? Had I the remotest clue, I would follow him barefoot to the end of the world."

"I think you ought to search all the rivers—you would have to do that barefoot. He must have fallen in somewhere, or fallen down some place."

"No, no. Do you think I should be here if I thought his life in danger? I have reasons—I know that he is only gone away."

"Oh, indeed! He took his portmanteau with him, did he? Perhaps he has gone to Paris to buy you something nice and give you a pleasant surprise."

"No," said Henrietta dejectedly. "He knew that I wanted nothing."

"Then I suppose he got tired of you and ran away."

Henrietta's peculiar scarlet blush flowed rapidly over her cheeks as she flung Agatha's arm away, exclaiming, "How dare you say so! You have no heart. He adored me."

"Bosh!" said Agatha. "People always grow tired of one another. I grow tired of myself whenever I am left alone for ten minutes, and I am certain that I am fonder of myself than any one can be of another person."

"I know you are," said Henrietta, pained and spiteful. "You have always been particularly fond of yourself."

"Very likely he resembles me in that respect. In that case he will grow tired of himself and come back, and you will both coo like turtle-doves until he runs away again. Ugh! Serve you right for getting married. I wonder how people can be so mad as to do it, with the example of their married acquaintances all warning them against it."

"You dont know what it is to love," said Henrietta plaintively, and yet patronizingly. "Besides, we were not like other couples."

"So it seems. But never mind, take my word for it, he will return to you as soon as he has had enough of his own company. Dont worry thinking about him, but come and have a game at lawn tennis."

During this conversation they had left the drawing room and made a detour through the grounds. They were now approaching the tennis courts by a path which wound between two laurel hedges through the shrubbery.

Meanwhile, Smilash, waiting on the guests in his white apron and gloves (which he had positively refused to take off, alleging that he was a common man, with common hands such as born ladies and gentlemen could not be expected to take meat and drink from), had behaved himself irreproachably until the arrival of Miss Wilson and her visitors, which occurred as he was returning to the table with an empty tray, moving so swiftly that he nearly came into collision with Mrs Jansenius. Instead of apologizing, he changed countenance, hastily held up the tray like a shield before his face, and began to walk backward from her, stumbling presently against Miss Lindsay, who was running to return a ball. Without heeding her angry look and curt rebuke, he half turned, and sidled away into the shrubbery, whence the tray presently rose into the air, flew across the laurel hedge, and descended with a peal of stage thunder on the stooped shoulders of Josephs. Miss Wilson, after asking the housekeeper with some asperity why she had allowed that man to interfere in the attendance, explained to the guests that he was the idiot of the countryside. Mr Jansenius laughed, and said that he had not seen the man's face, but that his figure reminded him forcibly of some one; he could not just then recollect exactly whom.

Smilash, making off through the shrubbery, found the end of his path blocked by Agatha and a young lady whose appearance alarmed him more than had that of Mrs Jansenius. He attempted to force his way through the hedge, but in vain; the laurel was impenetrable, and the noise he made attracted the attention of

53

the approaching couple. He made no further effort to escape, but threw his borrowed apron over his head and stood bolt upright with his back against the bushes.

"What is that man doing there?" said Henrietta, stopping mistrustfully.

Agatha laughed, and said loudly, so that he might hear: "It is only a harmless madman that Miss Wilson employs. He is fond of disguising himself in some silly way and trying to frighten us. Dont be afraid. Come on."

Henrietta hung back, but her arm was linked in Agatha's, and she was drawn along in spite of herself. Smilash did not move. Agatha strolled on coolly, and as she passed him, adroitly caught the apron between her finger and thumb and twitched it from his face. Instantly Henrietta uttered a piercing scream, and Smilash caught her in his arms.

"Quick," he said to Agatha, "she is fainting. Run for some water. Run!" And he bent over Henrietta, who clung to him frantically. Agatha, bewildered by the effect of her practical joke, hesitated a moment, and then ran to the lawn.

"What is the matter?" said Fairholme.

"Nothing. I want some water—quick, please. Henrietta has fainted in the shrubbery, that is all."

"Please do not stir," said Miss Wilson authoritatively, "you will crowd the path and delay useful assistance. Miss Ward, kindly get some water and bring it to us. Agatha, come with me and point out where Mrs Trefusis is. You may come too, Miss Carpenter; you are so strong. The rest will please remain where they are."

Followed by the two girls, she hurried into the shrubbery, where Mr Jansenius was already looking anxiously for his daughter. He was the only person they found there. Smilash and Henrietta were gone.

At first the seekers, merely puzzled, did nothing but question Agatha incredulously as to the exact spot on which Henrietta had fallen. But Mr Jansenius soon made them understand that the position of a lady in the hands of a half-witted laborer was one of danger. His agitation infected them, and when Agatha endeavored to reassure him by declaring that Smilash was a disguised gentleman, Miss Wilson, supposing this to be a mere repetition of her former idle conjecture, told her sharply to hold her tongue, as the time was not one for talking nonsense. The news now spread through the whole company, and the excitement became intense. Fairholme shouted for volunteers to make up a searching party. All the men present responded, and they were about to rush to the college gates in a body when it occurred to the cooler among them that they had better divide into several parties, in order that search might be made at once in different quarters. Ten minutes of confusion followed. Mr Jansenius started several times in quest of Henrietta, and, when he had gone a few steps, returned and begged that no more time should be wasted. Josephs, whose faith was simple, retired to pray, and did good, as far as it went, by withdrawing one voice from the din of plans, objections, and suggestions which the rest were making; each person trying to be heard above the others.

At last Miss Wilson quelled the prevailing anarchy. Servants were sent to alarm the neighbors and call in the village police. Detachments were sent in various directions under the command of Fairholme and other energetic spirits. The girls formed parties among themselves, which were reinforced by male deserters from the previous levies. Miss Wilson then went indoors and conducted a search through the interior of the college. Only two persons were left on the tennis ground—Agatha and Mrs Jansenius, who had been surprisingly calm throughout.

"You need not be anxious," said Agatha, who had been standing aloof since her rebuff by Miss Wilson. "I am sure there is no danger. It is most extraordinary that they have gone away; but the man is no more mad than I am, and I know he is a gentleman. He told me so."

"Let us hope for the best," said Mrs Jansenius smoothly. "I think I will sit down—I feel so tired. Thanks." (Agatha had handed her a chair.) "What did you say he told you—this man?"

Agatha related the circumstances of her acquaintance with

Smilash, adding, at Mrs Jansenius's request, a minute description of his personal appearance. Mrs Jansenius remarked that it was very singular, and that she was sure Henrietta was quite safe. She then partook of claret-cup and sandwiches. Agatha, though glad to find some one disposed to listen to her, was puzzled by her aunt's coolness, and was goaded into pointing out that though Smilash was not a laborer, it did not follow that he was an honest man. But Mrs Jansenius only said: "Oh, she is safe—quite safe! At least, of course, I can only hope so. We shall have news presently," and took another sandwich.

The searchers soon began to return, baffled. A few shepherds, the only persons in the vicinity, had been asked whether they had seen a young lady and a laborer. Some of them had seen a young woman with a basket of clothes, if that mout be her. Some thought that Phil Martin the carrier would see her if anybody would. None of them had any positive information to give.

As the afternoon wore on, and party after party returned tired and unsuccessful, depression replaced excitement; conversation, no longer tumultuous, was carried on in whispers, and some of the local visitors slipped away to their homes with a growing conviction that something unpleasant had happened, and that it would be as well not to be mixed up in it. Mr Jansenius, though a few words from his wife had surprised and somewhat calmed him, was still pitiably restless and uneasy.

At last the police arrived. At sight of their uniforms excitement revived; there was a general conviction that something effectual would be done now. But the constables were only mortal, and in a few moments a whisper spread that they were fools. They doubted everything told them, and expressed their contempt for amateur searching by entering on a fresh investigation, prying with the greatest care into the least probable places. Two of them went off to the chalet to look for Smilash. Then Fairholme, sunburnt, perspiring, and dusty, but still energetic, brought back the exhausted remnant of his party, with a sullen boy, who scowled defiantly at the police, evidently believing that he was about to be delivered into their custody.

Fairholme had been everywhere, and, having seen nothing of the missing pair, had come to the conclusion that they were nowhere. He had asked everybody for information, and had let them know that he meant to have it too, if it was to be had. But it was not to be had. The sole result of his labor was the evidence of the boy, whom he didnt believe.

"Hm!" said the inspector, not quite pleased by Fairholme's zeal, and yet overborne by it. "Youre Wickens's boy, aint you?"

"Yes, I am Wickens's boy," said the witness, partly fierce, partly lachrymose, "and I say I seen him, and if any one sez I didnt see him, he's a lie."

"Come," said the inspector sharply, "give us none of your cheek, but tell us what you saw, or youll have to deal with me afterwards."

"I dont care who I deal with," said the boy, at bay. "I cant be took for seein him, because theres no lor agin it. I was in the gravel-pit in the canal meadow—"

"What business had you there?" said the inspector, interrupting.

"I got leave to be there," said the boy insolently, but reddening.

"Who gave you leave?" said the inspector, collaring him. "Ah," he added, as the captive burst into tears, "I told you youd have to deal with me. Now hold your noise, and remember where you are and who youre speakin to; and perhaps I maynt lock you up this time. Tell me what you saw when you were trespassin in the meadow."

"I sor a young 'oman and a man. And I see her kissin him; and the gentleman wont believe me."

"You mean you saw him kissing her, more likely."

"No, I dont. I know wot it is to have a girl kiss you when you dont want. And I gev a screech to friken em. And he called me and gev me tuppence, and sez, 'You go to the devil,' he sez, 'and dont tell no one you seen me here, or else,' he sez, 'I might be tempted to drownd you,' he sez, 'and wot a shock that would be to your parents!' 'Oh, yes, very likely,' I sez, jes like that. Then I went away, because he knows Mr Wickens, and I was afeerd of his telling on me."

The boy being now subdued, questions were put to him from all sides. But his powers of observation and description went no further. As he was anxious to propitiate his captors, he answered as often as possible in the affirmative. Mr Jansenius asked him whether the young woman he had seen was a lady, and he said yes. Was the man a laborer? Yes—after a moment's hesitation. How was she dressed? He hadnt taken notice. Had she red flowers in her hat? Yes. Had she a green dress? Yes. Were the flowers in her hat yellow? (Agatha's question.) Yes. Was her dress pink? Yes. Sure it wasnt black? No answer.

"I told you he was a liar," said Fairholme contemptuously.

"Well, I expect he's seen something," said the inspector, "but what it was, or who it was, is more than I can get out of him."

There was a pause, and they looked askance upon Wickens's boy. His account of the kissing made it almost an insult to the Janseniuses to identify with Henrietta the person he had seen. Jane suggested dragging the canal, but was silenced by an indignant "sh-sh-sh," accompanied by apprehensive and sympathetic glances at the bereaved parents. She was displaced from the focus of attention by the appearance of the two policemen who had been sent to the chalet. Smilash was between them, apparently a prisoner. At a distance, he seemed to have suffered some frightful injury to his head, but when he was brought into the midst of the company it appeared that he had twisted a red handkerchief about his face as if to soothe a toothache. He had a particularly hangdog expression as he stood before the inspector with his head bowed and his countenance averted from Mr Jansenius, who, attempting to scrutinize his features, could see nothing but a patch of red handkerchief.

One of the policemen described how they had found Smilash in the act of entering his dwelling; how he had refused to give any information or to go to the college, and had defied them to take him there against his will; and how, on their at last proposing to send for the inspector and Mr Jansenius, he had called them asses, and consented to accompany them. The policeman concluded by declaring that the man was either drunk or designing, as he could not or would not speak sensibly.

"Look here, governor," began Smilash to the inspector, "I am a common man—no commoner goin, as you may see for—"

"Thats 'im," cried Wickens's boy, suddenly struck with a sense of his own importance as a witness. "Thats 'im that the lady kissed, and that gev me tuppence and threatened to drownd me."

"And with a 'umble and contrite 'art do I regret that I did not drownd you, you young rascal," said Smilash. "It aint manners to interrupt a man who, though common, might be your father for years and wisdom."

"Hold your tongue," said the inspector to the boy. "Now, Smilash, do you wish to make any statement? Be careful, for whatever you say may be used against you hereafter."

"If you was to lead me straight away to the scaffold, colonel, I could tell you no more than the truth. If any man can say that he has heard Jeff Smilash tell a lie, let him stand forth."

"We dont want to hear about that," said the inspector. "As you are a stranger in these parts, nobody here knows any bad of you. No more do they know any good of you neither."

"Colonel," said Smilash, deeply impressed, "you have a penetrating mind, and you know a bad character at sight. Not to deceive you, I am that given to lying, and laziness, and self-indulgence of all sorts, that the only excuse I can find for myself is that it is the nature of the race so to be; for most men is just as bad as me, and some of em worser. I do not speak pers'nal to you, governor, nor to the honorable gentlemen here assembled. But then you, colonel, are a hinspector of police, which I take to be more than merely human; and as to the gentlemen here, a gentleman aint a man—leastways not a common man—the common man bein but the slave wot feeds and clothes the gentleman beyond the common."

"Come," said the inspector, unable to follow these observations, "you are a clever dodger, but you cant dodge me. Have you any statement to make with reference to the lady that was last seen in your company?"

"Make a statement about a lady!" said Smilash indignantly. "Far be the thought from my mind!"

"What have you done with her?" said Agatha impetuously. "Dont be silly."

"Youre not bound to answer that, you know," said the inspector, a little put out by Agatha's taking advantage of her irresponsible unofficial position to come so directly to the point. "You may if you like, though. If youve done any harm, youd better hold your tongue. If not, youd better say so."

"I will set the young lady's mind at rest respecting her honorable sister," said Smilash. "When the young lady caught sight of me she fainted. Bein but a young man, and not used to ladies, I will not deny but that I were a bit scared, and that my mind were not open to the sensiblest considerations. When she unveils her orbs, so to speak, she ketches me round the neck, not knowin me from Adam the father of us all, and sez, 'Bring me some water, and dont let the girls see me.' Through not 'avin the intelligence to think for myself, I done just what she told me. I ups with her in my arms—she bein a light weight and a slender figure—and makes for the canal as fast as I could. When I got there, I lays her on the bank and goes for the water. But what with factories, and pollutions, and high civilizations of one sort and another, English canal water aint fit to sprinkle on a lady, much less for her to drink. Just then, as luck would have it, a barge came along and took her aboard, and—"

"No such a thing," said Wickens's boy stubbornly, emboldened by witnessing the effrontery of one apparently of his own class. "I sor you two standin together, and her a kissin of you. There wornt no barge."

"Is the maiden modesty of a born lady to be disbelieved on the word of a common boy that only walks the earth by the sufferance of the landlords and money-lords he helps to feed?" cried Smilash indignantly. "Why, you young infidel, a lady aint made of common brick like you. She dont know what a kiss means, and if she did, is it likely that she'd kiss me when a fine man like the inspector here would be only too happy to oblige her. Fie, for shame! The barge were red and yellow, with a green dragon for a figurehead, and a white horse towin of it. Perhaps youre colour-blind, and cant distinguish red and yellow. The bargee was moved to compassion by the sight of the poor faintin lady, and the offer of arf-a-crown, and he had a mother that acted as a mother should. There was a cabin in that barge about as big as the locker where your ladyship keeps your jam and pickles, and in that locker the bargee lives, quite domestic, with his wife and mother and five children. Them canal boats is what you may call the wooden walls of England."

"Come, get on with your story," said the inspector. "We know what barges is as well as you."

"I wish more knew of em," retorted Smilash; "perhaps it 'ud lighten your work a bit. However, as I was sayin, we went right down the canal to Lyvern, where we got off, and the lady she took the railway omnibus and went away in it. With the noble open-handedness of her class, she gave me sixpence; here it is, in proof that my words is true. And I wish her safe home, and if I was on the rack I could tell no more, except that when I got back I were laid hands on by these here bobbies, contrary to the British con-stitooshun, and if your ladyship will kindly go to where that constitooshun is wrote down, and find out wot it sez about my rights and liberties—for I have been told that the working-man has his liberties, and have myself seen plenty took with him—you will oblige a common chap more than his education will enable him to express."

"Sir," cried Mr Jansenius suddenly, "will you hold up your head and look me in the face?"

Smilash did so, and immediately started theatrically, exclaiming, "Whom do I see?"

"You would hardly believe it," he continued, addressing the company at large, "but I am well beknown to this honorable gentleman. I see it upon your lips, governor, to ask after my missus, and I thank you for your condescending interest. She is well, sir, and my residence here is fully agreed upon between us. What little cloud may have rose upon our domestic horizon has passed away; and, governor"—here Smilash's voice fell with graver emphasis—"them as interferes betwixt man and wife now will incur a nevvy responsibility. Here I am, such as you see me, and here I mean to stay, likewise such as you see me. That is, if what you may call destiny permits. For destiny is a rum thing, governor. I came here thinking it was the last place in the world I should ever set eyes on you in, and blow me if you aint a'most the first person I pops on."

"I do not choose to be a party to this mummery of—"

"Asking your leave to take the word out of your mouth, governor, I make you a party to nothink. Respecting my past conduct, you may out with it or you may keep it to yourself. All I say is that if you out with some of it I will out with the rest. All or none. You are free to tell the inspector here that I am a bad un. His penetrating mind have discovered that already. But if you go into names and particulars, you will not only be acting against the wishes of my missus, but you will lead to my tellin the whole story right out afore every one here, and then goin away where no one wont never find me."

"I think the less said the better," said Mrs Jansenius, uneasily observant of the curiosity and surprise this dialogue was causing. "But understand this, Mr—"

"Smilash, dear lady; Jeff Smilash."

"Mr Smilash, whatever arrangement you may have made with your wife, it has nothing to do with me. You have behaved infamously, and I desire to have as little as possible to say to you in future."

"I desire to have *nothing* to say to you—*nothing!*" said Mr Jansenius. "I look on your conduct as an insult to me, personally. You may live in any fashion you please, and where you please. All England is open to you except one place—my house. Come, Ruth." He offered his arm to his wife; she took it, and they turned away, looking about for Agatha, who, disgusted at the gaping curiosity of the rest, had pointedly withdrawn beyond earshot of the conversation.

Miss Wilson looked from Smilash—who had watched Mr Jansenius's explosion of wrath with friendly interest, as if it concerned him as a curious spectator only—to her two visitors as they retreated. "Pray do not consider this man's statement satisfactory," she said to them. "*I* do not."

"I am far too common a man to be able to make any statement that could satisfy a mind cultivated as yours has been," said Smilash, "but I would 'umbly pint out to you that there is a boy yonder with a telegram trying to shove hisself through the 'iborn throng."

"Miss Wilson!" cried the boy shrilly.

She took the telegram, read it, and frowned. "We have had all our trouble for nothing, ladies and gentlemen," she said, with suppressed vexation. "Mrs Trefusis says here that she has gone back to London. She has not considered it necessary to add any explanation."

There was a general murmur of disappointment.

"Dont lose heart, ladies," said Smilash. "She may be drowned or murdered for all we know. Any one may send a telegram in a false name. Perhaps it's a plant. Lets hope for your sakes that some little accident—on the railway, for instance—may happen yet."

Miss Wilson turned upon him, glad to find some one with whom she might justly be angry. "*You* had better go about your business," she said. "And dont let me see you here again."

"This is 'ard," said Smilash plaintively. "My intentions was nothing but good. But I know wot it is. It's that young varmint a-saying that the young lady kissed me."

"Inspector," said Miss Wilson, "will you oblige me by seeing that he leaves the college as soon as possible?"

"Wheres my wages?" he retorted reproachfully. "Wheres my lawful wages? I am su'prised at a lady like you, chock full o' moral science and political economy, wanting to put a poor man off. Wheres your wages fund? Wheres your remuneratory capital?"

"Dont you give him anything, maam," said the inspector.

"The money he's had from the lady will pay him very well. Move on here, or we'll precious soon hurry you."

"Very well," grumbled Smilash. "I bargained for ninepence, and what with the roller, and opening the soda-water, and shoving them heavy tables about, there was a decomposition of tissue in me to the tune of two shillings. But all I ask is the ninepence, and let the lad keep the one and threppence as the reward of abstinence. Exploitation of labor at the rate of a hundred and twenty-five per cent., that is. Come, give us ninepence, and I'll get straight off."

"Here is a shilling," said Miss Wilson. "Now go."

"Threppence change!" cried Smilash. "Honesty has ever been—"

"You may keep the change."

"You have a noble 'art, lady; but youre flying in the face of the law of supply and demand. If you keep payin at this rate, there'll be a rush of laborers to the college, and competition'll soon bring you down from a shilling to sixpence, let alone ninepence. Thats the way wages go down and death rates goes up, worse luck for the likes of hus, as has to sell ourselves like pigs in the market."

He was about to continue when the policeman took him by the arm, turned him towards the gate, and pointed expressively in that direction. Smilash looked vacantly at him for a moment. Then, with a wink at Fairholme, he walked gravely away, amid general staring and silence.

CHAPTER V

WHAT had passed between Smilash and Henrietta remained unknown except to themselves. Agatha had seen Henrietta clasping his neck in her arms, but had not waited to hear the exclamation of "Sidney, Sidney," which followed, nor to see him press her face to his breast in his anxiety to stifle her voice as he said, "My darling love, dont screech, I implore you. Confound it, we shall have the whole pack here in a moment. Hush!"

"Dont leave me again, Sidney," she entreated, clinging faster to him as his perplexed gaze, wandering towards the entrance to the shrubbery, seemed to forsake her. A din of voices in that direction precipitated his irresolution.

"We must run away, Hetty," he said. "Hold fast about my neck, and dont strangle me. Now then." He lifted her upon his shoulder and ran swiftly through the grounds. When they were stopped by the wall, he placed her atop of it, scrambled over, and made her jump into his arms. Then he staggered away with her across the fields, gasping out, in reply to the inarticulate remonstrances which burst from her as he stumbled and reeled at every hillock, "Your weight is increasing at the rate of a stone a second, my love. If you stoop you will break my back. Oh, Lord, here's a ditch!"

"Let me down," screamed Henrietta in an ecstasy of delight and apprehension. "You will hurt yourself, and— Oh, *do* take—"

He struggled through a dry ditch as she spoke, and came out upon a grassy place that bordered the tow-path of the canal. Here, on the bank of a hollow where the moss was dry and soft, he seated her, threw himself prone on his elbows before her, and said, panting:

"Nessus carrying off Dejanira was nothing to this! Whew! Well, my darling, are you glad to see me?"

"But—"

"But me no buts, unless you wish me to vanish again and for ever. Wretch that I am, I have longed for you unspeakably, more than once since I ran away from you. You didnt care, of course?"

"I did. I did, indeed. Why did you leave me, Sidney?"

"Lest a worse thing might befall. Come, dont let us waste in explanations the few minutes we have left. Give me a kiss."

"Then you are going to leave me again. Oh, Sidney—"

"Never mind to-morrow, Hetty. Be like the sun and the meadow, which are not in the least concerned about the coming winter. Why do you stare at that cursed canal, blindly dragging its load of filth from place to place until it pitches it into the sea—just as a crowded street pitches its load into the cemetery? Stare at *me*, and give me a kiss."

She gave him several, and said coaxingly, with her arm still upon his shoulder: "You only talk that way to frighten me, Sidney; I know you do."

"You are the bright sun of my senses," he said, embracing her. "I feel my heart and brain wither in your smile, and I fling them to you for your prey with exultation. How happy I am to have a wife who does not despise me for doing so—who rather loves me the more!"

"Dont be silly," said Henrietta, smiling vacantly. Then, stung by a half intuition of his meaning, she repulsed him and said angrily, "*You* despise *me*."

"Not more than I despise myself. Indeed, not so much; for many emotions that seem base from within, seem lovable from without."

"You intend to leave me again. I feel it. I know it."

"You think you know it because you feel it. Not a bad reason, either."

"Then you *are* going to leave me?"

"Do you not feel it and know it? Yes, my cherished Hetty, I assuredly am."

She broke into wild exclamations of grief, and he drew her head down and kissed her with a tender action which she could not resist, and a wry face which she did not see.

"My poor Hetty, you dont understand me."

"I only understand that you hate me, and want to go away from me."

"That would be easy to understand. But the strangeness is that I *love* you and want to go away from you. Not for ever. Only for a time."

"But I dont want you to go away. I wont let you go away," she said, a trace of fierceness mingling with her entreaty. "Why do you want to leave me if you love me?"

"How do I know? I can no more tell you the whys and wherefores of myself than I can lift myself up by the waistband and carry myself into the next county, as some one challenged a speculator in perpetual motion to do. I am too much a pessimist to respect my own affections. Do you know what a pessimist is?"

"A man who thinks everybody as nasty as himself, and hates them for it."

"So, or thereabout. Modern English polite society, my native sphere, seems to me as corrupt as consciousness of culture and absence of honesty can make it. A canting, lie-loving, fact-hating, scribbling, chattering, wealth-hunting, pleasure-hunting, celebrity-hunting mob, that, having lost the fear of hell, and not replaced it by the love of justice, cares for nothing but the lion's share of the wealth wrung by threat of starvation from the hands of the classes that create it. If you interrupt me with a silly speech, Hetty, I will pitch you into the canal, and die of sorrow for my lost love afterwards. You know what I am, according to the conventional description: a gentleman with lots of money. Do you know the wicked origin of that money and gentility?"

"Oh, Sidney; have you been doing anything?"

"No, my best beloved; I am a gentleman, and have been doing nothing. That a man can do so and not starve is nowadays not even a paradox. Every halfpenny I possess is stolen money; but it has been stolen legally, and, what is of some practical importance to you, I have no means of restoring it to the rightful owners even if I felt inclined to. Do you know what my father was?"

"What difference can that make now? Dont be disagreeable and full of ridiculous fads, Sidney dear. I didnt marry your father."

"No; but you married—only incidentally, of course—my father's fortune. That necklace of yours was purchased with his money; and I can almost fancy stains of blood—"

"Stop, Sidney. I dont like this sort of romancing. It's all nonsense. *Do* be nice to me."

"There are stains of sweat on it, I know."

"You nasty wretch!"

"I am thinking, not of you, my dainty one, but of the unfortunate people who slave that we may live idly. Let me explain to you why we are so rich. My father was a shrewd, energetic, and ambitious Manchester man, who understood an exchange of any sort as a transaction by which one man should lose and the other gain. He made it his object to make as many exchanges as possible, and to be always the gaining party in them. I do not know exactly what he was, for he was ashamed both of his antecedents and of his relatives, from which I can only infer that they were honest, and, therefore, unsuccessful people. However, he acquired some knowledge of the cotton trade, saved some money, borrowed some more on the security of his reputation for getting the better of other people in business, and, as he accurately told me afterwards, started *for himself.* He bought a factory and some raw cotton. Now you must know that a man, by laboring some time on a piece of raw cotton, can turn it into a piece of manufactured cotton fit for making into sheets and shifts and the like. The manufactured cotton is more valuable than the raw cotton, because the manufacture costs wear and tear of machinery, wear and tear of the factory, rent of the ground upon which the factory is built, and human labor, or wear and tear of live men, which has to be made good by food, shelter, and rest. Do you understand that?"

"We used to learn all about it at college. I dont see what it has to do with us, since you are not in the cotton trade."

"You learned as much as it was thought safe to teach you,

no doubt; but not quite all, I should think. When my father started for himself, there were many men in Manchester who were willing to labor in this way, but they had no factory to work in, no machinery to work with, and no raw cotton to work on, simply because all this indispensable plant, and the materials for producing a fresh supply of it, had been appropriated by earlier comers. So they found themselves with gaping stomachs, shivering limbs, and hungry wives and children, in a place called their own country, in which, nevertheless, every scrap of ground and possible source of subsistence was tightly locked up in the hands of others and guarded by armed soldiers and policemen. In this helpless condition, the poor devils were ready to beg for access to a factory and to raw cotton on any conditions compatible with life. My father offered them the use of his factory, his machines, and his raw cotton on the following conditions: They were to work long and hard, early and late, to add fresh value to his raw cotton by manufacturing it. Out of the value thus created by them, they were to recoup him for what he supplied them with: rent, shelter, gas, water, machinery, raw cotton— everything, and to pay him for his own services as superintendent, manager, and salesman. So far he asked nothing but just remun- eration. But after this had been paid, a balance due solely to their own labor remained. 'Out of this,' said my father, 'you shall keep just enough to save you from starving, and of the rest you shall make me a present to reward me for my virtue in saving money. Such is the bargain I propose. It is, in my opinion, fair and calcu- lated to encourage thrifty habits. If it does not strike you in that light, you can get a factory and raw cotton for yourselves; you shall not use mine.' In other words, they might go to the devil and starve—Hobson's choice!—for all the other factories were owned by men who offered no better terms. The Manchesterians could not bear to starve or to see their children starve, and so they accepted his terms and went into the factory. The terms, you see, did not admit of their beginning to save for themselves as he had done. Well, they created great wealth by their labor, and lived on very little, so that the balance they gave for nothing to my father was large. He bought more cotton, and more machinery, and more factories with it; employed more men to make wealth for him, and saw his fortune increase like a rolling snowball. He prospered enormously, but the workmen were no better off than at first, and they dared not rebel and demand more of the money they had made, for there were always plenty of starving wretches outside willing to take their places on the old terms. Sometimes he met with a check, as, for instance, when, in his eagerness to increase his store, he made the men manufacture more cotton than the public needed; or when he could not get enough of raw cotton, as happened during the Civil War in America. Then he adapted himself to circumstances by turning away as many workmen as he could not find customers or cotton for; and they, of course, starved or subsisted on charity. During the war-time a big subscription was got up for these poor wretches, and my father subscribed one hundred pounds, in spite, he said, of his own great losses. Then he bought new machines; and, as women and children could work these as well as men, and were cheaper and more docile, he turned away about seventy out of every hundred of his *hands* (so he called the men), and replaced them by their wives and children, who made money for him faster than ever. By this time he had long ago given up managing the factories, and paid clever fellows who had no money of their own a few hundreds a year to do it for him. He also purchased shares in other concerns conducted on the same principle; pocketed dividends made in countries which he had never visited by men whom he had never seen; bought a seat in Parliament from a poor and corrupt constituency, and helped to preserve the laws by which he had thriven. Afterwards, when his wealth grew famous, he had less need to bribe; for modern men worship the rich as gods, and will elect a man as one of their rulers for no other reason than that he is a millionaire. He aped gentility, lived in a palace at Kensington, and bought a part of Scotland to make a deer forest of. It is easy enough to make a deer forest, as trees are not necessary there. You simply drive off the peasants, destroy their houses, and make a desert of the land. However, my father did not shoot much himself; he generally let the forest out by the season to those who did. He purchased a wife of gentle blood too, with the unsatisfactory result now before you. That is how Jesse Trefusis, a poor Manchester bagman, contrived to become a plutocrat and gentleman of landed estate. And also how I, who never did a stroke of work in my life, am overburdened with wealth; whilst the children of the men who made that wealth are slaving as their fathers slaved, or starving, or in the workhouse, or on the streets, or the deuce knows where. What do you think of that, my love?"

"What is the use of worrying about it, Sidney? It cannot be helped now. Besides, if your father saved money, and the others were improvident, he deserved to make a fortune."

"Granted; but he didnt make a fortune. He took a fortune that others made. At Cambridge they taught me that his profits were the reward of abstinence—the abstinence which enabled him to save. That quieted my conscience until I began to wonder why one man should make another pay him for exercising one of the virtues. Then came the question: what did my father abstain from? The workmen abstained from meat, drink, fresh air, good clothes, decent lodging, holidays, money, the society of their families, and pretty nearly everything that makes life worth living, which was perhaps the reason why they usually died twenty years or so sooner than people in our circumstances. Yet no one rewarded them for their abstinence. The reward came to my father, who abstained from none of these things, but indulged in them all to his heart's content. Besides, if the money was the reward of abstinence, it seemed logical to infer that he must abstain ten times as much when he had fifty thousand a year as when he had only five thousand. Here was a problem for my young mind. Required, something from which my father abstained and in which his workmen exceeded, and which he abstained from more and more as he grew richer and richer. The only thing that answered this description was hard work, and as I never met a sane man willing to pay another for idling, I began to see that these prodigious payments to my father were extorted by force. To do him justice, he never boasted of abstinence. He considered himself a hard-worked man, and claimed his fortune as the reward of his risks, his calculations, his anxieties, and the journeys he had to make at all seasons and at all hours. This comforted me somewhat until it occurred to me that if he had lived a century earlier, invested his money in a horse and a pair of pistols, and taken to the road, his object—that of wresting from others the fruits of their labor without rendering them an equivalent—would have been exactly the same, and his risk far greater, for it would have included risk of the gallows. Constant travelling with the constable at his heels, and calculations of the chances of robbing the Dover mail, would have given him his fill of activity and anxiety. On the whole, if Jesse Trefusis, M.P., who died a millionaire in his palace at Kensington, had been a highwayman, I could not more heartily loathe the social arrangements that rendered such a career as his not only possible, but eminently creditable to himself in the eyes of his fellows. Most men make it their business to imitate him, hoping to become rich and idle on the same terms. Therefore I turn my back on them. I cannot sit at their feasts knowing how much they cost in human misery, and seeing how little they produce of human happiness. What is your opinion, my treasure?"

Henrietta seemed a little troubled. She smiled faintly, and said caressingly: "It is not your fault, Sidney. *I* dont blame you."

"Immortal powers!" he exclaimed, sitting bolt upright and appealing to the skies, "here is a woman who believes that the only concern all this causes me is whether she thinks any the worse of me personally on account of it!"

"No, no, Sidney. It is not I alone. Nobody thinks the worse of you for it."

"Quite so," he returned, in a polite frenzy. "Nobody sees any harm in it. That is precisely the mischief of it."

"Besides," she urged, "your mother belonged to one of the oldest families in England."

"And what more can man desire than wealth with descent

from a county family! Could a man be happier than I ought to
be, sprung as I am from monopolists of all the sources and
instruments of production—of land on the one side, and of
machinery on the other? This very ground on which we are
resting was the property of my mother's father. At least, the law
allowed him to use it as such. When he was a boy, there was a
fairly prosperous race of peasants settled here, tilling the soil,
paying him rent for permission to do so, and making enough
out of it to satisfy his large wants and their own narrow needs
without working themselves to death. But my grandfather was
a shrewd man. He perceived that cows and sheep produced more
money by their meat and wool than peasants by their husbandry.
So he cleared the estate. That is, he drove the peasants from
their homes, as my father did afterwards in his Scotch deer
forest. Or, as his tombstone has it, he developed the resources
of his country. I dont know what became of the peasants; *he*
didnt know, and, I presume, didnt care. I suppose the old ones
went into the workhouse, and the young ones crowded the towns,
and worked for men like my father in factories. Their places
were taken by cattle, which paid for their food so well that my
grandfather, getting my father to take shares in the enterprise,
hired laborers on the Manchester terms to cut that canal for him.
When it was made, he took toll upon it; and his heirs still take
toll, and the sons of the navvies who dug it and of the engineer
who designed it pay the toll when they have occasion to travel
by it, or to purchase goods which have been conveyed along it.
I remember my grandfather well. He was a well-bred man, and
a perfect gentleman in his manners; but on the whole, I think
he was wickeder than my father, who, after all, was caught in
the wheels of a vicious system, and had either to spoil others or
be spoiled by them. But my grandfather—the old rascal!—was
in no such dilemma. Master as he was of his bit of merry England,
no man could have enslaved him, and he might at least have
lived and let live. My father followed his example in the matter
of the deer forest, but that was the climax of his wickedness,
whereas it was only the beginning of my grandfather's. Howbeit,

whichever bears the palm, there they were, the types after which we all strive."

"Not all, Sidney. Not we two. I hate tradespeople and country squires. We belong to the artistic and cultured classes, and we can keep aloof from shopkeepers."

"Living, meanwhile, at the rate of several thousand a year on rent and interest. No, my dear, this is the way of those people who insist that when they are in heaven they shall be spared the recollection of such a place as hell, but are quite content that it shall exist outside their consciousness. I respect my father more—I mean I despise him less—for doing his own sweating and filching than I do the sensitive sluggards and cowards who lent him their money to sweat and filch with, and asked no questions provided the interest was paid punctually. And as to your friends the artists, they are the worst of all."

"Oh, Sidney, you are determined not to be pleased. Artists dont keep factories."

"No; but the factory is only a part of the machinery of the system. Its basis is the tyranny of brain force, which, among civilized men, is allowed to do what muscular force does among schoolboys and savages. The schoolboy proposition is: 'I am stronger than you, therefore you shall fag for me.' Its grown-up form is: 'I am cleverer than you, therefore you shall fag for me.' The state of things we produce by submitting to this, bad enough even at first, becomes intolerable when the mediocre or foolish descendants of the clever fellows claim to have inherited their privileges. Now, no men are greater sticklers for the arbitrary dominion of genius and talent than your artists. The great painter is not satisfied with being sought after and admired because his hands can do more than ordinary hands, which they truly can, but he wants to be fed as if his stomach needed more food than ordinary stomachs, which it does not. A day's work is a day's work, neither more nor less, and the man who does it needs a day's sustenance, a night's repose, and due leisure, whether he be painter or ploughman. But the rascal of a painter, poet, novelist, or other voluptuary in labor, is not content with his advantage in popular esteem over the ploughman; he also wants an advantage in money, as if there were more hours in a day spent in the studio or library than in the field; or as if he needed more food to enable him to do his work than the ploughman to enable him to do his. He talks of the higher quality of his work, as if the higher quality of it were of his own making—as if it gave him a right to work less for his neighbor than his neighbor works for him—as if the ploughman could not do better without him than he without the ploughman—as if the value of the most celebrated pictures has not been questioned more than that of any straight furrow in the arable world—as if it did not take an apprenticeship of as many years to train the hand and eye of a mason or blacksmith as of an artist—as if, in short, the fellow were a god, as canting brain-worshippers have for years past been assuring him he is. Artists are the high priests of the modern Moloch. Nine out of ten of them are diseased creatures, just sane enough to trade on their own neuroses. The only quality of theirs which extorts my respect is a certain sublime selfishness which makes them willing to starve and to let their families starve sooner than do any work they dont like."

"*Indeed* you are quite wrong, Sidney. There was a girl at the Slade School who supported her mother and two sisters by her drawing. Besides, what can you do? People were made so."

"Yes; I was made a landlord and capitalist by the folly of the people; but they can unmake me if they will. Meanwhile I have absolutely no means of escape from my position except by giving away my slaves to fellows who will use them no better than I, and becoming a slave myself; which, if you please, you shall not catch me doing in a hurry. No, my beloved, I must keep my foot on their necks for your sake as well as for my own. But you do not care about all this prosy stuff. I am consumed with remorse for having bored my darling. You want to know why I am living here like a hermit in a vulgar two-roomed hovel instead of tasting the delights of London society with my beautiful and devoted young wife."

"But you dont intend to stay here, Sidney?"

"Yes, I do; and I will tell you why. I am helping to liberate those Manchester laborers who were my father's slaves. To bring that about, their fellow-slaves all over the world must unite in a vast international association of men pledged to share the world's work justly; to share the produce of the work justly; to yield not a farthing—charity apart—to any full-grown and able-bodied idler or malingerer, and to treat as vermin in the commonwealth persons attempting to get more than their share of wealth or give less than their share of work. This is a very difficult thing to accomplish, because working-men, like the people called their betters, do not always understand their own interests, and will often actually help their oppressors to exterminate their saviours to the tune of 'Rule Britannia,' or some such lying doggerel. We must educate them out of that, and, meanwhile, push forward the international association of laborers diligently. I am at present occupied in propagating its principles. Capitalism, organized for repressive purposes under pretext of governing the nation, would very soon stop the association if it understood our aim; but it thinks that we are engaged in gunpowder plots and conspiracies to assassinate crowned heads; and so, whilst the police are blundering in search of evidence of these, our brain work goes on unmolested. Whether I am really advancing the cause is more than I can say. I use heaps of postage stamps, pay the expenses of many indifferent lecturers, defray the cost of printing reams of pamphlets and hand-bills which hail the laborer flatteringly as the salt of the earth, write and edit a little socialist journal, and do what lies in my power generally. I had rather spend my ill-gotten wealth in this way than upon an expensive house and a retinue of servants. And I prefer my corduroys and my two-roomed chalet here to our pretty little house and your pretty little ways, and my pretty little neglect of the work that my heart is set upon. Some day, perhaps, I will take a holiday; and then we shall have a new honeymoon."

For a moment Henrietta seemed about to cry. Suddenly she exclaimed with enthusiasm: "I will stay with you, Sidney. I will share your work, whatever it may be. I will dress as a dairymaid, and have a little pail to carry milk in. The world is nothing to me except when you are with me; and I should love to live here and sketch from nature."

He blenched, and partially rose, unable to conceal his dismay. She, resolved not to be cast off, seized him and clung to him. This was the movement that excited the derision of Wickens's boy in the adjacent gravel-pit. Trefusis was glad of the interruption; and, when he gave the boy twopence and bade him begone, half hoped that he would insist on remaining. But though an obdurate boy on most occasions, he proved complaisant on this, and withdrew to the high road, where he made over one of his pennies to a phantom gambler, and tossed with him until recalled from his dual state by the appearance of Fairholme's party.

In the meantime, Henrietta urgently returned to her proposition.

"We should be so happy," she said. "I would housekeep for you, and you could work as much as you pleased. Our life would be a long idyll."

"My love," he said, shaking his head as she looked beseechingly at him, "I have too much Manchester cotton in my constitution for long idylls. And the truth is, that the first condition of work with me is your absence. When you are with me, I can do nothing but make love to you. You bewitch me. When I escape from you for a moment, it is only to groan remorsefully over the hours you have tempted me to waste and the energy you have futilized."

"If you wont live with me you had no right to marry me."

"True. But that is neither your fault nor mine. We have found that we love each other too much—that our intercourse hinders our usefulness—and so we must part. Not for ever, my dear; only until you have cares and business of your own to fill up your life and prevent you from wasting mine."

"I believe you are mad," she said petulantly.

"The world is mad nowadays, and is galloping to the deuce

as fast as greed can goad it. I merely stand out of the rush, not liking its destination. Here comes a barge, the commander of which is devoted to me because he believes that I am organizing a revolution for the abolition of lock dues and tolls. We will go aboard and float down to Lyvern, whence you can return to London. You had better telegraph from the junction to the college; there must be a hue and cry out after us by this time. You shall have my address, and we can write to one another or see one another whenever we please. Or you can divorce me for deserting you."

"You would like me to, I know," said Henrietta, sobbing.

"I should die of despair, my darling," he said complacently. "Ship aho-o-o-oy! Stop crying, Hetty, for God's sake. You lacerate my very soul."

"Ah-o-o-o-o-o-o-oy, master!" roared the bargee.

"Good arternoon, sir," said a man who, with a short whip in his hand, trudged beside the white horse that towed the barge. "Come up!" he added malevolently to the horse.

"I want to get on board, and go up to Lyvern with you," said Trefusis. "He seems a well-fed brute that."

"Better fed nor me," said the man. "You cant get the work out of a hunderfed orse that you can out of a hunderfed man or woman. I've bin in parts of England where women pulled the barges. They come cheaper nor orses, because it didnt cost nothing to get new ones when the old ones was wore out."

"Then why not employ them?" said Trefusis, with ironical gravity. "The principle of buying labor-force in the cheapest market and selling its product in the dearest has done much to make Englishmen—what they are."

"The railway comp'nies keeps orspittles for the like of '*im*,'" said the man, with a cunning laugh, indicating the horse by smacking him on the belly with the butt of the whip. "If ever you try bein a laborer in earnest, governor, try it on four legs. Youll find it far preferable to trying on two."

"This man is one of my converts," said Trefusis apart to Henrietta. "He told me the other day that since I set him thinking he never sees a gentleman without feeling inclined to heave a brick at him. I find that socialism is often misunderstood by its least intelligent supporters and opponents to mean simply unrestrained indulgence of our natural propensity to heave bricks at respectable persons. Now I am going to carry you along this plank. If you keep quiet, we may reach the barge. If not, we shall reach the bottom of the canal."

He carried her safely over, and exchanged some friendly words with the bargee. Then he took Henrietta forward, and stood watching the water as they were borne along noiselessly between the hilly pastures of the country.

"This would be a fairy journey," he said, "if one could forget the woman down below, cooking her husband's dinner in a stifling hole about as big as your wardrobe, and—"

"Oh, dont talk any more of these things," she said crossly; "I cannot help them. I have my own troubles to think of. *Her* husband lives with her."

"She will change places with you, my dear, if you make her the offer."

She had no answer ready. After a pause he began to speak poetically of the scenery and to offer her lover-like speeches and compliments. But she felt that he intended to get rid of her, and he knew that it was useless to try to hide that design from her. She turned away and sat down on a pile of bricks, only writhing angrily when he pressed her for a word. As they neared the end of her voyage, and her intense protest against desertion remained, as she thought, only half expressed, her sense of injury grew almost unbearable.

They landed on a wharf, and went through an unswept, deeply-rutted lane up to the main street of Lyvern. Here he became Smilash again, walking deferentially a little before her, as if she had hired him to point out the way. She then saw that her last opportunity of appealing to him had gone by, and she nearly burst into tears at the thought. It occurred to her that she might prevail upon him by making a scene in public. But the street was a busy one, and she was a little afraid of him. Neither consideration would have checked her in one of her ungovernable moods, but now she was in an abject one. Her moods seemed to come only when they were harmful to her. She suffered herself to be put into the railway omnibus, which was on the point of starting from the inn yard when they arrived there, and though he touched his hat, asked whether she had any message to give him, and in a tender whisper wished her a safe journey, she would not look at or speak to him. So they parted, and he returned alone to the chalet, where he was received by the two policemen who subsequently brought him to the college.

CHAPTER VI

THE year wore on, and the long winter evenings set in. The studious young ladies at Alton College, elbows on desks and hands over ears, shuddered chillily in fur tippets whilst they loaded their memories with the statements of writers on moral science, or, like men who swim upon corks, reasoned out mathematical problems upon postulates. Whence it sometimes happened that the more reasonable a student was in mathematics, the more unreasonable she was in the affairs of real life, concerning which few trustworthy postulates have yet been ascertained.

Agatha, not studious, and apt to shiver in winter, began to break Rule No. 17 with increasing frequency. Rule No. 17 forbade the students to enter the kitchen, or in any way to disturb the servants in the discharge of their duties. Agatha broke it because she was fond of making toffee, of eating it, of a good fire, of doing any forbidden thing, and of the admiration with which the servants listened to her ventriloquial and musical feats. Gertrude accompanied her because she too liked toffee, and because she plumed herself on her condescension to her inferiors. Jane went because her two friends went, and the spirit of adventure, the force of example, and the love of toffee often brought more volunteers to these expeditions than Agatha thought it safe to enlist. One evening, Miss Wilson, going downstairs alone to her private wine cellar, was arrested near the kitchen by sounds of revelry, and, stopping to listen, overheard the castanet dance (which reminded her of the emphasis with which Agatha had snapped her fingers at Mrs Miller), the bee on the window pane, Robin Adair (encored by the servants), and an imitation of herself in the act of appealing to Jane Carpenter's better nature to induce her to study for the Cambridge Local. She waited until the cold and her fear of being discovered spying forced her to creep upstairs, ashamed of having enjoyed a silly entertainment, and of conniving at a breach of the rules rather than face a fresh quarrel with Agatha.

There was one particular in which matters between Agatha and the college discipline did not go on exactly as before. Although she had formerly supplied a disproportionately large number of the confessions in the fault book, the entry which had nearly led to her expulsion was the last she ever made in it. Not that her conduct was better—it was rather the reverse. Miss Wilson never mentioned the matter, the fault book being sacred from all allusion on her part. But she saw that though Agatha would not confess her own sins, she still assisted others to unburden their consciences. The witticisms with which Jane unsuspectingly enlivened the pages of the Recording Angel were conclusive on this point.

Smilash had now adopted a profession. In the last days of autumn he had whitewashed the chalet, painted the doors, windows, and veranda, repaired the roof and interior, and improved the place so much that the landlord had warned him that the rent would be raised at the expiration of his twelve-month's tenancy, remarking that a tenant could not reasonably expect to have a pretty, rain-tight dwelling-house for the same money as a hardly habitable ruin. Smilash had immediately promised to dilapidate it to its former state at the end of the year. He had put up a board at the gate with an inscription copied from some printed cards which he presented to persons who happened to converse with him.

JEFFERSON SMILASH

PAINTER, DECORATOR, GLAZIER, PLUMBER & GARDENER

Pianofortes tuned. Domestic Engineering in all its Branches. Families waited upon at table or otherwise.

CHAMOUNIX VILLA,
LYVERN.

(N.B.—ADVICE GRATIS.
No reasonable offer refused.)

The business thus announced, comprehensive as it was, did not flourish. When asked by the curious for testimony to his competence and respectability, he recklessly referred them to Fairholme, to Josephs, and in particular to Miss Wilson, who, he said, had known him from his earliest childhood. Fairholme, glad of an opportunity to show that he was no mealy-mouthed parson, declared, when applied to, that Smilash was the greatest rogue in the country. Josephs, partly from benevolence, and partly from a vague fear that Smilash might at any moment take an action against him for defamation of character, said he had no doubt that he was a very cheap workman, and that it would be a charity to give him some little job to encourage him. Miss Wilson confirmed Fairholme's account; and the church organist, who had tuned all the pianofortes in the neighborhood once a year for nearly a quarter of a century, denounced the newcomer as Jack of all trades and master of none. Hereupon the radicals of Lyvern, a small and disreputable party, began to assert that there was no harm in the man, and that the parsons and Miss Wilson, who lived in a fine house and did nothing but take in the daughters of rich swells as boarders, might employ their leisure better than in taking the bread out of a poor workman's mouth. But as none of this faction needed the services of a domestic engineer, he was none the richer for their support, and the only patron he obtained was a housemaid who was leaving her situation at a country-house in the vicinity, and wanted her box repaired, the lid having fallen off. Smilash demanded half-a-crown for the job, but on her demurring, immediately apologized and came down to a shilling. For this sum he repainted the box, traced her initials on it, and affixed new hinges, a Bramah lock, and brass handles, at a cost to himself of ten shillings and several hours' labor. The housemaid found fault with the color of the paint, made him take off the handles, which, she said, reminded her of a coffin, complained that a lock with such a small key couldnt be strong enough for a large box, but admitted that it was all her own fault for not employing a proper man. It got about that he had made a poor job of the box; and as he, when taxed with this, emphatically confirmed it, he got no other commission; and his signboard served thenceforth only for the amusement of pedestrian tourists and of shepherd boys with a taste for stone-throwing.

One night a great storm blew over Lyvern, and those young ladies at Alton College who were afraid of lightning said their prayers with some earnestness. At half-past twelve the rain, wind, and thunder made such a din that Agatha and Gertrude wrapped themselves in shawls, stole downstairs to the window on the landing outside Miss Wilson's study, and stood watching the flashes give vivid glimpses of the landscape, and discussing in whispers whether it was dangerous to stand near a window, and whether brass stair-rods could attract lightning. Agatha, as serious and friendly with a single companion as she was mischievous and satirical before a larger audience, enjoyed the scene quietly. The lightning did not terrify her, for she knew little of the value of life, and fancied much concerning the heroism of being indifferent to it. The tremors which the more startling flashes caused her, only made her more conscious of her own courage and its contrast with the uneasiness of Gertrude, who at last, shrinking from a forked zig-zag of blue flame, said:

"Let us go back to bed, Agatha. I feel sure that we are not safe here."

"Quite as safe as in bed, where we cannot see anything. How the house shakes! I believe the rain will batter in the windows before—"

"Hush," whispered Gertrude, catching her arm in terror. "What was that?"

"What?"

"I am sure I heard the bell—the gate bell. Oh, do let us go back to bed."

"Nonsense! Who would be out on such a night as this? Perhaps the wind rang it."

They waited for a few moments; Gertrude trembling, and Agatha feeling, as she listened in the darkness, a sensation familiar to persons who are afraid of ghosts. Presently a veiled clangor mingled with the wind. A few sharp and urgent snatches of it came unmistakably from the bell at the gate of the college grounds. It was a loud bell, used to summon a servant from the college to open the gates; for though there was a porter's lodge, it was uninhabited.

"Who on earth can it be?" said Agatha. "Cant they find the wicket, the idiots?"

"Oh, I hope not! Do come upstairs, Agatha."

"No, I wont. Go you, if you like." But Gertrude was afraid to go alone. "I think I had better waken Miss Wilson, and tell her," continued Agatha. "It seems awful to shut anybody out on such a night as this."

"But we dont know who it is."

"Well, I suppose you are not afraid of them, in any case," said Agatha, knowing the contrary, but recognizing the convenience of shaming Gertrude into silence.

They listened again. The storm was now very boisterous, and they could not hear the bell. Suddenly there was a loud knocking at the house door. Gertrude screamed, and her cry was echoed from the rooms above, where several girls had heard the knocking also, and had been driven by it into the state of mind which accompanies the climax of a nightmare. Then a candle flickered on the stairs, and Miss Wilson's voice, reassuringly firm, was heard.

"Who is that?"

"It is I, Miss Wilson, and Gertrude. We have been watching the storm, and there is some one knocking at the—" A tremendous battery with the knocker, followed by a sound, confused by the gale, as of a man shouting, interrupted her.

"They had better not open the door," said Miss Wilson, in some alarm. "You are very imprudent, Agatha, to stand here. You will catch your death of— Dear me! What can be the matter?"

She hurried down, followed by Agatha, Gertrude, and some of the braver students, to the hall, where they found a few shivering servants watching the housekeeper, who was at the keyhole of the house door, querulously asking who was there. She was evidently not heard by those without, for the knocking recommenced whilst she was speaking, and she recoiled as if she had received a blow on the mouth. Miss Wilson then rattled the chain to attract attention, and demanded again who was there.

"Let us in," was returned in a hollow shout through the key-hole. "There is a dying woman and three children here. Open the door."

Miss Wilson lost her presence of mind. To gain time, she replied, "I—I cant hear you. What do you say?"

"Damnation!"said the voice, speaking this time to some one outside. "They cant hear." And the knocking recommenced with increased urgency. Agatha, excited, caught Miss Wilson's dressing gown, and repeated to her what the voice had said. Miss Wilson had heard distinctly enough, and she felt, without knowing clearly why, that the door must be opened, but she was almost overmastered by a vague dread of what was to follow. She began to undo the chain, and Agatha helped with the bolts. Two of the servants exclaimed that they were all about to be murdered in their beds, and ran away. A few of the students seemed inclined to follow their example. At last the door, loosed, was blown wide open, flinging Miss Wilson and Agatha back, and admitting a whirlwind that tore round the hall, snatched at the women's draperies, and blew out the lights. Agatha, by a flash of lightning, saw for an instant two men straining at the door like sailors at a capstan. Then she knew by the cessation of the whirlwind that they had shut it. Matches were struck, the candles relighted, and the newcomers clearly perceived.

Smilash, bareheaded, without a coat, his corduroy vest and trousers heavy with rain; a rough-looking middle-aged man, poorly dressed like a shepherd, wet as Smilash, with the expression, piteous, patient, and desperate, of one hard driven by ill-fortune, and at the end of his resources; two little children, a boy and a girl, almost naked, cowering under an old sack that had served them as an umbrella; and, lying on the settee where the two men had laid it, a heap of wretched wearing apparel, sacking, and

86

rotten matting, with Smilash's coat and sou'wester, the whole covering a bundle which presently proved to be an exhausted woman with a tiny infant at her breast. Smilash's expression, as he looked at her, was ferocious.

"Sorry fur to trouble you, lady," said the man, after glancing anxiously at Smilash, as if he had expected him to act as spokesman; "but my roof and the side of my house has gone in the storm, and my missus has been having another little one, and I am sorry to ill-convenience you, Miss; but—but—"

"Inconvenience!" exclaimed Smilash. "It is the lady's privilege to relieve you—her highest privilege!"

The little boy here began to cry from mere misery, and the woman roused herself to say, "For shame, Tom! before the lady," and then collapsed, too weak to care for what might happen next in the world. Smilash looked impatiently at Miss Wilson, who hesitated, and said to him:

"What do you expect me to do?"

"To help us," he replied. Then, with an explosion of nervous energy, he added: "Do what your heart tells you to do. Give your bed and your clothes to the woman, and let your girls pitch their books to the devil for a few days and make something for these poor little creatures to wear. The poor have worked hard enough to clothe *them*. Let them take their turn now and clothe the poor."

"No, no. Steady, master," said the man, stepping forward to propitiate Miss Wilson, and evidently much oppressed by a sense of unwelcomeness. "It aint any fault of the lady's. Might I make so bold as to ask you to put this woman of mine anywhere that may be convenient until morning? Any sort of a place will do; she's accustomed to rough it. Just to have a roof over her until I find a room in the village where we can shake down." Here, led by his own words to contemplate the future, he looked desolately round the cornice of the hall, as if it were a shelf on which somebody might have left a suitable lodging for him.

Miss Wilson turned her back decisively and contemptuously on Smilash. She had recovered herself. "I will keep your wife here," she said to the man. "Every care shall be taken of her. The children can stay too."

"Three cheers for moral science!" cried Smilash, ecstatically breaking into the outrageous dialect he had forgotten in his wrath. "Wot was my words to you, neighbor, when I said we should bring your missus to the college, and you said, ironical-like, 'Aye, and bloomin glad theyll be to see us there.' Did I not say to you that the lady had a noble 'art, and would show it when put to the test by sech a calamity as this?"

"Why should you bring my hasty words up again' me now, master, when the lady has been so kind?" said the man, with emotion. "I am humbly grateful to you, Miss; and so is Bess. We are sensible of the ill-convenience we—"

Miss Wilson, who had been conferring with the housekeeper, cut his speech short by ordering him to carry his wife to bed, which he did with the assistance of Smilash, now jubilant. Whilst they were away, one of the servants, bidden to bring some blankets to the woman's room, refused, saying that she was not going to wait on that sort of people. Miss Wilson gave her warning almost fiercely to quit the college next day. This excepted, no ill-will was shown to the refugees. The young ladies were then requested to return to bed.

Meanwhile the man, having laid his wife in a chamber palatial in comparison with that which the storm had blown about her ears, was congratulating her on her luck, and threatening the children with the most violent chastisement if they failed to behave themselves with strict propriety whilst they remained in that house. Before leaving them he kissed his wife; and she, reviving, asked him to look at the baby. He did so, and pensively apostrophized it with a shocking epithet in anticipation of the time when its appetite must be satisfied from the provision shop instead of from its mother's breast. She laughed and cried shame on him; and so they parted cheerfully. When he returned to the hall with Smilash they found two mugs of beer waiting for them. The girls had retired, and only Miss Wilson and the housekeeper remained.

"Heres your health, mum," said the man, before drinking; "and may you find such another as yourself to help you when youre in trouble, which Lord send may never come!"

"Is your house quite destroyed?" said Miss Wilson. "Where will you spend the night?"

"Dont you think of me, mum. Master Smilash here will kindly put me up 'til morning."

"His health!" said Smilash, touching the mug with his lips.

"The roof and south wall is blowed right away," continued the man, after pausing for a moment to puzzle over Smilash's meaning. "I doubt if theres a stone of it standing by this."

"But Sir John will build it for you again. You are one of his herds, are you not?"

"I am, Miss. But not he; he'll be glad it's down. He dont like people livin on the land. I have told him time and again that the place was ready to fall; but he said I couldnt expect him to lay out money on a house that he got no rent for. You see, Miss, I didnt pay any rent. I took low wages; and the bit of a hut was a sort of set-off again' what I was paid short of the other men. I couldnt afford to have it repaired, though I did what I could to patch and prop it. And now most like I shall be blamed for letting it be blew down, and shall have to live in half a room in the town and pay two or three shillins a week, besides walkin three miles to and from my work every day. A gentleman like Sir John dont hardly know what the value of a penny is to us laborin folk, nor how cruel hard his estate rules and the like comes on us."

"Sir John's health!" said Smilash, touching the mug as before. The man drank a mouthful humbly, and Smilash continued, "Heres to the glorious landed gentry of old England: bless em!"

"Master Smilash is only jokin," said the man apologetically. "It's his way."

"You should not bring a family into the world if you are so poor," said Miss Wilson severely. "Can you not see that you impoverish yourself by doing so?—to put the matter on no higher grounds."

"Reverend Mr Malthus's health!" remarked Smilash, repeating his pantomime.

"Some say it's the children, and some say it's the drink, Miss," said the man submissively. "But from what I see, family or no family, drunk or sober, the poor gets poorer and the rich richer every day."

"Aint it disgustin to hear a man so ignorant of the improvement in the condition of his class?" said Smilash, appealing to Miss Wilson.

"If you intend to take this man home with you," she said, turning sharply on him, "you had better do it at once."

"I take it kind on your part that you ask me to do anythink, after your up and telling Mr Wickens that I am the last person in Lyvern you would trust with a job."

"So you are—the very last. Why dont you drink your beer?"

"Not in scorn of your brewing, lady; but because, bein a common man, water is good enough for me."

"I wish you goodnight, Miss," said the man; "and thank you kindly for Bess and the children."

"Goodnight," she replied, stepping aside to avoid any salutation from Smilash. But he went up to her and said in a low voice, and with the Trefusis manner and accent:

"Goodnight, Miss Wilson. If you should ever be in want of the services of a dog, a man, or a domestic engineer, remind Smilash of Bess and the children, and he will act for you in any of those capacities."

They opened the door cautiously, and found that the wind, conquered by the rain, had abated. Miss Wilson's candle, though it flickered in the draught, was not extinguished this time; and she was presently left with the housekeeper, bolting and chaining the door, and listening to the crunching of feet on the gravel outside dying away through the steady pattering of the rain.

CHAPTER VII

AGATHA was at this time in her seventeenth year. She had a lively perception of the foibles of others, and no reverence for her seniors, whom she thought dull, cautious, and ridiculously amenable by commonplaces. But she was subject to the illusion which disables youth in spite of its superiority to age. She thought herself an exception. Crediting Mr Jansenius and the general mob of mankind with nothing but a grovelling consciousness of some few material facts, she felt in herself an exquisite sense and all-embracing conception of nature, shared only by her favorite poets and heroes of romance and history. Hence she was in the common youthful case of being a much better judge of other people's affairs than of her own. At the fellow-student who adored some Henry or Augustus, not from the drivelling senti-mentality which the world calls love, but because this particular Henry or Augustus was a phœnix to whom the laws that govern the relations of ordinary lads and lasses did not apply, Agatha laughed in her sleeve. The more she saw of this weakness in her fellows, the more satisfied she was that, being forewarned, she was also forearmed against any attack of it on herself. Much as if a doctor were to conclude that he could not catch smallpox because he had seen many cases of it; or as if a master mariner, knowing that many ships are wrecked in the British Channel, should venture there without a pilot, thinking that he knew its perils too well to run any risk of them. Yet, as the doctor might hold such an opinion if he believed himself to be constituted differently from ordinary men; or the shipmaster adopt such a course under the impression that his vessel was a star, Agatha found false security in the subjective difference between her fellows seen from without and herself known from within. When, for instance, she fell in love with Mr Jefferson Smilash (a step upon which she resolved the day after the storm), her imagination invested the pleasing emotion with a sacredness which, to her, set it far apart and distinct from the frivolous fancies of which

Henry and Augustus had been the subject, and she the confidant.

"I can look at him quite coolly and dispassionately," she said to herself. "Though his face has a strange influence that must, I know, correspond to some unexplained power within me, yet it is not a perfect face. I have seen many men who are, strictly speaking, far handsomer. If the light that never was on sea or land is in his eyes, yet they are not pretty eyes—not half so clear as mine. Though he wears his common clothes with a nameless grace that betrays his true breeding at every step, yet he is not tall, dark, and melancholy, as my ideal hero would be if I were as great a fool as girls of my age usually are. If I am in love, I have sense enough not to let my love blind my judgment."

She did not tell any one of her new interest in life. Strongest in that student community, she had used her power with good-nature enough to win the popularity of a school leader, and occasionally with unscrupulousness enough to secure the privileges of a school bully. Popularity and privilege, however, only satisfied her when she was in the mood for them. Girls, like men, want to be petted, pitied, and made much of, when they are diffident, in low spirits, or in unrequited love. These are services which the weak cannot render to the strong and which the strong will not render to the weak, except when there is also a difference of sex. Agatha knew by experience that though a weak woman cannot understand why her stronger sister should wish to lean upon her, she may triumph in the fact without understanding it, and give chaff instead of consolation. Agatha wanted to be understood and not to be chaffed. Finding herself unable to satisfy both these conditions, she resolved to do without sympathy and to hold her tongue. She had often had to do so before, and she was helped on this occasion by a sense of the ridiculous appearance her passion might wear in the vulgar eye.

Her secret kept itself, as she was supposed in the college to be insensible to the softer emotions. Love wrought no external change upon her. It made her believe that she had left her girl-hood behind her and was now a woman with a newly-developed heart capacity at which she would childishly have scoffed a little while before. She felt ashamed of the bee on the window pane, although it somehow buzzed as frequently as before in spite of her. Her calendar, formerly a monotonous cycle of class times, meal times, play times, and bed time, was now irregularly divided by walks past the chalet and accidental glimpses of its tenant.

Early in December came a black frost, and navigation on the canal was suspended. Wickens's boy was sent to the college with news that Wickens's pond would bear, and that the young ladies should be welcome at any time. The pond was only four feet deep, and as Miss Wilson set much store by the physical education of her pupils, leave was given for skating. Agatha, who was expert on the ice, immediately proposed that a select party should go out before breakfast next morning. Actions not in themselves virtuous often appear so when performed at hours that compel early rising, and some of the candidates for the Cambridge Local, who would not have sacrificed the afternoon to amusement, at once fell in with her suggestion. But for them it might never have been carried out; for when they summoned Agatha, before sunrise next morning, to leave her warm bed and brave the biting air, she would have refused without hesitation had she not been shamed into compliance by these laborious ones who stood by her bedside, blue-nosed and hungry, but ready for the ice. When she had dressed herself with much shuddering and chattering, they allayed their internal discomfort by a slender meal of biscuits, got their skates, and went out across the rimy meadows, past patient cows breathing clouds of steam, to Wickens's pond. Here, to their surprise, was Smilash, on electro-plated acme skates, practising complicated figures with intense diligence. It soon appeared that his skill came short of his ambition; for, after several narrow escapes and some frantic staggering, his calves, elbows, and occiput smote the ice almost simultaneously. On rising ruefully to a sitting posture, he became aware that eight young ladies were watching his proceedings with interest.

"This comes of a common man putting himself above his station by getting into gentlemen's skates," he said. "Had I been content with a humble slide, as my fathers was, I should ha' been a happier man at the present moment." He sighed, rose, touched his hat to Miss Ward, and took off his skates, adding: "Good morning, Miss. Miss Wilson sent me word to be here sharp by six to put on the young ladies' skates, and I took the liberty of trying a figure or two to keep out the cold."

"Miss Wilson did not tell me that she ordered you to come," said Miss Ward.

"Just like her to be thoughtful and yet not let on to be! She is a kind lady, and a learned—like yourself, Miss. Sit yourself down on the camp-stool, and give me your heel, if I may be so bold as to stick a gimlet into it."

His assistance was welcome, and Miss Ward allowed him to put on her skates. She was a Canadian, and could skate well. Jane, the first to follow her, was anxious as to the strength of the ice; but when reassured, she acquitted herself admirably, for she was proficient in outdoor exercises, and had the satisfaction of laughing in the field at those who laughed at her in the study. Agatha, contrary to her custom, gave way to her companions, and her boots were the last upon which Smilash operated.

"How d'you do, Miss Wylie?" he said, dropping the Smilash manner now that the rest were out of earshot.

"I am very well, thank you," said Agatha, shy and constrained. This phase of her being new to him, he paused with her heel in his hand and looked up at her curiously. She collected herself, returned his gaze steadily, and said: "How did Miss Wilson send you word to come? She only knew of our party at half-past nine last night."

"Miss Wilson did not send for me."

"But you have just told Miss Ward that she did."

"Yes. I find it necessary to tell almost as many lies now that I am a simple laborer as I did when I was a gentleman. More, in fact."

"I shall know how much to believe of what you say in the future."

"The truth is this. I am perhaps the worst skater in the world, and therefore, according to a natural law, I covet the faintest distinction on the ice more than immortal fame for the things in which nature has given me aptitude to excel. I envy that large friend of yours—Jane is her name, I think—more than I envy Plato. I came down here this morning, thinking that the skating world was all a-bed, to practise in secret."

"I am glad we caught you at it," said Agatha maliciously, for he was disappointing her. She wanted him to be heroic in his conversation; and he would not.

"I suppose so," he replied. "I have observed that Woman's dearest delight is to wound Man's self-conceit, though Man's dearest delight is to gratify hers. There is at least one creature lower than Man. Now, off with you. Shall I hold you until your ankles get firm?"

"Thank you," she said, disgusted: "*I* can skate pretty well, and I dont think you could give me any useful assistance." And she went off cautiously, feeling that a mishap would be very disgraceful after such a speech.

He stood on the shore, listening to the grinding, swaying sound of the skates, and watching the growing complexity of the curves they were engraving on the ice. As the girls grew warm and accustomed to the exercise they laughed, jested, screamed recklessly when they came into collision, and sailed before the wind down the whole length of the pond at perilous speed. The more animated they became, the gloomier looked Smilash.

"Not two-penn'orth of choice between them and a parcel of puppies," he said; "except that some of them are conscious that there is a man looking at them, although he is only a blackguard laborer. They remind me of Henrietta in a hundred ways. Would I laugh, now, if the whole sheet of ice were to burst into little bits under them?"

Just then the ice cracked with a startling report, and the skaters, except Jane, skimmed away in all directions.

"You are breaking the ice to pieces, Jane," said Agatha, calling from a safe distance. "How can you expect it to bear your weight?"

"Pack of fools!" retorted Jane indignantly. "The noise only shows how strong it is."

The shock which the report had given Smilash answered him his question. "Make a note that wishes for the destruction of the human race, however rational and sincere, are contrary to nature," he said, recovering his spirits. "Besides, what a precious fool I should be if I were working at an international association of creatures only fit for destruction! Hi, lady! One word, Miss!" This was to Miss Ward, who had skated into his neighborhood. "It bein a cold morning, and me havin a poor and common circulation, would it be looked on as a liberty if I was to cut a slide here or take a turn in the corner all to myself?"

"You may skate over there if you wish," she said, after a pause for consideration, pointing to a deserted spot at the leeward end of the pond, where the ice was too rough for comfortable skating.

"Nobly spoke!" he cried, with a grin, hurrying to the place indicated, where, skating being out of the question, he made a pair of slides, and gravely exercised himself upon them until his face glowed and his fingers tingled in the frosty air. The time passed quickly; when Miss Ward sent for him to take off her skates there was a general groan and declaration that it could not possibly be half-past eight o'clock yet. Smilash knelt before the camp-stool, and was presently busy unbuckling and unscrewing. When Jane's turn came, the camp-stool creaked beneath her weight. Agatha again remonstrated with her, but immediately reproached herself with flippancy before Smilash, to whom she wished to convey an impression of deep seriousness of character.

"Smallest foot of the lot," he said critically, holding Jane's foot between his finger and thumb as if it were an art treasure which he had been invited to examine. "And belonging to the finest-built lady."

Jane snatched away her foot, blushed, and said:

"Indeed! What next, I wonder?"

"Tother un next," he said, setting to work on the remaining skate. When it was off, he looked up at her, and she darted a glance at him as she rose which showed that his compliment (her feet were, in fact, small and pretty) was appreciated.

"Allow me, Miss," he said to Gertrude, who was standing on

one leg, leaning on Agatha, and taking off her own skates.

"No, thank you," she said coldly. "I dont need your assistance."

"I am well aware that the offer was overbold," he replied, with a self-complacency that made his profession of humility exasperating, "If all the skates is off, I will, by Miss Wilson's order, carry them and the camp-stool back to the college."

Miss Ward handed him her skates and turned away. Gertrude placed hers on the stool and went with Miss Ward. The rest followed, leaving him to stare at the heap of skates and consider how he should carry them. He could think of no better plan than to interlace the straps and hang them in a chain over his shoulder. By the time he had done this the young ladies were out of sight, and his intention of enjoying their society during the return to the college was defeated. They had entered the building long before he came in sight of it.

Somewhat out of conceit with his folly, he went to the servants' entrance and rang the bell there. When the door was opened, he saw Miss Ward standing behind the maid who admitted him.

"Oh," she said, looking at the string of skates as if she had hardly expected to see them again, "so you have brought our things back?"

"Such were my instructions," he said, taken aback by her manner.

"You had no instructions. What do you mean by getting our skates into your charge under false pretences? I was about to send the police to take them from you. How dare you tell me that you were sent to wait on me, when you know very well that you were nothing of the sort?"

"I couldnt help it, Miss," he replied submissively. "I am a natural born liar—always was. I know that it must appear dreadful to you that never told a lie, and dont hardly know what a lie is, belonging as you do to a class where none is ever told. But common people like me tells lies just as a duck swims. I ask your pardon, Miss, most humble, and I hope the young ladies'll be able to tell one set of skates from tother; for I'm blest if I can."

"Put them down. Miss Wilson wishes to speak to you before you go. Susan, show him the way."

"Hope you aint been and got a poor cove into trouble, Miss?"

"Miss Wilson knows how you have behaved."

He smiled at her benevolently and followed Susan upstairs. On their way they met Jane, who stole a glance at him, and was about to pass by, when he said:

"Wont you say a word to Miss Wilson for a poor common fellow, honored young lady? I have got into dreadful trouble for having made bold to assist you this morning."

"You neednt give yourself the pains to talk like that," replied Jane in an impetuous whisper. "We all know that you are only pretending."

"Well, you can guess my motive," he whispered, looking tenderly at her.

"Such stuff and nonsense! I never heard of such a thing in my life," said Jane, and ran away, plainly understanding that he had disguised himself in order to obtain admission to the college and enjoy the happiness of looking at her.

"Cursed fool that I am!" he said to himself; "I cannot act like a rational creature for five consecutive minutes."

The servant led him to the study and announced, "The man, if you please, maam."

"Jeff Smilash," he added in explanation.

"Come in," said Miss Wilson sternly.

He went in, and met the determined frown which she cast on him from her seat behind the writing-table, by saying courteously:

"Good morning, Miss Wilson."

She bent forward involuntarily, as if to receive a gentleman. Then she checked herself and looked implacable.

"I have to apologize," he said, "for making use of your name unwarrantably this morning—telling a lie, in fact. I happened to be skating when the young ladies came down, and as they needed some assistance which they would hardly have accepted from a common man—excuse my borrowing that tiresome expression from our acquaintance Smilash—I set their minds at ease by saying that you had sent for me. Otherwise, as you have given me a bad character—though not worse than I deserve—they would probably have refused to employ me, or at least I should have been compelled to accept payment, which I, of course, do not need."

Miss Wilson affected surprise. "I do not understand," she said.

"Not altogether," he said, smiling. "But you understand that I am what is called a gentleman."

"No. The gentlemen with whom I am conversant do not dress as you dress, nor speak as you speak, nor act as you act."

He looked at her, and her countenance confirmed the hostility of her tone. He instantly relapsed into an aggravated phase of Smilash.

"I will no longer attempt to set myself up as a gentleman," he said. "I am a common man, and your ladyship's hi recognizes me as such and is not to be deceived. But dont go for to say that I am not candid when I am as candid as ever you will let me be. What fault, if any, do you find with my putting the skates on the young ladies, and carryin the camp-stool for them?"

"If you are a gentleman," said Miss Wilson, reddening, "your conduct in persisting in these antics in my presence is insulting to me. Extremely so."

"Miss Wilson," he replied, unruffled, "if you insist on Smilash, you shall have Smilash; I take an insane pleasure in personating him. If you want Sidney—my real Christian name—you can command him. But allow me to say that you must have either one or the other. If you become frank with me, I will understand that you are addressing Sidney. If distant and severe, Smilash."

"No matter what your name may be," said Miss Wilson, much annoyed, "I forbid you to come here or to hold any communication whatever with the young ladies in my charge."

"Why?"

"Because I choose."

"There is much force in that reason, Miss Wilson; but it is not moral force in the sense conveyed by your college prospectus, which I have read with great interest."

Miss Wilson, since her quarrel with Agatha, had been sore on the subject of moral force. "No one is admitted here," she said, "without a trustworthy introduction or recommendation. A disguise is not a satisfactory substitute for either."

"Disguises are generally assumed for the purpose of concealing crime," he remarked sententiously.

"Precisely so," she said emphatically.

"Therefore, I bear, to say the least, a doubtful character. Nevertheless, I have formed with some of the students here a slight acquaintance, of which, it seems, you disapprove. You have given me no good reason why I should discontinue that acquaintance, and you cannot control me except by your wish—a sort of influence not usually effective with doubtful characters. Suppose I disregard your wish, and that one or two of your pupils come to you and say: 'Miss Wilson, in our opinion Smilash is an excellent fellow; we find his conversation most improving. As it is your principle to allow us to exercise our own judgment, we intend to cultivate the acquaintance of Smilash.' How will you act in that case?"

"Send them home to their parents at once."

"I see that your principles are those of the Church of England. You allow the students the right of private judgment on condition that they arrive at the same conclusions as you. Excuse my saying that the principles of the Church of England, however excellent, are not those your prospectus led me to hope for. Your plan is coercion, stark and simple."

"I do not admit it," said Miss Wilson, ready to argue, even with Smilash, in defence of her system. "The girls are quite at liberty to act as they please, but I reserve my equal liberty to exclude them from my college if I do not approve of their behaviour."

"Just so. In most schools children are perfectly at liberty to learn their lessons or not, just as they please; but the principal reserves an equal liberty to whip them if they cannot repeat their tasks."

"I do not whip my pupils," said Miss Wilson indignantly.

"The comparison is an outrage."

"But you expel them; and, as they are devoted to you and to the place, expulsion is a dreaded punishment. Yours is the old system of making laws and enforcing them by penalties, and the superiority of Alton College to other colleges is due, not to any difference of system, but to the comparative reasonableness of its laws and the mildness and judgment with which they are enforced."

"My system is radically different from the old one. However, I will not discuss the matter with you. A mind occupied with the prejudices of the old coercive despotism can naturally only see in the new a modification of the old, instead of, as my system is, an entire reversal or abandonment of it."

He shook his head sadly and said: "You seek to impose your ideas on others, ostracizing those who reject them. Believe me, mankind has been doing nothing else ever since it began to pay some attention to ideas. It has been said that a benevolent despotism is the best possible form of government. I do not believe that saying, because I believe another one to the effect that hell is paved with benevolence, which most people, the proverb being too deep for them, misinterpret as unfulfilled intentions. As if a benevolent despot might not by any error of judgment destroy his kingdom, and then say, like Romeo when he got his friend killed, 'I thought all for the best!' Excuse my rambling. I meant to say, in short, that though you are benevolent and judicious you are none the less a despot."

Miss Wilson, at a loss for a reply, regretted that she had not, before letting him gain so far on her, dismissed him summarily instead of tolerating a discussion which she did not know how to end with dignity. He relieved her by adding unexpectedly:

"Your system was the cause of my absurd marriage. My wife acquired a degree of culture and reasonableness from her training here which made her seem a superior being among the chatterers who form the female seasoning in ordinary society. I admired her dark eyes, and was only too glad to seize the excuse her education offered me for believing her a match for me in mind as well as in body."

Miss Wilson, astonished, determined to tell him coldly that her time was valuable. But curiosity took possession of her in the act of utterance, and the words that came were: "Who was she?"

"Henrietta Jansenius. She is Henrietta Trefusis, and I am Sidney Trefusis, at your mercy. I see I have aroused your compassion at last."

"Nonsense!" said Miss Wilson hastily; for her surprise was indeed tinged by a feeling that he was thrown away on Henrietta.

"I ran away from her and adopted this retreat and this disguise in order to avoid her. The usual rebuke to human forethought followed. I ran straight into her arms—or rather she ran into mine. You remember the scene, and were probably puzzled by it."

"You seem to think your marriage contract a very light matter, Mr Trefusis. May I ask whose fault was the separation? Hers, of course."

"I have nothing to reproach her with. I expected to find her temper hasty, but it was not so—her behaviour was unexceptionable. So was mine. Our bliss was perfect, but unfortunately I was not made for domestic bliss—at all events I could not endure it—so I fled, and when she caught me again I could give no excuse for my flight, though I made it clear to her that I would not resume our connubial relations just yet. We parted on bad terms. I fully intended to write her a sweet letter to make her forgive me in spite of herself, but somehow the weeks have slipped away and I am still fully intending. She has never written, and I have never written. This is a pretty state of things, isnt it, Miss Wilson, after all her advantages under the influence of moral force and the movement for the higher education of women?"

"By your own admission, the fault seems to lie upon your moral training and not upon hers."

"The fault was in the conditions of our association. Why they should have attracted me so strongly at first, and repelled me so horribly afterwards, is one of those devil's riddles which will not be answered until we shall have traced all the yet unsuspected reactions of our inveterate dishonesty. But I am wasting your time,

I fear. You sent for Smilash, and I have responded by practically annihilating him. In public, however, you must still bear with his antics. One moment more. I had forgotten to ask you whether you are interested in the shepherd whose wife you sheltered on the night of the storm?"

"He assured me, before he took his wife away, that he was comfortably settled in a lodging in Lyvern."

"Yes. Very comfortably settled indeed. For half-a-crown a week he obtained permission to share a spacious drawing room with two other families in a ten-roomed house in not much better repair than his blown-down hovel. This house yields to its landlord over two hundred a year, or rather more than the rent of a commodious mansion in South Kensington. It is a troublesome rent to collect, but on the other hand there is no expenditure for repairs or sanitation, which are not considered necessary in tenement houses. Our friend has to walk three miles to his work and three miles back. Exercise is a capital thing for a student or a city clerk, but to a shepherd who has been in the fields all day, a long walk at the end of his work is somewhat too much of a good thing. He begged for an increase of wages to compensate him for the loss of the hut, but Sir John pointed out to him that if he was not satisfied his place could be easily filled by less exorbitant shepherds. Sir John even condescended to explain that the laws of political economy bind employers to buy labor in the cheapest market, and our poor friend, just as ignorant of economics as Sir John, of course did not know that this was untrue. However, as labor is actually so purchased everywhere except in Downing Street and a few other privileged spots, I suggested that our friend should go to some place where his market price would be higher than in merry England. He was willing enough to do so, but unable from want of means. So I lent him a trifle, and now he is on his way to Australia. Workmen are the geese that lay the golden eggs, but they fly away sometimes. I hear a gong sounding, to remind me of the flight of time and the value of your share of it. Good morning!"

Miss Wilson was suddenly moved not to let him go without

an appeal to his better nature. "Mr Trefusis," she said, "excuse me, but are you not, in your generosity to others, a little forgetful of your duty to yourself; and—"

"The first and hardest of all duties!" he exclaimed. "I beg your pardon for interrupting you. It was only to plead guilty."

"I cannot admit that it is the first of all duties, but it is sometimes perhaps the hardest, as you say. Still, you could surely do yourself more justice without any great effort. If you wish to live humbly, you can do so without pretending to be an uneducated man and without taking an irritating and absurd name. Why on earth do you call yourself Smilash?"

"I confess that the name has been a failure. I took great pains, in constructing it, to secure a pleasant impression. It is not a mere invention, but a compound of the words smile and eyelash. A smile suggests good humour; eyelashes soften the expression and are the only features that never blemish a face. Hence Smilash is a sound that should cheer and propitiate. Yet it exasperates. It is really very odd that it should have that effect, unless it is that it raises expectations which I am unable to satisfy."

Miss Wilson looked at him doubtfully. He remained perfectly grave. There was a pause. Then, as if she had made up her mind to be offended, she said "Good morning," shortly.

"Good morning, Miss Wilson. The son of a millionaire, like the son of a king, is seldom free from mental disease. I am just mad enough to be a mountebank. If I were a little madder, I should perhaps really believe myself Smilash instead of merely acting him. Whether you ask me to forget myself for a moment, or to remember myself for a moment, I reply that I am the son of my father, and cannot. With my egotism, my charlatanry, my tongue, and my habit of having my own way, I am fit for no calling but that of saviour of mankind—just of the sort they like." After an impressive pause he turned slowly and left the room.

"I wonder," he said, as he crossed the landing, "whether, by judiciously losing my way, I can catch a glimpse of that girl who is like a golden idol?"

Downstairs, on his way to the door, he saw Agatha coming

towards him, occupied with a book which she was tossing up to the ceiling and catching. Her melancholy expression, habitual in her lonely moments, showed that she was not amusing herself, but giving vent to her restlessness. As her gaze travelled upward, following the flight of the volume, it was arrested by Smilash. The book fell to the floor. He picked it up and handed it to her, saying:

"And, in good time, here *is* the golden idol!"

"What?" said Agatha, confused.

"I call you the golden idol," he said. "When we are apart I always imagine your face as a face of gold, with eyes and teeth of bdellium, or chalcedony, or agate, or any wonderful unknown stones of appropriate colours."

Agatha, witless and dumb, could only look down deprecatingly.

"You think you ought to be angry with me, and you do not know exactly how to make me feel that you are so. Is that it?"

"No. Quite the contrary. At least—I mean that you are wrong. I am the most commonplace person you can imagine—if you only knew. No matter what I may look, I mean."

"How do you know that you are commonplace?"

"Of course I know," said Agatha, her eyes wandering uneasily.

"Of course you do not know; you cannot see yourself as others see you. For instance, you have never thought of yourself as a golden idol."

"But that is absurd. You are quite mistaken about me."

"Perhaps so. I know, however, that your face is not really made of gold and that it has not the same charm for you that it has for others—for me."

"I must go," said Agatha, suddenly, in haste.

" When shall we meet again?"

"I dont know," she said, with a growing sense of alarm. "I really must go."

"Believe me, your hurry is only imaginary. Do you fancy that you are behaving in a manner quite unworthy of yourself, and that a net is closing round you?"

"No. Nothing of the sort!"

"Then why are you so anxious to get away?"

"I don't know," said Agatha, affecting to laugh as he looked sceptically at her from beneath his lowered eyelids. "Perhaps I do feel a little like that; but not so much as you say."

"I will explain the emotion to you," he said, with a subdued ardour that affected Agatha strangely. "But first tell me whether it is new to you or not."

"It is not an emotion at all. I did not say that it was."

"Do not be afraid of it. It is only being alone with a man whom you have bewitched. You would be mistress of the situation if you only knew how to manage a lover. It is far easier than managing a horse, or skating, or playing the piano, or half a dozen other feats of which you think nothing."

Agatha colored and raised her head.

"Forgive me," he said, interrupting the action. "I am trying to offend you in order to save myself from falling in love with you, and I have not the heart to let myself succeed. On your life, do not listen to me or believe me. I have no right to say these things to you. Some fiend enters into me when I am at your side. You should wear a veil, Agatha."

She blushed, and stood burning and tingling, her presence of mind gone, and her chief sensation one of relief to hear—for she did not dare to see—that he was departing. Her consciousness was in a delicious confusion, with the one definite thought in it that she had won her lover at last. The tone of Trefusis's voice, rich with truth and earnestness, his quick insight, and his passionate warning to her not to heed him, convinced her that she had entered into a relation destined to influence her whole life.

"And yet," she said remorsefully, "I cannot love him as he loves me. I am selfish, cold, calculating, worldly, and have doubted until now whether such a thing as love really existed. If I could only love him recklessly and wholly, as he loves me!"

Smilash was also soliloquizing as he went on his way.

"Now I have made the poor child—who was so anxious that

I should not mistake her for a supernaturally gifted and lovely woman—as happy as an angel; and so is that fine girl whom they call Jane Carpenter. I hope they wont exchange confidences on the subject."

CHAPTER VIII

MRS TREFUSIS found her parents so unsympathetic on the subject of her marriage that she left their house shortly after her visit to Lyvern, and went to reside with a hospitable friend. Unable to remain silent upon the matter constantly in her thoughts, she discussed her husband's flight with this friend, and elicited an opinion that the behaviour of Trefusis was scandalous and wicked. Henrietta could not bear this, and sought shelter with a relative. The same discussion arising, the relative said:

"Well, Hetty, if I am to speak candidly, I must say that I have known Sidney Trefusis for a long time, and he is the easiest person to get on with I ever met. And you know, dear, that you are very trying sometimes."

"And so," cried Henrietta, bursting into tears, "after the infamous way he has treated me I am to be told that it is all my own fault."

She left the house next day, having obtained another invitation from a discreet lady who would not discuss the subject at all. This proved quite intolerable, and Henrietta went to stay with her uncle Daniel Jansenius, a jolly and indulgent man. He opined that things would come right as soon as both parties grew more sensible; and, as to which of them was in fault, his verdict was, six of one and half a dozen of the other. Whenever he saw his niece pensive or tearful he laughed at her and called her a grass widow. Henrietta found that she could endure anything rather than this. Declaring that the world was hateful to her, she hired a furnished villa in St John's Wood, whither she moved in December. But, suffering much there from loneliness, she soon wrote a pathetic letter to Agatha, entreating her to spend the approaching Christmas vacation with her, and promising her every luxury and amusement that boundless affection could suggest and boundless means procure. Agatha's reply contained some unlooked-for information.

"ALTON COLLEGE, LYVERN, 14*th December*.

"Dearest Hetty—I dont think I can do exactly what you want, as I must spend Xmas with Mamma at Chiswick; but I need not get there until Xmas Eve, and we break up here on yesterday week, the 20th. So I will go straight to you and bring you with me to Mamma's, where you will spend Xmas much better than moping in a strange house. It is not quite settled yet about my leaving the college after this term. You must promise not to tell any one; but I have a new friend here—a lover. Not that I am in love with him, though I think very highly of him—you know I am not a romantic fool; but he is very much in love with me; and I wish I could return it as he deserves. The French say that one person turns the cheek and the other kisses it. It has not got quite so far as that with us; indeed, since he declared what he felt he has only been able to snatch a few words with me when I have been skating or walking. But there has always been at least one word or look that meant a great deal.

"And now, who do you think he is? He says he knows you. Can you guess? He says you know all his secrets. He says he knows your husband well; that he treated you very badly, and that you are greatly to be pitied. Can you guess now? He says he has kissed you—for shame, Hetty! Have you guessed yet? He was going to tell me something more when we were interrupted, and I have not seen him since except at a distance. He is the man with whom you eloped that day when you gave us all such a fright—Mr Sidney. I was the first to penetrate his disguise; and that very morning I had taxed him with it, and he had confessed it. He said then that he was hiding from a woman who was in love with him; and I should not be surprised if it turned out to be true; for he is wonderfully original—in fact what makes me like him is that he is by far the cleverest man I have ever met; and yet he thinks nothing of himself. I cannot imagine what he sees in me to care for, though he is evidently ensnared by my charms. I hope he wont find out how silly I am. He calls me his golden idol—"

Henrietta, with a scream of rage, tore the letter across, and stamped upon it. When the paroxysm subsided she picked up the pieces, held them together as accurately as her trembling hands could, and read on.

"—but he is not all honey, and will say the most severe things sometimes if he thinks he ought to. He has made me so ashamed of my ignorance that I am resolved to stay here for another term at least, and study as hard as I can. I have not begun yet, as it is not worth while at the eleventh hour of this term; but when I return in January I will set to work in earnest. So you may see that his influence over me is an entirely good one. I will tell you all about him when we meet; for I have no time to say anything now, as the girls are bothering me to go skating with them. He pretends to be a workman, and puts on our skates for us; and Jane Carpenter believes that he is in love with her. Jane is exceedingly kind-hearted; but she has a talent for making herself ridiculous that nothing can suppress. The ice is lovely, and the weather jolly; we do not mind the cold in the least. They are threatening to go without me—goodbye!—Ever your affectionate.

                                                        "AGATHA."

Henrietta looked round for something sharp. She grasped a pair of scissors greedily and stabbed the air with them. Then she became conscious of her murderous impulse, and she shuddered at it; but in a moment more her jealousy swept back upon her. She cried, as if suffocating: "I dont care; I should like to kill her!" But she did not take up the scissors again.

At last she rang the bell violently and asked for a railway guide. On being told that there was not one in the house, she scolded her maid so unreasonably that the girl said pertly that if she were to be spoken to like that she should wish to leave when her month was up. This check brought Henrietta to her senses. She went upstairs and put on the first cloak at hand, which was fortunately a heavy fur one. Then she took her bonnet and purse, left the house, hailed a passing hansom, and bade the cabman drive her to St Pancras.

When the night came the air at Lyvern was like iron in the intense cold. The trees and the wind seemed ice-bound, as the water was, and silence, stillness, and starlight, frozen hard, brooded over the country. At the chalet, Smilash, indifferent to the price of coals, kept up a roaring fire that glowed through the uncurtained windows, and tantalized the chilled wayfarer who did not happen to know, as the herdsmen of the neighborhood did, that he was welcome to enter and warm himself without risk of rebuff from the tenant. Smilash was in high spirits. He had become a proficient skater, and frosty weather was now a luxury to him. It braced him, and drove away his gloomy fits, whilst his sympathies were kept awake and his indignation maintained at an exhilarating pitch by the sufferings of the poor, who, unable to afford fires or skating, warmed themselves in such sweltering heat as overcrowding produces in all seasons.

It was Smilash's custom to make a hot drink of oatmeal and water for himself at half-past nine o'clock each evening, and to go to bed at ten. He opened the door to throw out some water that remained in the saucepan from its last cleansing. It froze as it fell upon the soil. He looked at the night, and shook himself to throw off an oppressive sensation of being clasped in the icy ribs of the air, for the mercury had descended below the familiar region of crisp and crackly cold and marked a temperature at which the numb atmosphere seemed on the point of congealing into black solidity. Nothing was stirring.

"By George!" he said, "this is one of those nights on which a rich man darent think!"

He shut the door, hastened back to his fire, and set to work at his caudle, which he watched and stirred with a solicitude that would have amused a professed cook. When it was done he poured it into a large mug, where it steamed invitingly. He took up some in a spoon and blew upon it to cool it. Tap, tap, tap, tap! hurriedly at the door.

"Nice night for a walk," he said, putting down the spoon; then shouting, "Come in."

The latch rose unsteadily, and Henrietta, with frozen tears

on her cheeks, and an unintelligible expression of wretchedness and rage, appeared. After an instant of amazement, he sprang to her and clasped her in his arms, and she, against her will, and protesting voicelessly, stumbled into his embrace.

"You are frozen to death," he exclaimed, carrying her to the fire. "This seal jacket is like a sheet of ice. So is your face" (kissing it). "What is the matter? Why do you struggle so?"

"Let me go," she gasped, in a vehement whisper. "I h—hate you."

"My poor love, you are too cold to hate any one—even your husband. You must let me take off these atrocious French boots. Your feet must be perfectly dead."

By this time her voice and tears were thawing in the warmth of the chalet and of his caresses. "You shall not take them off," she said, crying with cold and sorrow. "Let me alone. Dont touch me. I am going away—straight back. I will not speak to you, nor take off my things here, nor touch anything in the house."

"No, my darling," he said, putting her into a capacious wooden armchair and busily unbuttoning her boots, "you shall do nothing that you dont wish to do. Your feet are like stones. Yes, yes, my dear, I am a wretch unworthy to live. I know it."

"Let me alone," she said piteously. "I dont want your attentions. I have done with you for ever."

"Come, you must drink some of this nasty stuff. You will need strength to tell your husband all the unpleasant things your soul is charged with. Take just a little."

She turned her face away and would not answer. He brought another chair and sat down beside her. "My lost, forlorn, betrayed one—"

"I am," she sobbed. "You dont mean it, but I am."

"You are also my dearest and best of wives. If you ever loved me, Hetty, do, for my once dear sake, drink this before it gets cold."

She pouted, sobbed, and yielded to some gentle force which he used, as a child allows herself to be half persuaded, half compelled, to take physic.

"Do you feel better and more comfortable now?" he said.

"No," she replied, angry with herself for feeling both.

"Then," he said cheerfully, as if she had uttered a hearty affirmative, "I will put some more coals on the fire, and we shall be as snug as possible. It makes me wildly happy to see you at my fireside, and to know that you are my own wife."

"I wonder how you can look me in the face and say so," she cried.

"I should wonder at myself if I could look at your face and say anything else. Oatmeal is a capital restorative; all your energy is coming back. There, that will make a magnificent blaze presently."

"I never thought you deceitful, Sidney, whatever other faults you might have had."

"Precisely, my love. I understand your feelings. Murder, burglary, intemperance, or the minor vices you could have borne; but deceit you cannot abide."

"I will go away," she said despairingly, with a fresh burst of tears. "I will not be laughed at and betrayed. I will go barefooted." She rose and attempted to reach the door; but he intercepted her and said—

"My love, there is something serious the matter. What is it? Dont be angry with me."

He brought her back to the chair. She took Agatha's letter from the pocket of her fur cloak, and handed it to him with a faint attempt to be tragic.

"Read that," she said. "And never speak to me again. All is over between us."

He took it curiously, and turned it to look at the signature. "Aha!" he said, "my golden idol has been making mischief, has she?"

"There!" exclaimed Henrietta. "You have said it to my face! You have convicted yourself out of your own mouth!"

"Wait a moment, my dear. I have not read the letter yet."

He rose and walked to and fro through the room, reading.

She watched him, angrily confident that she should presently see him change countenance. Suddenly he drooped as if his spine had partly given way; and in this ungraceful attitude he read the remainder of the letter. When he had finished he threw it on the table, thrust his hands deep into his pockets, and roared with laughter, huddling himself together as if he could concentrate the joke by collecting himself into the smallest possible compass. Henrietta, speechless with indignation, could only look her feelings. At last he came and sat down beside her.

"And so," he said, "on receiving this you rushed out in the cold and came all the way to Lyvern. Now, it seems to me that you must either love me very much—"

"I dont. I hate you."

"Or else love yourself very much."

"Oh!" And she wept afresh. "You are a selfish brute, and you do just as you like without considering any one else. No one ever thinks of me. And now you wont even take the trouble to deny that shameful letter."

"Why should I deny it? It is true. Do you not see the irony of all this? I amuse myself by paying a few compliments to a schoolgirl for whom I do not care two straws more than for any agreeable and passably clever woman I meet. Nevertheless, I occasionally feel a pang of remorse because I think that she may love me seriously, although I am only playing with her. I pity the poor heart I have wantonly ensnared. And, all the time, she is pitying me for exactly the same reason! She is conscience-stricken because she is only indulging in the luxury of being adored by 'by far the cleverest man she has ever met,' and is as heart-whole as I am! Ha, ha! That is the basis of the religion of love of which poets are the high-priests. Each worshipper knows that his own love is either a transient passion or a sham copied from his favorite poem; but he believes honestly in the love of others for him. Ho, ho! Is it not a silly world, my dear?"

"You had no right to make love to Agatha. You have no right to make love to any one but me; and I wont bear it."

"You are angry because Agatha has infringed your monopoly. Always monopoly! Why, you silly girl, do you suppose that I belong to you, body and soul?—that I may not be moved except by your affection, or think except of your beauty?"

"You may call me as many names as you please, but you have no right to make love to Agatha."

"My dearest, I do not recollect calling you any names. I think you said something about a selfish brute."

"I did not. You called me a silly girl."

"But, my love, you are."

"And so *you* are. You are thoroughly selfish."

"I dont deny it. But let us return to our subject. What did we begin to quarrel about?"

"I am not quarrelling, Sidney. It is you."

"Well, what did I begin to quarrel about?"

"About Agatha Wylie."

"Oh, pardon me, Hetty; I certainly did not begin to quarrel about her. I am very fond of her—more so, it appears, than she is of me. One moment, Hetty, before you recommence your reproaches. Why do you dislike my saying pretty things to Agatha?"

Henrietta hesitated, and said: "Because you have no right to. It shows how little you care for me."

"It has nothing to do with you. It only shews how much I care for her."

"I will not stay here to be insulted," said Hetty, her distress returning. "I will go home."

"Not tonight; there is no train."

"I will walk."

"It is too far."

"I dont care. I will not stay here, though I die of cold by the roadside."

"My cherished one, I have been annoying you purposely because you shew by your anger that you have not ceased to care for me. I am in the wrong, as I usually am, and it is all my fault. Agatha knows nothing about our marriage."

"I do not blame you so much," said Henrietta, suffering him to place her head on his shoulder; "but I will never speak to Agatha again. She has behaved shamefully to me, and I will tell her so."

"No doubt she will opine that it is all your fault, dearest, and that I have behaved admirably. Between you I shall stand exonerated. And now, since it is too cold for walking, since it is late, since it is far to Lyvern and farther to London, I must improvise some accommodation for you here."

"But—"

"But there is no help for it. You must stay."

CHAPTER IX

Next day Smilash obtained from his wife a promise that she would behave towards Agatha as if the letter had given no offence. Henrietta pleaded as movingly as she could for an immediate return to their domestic state, but he put her off with endearing speeches, promised nothing but eternal affection, and sent her back to London by the twelve o'clock express. Then his countenance changed; he walked back to Lyvern, and thence to the chalet, like a man pursued by disgust and remorse. Later in the afternoon, to raise his spirits, he took his skates and went to Wickens's pond, where, it being Saturday, he found the ice crowded with the Alton students and their half-holiday visitors. Fairholme, describing circles with his habitual air of compressed hardihood, stopped and stared with indignant surprise as Smilash lurched past him.

"Is that man here by your permission?" he said to Farmer Wickens, who was walking about as if superintending a harvest.

"He is here because he likes, I take it," said Wickens stubbornly. "He is a neighbor of mine and a friend of mine. Is there any objections to my having a friend on my own pond, seein that there is nigh on two or three ton of other people's friends on it without as much as a with-your-leave or a by-your-leave?"

"Oh, no," said Fairholme, somewhat dashed. "If you are satisfied there can be no objection."

"I'm glad on it. I thought there mout be."

"Let me tell you," said Fairholme, nettled, "that your landlord would not be pleased to see him here. He sent one of Sir John's best shepherds out of the country, after filling his head with ideas above his station. I heard Sir John speak very warmly about it last Sunday."

"Mayhap you did, Muster Fairholme. I have a lease of this land—and gravelly, poor stuff it is—and I am no ways beholden to Sir John's likings and dislikings. A very good thing too for

117

Sir John that I have a lease, for there aint a man in the country 'ud tak' a present o' the farm if it was free tomorrow. And what's a' more, though that young man do talk foolish things about the rights of farm laborers and such-like nonsense, if Sir John was to hear him layin it down concernin rent and improvements, and the way we tenant farmers is put upon, p'raps he'd speak warmer than ever next Sunday."

And Wickens, with a smile expressive of his sense of having retorted effectively upon the parson, nodded and walked away.

Just then Agatha, skating hand in hand with Jane Carpenter, heard these words in her ear: "I have something very funny to tell you. Dont look round."

She recognized the voice of Smilash and obeyed.

"I am not quite sure that you will enjoy it as it deserves," he added, and darted off again, after casting an eloquent glance at Miss Carpenter.

Agatha disengaged herself from her companion, made a circuit, and passed near Smilash, saying: "What is it?"

Smilash flitted away like a swallow, traced several circles around Fairholme, and then returned to Agatha and proceeded side by side with her.

"I have read the letter you wrote to Hetty," he said.

Agatha's face began to glow. She forgot to maintain her balance, and almost fell.

"Take care. And so you are not fond of me—in the romantic sense?"

No answer. Agatha dumb and afraid to lift her eyelids.

"That is fortunate," he continued, "because—good evening, Miss Ward; I have done nothing but admire your skating for the last hour—because men were deceivers ever; and I am no exception, as you will presently admit."

Agatha murmured something, but it was unintelligible amid the din of skating.

"You think not? Well, perhaps you are right; I have said nothing to you that is not in a measure true. You have always had a peculiar charm for me. But I did not mean you to tell

Hetty. Can you guess why?"

Agatha shook her head.

"Because she is my wife."

Agatha's ankles became limp. With an effort she kept upright until she reached Jane, to whom she clung for support.

"Dont," screamed Jane. "Youll upset me."

"I must sit down," said Agatha. "I am tired. Let me lean on you until we get to the chairs."

"Bosh! I can skate for an hour without sitting down," said Jane. However, she helped Agatha to a chair and left her. Then Smilash, as if desiring a rest also, sat down close by on the margin of the pond.

"Well," he said, without troubling himself as to whether their conversation attracted attention or not, "what do you think of me now?"

"Why did you not tell me before, Mr Trefusis?"

"That is the cream of the joke," he replied, poising his heels on the ice so that his skates stood vertically at legs' length from him, and looking at them with a cynical air. "I thought you were in love with me, and that the truth would be too severe a blow to you. Ha! ha! And, for the same reason, you generously forbore to tell me that you were no more in love with me than with the man in the moon. Each played a farce, and palmed it off on the other as a tragedy."

"There are some things so unmanly, so unkind, and so cruel," said Agatha, "that I cannot understand any gentleman saying them to a girl. Please do not speak to me again. Miss Ward! Come to me for a moment. I—I am not well."

Miss Ward hurried to her side. Smilash, after staring at her for a moment in astonishment, and in some concern, skimmed away into the crowd. When he reached the opposite bank he took off his skates, and asked Jane, who strayed intentionally in his direction, to tell Miss Wylie that he was gone, and would skate no more there. Without adding a word of explanation he left her and made for his dwelling. As he went down into the hollow where the road passed through the plantation on the college side of the chalet he descried a boy, in the uniform of the post office, sliding along the frozen ditch. A presentiment of evil tidings came upon him like a darkening of the sky. He quickened his pace.

"Anything for me?" he said.

The boy, who knew him, fumbled in a letter case and produced a buff envelope. It contained a telegram.

From JANSENIUS, London.

To J. SMILASH, Chamounix Villa, Lyvern.

Henrietta	*dangerously*	*ill*	*after*	*journey*
wants	*to*	*see*	*you*	*doctors*
say	*must*	*come*	*at*	*once*

There was a pause. Then he folded the paper methodically and put it in his pocket, as if quite done with it.

"And so," he said, "perhaps the tragedy is to follow the farce after all."

He looked at the boy, who retreated, not liking his expression.

"Did you slide all the way from Lyvern?"

"Only to come quicker," said the messenger, faltering. "I came as quick as I could."

"You carried news heavy enough to break the thickest ice ever frozen. I have a mind to throw you over the top of that tree instead of giving you this half-crown."

"You let me alone," whimpered the boy, retreating another pace.

"Get back to Lyvern as fast as you can run or slide, and tell Mr Marsh to send me the fastest trap he has, to drive me to the railway station. Here is your half-crown. Off with you; and if I do not find the trap ready when I want it, woe betide you."

The boy came for the money mistrustfully, and ran off with it as fast as he could. Smilash went into the chalet and never reappeared. Instead, Trefusis, a gentleman in an ulster, carrying a rug, came out, locked the door, and hurried along the road to

Lyvern, where he was picked up by the trap, and carried swiftly to the railway station, just in time to catch the London train.

"Evening paper, sir?" said a voice at the window, as he settled himself in the corner of a first-class carriage.

"No, thank you."

"Footwarmer, sir?" said a porter, appearing in the newsvendor's place.

"Ah, that's a good idea. Yes, let me have a footwarmer."

The footwarmer was brought, and Trefusis composed himself comfortably for his journey. It seemed very short to him; he could hardly believe, when the train arrived in London, that he had been nearly three hours on the way.

There was a sense of Christmas about the travellers and the people who were at the terminus to meet them. The porter who came to the carriage door reminded Trefusis by his manner and voice that the season was one at which it becomes a gentleman to be festive and liberal.

"Wot luggage, sir? Ensom or fourweoll, sir?"

For a moment Trefusis felt a vagabond impulse to resume the language of Smilash and fable to the man of hampers of turkey and plum-pudding in the van. But he repressed it, got into a hansom, and was driven to his father-in-law's house in Belsize Avenue, studying in a gloomily critical mood the anxiety that surged upon him and made his heart beat like a boy's as he drew near his destination. There were two carriages at the door when he alighted. The reticent expression of the coachman sent a tremor through him.

The door opened before he rang. "If you please, sir," said the maid in a low voice, "will you step into the library; and the doctor will see you immediately."

On the first landing of the staircase two gentlemen were speaking to Mr Jansenius, who hastily moved out of sight, not before a glimpse of his air of grief and discomfiture had given Trefusis a strange twinge, succeeded by a sensation of having been twenty years a widower. He smiled unconcernedly as he followed the girl into the library, and asked her how she did. She murmured some reply and hurried away, thinking that the poor young man would alter his tone presently.

He was joined at once by a grey-whiskered gentleman, scrupulously dressed and mannered. Trefusis introduced himself, and the physician looked at him with some interest. Then he said:

"You have arrived too late, Mr Trefusis. All is over, I am sorry to say."

"Was the long railway journey she took in this cold weather the cause of her death?"

Some bitter words that the physician had heard upstairs made him aware that this was a delicate question. But he said quietly: "The proximate cause, doubtless. The proximate cause."

"She received some unwelcome and quite unlooked-for intelligence before she started. Had that anything to do with her death, do you think?"

"It may have produced an unfavorable effect," said the physician, growing restive and taking up his gloves. "The habit of referring such events to such causes is carried too far, as a rule."

"No doubt. I am curious because the event is novel in my experience. I suppose it is a commonplace in yours."

"Pardon me. The loss of a lady so young and so favorably circumstanced is not a commonplace either in my experience or in my opinion." The physician held up his head as he spoke, in protest against any assumption that his sympathies had been blunted by his profession.

"Did she suffer?"

"For some hours, yes. We were able to do a little to alleviate her pain—poor thing!" He almost forgot Trefusis as he added the apostrophe.

"Hours of pain! Can you conceive any good purpose that those hours may have served?"

The physician shook his head, leaving it doubtful whether he meant to reply in the negative or to deplore considerations of that nature. He also made a movement to depart, being uneasy in conversation with Trefusis, who would, he felt sure, presently ask questions or make remarks with which he could hardly deal without committing himself in some direction. His conscience was not quite at rest. Henrietta's pain had not, he thought, served any good purpose; but he did not want to say so, lest he should acquire a reputation for impiety and lose his practice. He believed that the general practitioner who attended the family, and had called him in when the case grew serious, had treated Henrietta unskilfully, but professional etiquette bound him so strongly that, sooner than betray his colleague's inefficiency, he would have allowed him to decimate London.

"One word more," said Trefusis. "Did she know that she was dying?"

"No. I considered it best that she should not be informed of her danger. She passed away without any apprehension."

"Then one can think of it with equanimity. She dreaded death, poor child. The wonder is that there was not enough folly in the household to prevail against your good sense."

The physician bowed and took his leave, esteeming himself somewhat fortunate in escaping without being reproached for his humanity in having allowed Henrietta to die unawares.

A moment later the general practitioner entered. Trefusis, having accompanied the consulting physician to the door, detected the family doctor in the act of pulling a long face just outside it. Restraining a desire to seize him by the throat, he seated himself on the edge of the table and said cheerfully:

"Well, doctor, how has the world used you since we last met?"

The doctor was taken aback, but the solemn disposition of his features did not relax as he almost intoned: "Has Sir Francis told you the sad news, Mr Trefusis?"

"Yes. Frightful, isnt it? Lord bless me, we're here today and gone tomorrow."

"True, very true!"

"Sir Francis has a high opinion of you."

The doctor looked a little foolish. "Everything was done that could be done, Mr Trefusis; but Mrs Jansenius was very anxious that no stone should be left unturned. She was good enough to say that her sole reason for wishing me to call in Sir Francis was that you should have no cause to complain."

"Indeed!"

"An excellent mother! A sad event for her! Ah, yes, yes! Dear me! A very sad event!"

"Most disagreeable. Such a cold day too. Pleasanter to be in heaven than here in such weather, possibly."

"Ah!" said the doctor, as if much sound comfort lay in that. "I hope so; I hope so; I do not doubt it. Sir Francis did not permit us to tell her, and I, of course, deferred to him. Perhaps it was for the best."

"You would have told her, then, if Sir Francis had not objected?"

"Well, there are, you see, considerations which we must not ignore in our profession. Death is a serious thing, as I am sure I need not remind you, Mr Trefusis. We have sometimes higher duties than indulgence to the natural feelings of our patients."

"Quite so. The possibility of eternal bliss and the probability of eternal torment are consolations not to be lightly withheld from a dying girl, eh? However, whats past cannot be mended. I have much to be thankful for, after all. I am a young man, and shall not cut a bad figure as a widower. And now tell me, doctor, am I not in very bad repute upstairs?"

"Mr Trefusis! Sir! I cannot meddle in family matters. I understand my duties and never overstep them." The doctor, shocked at last, spoke as loftily as he could.

"Then I will go and see Mr Jansenius," said Trefusis, getting off the table.

"Stay, sir! One moment. I have not finished. Mrs Jansenius has asked me to ask—I was about to say that I am not speaking now as the medical adviser of this family; but although an old friend—and—ahem! Mrs Jansenius has asked me to ask—to request you to excuse Mr Jansenius, as he is prostrated by grief, and is, as I can—as a medical man—assure you, unable to see any one. She will speak to you herself as soon as she feels able to do so—at some time this evening. Meanwhile, of course, any orders you may give—you must be fatigued by your journey, and I always recommend people not to fast too long; it produces an acute form of indigestion—any orders you may wish to give will, of course, be attended to at once."

"I think," said Trefusis, after a moment's reflection, "I will order a hansom."

"There is no ill-feeling," said the doctor, who, as a slow man, was usually alarmed by prompt decisions, even when they seemed wise to him, as this one did. "I hope you have not gathered from anything I have said—"

"Not at all; you have displayed the utmost tact. But I think I had better go. Jansenius can bear death and misery with perfect fortitude when it is on a large scale and hidden in a back slum. But when it breaks into his own house, and attacks his property —his daughter was his property until very recently—he is just the man to lose his head and quarrel with me for keeping mine."

The doctor was unable to cope with this speech, which conveyed vaguely monstrous ideas to him. Seeing Trefusis about to leave, he said in a low voice: "Will you go upstairs?"

"Upstairs! Why?"

"I—I thought you might wish to see—" He did not finish the sentence, but Trefusis flinched; the blank had expressed what was meant.

"To see something that was Henrietta, and that is a thing we must cast out and hide, with a little superstitious mumming to save appearances. Why did you remind me of it?"

"But, sir, whatever your views may be, will you not, as a matter of form, in deference to the feelings of the family—"

"Let them spare their feelings for the living, on whose behalf I have often appealed to them in vain," cried Trefusis, losing patience. "Damn their feelings!" And, turning to the door, he found it open, and Mrs Jansenius there listening.

Trefusis was confounded. He knew what the effect of his speech must be, and felt that it would be folly to attempt excuse or explanation. He put his hands into his pockets, leaned against the table, and looked at her, mutely wondering what would follow on her part.

The doctor broke the silence by saying tremulously, "I have communicated the melancholy intelligence to Mr Trefusis."

"I hope you told him also," she said sternly, "that, however deficient we may be in feeling, we did everything that lay in our power for our child."

"I am quite satisfied," said Trefusis.

"No doubt you are—with the result," said Mrs Jansenius, hardly. "I wish to know whether you have anything to complain of."

"Nothing."

"Please do not imply that anything has happened through our neglect."

"What have I to complain of? She had a warm room and a luxurious bed to die in, with the best medical advice in the world. Plenty of people are starving and freezing today that we may have the means to die fashionably; ask *them* if they have any cause for complaint. Do you think I will wrangle over her body about the amount of money spent on her illness? What measure is that of the cause she had for complaint? I never grudged money to her—how could I, seeing that more than I can waste is given to me for nothing? Or how could you? Yet she had great reason to complain of me. You will allow that to be so."

"It is perfectly true."

"Well, when I am in the humor for it, I will reproach myself and not you." He paused, and then turned forcibly on her, saying, "Why do you select this time, of all others, to speak so bitterly to me?"

"I am not aware that I have said anything to call for such a remark. Did *you*" (appealing to the doctor) "hear me say anything?"

"Mr Trefusis does not mean to say that you did, I am sure. Oh, no. Mr Trefusis's feelings are naturally—are harrowed. That is all."

"My feelings!" cried Trefusis impatiently. "Do you suppose

my feelings are a trumpery set of social observances, to be harrowed to order and exhibited at funerals? She has gone as we three shall go soon enough. If we were immortal, we might reasonably pity the dead. As we are not, we had better save our energies to minimize the harm we are likely to do before we follow her."

The doctor was deeply offended by this speech, for the statement that he should one day die seemed to him a reflection upon his professional mastery over death. Mrs Jansenius was glad to see Trefusis confirming her bad opinion and report of him by his conduct and language in the doctor's presence. There was a brief pause, and then Trefusis, too far out of sympathy with them to be able to lead the conversation into a kinder vein, left the room. In the act of putting on his overcoat in the hall, he hesitated, and hung it up again irresolutely. Suddenly he ran upstairs. At the sound of his steps a woman came from one of the rooms and looked inquiringly at him.

"Is it here?" he said.

"Yes, sir," she whispered.

A painful sense of constriction came in his chest, and he turned pale and stopped with his hand on the lock.

"Dont be afraid, sir," said the woman, with an encouraging smile. "She looks beautiful."

He looked at her with a strange grin, as if she had uttered a ghastly but irresistible joke. Then he went in, and, when he reached the bed, wished he had stayed without. He was not one of those who, seeing little in the faces of the living, miss little in the faces of the dead. The arrangement of the black hair on the pillow, the soft drapery, and the flowers placed there by the nurse to complete the artistic effect to which she had so confidently referred, were lost on him; he saw only a lifeless mask that had been his wife's face, and at sight of it his knees failed, and he had to lean for support on the rail at the foot of the bed.

When he looked again the face seemed to have changed. It was no longer a waxlike mask, but Henrietta, girlish and pathetically at rest. Death seemed to have cancelled her marriage and womanhood; he had never seen her look so young. A minute passed, and then a tear dropped on the coverlet. He started; shook another tear on his hand, and stared at it incredulously.

"This is a fraud of which I have never even dreamed," he said. "Tears and no sorrow! Here am I crying! growing maudlin! whilst I am glad that she is gone and I free. I have the mechanism of grief in me somewhere; it begins to turn at sight of her, though I have no sorrow; just as she used to start the mechanism of passion when I had no love. And that made no difference to her; whilst the wheels went round she was satisfied. I hope the mechanism of grief will flag and stop in its spinning as soon as the other used to. It is stopping already, I think. What a mockery! Whilst it lasts I suppose I am really sorry. And yet, would I restore her to life if I could? Perhaps so; I am therefore thankful that I cannot." He folded his arms on the rail and gravely addressed the dead figure, which still affected him so strongly that he had to exert his will to face it with composure. "If you really loved me, it is well for you that you are dead—idiot that I was to believe that the passion you could inspire, you poor child, would last. We are both lucky; I have escaped from you, and you have escaped from yourself."

Presently he breathed more freely and looked round the room to help himself into a matter-of-fact vein by a little unembarrassed action, and the commonplace aspect of the bedroom furniture. He went to the pillow, and bent over it, examining the face closely.

"Poor child!" he said again, tenderly. Then, with sudden reaction, apostrophizing himself instead of his wife, "Poor ass! Poor idiot! Poor jackanapes! Here is the body of a woman who was nearly as old as myself, and perhaps wiser, and here am I moralizing over it as if I were God Almighty and she a baby! The more you remind a man of what he is, the more conceited he becomes. Monstrous! I shall feel immortal presently."

He touched the cheek with a faint attempt at roughness, to feel how cold it was. Then he touched his own, and remarked:

"This is what I am hastening toward at the express speed of

sixty minutes an hour!" He stood looking down at the face and tasting this sombre reflection for a long time. When it palled on him, he roused himself, and exclaimed more cheerfully:

"After all, she is not dead. Every word she uttered, every idea she formed and expressed, was an inexhaustible and indestructible impulse." He paused, considered a little further, and relapsed into gloom, adding: "And the dozen others whose names will be with hers in the Times tomorrow? Their words too are still in the air, to endure there to all eternity. Hm! How the air must be crammed with nonsense! Two sounds sometimes produce a silence; perhaps ideas neutralize one another in some analogous way. No, my dear; you are dead and gone and done with, and I shall be dead and gone and done with too soon to leave me leisure to fool myself with hopes of immortality. Poor Hetty! Well, good-bye, my darling. Let us pretend for a moment that you can hear that; I know it will please you."

All this was in a half-articulate whisper. When he ceased he still bent over the body, gazing intently at it. Even when he had exhausted the subject, and turned to go, he changed his mind, and looked again for a while. Then he stood erect, apparently nerved and refreshed, and left the room with a firm step. The woman was waiting outside. Seeing that he was less distressed than when he entered, she said:

"I hope you are satisfied, sir!"

"Delighted! Charmed! The arrangements are extremely pretty and tasteful. Most consolatory." And he gave her half a sovereign.

"I thank you, sir," she said, dropping a curtsey. "The poor young lady! She was anxious to see you, sir. To hear her say that you were the only one that cared for her! And so fretful with her mother, too. 'Let him be told that I am dangerously ill,' says she, 'and he'll come.' She didnt know how true her word was, poor thing; and she went off without being aware of it."

"Flattering herself and flattering me. Happy girl!"

"Bless you, I know what her feelings were, sir; I have had

experience." Here she approached him confidentially, and whispered: "The family were again' you, sir, and she knew it. But she wouldnt listen to them. She thought of nothing, when she was easy enough to think at all, but of your coming. And— hush! Here's the old gentleman."

Trefusis looked round and saw Mr Jansenius, whose handsome face was white and seamed with grief and annoyance. He drew back from the proffered hand of his son-in-law, like an over-worried child from an ill-timed attempt to pet it. Trefusis pitied him. The nurse coughed and retired.

"Have you been speaking to Mrs Jansenius?" said Trefusis.

"Yes," said Jansenius offensively.

"So have I, unfortunately. Pray make my apologies to her. I was rude. The circumstances upset me."

"You are not upset, sir," said Jansenius loudly. "You do not care a damn."

Trefusis recoiled.

"You damned my feelings, and I will damn yours," continued Jansenius in the same tone. Trefusis involuntarily looked at the door through which he had lately passed. Then, recovering him-self, he said quietly—

"It does not matter. She cant hear us."

Before Jansenius could reply his wife hurried upstairs, caught him by the arm, and said, "Dont speak to him, John. And you," she added, to Trefusis, "*will* you begone?"

"What!" he said, looking cynically at her. "Without my dead! Without my property! Well, be it so."

"What do you know of the feelings of a respectable man?" persisted Jansenius, breaking out again in spite of his wife. "Nothing is sacred to you. This shows what Socialists are!"

"And what fathers are, and what mothers are," retorted Trefusis, giving way to his temper. "I thought you loved Hetty, but I see that you only love your feelings and your respectability. The devil take both! She was right; my love for her, incomplete as it was, was greater than yours." And he left the house in dudgeon.

But he stood awhile in the avenue to laugh at himself and his father-in-law. Then he took a hansom and was driven to the house of his solicitor, whom he wished to consult on the settlement of his late wife's affairs.

CHAPTER X

The remains of Henrietta Trefusis were interred in Highgate Cemetery the day before Christmas Eve. Three noblemen sent their carriages to the funeral, and the friends and clients of Mr Jansenius, to a large number, attended in person. The bier was covered with a profusion of costly flowers. The undertaker, instructed to spare no expense, provided long-tailed black horses, with black palls on their backs and black plumes upon their foreheads; coachmen decorated with scarves and jack-boots, black hammercloths, cloaks, and gloves, with many hired mourners, who, however, would have been instantly discharged had they presumed to betray emotion, or in any way overstep their function of walking beside the hearse with brass-tipped batons in their hands.

Among the genuine mourners were Mr Jansenius, who burst into tears at the ceremony of casting earth on the coffin; the boy Arthur, who, preoccupied by the novelty of appearing in a long cloak at the head of a public procession, felt that he was not so sorry as he ought to be when he saw his papa cry; and a cousin who had once asked Henrietta to marry him, and who now, full of tragic reflections, was enjoying his despair intensely.

The rest whispered, whenever they could decently do so, about a strange omission in the arrangements. The husband of the deceased was absent. Members of the family and intimate friends were told by Daniel Jansenius that the widower had acted in a blackguard way, and that the Janseniuses did not care twopence whether he came or stayed at home; that, but for the indecency of the thing, they were just as glad that he was keeping away. Others, who had no claim to be privately informed, made inquiries of the undertaker's foreman, who said he understood the gentleman objected to large funerals. Asked why, he said he supposed it was on the ground of expense. This being met by a remark that Mr Trefusis was very wealthy, he added that he had been told so, but believed the money had not come from the lady; that people seldom cared to go to a great expense for a funeral unless they came into something good by the death; and that some parties the more they had the more they grudged. Before the funeral guests dispersed, the report spread by Mr Jansenius's brother had got mixed with the views of the foreman, and had given rise to a story of Trefusis expressing joy at his wife's death with frightful oaths in her father's house whilst she lay dead there, and refusing to pay a farthing of her debts or funeral expenses.

Some days later, when gossip on the subject was subsiding, a fresh scandal revived it. A literary friend of Mr Jansenius's helped him to compose an epitaph, and added to it a couple of pretty and touching stanzas, setting forth that Henrietta's character had been one of rare sweetness and virtue, and that her friends would never cease to sorrow for her loss. A trades-man who described himself as a "monumental mason" furnished a book of tomb designs, and Mr Jansenius selected a highly ornamental one, and proposed to defray half the cost of its erection. Trefusis objected that the epitaph was untrue, and said that he did not see why tombstones should be privileged to publish false statements. It was reported that he had followed up his former misconduct by calling his father-in-law a liar, and that he had ordered a common tombstone from some cheap-jack at the East End. He had, in fact, spoken contemptuously of the monumental tradesman as an "exploiter" of labor, and had asked a young working mason, a member of the International Associa-tion, to design a monument for the gratification of Jansenius.

The mason, with much pains and misgiving, produced an original design. Trefusis approved of it, and resolved to have it executed by the hands of the designer. He hired a sculptor's studio, purchased blocks of marble of the dimensions and quality described to him by the mason, and invited him to set to work forthwith.

Trefusis now encountered a difficulty. He wished to pay the mason the just value of his work, no more and no less. But this he could not ascertain. The only available standard was the market price, and this he rejected as being fixed by competition among capitalists who could only secure profit by obtaining from their workmen more products than they paid them for, and could only tempt customers by offering a share of the unpaid-for part of the products as a reduction in price. Thus he found that the system of withholding the indispensable materials for production and subsistence from the laborers, except on condition of their supporting an idle class whilst accepting a lower standard of comfort for themselves than for that idle class, rendered the determination of just ratios of exchange, and consequently the practice of honest dealing, impossible. He had at last to ask the mason what he would consider fair payment for the execution of the design, though he knew that the man could no more solve the problem than he, and that, though he would certainly ask as much as he thought he could get, his demand must be limited by his poverty and by the competition of the monumental tradesman. Trefusis settled the matter by giving double what was asked, only imposing such conditions as were necessary to compel the mason to execute the work himself, and not make a profit by hiring other men at the market rate of wages to do it.

But the design was, to its author's astonishment, to be paid for separately. The mason, after hesitating a long time between two-pounds-ten and five pounds, was emboldened by a fellow-workman, who treated him to some hot whiskey and water, to name the larger sum. Trefusis paid the money at once, and then set himself to find out how much a similar design would have cost from the hands of an eminent Royal Academician. Happening to know a gentleman in this position, he consulted him, and was informed that the probable cost would be from five hundred to one thousand pounds. Trefusis expressed his opinion that the mason's charge was the more reasonable, somewhat to the indignation of his artist friend, who reminded him of the years which a Royal Academician has to spend in acquiring his skill. Trefusis mentioned that the apprenticeship of a mason was quite as long, twice as laborious, and not half so pleasant. The artist now began to find Trefusis's socialistic views, with which he had previously fancied himself in sympathy, both odious and dangerous. He demanded whether nothing was to be allowed for genius. Trefusis warmly replied that genius costs its possessor nothing; that it was the inheritance of the whole race incidentally vested in a single individual; and that if that individual employed his monopoly of it to extort money from others, he deserved nothing better than hanging. The artist lost his temper, and suggested that if Trefusis could not feel that the prerogative of art was divine, perhaps he could understand that a painter was not such a fool as to design a tomb for five pounds when he might be painting a portrait for a thousand. Trefusis retorted that the fact of a man paying a thousand pounds for a portrait proved that he had not earned the money and was therefore either a thief or a beggar. The common workman who sacrificed sixpence from his week's wages for a cheap photograph to present to his sweetheart, or a shilling for a pair of chromo-lithographic pictures or delft figures to place on his mantelboard, suffered greater privation for the sake of possessing a work of art than the great landlord or shareholder who paid a thousand pounds, which he was too rich to miss, for a portrait that, like Hogarth's Jack Sheppard, was only interesting to students of criminal physiognomy. A lively quarrel ensued, Trefusis denouncing the folly of artists in fancying themselves a priestly caste when they were obviously only the parasites and favored slaves of the moneyed classes, and his friend (temporarily his enemy) sneering bitterly at levellers who were for levelling down instead of levelling up. Finally, tired of disputing, and remorseful for their acrimony, they dined amicably together.

The monument was placed in Highgate Cemetery by a small band of workmen whom Trefusis found out of employment.

It bore the following inscription:

THIS IS THE MONUMENT OF

HENRIETTA JANSENIUS

WHO WAS BORN ON THE 26TH JULY, 1856,

MARRIED TO SIDNEY TREFUSIS ON THE 23RD AUGUST, 1875,

AND WHO DIED ON THE 21ST DECEMBER IN THE SAME YEAR.

Mr Jansenius took this as an insult to his daughter's memory, and, as the tomb was much smaller than many which had been erected in the cemetery by families to whom the Janseniuses claimed superiority, cited it as an example of the widower's meanness. But by other persons it was so much admired that Trefusis hoped it would ensure the prosperity of its designer. The contrary happened. When the mason attempted to return to his ordinary work he was informed that he had contravened trade usage, and that his former employers would have nothing more to say to him. On applying for advice and assistance to the trades-union of which he was a member he received the same reply, and was further reproached for treachery to his fellow-workmen. He returned to Trefusis to say that the tombstone job had ruined him. Trefusis, enraged, wrote an argumentative letter to the Times, which was not inserted, a sarcastic one to the trades-union, which did no good, and a fierce one to the employers, who threatened to take an action for libel. He had to content himself with setting the man to work again on mantel-pieces and other decorative stone-work for use in house property on the Trefusis estate. In a year or two his liberal payments enabled the mason to save sufficient to start as an employer, in which capacity he soon began to grow rich, as he knew by experience exactly how much his workmen could be forced to do, and how little they could be forced to take. Shortly after this change in his circumstances he became an advocate of thrift, temperance, and steady industry, and quitted the International Association, of which he had been an enthusiastic supporter when dependent on his own skill and taste as a working mason.

During these occurrences Agatha's school-life ended. Her resolution to study hard during another term at the college had been formed, not for the sake of becoming learned, but that she might become more worthy of Smilash; and when she learned the truth about him from his own lips, the idea of returning to the scene of that humiliation became intolerable to her. She left under the impression that her heart was broken, for her smarting vanity, by the law of its own existence, would not perceive that it was the seat of the injury. So she bade Miss Wilson adieu; and the bee on the window pane was heard no more at Alton College.

The intelligence of Henrietta's death shocked her the more because she could not help being glad that the only other person who knew of her folly with regard to Smilash (himself excepted) was now silenced for ever. This seemed to her a terrible discovery of her own depravity. Under its influence she became almost religious, and caused some anxiety about her health to her mother, who was puzzled by her unwonted seriousness, and, in particular, by her determination not to speak of the misconduct of Trefusis, which was now the prevailing topic of conversation in the family. She listened in silence to gossiping discussions of his desertion of his wife, his heartless indifference to her decease, his violence and bad language by her deathbed, his parsimony, his malicious opposition to the wishes of the Janseniuses, his cheap tombstone with the insulting epitaph, his association with common workmen and low demagogues, his suspected connection with a secret society for the assassination of the royal family and blowing up of the army, his atheistic denial, in a pamphlet addressed to the clergy, of a statement by the Archbishop of Canterbury that spiritual aid alone could improve the condition of the poor in the East End of London, and the crowning disgrace of his trial for seditious libel at the Old Bailey, where he was condemned to six months' imprisonment; a penalty from which he was rescued by the ingenuity of his counsel, who discovered a flaw in the indictment, and succeeded, at great cost to Trefusis, in getting the sentence quashed. Agatha at last got tired of hearing of his misdeeds. She believed him to be heartless, selfish, and misguided, but she knew that he was not the loud, coarse, sensual, and ignorant brawler most of her mother's gossips supposed him to be. She even felt, in spite of herself, an emotion of gratitude to the few who ventured to defend him.

Preparation for her first season helped her to forget her misadventure. She "came out" in due time, and an extremely dull season she found it. So much so, that she sometimes asked herself whether she should ever be happy again. At the college there had been good-fellowship, fun, rules, and duties which were a source of strength when observed and a source of delicious excitement when violated, freedom from ceremony, toffee-making, flights on the banisters, and appreciative audiences for the soldier in the chimney. In society there were silly conversations lasting half a minute, cool acquaintanceships founded on such half-minutes, general reciprocity of suspicion, overcrowding, insufficient ventilation, bad music badly executed, late hours, unwholesome food, intoxicating liquors, jealous competition in useless expenditure, husband-hunting, flirting, dancing, theatres, and concerts. The last three, which Agatha liked, helped to make the contrast between Alton and London tolerable to her, but they had their drawbacks, for good partners at the dances, and good performances at the spiritless opera and concerts, were disappointingly scarce. Flirting she could no tendure; she drove men away when they became tender, seeing in them the falsehood of Smilash without his wit. She was considered rude by the younger gentlemen of her circle. They discussed her bad manners among themselves, and agreed to punish her by not asking her to dance. She thus got rid, without knowing why, of the attentions she cared for least (she retained a schoolgirl's cruel contempt for "boys"), and enjoyed herself as best she could with such of the older or more sensible men as were not intolerant of girls.

At best the year was the least happy she had ever spent. She repeatedly alarmed her mother by broaching projects of becoming a hospital nurse, a public singer, or an actress. These projects led to some desultory studies. In order to qualify herself as a nurse she read a handbook of physiology, which Mrs Wylie thought so improper a subject for a young lady that she went in tears to beg Mrs Jansenius to remonstrate with her unruly girl. Mrs Jansenius, better advised, was of opinion that the more a woman knew the more wisely she was likely to act, and that Agatha would soon drop the physiology of her own accord. This proved true. Agatha, having finished her book by dint of extensive skipping, proceeded to study pathology from a volume of clinical lectures. Finding her own sensations exactly like those described in the book as symptoms of the direst diseases, she put it by in alarm, and took up a novel, which was free from the fault she had found in the lectures, inasmuch as none of the emotions it described in the least resembled any she had ever experienced.

After a brief interval, she consulted a fashionable teacher of singing as to whether her voice was strong enough for the operatic stage. He recommended her to study with him for six years, assuring her that at the end of that period—if she followed his directions—she should be the greatest singer in the world. To this there was, in her mind, the conclusive objection that in six years she should be an old woman. So she resolved to try privately whether she could not get on more quickly by herself. Meanwhile, with a view to the drama in case her operatic scheme should fail, she took lessons in elocution and gymnastics. Practice in these improved her health and spirits so much that her previous aspirations seemed too limited. She tried her hand at all the arts in succession, but was too discouraged by the weakness of her first attempts to persevere. She knew that as a general rule there are feeble and ridiculous beginnings to all excellence, but she never applied general rules to her own case, still thinking of herself as an exception to them, just as she had done when she romanced about Smilash. The illusions of adolescence were thick upon her.

Meanwhile her progress was creating anxieties in which she had no share. Her paroxysms of exhilaration, followed by a gnawing sense of failure and uselessness, were known to her mother only as "wildness" and "low spirits," to be combated by needlework as a sedative, or beef tea as a stimulant. Mrs Wylie had learnt by rote that the whole duty of a lady is to be graceful, charitable, helpful, modest, and disinterested, whilst awaiting passively whatever lot these virtues may induce. But she had learnt by experience that a lady's business in society is to get married, and that virtues and accomplishments alike are important only as attractions to eligible bachelors. As this truth is shameful, young ladies are left for a year or two to find it out for themselves; it is seldom explicitly conveyed to them at their entry into society. Hence they often throw away capital bargains in their first season, and are compelled to offer themselves at greatly reduced prices subsequently, when their attractions begin to stale. This was the fate which Mrs Wylie, warned by Mrs Jansenius, feared for Agatha, who, time after time when a callow gentleman of wealth and position was introduced to her, drove him brusquely away as soon as he ventured to hint that his affections were concerned in their acquaintanceship. The anxious mother had to console herself with the fact that her daughter drove away the ineligible as ruthlessly as the eligible, formed no unworldly attachments, was still very young, and would grow less coy as she advanced in years and in what Mrs Jansenius called sense.

But as the seasons went by it remained questionable whether Agatha was the more to be congratulated on having begun life after leaving school or Henrietta on having finished it.

CHAPTER XI

BRANDON BEECHES, in the Thames valley, was the seat of Sir Charles Brandon, seventh baronet of that name. He had lost his father before attaining his majority, and had married shortly afterwards; so that in his twenty-fifth year he was father to three children. He was a little worn, in spite of his youth, but he was tall and agreeable, had a winning way of taking a kind and soothing view of the misfortunes of others, could tell a story well, liked music and could play and sing a little, loved the arts of design and could sketch a little in water-colors, read every magazine from London or Paris that criticized pictures, had travelled a little, fished a little, shot a little, botanized a little, wandered restlessly in the footsteps of women, and dissipated his energies through all the small channels that his wealth opened and his talents made easy to him. He had no large knowledge of any subject, though he had looked into many just far enough to replace absolute unconsciousness of them with measurable ignorance. Never having enjoyed the sense of achievement, he was troubled with unsatisfied aspirations that filled him with melancholy and convinced him that he was a born artist. His wife found him selfish, peevish, hankering after change, and prone to believe that he was attacked by dangerous diseases when he was only catching cold.

Lady Brandon, who believed that he understood all the subjects he talked about because she did not understand them herself, was one of his disappointments. In person she resembled none of the types of beauty striven after by the painters of her time, but she had charms to which few men are insensible. She was tall, soft, and stout, with ample and shapely arms, shoulders, and hips. With her small head, little ears, pretty lips, and roguish eye, she, being a very large creature, presented an immensity of half womanly, half infantile loveliness which smote even grave men with a desire to clasp her in their arms and kiss her. This desire had scattered the desultory intellectual culture of Sir

Charles at first sight. His imagination invested her with the taste for the fine arts which he required from a wife, and he married her in her first season, only to discover that the amativeness in her temperament was so little and languid that she made all his attempts at fondness ridiculous, and robbed the caresses for which he had longed of all their anticipated ecstasy. Intellectually she fell still further short of his hopes. She looked upon his favorite art of painting as a pastime for amateur and a branch of the house-furnishing trade for professional artists. When he was discussing it among his friends, she would offer her opinion with a presumption which was the more trying as she frequently blundered upon a sound conclusion whilst he was reasoning his way to a hollow one with his utmost subtlety and seriousness. On such occasions his disgust did not trouble her in the least; she triumphed in it. She had concluded that marriage was a greater folly, and men greater fools, than she had supposed; but such beliefs rather lightened her sense of responsibility than disappointed her, and, as she had plenty of money, plenty of servants, plenty of visitors, and plenty of exercise on horseback, of which she was immoderately fond, her time passed pleasantly enough. Comfort seemed to her the natural order of life; trouble always surprised her. Her husband's friends, who mistrusted every future hour, and found matter for bitter reflection in many past ones, were to her only examples of the power of sedentary habits and excessive reading to make men hipped and dull.

One fine May morning, as she cantered along the avenue at Brandon Beeches on a powerful bay horse, the gates at the end opened and a young man sped through them on a bicycle. He was of slight frame, with fine dark eyes and delicate nostrils. When he recognized Lady Brandon he waved his cap, and when they met he sprang from his inanimate steed, at which the bay horse shied.

"Dont, you silly beast!" she cried, whacking the animal with the butt of her whip. "Though it's natural enough, goodness knows! How d'ye do? The idea of any one rich enough to afford a horse riding on a wheel like that!"

"But I am not rich enough to afford a horse," he said, approaching her to pat the bay, having placed the bicycle against a tree. "Besides, I am afraid of horses, not being accustomed to them; and I know nothing about feeding them. My steed needs no food. He doesnt bite nor kick. He never goes lame, nor sickens, nor dies, nor needs a groom, nor—"

"Thats all bosh," said Lady Brandon impetuously. "It stumbles, and gives you the most awful tosses, and it goes lame by its treadles and thingamyjigs coming off, and it wears out, and is twice as much trouble to keep clean and scrape the mud off as a horse, and all sorts of things. I think the most ridiculous sight in the world is a man on a bicycle, working away with his feet as hard as he possibly can, and believing that his horse is carrying him instead of, as any one can see, he carrying the horse. You neednt tell me that it isnt easier to walk in the ordinary way than to drag a great dead iron thing along with you. It's not good sense."

"Nevertheless I can carry it a hundred miles further in a day than I can carry myself alone. Such are the marvels of machinery. But I know that we cut a very poor figure beside you and that magnificent creature—not that any one will look at me whilst you are by to occupy their attention so much more worthily."

She darted a glance at him which clouded his vision and made his heart beat more strongly. This was an old habit of hers. She kept it up from love of fun, having no idea of the effect it produced on more ardent temperaments than her own. He continued hastily:

"Is Sir Charles at home?"

"Oh, it's the most ridiculous thing I ever heard of in my life," she exclaimed. "A man that lives by himself in a place down by the Riverside Road like a toy savings bank—dont you know the things I mean?—called Sallust's House, says there is a right of way through our new pleasure ground. As if any one could have any right there after all the money we have spent fencing it on three sides, and building up the wall by the road, and levelling, and planting, and draining, and goodness knows what else! And now the man says that all the common people and tramps in the neighborhood have a right to walk across it because they are too lazy to go round by the road. Charlie has gone to see the man about it. Of course he wouldnt do as I wanted him."

"What was that?"

"Write to tell the man to mind his own business, and to say that the first person we found attempting to trespass on our property should be given to the police."

"Then I shall find no one at home. I beg your pardon for calling it so; but it is the only place like home to me."

"Yes: it is so comfortable since we built the billiard room and took away those nasty hangings in the hall. I was ever so long trying to pers—"

She was interrupted by an old laborer, who hobbled up as fast as his rheumatism would allow him, and began to speak without further ceremony than snatching off his cap.

"Th'ave coom to the noo grouns, my lady, crowds of em. An' a parson with em, an' a flag! Sur Chorles he dont know what to say; an' sooch doins never was."

Lady Brandon turned pale and pulled at her horse as if to back him out of some danger. Her visitor, puzzled, asked the old man what he meant.

"There's goin to be a proceyshon through the noo grouns," he replied, "an' the master cant stop em. Th'ave throon down the wall; three yards of it is lyin on Riverside Road. An' there's a parson with em, an' a flag. An' him that lives in Sallust's Hoos, he's there, hoddin em on."

"Thrown down the wall!" exclaimed Lady Brandon, scarlet with indignation and pale with apprehension by turns. "What a disgraceful thing! Where are the police? Chester, will you come with me and see what they are doing? Charlie is no use. Do you think there is any danger?"

"There's two police," said the old man, "an' him that lives at Sallust's dar'd em stop him. Theyre lookin on. An' there's a parson among em. I see him pullin away at the wall with his own han's."

"Let's go and see the fun," said Chester.

Lady Brandon hesitated. But her anger and curiosity vanquished her fears. She overtook the bicycle, and they went together through the gates and by the high road to the scene the old man had described. A heap of bricks and mortar lay in the roadway on each side of a breach in the newly built wall, over which Lady Brandon, from her eminence on horseback, could see, coming towards her across the pleasure ground, a column of about thirty persons. They marched three abreast in good order and in silence; the expression of all except a few mirthful faces being that of devotees fulfilling a rite. The gravity of the procession was deepened by the appearance of a clergyman in its ranks, which were composed of men of the middle class, and a few workmen carrying a banner inscribed THE SOIL OF ENGLAND THE BIRTHRIGHT OF ALL HER PEOPLE. There were also four women, upon whom Lady Brandon looked with intense indignation and contempt. None of the men of the neighborhood had dared to join; they stood in the road whispering, and occasionally venturing to laugh at the jests of a couple of tramps who had stopped to see the fun, and who cared nothing for Sir Charles.

He, standing a little way within the field, was remonstrating angrily with a man of his own class, who stood with his back to the breach and his hands in the pockets of his snuff-colored clothes, contemplating the procession with elate satisfaction. Lady Brandon, at once suspecting that this was the man from Sallust's House, and encouraged by the loyalty of the crowd, most of whom made way for her and touched their hats, hit the bay horse smartly with her whip and rode him, with a clatter of hoofs and scattering of clods, right at the snuff-colored enemy, who had to spring hastily aside to avoid her. There was a roar of laughter from the roadway, and the man turned sharply on her. But he suddenly smiled affably, replaced his hands in his pockets after raising his hat, and said:

"How do you do, Miss Carpenter? I thought you were a

145

charge of cavalry."

"I am not Miss Carpenter, I am Lady Brandon; and you ought to be ashamed of yourself, Mr Smilash, if it is you that have brought these disgraceful people here."

His eyes as he replied were eloquent with reproach to her for being no longer Miss Carpenter. "I am not Smilash," he said; "I am Sidney Trefusis. I have just had the pleasure of meeting Sir Charles for the first time, and we shall be the best friends possible when I have convinced him that it is hardly fair to seize on a path belonging to the people and compel them to walk a mile and a half round his estate instead of four hundred yards between two portions of it."

"I have already told you, sir," said Sir Charles, "that I intend to open a still shorter path, and to allow all the well-conducted workpeople to pass through twice a day. This will enable them to go to their work and return from it; and I will be at the cost of keeping the path in repair."

"Thank you," said Trefusis dryly; "but why should we trouble you when we have a path of our own to use fifty times a day if we choose, without any man barring our way until our conduct happens to please him? Besides, your next heir would probably shut the path up the moment he came into possession."

"Offering them a path is just what makes them impudent," said Lady Brandon to her husband. "Why did you promise them anything? They would not think it a hardship to walk a mile and a half, or twenty miles, to a public-house, but when they go to their work they think it dreadful to have to walk a yard. Perhaps they would like us to lend them the wagonette to drive in?"

"I have no doubt they would," said Trefusis, beaming at her.

"Pray leave me to manage here, Jane; this is no place for you. Take Erskine to the house. He must be—"

"Why dont the police make them go away?" said Lady Brandon, too excited to listen to her husband.

"Hush, Jane, pray. What can three men do against thirty or forty?"

"They ought to take up somebody as an example to the rest."

"They have offered, in the handsomest manner, to arrest me if Sir Charles will give me in charge," said Trefusis.

"There!" said Lady Jane, turning to her husband. "Why dont you give him—or some one—in charge?"

"You know nothing about it," said Sir Charles, vexed by a sense that she was publicly making him ridiculous.

"If you dont, I will," she persisted. "The idea of having our ground broken into and our new wall knocked down! A nice state of things it would be if people were allowed to do as they liked with other people's property. I will give every one of them in charge."

"Would you consign me to a dungeon?" said Trefusis, in melancholy tones.

"I dont mean you exactly," she said, relenting. "But I will give that clergyman into charge, because he ought to know better. He is the ringleader of the whole thing."

"He will be delighted, Lady Brandon; he pines for martyrdom. But will you really give him into custody?"

"I will," she said vehemently, emphasizing the assurance by a plunge in the saddle that made the bay stagger.

"On what charge?" he said, patting the horse and looking up at her.

"I dont care what charge," she replied, conscious that she was being admired, and not displeased. "Let them take him up, thats all."

Human beings on horseback are so far centaurs that liberties taken with their horses are almost as personal as liberties taken with themselves. When Sir Charles saw Trefusis patting the bay he felt as much outraged as if Lady Brandon herself were being patted, and he felt bitterly towards her for permitting the familiarity. He was relieved by the arrival of the procession. It halted as the leaders came up to Trefusis, who said gravely:

"Gentlemen, I congratulate you on the firmness with which you have this day asserted the rights of the people of this place to the use of one of the few scraps of mother earth of which they have not been despoiled."

"Gentlemen," shouted an excited member of the procession, "three cheers for the resumption of the land of England by the people of England! Hip, hip, hurrah!"

The cheers were given with much spirit, Sir Charles's cheeks becoming redder at each repetition. He looked angrily at the clergyman, now distracted by the charms of Lady Brandon, whose scorn, as she surveyed the crowd, expressed itself by a pout which became her pretty lips extremely.

Then a middle-aged laborer stepped from the road into the field, hat in hand, ducked respectfully, and said: "Look 'e here, Sir Charles. Dont 'e mind them fellers. There aint a man belonging to this neighborhood among em; not one in your employ or on your land. Our dooty to you and your ladyship, and we will trust to you to do what is fair by us. We want no interlopers from Lunnon to get us into trouble with your honor, and—"

"You unmitigated cur," exclaimed Trefusis fiercely, "what right have you to give away to his unborn children the liberty of your own?"

"Theyre not unborn," said Lady Brandon indignantly. "That just shews how little you know about it."

"No, nor mine either," said the man, emboldened by her ladyship's support. "And who are you that call me a cur?"

"Who am I! I am a rich man—one of your masters, and privileged to call you what I please. You are a grovelling famine-broken slave. Now go and seek redress against me from the law. I can buy law enough to ruin you for less money than it would cost me to shoot deer in Scotland or vermin here. How do you like that state of things? Eh?"

The man was taken aback. "Sir Charles will stand by me," he said, after a pause, with assumed confidence, but with an anxious glance at the baronet.

"If he does, after witnessing the return you have made me for standing by you, he is a greater fool than I take him to be."

"Gently, gently," said the clergyman. "There is much excuse to be made for the poor fellow."

"As gently as you please with any man that is a freeman at heart," said Trefusis; "but slaves must be driven, and this fellow is a slave to the marrow."

"Still, we must be patient. He does not know——"

"He knows a great deal better than you do," said Lady Brandon, interrupting. "And the more shame for you, because you ought to know best. I suppose you were educated somewhere. You will not be satisfied with yourself when our bishop hears of this. Yes," she added, turning to Trefusis with an infantile air of wanting to cry and being forced to laugh against her will, "you may laugh as much as you please—dont trouble to pretend it's only coughing—but we will write to his bishop, as he shall find to his cost."

"Hold your tongue, Jane, for God's sake," said Sir Charles, taking her horse by the bridle and backing him from Trefusis.

"I will not. If you choose to stand here and allow them to walk away with the walls in their pockets, I dont, and wont. Why cannot you make the police do something?"

"They can do nothing," said Sir Charles, almost beside himself with humiliation. "I cannot do anything until I see my solicitor. How can you bear to stay here wrangling with these fellows? It is so undignified!"

"It's all very well to talk of dignity, but I dont see the dignity of letting people trample on our grounds without leave. Mr Smilash, will you make them all go away, and tell them that they shall all be prosecuted and put in prison?"

"They are going to the cross-roads, to hold a public meeting and—of course—make speeches. I am desired to say that they deeply regret that their demonstration should have disturbed you personally, Lady Brandon."

"So they ought," she replied. "They dont look very sorry. They are getting frightened at what they have done, and they would be glad to escape the consequences by apologizing, most likely. But they shant. I am not such a fool as they think."

"They dont think so. You have proved the contrary."

"Jane," said Sir Charles pettishly, "do you know this gentleman?"

"I should think I do," said Lady Brandon emphatically.

Trefusis bowed as if he had just been formally introduced to the baronet, who, against his will, returned the salutation stiffly, unable to ignore an older, firmer, and quicker man under the circumstances.

"This seems an unneighborly business, Sir Charles," said Trefusis, quite at his ease; "but as it is a public question, it need not prejudice our private relations. At least I hope not."

Sir Charles bowed again, more stiffly than before.

"I am, like you, a capitalist and landlord—"

"Which it seems to me you have no right to be, if you are in earnest," struck in Chester, who had been watching the scene in silence by Sir Charles's side.

"Which, as you say, I have undoubtedly no right to be," said Trefusis, surveying him with interest; "but which I nevertheless cannot help being. Have I the pleasure of speaking to Mr Chichester Erskine, author of a tragedy entitled The Patriot Martyrs, dedicated with enthusiastic devotion to the Spirit of Liberty and half a dozen famous upholders of that principle, and denouncing in forcible language the tyranny of the late Tsar of Russia, Bomba of Naples, and Napoleon the Third?"

"Yes, sir," said Erskine, reddening; for he felt that this description might make his drama seem ridiculous to those present who had not read it.

"Then," said Trefusis, extending his hand—Erskine at first thought for a hearty shake—"give me half a crown towards the cost of our expedition here today to assert the right of the people to tread the soil we are standing upon."

"You shall do nothing of the sort, Chester," cried Lady Brandon. "I never heard of such a thing in my life! Do *you* pay us for the wall and fence your people have broken, Mr Smilash; that would be more to the purpose."

"If I could find a thousand men as practical as you, Lady Brandon, I might accomplish the next great revolution before the end of this season." He looked at her for a moment curiously, as if trying to remember; and then added inconsequently: "How are your friends? There was a Miss—Miss—I am afraid I have forgotten all the names except your own."

"Gertrude Lindsay is staying with us. Do you remember her?"

"I think—no, I am afraid I do not. Let me see. Was she a haughty young lady?"

"Yes," said Lady Brandon eagerly, forgetting the wall and fence. "But who do you think is coming next Thursday? I met her accidentally the last time I was in town. She's not a bit changed. You cant forget her, so dont pretend to be puzzled."

"You have not told me who she is yet. And I shall probably not remember her. You must not expect me to recognize every one instantaneously, as I recognized you."

"What stuff! You will know Agatha fast enough."

"Agatha Wylie!" he said, with sudden gravity.

"Yes. She is coming on Thursday. Are you glad?"

"I fear I shall have no opportunity of seeing her."

"Oh, of course you must see her. It will be so jolly for us all to meet again just as we used. Why cant you come to luncheon on Thursday?"

"I shall be delighted, if you will really allow me to come after my conduct here."

"The lawyers will settle that. Now that you have found out who we are you will stop pulling down our walls, of course."

"Of course," said Trefusis, smiling, as he took out a pocket diary and entered the engagement. "I must hurry away to the cross-roads. They have probably voted me into the chair by this time, and are waiting for me to open their meeting. Goodbye. You have made this place, which I was growing tired of, unexpectedly interesting to me."

They exchanged glances of the old college pattern. Then he nodded to Sir Charles, waved his hand familiarly to Erskine, and followed the procession, which was by this time out of sight.

Sir Charles, who, waiting to speak, had been repeatedly baffled by the hasty speeches of his wife and the unhesitating replies of

Trefusis, now turned angrily upon her, saying:

"What do you mean by inviting that fellow to my house?"

"*Your* house, indeed! I will invite whom I please. You are getting into one of your tempers."

Sir Charles looked about him. Erskine had discreetly slipped away, and was in the road, tightening a screw in his bicycle. The few persons who remained were out of earshot.

"Who and what the devil is he, and how do you come to know him?" he demanded. He never swore in the presence of any lady except his wife, and then only when they were alone.

"He is a gentleman, which is more than you are," she retorted, and, with a cut of her whip that narrowly missed her husband's shoulder, sent the bay plunging through the gap.

"Come along," she said to Erskine. "We shall be late for luncheon."

"Had we not better wait for Sir Charles?" he asked injudiciously.

"Never mind Sir Charles, he is in the sulks," she said, without abating her voice. "Come along." And she went off at a canter, Erskine following her with a misgiving that his visit was unfortunately timed.

CHAPTER XII

On the following Thursday Gertrude, Agatha, and Jane met for the first time since they had parted at Alton College. Agatha was the shyest of the three, and externally the least changed. She fancied herself very different from the Agatha of Alton; but it was her opinion of herself that had altered, not her person. Expecting to find a corresponding alteration in her friends, she had looked forward to the meeting with much doubt and little hope of its proving pleasant.

She was more anxious about Gertrude than about Jane, concerning whom, at a brief interview in London, she had already discovered that Lady Brandon's manner, mind, and speech were just what Miss Carpenter's had been. But, even from Agatha, Jane commanded more respect than before, having changed from an overgrown girl into a fine woman, and made a brilliant match in her first season, whilst many of her pretty, proud, and clever contemporaries, whom she had envied at school, were still unmarried, and were having their homes made uncomfortable by parents anxious to get rid of the burthen of supporting them, and to profit in purse or position by their marriages.

This was Gertrude's case. Like Agatha, she had thrown away her matrimonial opportunities. Proud of her rank and exclusiveness, she had resolved to have as little as possible to do with persons who did not share both with her. She began by repulsing the proffered acquaintance of many families of great wealth and fashion, who either did not know their grandparents or were ashamed of them. Having shut herself out of their circle, she was presented at court, and thenceforth accepted the invitations of those only who had, in her opinion, a right to the same honor. And she was far stricter on that point than the Lord Chamberlain, who had, she held, betrayed his trust by practically turning Leveller. She was well educated, refined in her manners and habits, skilled in etiquette to an extent irritating to the ignorant, and gifted with a delicate complexion, pearly teeth, and a face that would have been Grecian but for a slight upward tilt of the nose and traces of a square, heavy type in the jaw. Her father was a retired admiral, with sufficient influence to have had a sinecure made by a Conservative Government expressly for the maintenance of his son pending alliance with some heiress. Yet Gertrude remained single, and the admiral, who had formerly spent more money than he could comfortably afford on her education, and was still doing so upon her state and personal adornment, was complaining so unpleasantly of her failure to get taken off his hands, that she could hardly bear to live at home, and was ready to marry any thoroughbred gentleman, however unsuitable his age or character, who would relieve her from her humiliating dependence. She was prepared to sacrifice her natural desire for youth, beauty, and virtue in a husband if she could escape from her parents on no easier terms, but she was resolved to die an old maid sooner than marry an upstart.

The difficulty in her way was pecuniary. The admiral was poor. He had not quite six thousand a year, and though he practised the utmost economy in order to keep up the most expensive habits, he could not afford to give his daughter a dowry. Now the well-born bachelors of her set, having more blue blood, but much less wealth, than they needed, admired her, paid her compliments, danced with her, but could not afford to marry her. Some of them even told her so, married rich daughters of tea merchants, iron founders, or successful stock-brokers, and then tried to make matches between her and their lowly-born brothers-in-law.

So, when Gertrude met Lady Brandon, her lot was secretly wretched, and she was glad to accept an invitation to Brandon Beeches in order to escape for a while from the admiral's daily sarcasms on the marriage list in the Times. The invitation was the more acceptable because Sir Charles was no mushroom noble, and, in the school days which Gertrude now remembered as the happiest of her life, she had acknowledged that Jane's family and connections were more aristocratic than those of any other student then at Alton, herself excepted. To Agatha, whose grandfather had amassed wealth as a proprietor of gasworks (novelties in his time), she had never offered her intimacy. Agatha had taken it by force, partly moral, partly physical. But the gasworks were never forgotten, and when Lady Brandon mentioned, as a piece of delightful news, that she had found out their old school companion, and had asked her to join them, Gertrude was not quite pleased. Yet, when they met, her eyes were the only wet ones there, for she was the least happy of the three, and, though she did not know it, her spirit was somewhat broken. Agatha, she thought, had lost the bloom of girlhood, but was bolder, stronger, and cleverer than before. Agatha had, in fact, summoned all her self-possession to hide her shyness. She detected the emotion of Gertrude, who at the last moment did not try to conceal it. It would have been poured out freely in words, had Gertrude's social training taught her to express her feelings as well as it had accustomed her to dissemble them.

"Do you remember Miss Wilson?" said Jane, as the three drove from the railway station to Brandon Beeches. "Do you remember Mrs Miller and her cat? Do you remember the Recording Angel? Do you remember how I fell into the canal?"

These reminiscences lasted until they reached the house and went together to Agatha's room. Here Jane, having some orders to give in the household, had to leave them—reluctantly; for she was jealous lest Gertrude should get the start of her in the renewal of Agatha's affection. She even tried to take her rival away with her; but in vain. Gertrude would not budge.

"What a beautiful house and splendid place!" said Agatha, when Jane was gone. "And what a nice fellow Sir Charles is! We used to laugh at Jane, but she can afford to laugh at the luckiest of us now. I always said she would blunder into the best of everything. Is it true that she married in her first season?"

"Yes. And Sir Charles is a man of great culture. I cannot understand it. Her size is really beyond everything, and her manners are bad."

"Hm!" said Agatha with a wise air. "There was always something about Jane that attracted men. And she is more knave than fool. But she is certainly a great ass."

Gertrude looked serious, to imply that she had grown out of the habit of using or listening to such language. Agatha, stimulated by this, continued:

"Here are you and I, who consider ourselves twice as presentable and conversable as she, two old maids." Gertrude winced, and Agatha hastened to add: "Why, as for you, you are perfectly lovely! And she has asked us down expressly to marry us."

"She would not presume—"

"Nonsense, my dear Gertrude. She thinks that we are a couple of fools who have mismanaged our own business, and that she, having managed so well for herself, can settle us in a jiffy. Come, did she not say to you, before I came, that it was time for me to be getting married?"

"Well, she did. But—"

"She said exactly the same thing to me about you when she invited me."

"I would leave her house this moment," said Gertrude, "if I thought she dared meddle in my affairs. What is it to her whether I am married or not?"

"Where have you been living all these years, if you do not know that the very first thing a woman wants to do when she has made a good match is to make one for all her spinster friends? Jane does not mean any harm. She does it out of pure benevolence."

"I do not need Jane's benevolence."

"Neither do I; but it doesnt do any harm, and she is welcome to amuse herself by trotting out her male acquaintances for my approval. Hush! Here she comes."

Gertrude subsided. She could not quarrel with Lady Brandon without leaving the house, and she could not leave the house without returning to her home. But she privately resolved to discourage the attentions of Erskine, suspecting that instead of being in love with her as he pretended, he had merely been recommended by Jane to marry her.

Chichester Erskine had made sketches in Palestine with Sir

Charles, and had tramped with him through many European picture galleries. He was a young man of gentle birth, and had inherited fifteen hundred a year from his mother, the bulk of the family property being his elder brother's. Having no profession, and being fond of books and pictures, he had devoted himself to fine art, a pursuit which offered him on the cheapest terms a high opinion of the beauty and capacity of his own nature. He had published a tragedy entitled The Patriot Martyrs, with an etched frontispiece by Sir Charles, and an edition of it had been speedily disposed of in presentations to the friends of the artist and poet, and to the reviews and newspapers. Sir Charles had asked an eminent tragedian of his acquaintance to place the work on the stage and to enact one of the patriot martyrs. But the tragedian had objected that the other patriot martyrs had parts of equal importance to that proposed for him. Erskine had indignantly refused to cut these parts down or out, and so the project had fallen through.

Since then Erskine had been bent on writing another drama, without regard to the exigencies of the stage, but he had not yet begun it, in consequence of his inspiration coming upon him at inconvenient hours, chiefly late at night, when he had been drinking, and had leisure for sonnets only. The morning air and bicycle riding were fatal to the vein in which his poetry struck him as being worth writing. In spite of the bicycle, however, the drama, which was to be entitled Hypatia, was now in a fair way to be written, for the poet had met and fallen in love with Gertrude Lindsay, whose almost Grecian features, and some knowledge of the differential calculus which she had acquired at Alton, helped him to believe that she was a fit model for his heroine.

When the ladies came downstairs they found their host and Erskine in the picture gallery, famous in the neighborhood for the sum it had cost Sir Charles. There was a new etching to be admired, and they were called on to observe what the baronet called its tones, and what Agatha would have called its degrees of smudginess. Sir Charles's attention often wandered from this work of art. He looked at his watch twice, and said to his wife:

"I have ordered them to be punctual with the luncheon."

"Oh, yes; it's all right," said Lady Brandon, who had given orders that luncheon was not to be served until the arrival of another gentleman. "Show Agatha the picture of the man in the—"

"Mr Trefusis," said a servant.

Mr Trefusis, still in snuff color, entered; coat unbuttoned and attention unconstrained; exasperatingly unconscious of any occasion for ceremony.

"Here you are at last," said Lady Brandon. "You know everybody, dont you?"

"How do you do?" said Sir Charles, offering his hand as a severe expression of his duty to his wife's guest, who took it cordially, nodded to Erskine, looked without recognition at Gertrude, whose frosty stillness repudiated Lady Brandon's implication that the stranger was acquainted with her, and turned to Agatha, to whom he bowed. She made no sign; she was paralysed. Lady Brandon reddened with anger. Sir Charles noted his guest's reception with secret satisfaction, but shared the embarrassment which oppressed all present except Trefusis, who seemed quite indifferent and assured, and unconsciously produced an impression that the others had not been equal to the occasion, as indeed they had not.

"We were looking at some etchings when you came in," said Sir Charles, hastening to break the silence. "Do you care for such things?" And he handed him a proof.

Trefusis looked at it as if he had never seen such a thing before and did not quite know what to make of it. "All these scratches seem to me to have no meaning," he said dubiously.

Sir Charles stole a contemptuous smile and significant glance at Erskine. He, seized already with an instinctive antipathy to Trefusis, said emphatically:

"There is not one of those scratches that has not a meaning."

"That one, for instance, like the limb of a daddy-long-legs. What does that mean?"

Erskine hesitated a moment; recovered himself; and said: "Obviously enough—to me at least—it indicates the marking of the roadway."

"Not a bit of it," said Trefusis. "There never was such a mark as that on a road. It may be a very bad attempt at a briar, but briars dont straggle into the middle of roads frequented as that one seems to be—judging by those overdone ruts." He put the etching away, showing no disposition to look further into the portfolio, and remarked: "The only art that interests me is photography."

Erskine and Sir Charles again exchanged glances, and the former said:

"Photography is not an art in the sense in which I understand the term. It is a process."

"And a much less troublesome and more perfect process than that," said Trefusis, pointing to the etching. "The artists are sticking to the old barbarous, difficult, and imperfect processes of etching and portrait painting merely to keep up the value of their monopoly of the required skill. They have left the new, more complexly organized, and more perfect, yet simple and beautiful method of photography in the hands of tradesmen, sneering at it publicly and resorting to its aid surreptitiously. The result is that the tradesmen are becoming better artists than they, and naturally so; for where, as in photography, the drawing counts for nothing, the thought and judgment count for everything; whereas in the etching and daubing processes, where great manual skill is needed to produce anything that the eye can endure, the execution counts for more than the thought, and if a fellow only fit to carry bricks up a ladder or the like has ambition and perseverance enough to train his hand and push into the van, you cannot afford to put him back into his proper place, because thoroughly trained hands are so scarce. Consider the proof of this that you have in literature. Our books are manually the work of printers and paper-makers; you may cut an author's hand off and he is as good an author as before. What is the result? There is more imagination in any number of a penny journal than in half a dozen of the Royal Academy rooms in the season. No author can live by his work and be as empty-headed as an average successful painter. Again, consider our implements of music—our pianofortes, for example. Nobody but an acrobat will voluntarily spend years at such a difficult mechanical puzzle as the keyboard, and so we have to take our impressions of Beethoven's sonatas from acrobats who vie with each other in the rapidity of their *prestos*, or the staying power of their left wrists. Thoughtful men will not spend their lives acquiring sleight-of-hand. Invent a piano which will respond as delicately to the turning of a handle as our present ones do to the pressure of the fingers, and the acrobats will be driven back to their carpets and trapezes, because the sole faculty necessary to the executant musician will be the musical faculty, and no other will enable him to obtain a hearing."

The company were somewhat overcome by this unexpected lecture. Sir Charles, feeling that such views bore adversely on him, and were somehow iconoclastic and low-lived, was about to make a peevish retort, when Erskine forestalled him by asking Trefusis what idea he had formed of the future of the arts. He replied promptly:

"Photography perfected in its recently discovered power of reproducing color as well as form! Historical pictures replaced by photographs of *tableaux vivants* formed and arranged by trained actors and artists, and used chiefly for the instruction of children! Nine-tenths of painting as we understand it at present extinguished by the competition of these photographs, and the remaining tenth only holding its own against them by dint of extraordinary excellence! Our mistuned and unplayable organs and pianofortes replaced by harmonious instruments, as manageable as barrel organs! Works of fiction superseded by interesting company and conversation, and made obsolete by the human mind outgrowing the childishness that delights in the tales told by grown-up children such as novelists and their like! An end to the silly confusion, under the one name of Art, of the tomfoolery and make-believe of our play hours with the higher methods of teaching men to know themselves! Every artist an amateur, and a consequent return to the healthy old disposition to look on every man who makes art a means of money-making as a vagabond not to be entertained as an equal by honest men!"

"In which case artists will starve, and there will be no more art."

"Sir," said Trefusis, excited by the word, "I, as a Socialist, can tell you that starvation is now impossible, except where, as in England, masterless men are forcibly prevented from producing the food they need. And you, as an artist, can tell me that at present great artists invariably do starve, except when they are kept alive by charity, private fortune, or some drudgery which hinders them in the pursuit of their vocation."

"Oh!" said Erskine. "Then Socialists have some little sympathy with artists after all."

"I fear," said Trefusis, repressing himself and speaking quietly again, "that when a Socialist hears of a hundred pounds paid for a drawing which Andrea del Sarto was glad to sell for tenpence, his heart is not wrung with pity for the artist's imaginary loss as that of a modern capitalist is. Yet that is the only way nowadays of enlisting sympathy for the old masters. Frightful disability, to be out of the reach of the dearest market when you want to sell your drawings! But," he added, giving himself a shake, and turning round gaily, "I did not come here to talk shop. So—pending the deluge—let us enjoy ourselves after our manner."

"No," said Jane. "Please go on about Art. It's such a relief to hear any one talking sensibly about it. I hate etching. It makes your eyes sore—at least the acid gets into Sir Charles's, and the difference between the first and second states is nothing but imagination, except that the last state is worse than the—Heres luncheon!"

They went downstairs then. Trefusis sat between Agatha and Lady Brandon, to whom he addressed all his conversation. They chatted without much interruption from the business of the table; for Jane, despite her amplitude, had a small appetite, and was fearful of growing fat; whilst Trefusis was systematically abstemious. Sir Charles was unusually silent. He was afraid to talk about art, lest he should be contradicted by Trefusis, who, he already felt, cared less and perhaps knew more about it than he.

Having previously commented to Agatha on the beauty of the ripening spring, and inquired whether her journey had fatigued her, he had said as much as he could think of at a first meeting. For her part, she was intent on Trefusis, who, though he must know, she thought, that they were all hostile to him except Jane, seemed as confident now as when he had befooled her long ago. That thought set her teeth on edge. She did not doubt the sincerity of her antipathy to him even when she detected herself in the act of protesting inwardly that she was not glad to meet him again, and that she would not speak to him. Gertrude, meanwhile, was giving short answers to Erskine and listening to Trefusis. She had gathered from the domestic squabbles of the last few days that Lady Brandon, against her husband's will, had invited a notorious demagogue, the rich son of a successful cotton-spinner, to visit the Beeches. She had made up her mind to snub any such man. But on recognizing the long-forgotten Smilash, she had been astonished, and had not known what to do. So, to avoid doing anything improper, she had stood stiffly silent and done nothing, as the custom of English ladies in such cases is. Subsequently, his unconscious self-assertion had wrought with her as with the others, and her intention of snubbing him had faded into the limbo of projects abandoned without trial. Erskine alone was free from the influence of the intruder. He wished himself elsewhere; but beside Gertrude the presence or absence of any other person troubled him very little.

"How are the Janseniuses?" said Trefusis, suddenly turning to Agatha.

"They are quite well, thank you," she said in measured tones.

"I met John Jansenius in the city lately. You know Jansenius?" he added parenthetically to Sir Charles. "Cotman's bank—the last Cotman died out of the firm before we were born. The Chairman of the Transcanadian Railway Company."

"I know the name. I am seldom in the city."

"Naturally," assented Trefusis; "for who would sadden himself by pushing his way through a crowd of such slaves, if he could help it? I mean slaves of Mammon, of course. To run the gauntlet of their faces in Cornhill is enough to discourage a thoughtful man for hours. Well, Jansenius, being high in the court of Mammon, is looking out for a good post in the household for his son. Jansenius, by the by, is Miss Wylie's guardian and the father of my late wife."

Agatha felt inclined to deny this; but, as it was true, she had to forbear. Resolved to shew that the relations between her family and Trefusis were not cordial ones, she asked deliberately: "Did Mr Jansenius speak to you?"

Gertrude looked up, as if she thought this scarcely ladylike.

"Yes," said Trefusis. "We are the best friends in the world— as good as possible, at any rate. He wanted me to subscribe to a fund for relieving the poor at the east end of London by assisting them to emigrate."

"I presume you subscribed liberally," said Erskine. "It was an opportunity of doing some *practical* good."

"I did not," said Trefusis, grinning at the sarcasm. "This Transcanadian Railway Company, having got a great deal of spare land from the Canadian government for nothing, thought it would be a good idea to settle British workmen on it and screw rent out of them. Plenty of British workmen, supplanted in their employment by machinery, or cheap foreign labor, or one thing or another, were quite willing to go; but as they couldnt afford to pay their passages to Canada, the Company appealed to the benevolent to pay for them by subscription, as the change would improve their miserable condition. I did not see why I should pay to provide a rich company with tenant farmers, and I told Jansenius so. He remarked that when money and not talk was required, the workmen of England soon found out who were their real friends."

"I know nothing about these questions," said Sir Charles with an air of conclusiveness; "but I see no objection to emigration."

"The fact is," said Trefusis, "the idea of emigration is a dangerous one for us. Familiarize the workman with it, and some day he may come to see what a capital thing it would be to pack off me, and you, with the peerage, and the whole tribe of unprofitable proprietors such as we are, to St Helena; making us a handsome present of the island by way of indemnity! We are such a restless, unhappy lot, that I doubt whether it would not prove a good thing for us too. The workmen would lose nothing but the contemplation of our elegant persons, exquisite manners, and refined tastes. They might provide against that loss by picking out a few of us to keep for ornament's sake. No nation with a sense of beauty would banish Lady Brandon, or Miss Lindsay, or Miss Wylie."

"Such nonsense!" said Jane.

"You would hardly believe how much I have spent in sending workmen out of the country against my own view of the country's interest," continued Trefusis, addressing Erskine. "When I make a convert among the working classes, the first thing he does is to make a speech somewhere declaring his new convictions. His employer immediately discharges him—'gives him the sack' is the technical phrase. The sack is the sword of the capitalist, and hunger keeps it sharp for him. His shield is the law, made for the purpose by his own class. Thus equipped, he gives the worst of it to my poor convert, who comes ruined to me for assistance. As I cannot afford to pension him for life, I get rid of him by assisting him to emigrate. Sometimes he prospers and repays me; sometimes I hear no more of him; sometimes he comes back with his habits unsettled. One man whom I sent to America made his fortune, but he was not a social democrat; he was a clerk who had embezzled, and who applied to me for assistance under the impression that I considered it rather meritorious to rob the till of a capitalist."

"He was a practical Socialist, in fact," said Erskine.

"On the contrary, he was a somewhat too grasping Individualist. Howbeit, I enabled him to make good his defalcation—in the city they consider a defalcation *made good* when the money is replaced—and to go to New York. I recommended him not to go there; but he knew better than I, for he made a fortune by speculating with money that existed only in the imagination of those with whom he dealt. *He* never repaid me; he is probably far too good a man of business to pay money that cannot be extracted from him by an appeal to the law or to his commercial credit. Mr Erskine," added Trefusis, lowering his voice, and turning to the poet, "you are wrong to take part with hucksters and money-hunters against your own nature, even though the attack upon them is led by a man who prefers photography to etching."

"But I assure you—You quite mistake me," said Erskine, taken aback. "I—" He stopped, looked to Sir Charles for support, and then said airily: "I dont doubt that you are quite right. I hate business and men of business; and as to social questions, I have only one article of belief, which is, that the sole refiner of human nature is fine art."

"Whereas I believe that the sole refiner of art is human nature. Art rises when men rise, and grovels when men grovel. What is your opinion?"

"I agree with you in many ways," replied Sir Charles nervously; for a lack of interest in his fellow-creatures, and an excess of interest in himself, had prevented him from obtaining that power of dealing with social questions which, he felt, a baronet ought to possess, and he was consequently afraid to differ from any one who alluded to them with confidence. "If you take an interest in art, I believe I can show you a few things worth seeing."

"Thank you. In return I will some day show you a remarkable collection of photographs I possess; many of them taken by me. I venture to think they will teach you something."

"No doubt," said Sir Charles. "Shall we return to the gallery? I have a few treasures there that photography is not likely to surpass for some time yet."

"Let's go through the conservatory," said Jane. "Dont you like flowers, Mr Smi—. I never can remember your proper name."

"Extremely," said Trefusis.

They rose and went out into a long hothouse. Here Lady Brandon, finding Erskine at her side, and Sir Charles before her with Gertrude, looked round for Trefusis, with whom she intended to enjoy a trifling flirtation under cover of showing him the flowers. He was out of sight; but she heard his footsteps in the passage on the opposite side of the greenhouse. Agatha was also invisible. Jane, not daring to rearrange their procession, lest her design should become obvious, had to walk on with Erskine.

Agatha had turned unintentionally into the opposite alley to that which the others had chosen. When she saw what she had done, and found herself virtually alone with Trefusis, who had followed her, she blamed him for it, and was about to retrace her steps when he said coolly:

"Were you shocked when you heard of Henrietta's sudden death?"

Agatha struggled with herself for a moment, and then said in a suppressed voice: "How dare you speak to me?"

"Why not?" said he, astonished.

"I am not going to enter into a discussion with you. You know what I mean very well."

"You mean that you are offended with me; that is plain enough. But when I part with a young lady on good terms, and after a lapse of years, during which we neither meet nor correspond, she asks me how I dare speak to her, I am naturally startled."

"We did not part on good terms."

Trefusis stretched his eyebrows, as if to stretch his memory. "If not," he said, "I have forgotten it, on my honour. When did we part, and what happened? It cannot have been anything very serious, or I should remember it."

His forgetfulness wounded Agatha. "No doubt you are well accustomed to—" She checked herself, and made a successful snatch at her normal manner with gentlemen. "I scarcely remember what it was, now that I begin to think. Some trifle, I suppose. Do you like orchids?"

"They have nothing to do with our affairs at present. You are not in earnest about the orchids, and you are trying to run away from a mistake instead of clearing it up. That is a short-sighted policy, always."

Agatha grew alarmed, for she felt his old influence over her returning. "I do not wish to speak of it," she said firmly.

Her firmness was lost on him. "I do not even know what *it* means yet," he said, "and I want to know, for I believe there is some misunderstanding between us, and it is the trick of your sex to perpetuate misunderstandings by forbidding all allusions to them. Perhaps, leaving Lyvern so hastily, I forgot to fulfil some promise, or to say farewell, or something of that sort. But do you know how suddenly I was called away? I got a telegram to say that Henrietta was dying, and I had only time to change my clothes—you remember my disguise—and catch the express. And, after all, she was dead when I arrived."

"I know that," said Agatha uneasily. "Please say no more about it."

"Not if it distresses you. Just let me hope that you did not suppose I blamed you for your share in the matter or that I told the Janseniuses of it. I did not. Yes, I like orchids. A plant that can subsist on a scrap of board is an instance of natural econ—"

"*You* blame *me!*" cried Agatha. "*I* never told the Janseniuses. What would they have thought of you if I had?"

"Far worse of you than of me, however unjustly. You were the immediate cause of the tragedy; I only the remote one. Jansenius is not far-seeing when his feelings are touched. Few men are."

"I dont understand you in the least. What tragedy do you mean?"

"Henrietta's death. I call it a tragedy conventionally. Seriously, of course, it was commonplace enough."

Agatha stopped and faced him. "What do you mean by what you said just now? You said that I was the immediate cause of the tragedy, and you say that you were talking of Henrietta's—of Henrietta. I had nothing to do with her illness."

Trefusis looked at her as if considering whether he would go any further. Then, watching her with the curiosity of a vivisector, he said: "Strange to say, Agatha" (she shrank proudly at the word), "Henrietta might have been alive now but for you. I am very glad she is not; so you need not reproach yourself on my account. She died of a journey she made to Lyvern in great excitement and distress, and in intensely cold weather. You caused her to make that journey by writing her a letter which made her

167

jealous."

"Do you mean to accuse me—"

"No; stop!" he said hastily, the vivisecting spirit in him exorcised by her shaking voice; "I accuse you of nothing. Why do you not speak honestly to me when you are at your ease? If you confess your real thoughts only under torture, who can resist the temptation to torture you? One must charge you with homicide to make you speak of anything but orchids."

But Agatha had drawn the new inference from the old facts, and would not be talked out of repudiating it. "It was not my fault," she said. "It was yours—altogether yours."

"Altogether," he assented, relieved to find her indignant instead of remorseful.

She was not to be soothed by a verbal acquiescence. "Your behaviour was most unmanly, and I told you so, and you could not deny it. You pretended that you— You pretended to have feelings— You tried to make me believe that— Oh, I am a fool to talk to you; you know perfectly well what I mean."

"Perfectly. I tried to make you believe that I was in love with you. How do you know I was not?"

She disdained to answer; but as he waited calmly she said, "You had no right to be."

"That does not prove that I was not. Come, Agatha, you pretended to like me when you did not care two straws about me. You confessed as much in that fatal letter, which I have somewhere at home. It has a great rent right across it, and the mark of her heel; she must have stamped on it in her rage, poor girl! So that I can shew your own hand for the very deception you accused me— without proof—of having practised on you."

"You are clever, and can twist things. What pleasure does it give you to make me miserable?"

"Ha!" he exclaimed, in an abrupt, sardonic laugh. "I dont know; you bewitch me, I think."

Agatha made no reply, but walked on quickly to the end of the conservatory, where the others were waiting for them.

"Where have you been, and what have you been doing all this

time?" said Jane, as Trefusis came up, hurrying after Agatha. "I dont know what you call it, but I call it perfectly disgraceful!"

Sir Charles reddened at his wife's bad taste, and Trefusis replied gravely: "We have been admiring the orchids, and talking about them. Miss Wylie takes an interest in them."

CHAPTER XIII

ONE morning Gertrude got a letter from her father:

"My Dear Gerty—I have just received a bill for £110 from Madame Smith for your dresses. May I ask you how long this sort of thing is to go on? I need not tell you that I have not the means to support you in such extravagance. I am, as you know, always anxious that you should go about in a style worthy of your position, but unless you can manage without calling on me to pay away hundreds of pounds every season to Madame Smith, you had better give up society and stay at home. I positively cannot afford it. As far as I can see, going into society has not done you much good. I had to raise £500 last month on Franklands; and it is too bad if I must raise more to pay your dressmaker. You might at least employ some civil person, or one whose charges are moderate. Madame Smith tells me that she will not wait any longer, and charges £60 for a single dress. I hope you fully understand that there must be an end to this.

"I hear from your mother that young Erskine is with you at Brandon's. I do not think much of him. He is not well off, nor likely to get on, as he has taken to poetry and so forth. I am told also that a man named Trefusis visits at the Beeches a good deal now. He must be a fool, for he contested the last Birmingham election, and came out at the foot of the poll with thirty-two votes through calling himself a Social Democrat or some such foreign rubbish, instead of saying out like a man that he was a Radical. I suppose the name stuck in his throat, for his mother was one of the Howards of Breconcastle; so he has good blood in him, though his father was nobody. I wish he had your bills to pay; he could buy and sell me ten times over, after all my twenty-five years' service.

"As I am thinking of getting something done to the house, I had rather you did not come back this month, if you can possibly hold on at Brandon's. Remember me to him, and give our kind regards to his wife. I should be obliged if you would gather some

hemlock leaves and send them to me. I want them for my oint-
ment; the stuff the chemists sell is no good. Your mother's eyes
are bad again; and your brother Berkeley has been gambling, and
seems to think I ought to pay his debts for him. I am greatly
worried over it all, and I hope that, until you have settled yourself, you will be more reasonable, and not run these everlasting
bills upon me. You are enjoying yourself out of reach of all the
unpleasantness; but it bears hardly upon your affectionate father,
"C. B. LINDSAY."

A faint sketch of the lines Time intended to engrave on
Gertrude's brow appeared there as she read the letter; but she
hastened to give the admiral's kind regards to her host and
hostess, and discussed her mother's health feelingly with them.
After breakfast she went to the library, and wrote her reply:

"BRANDON BEECHES, *Tuesday.*

"Dear Papa—Considering that it is more than three years
since you paid Madame Smith last, and that then her bill, which
included my court dress, was only £150, I cannot see how I could
possibly have been more economical, unless you expect me to go
in rags. I am sorry that Madame Smith has asked for the money
at such an inconvenient time, but when I begged you to pay her
something in March last year you told me to keep her quiet by
giving her a good order. I am not surprised at her not being
very civil, as she has plenty of tradesmen's daughters among her
customers who pay her more than £300 a year for their dresses.
I am wearing a skirt at present which I got two years ago.

"Sir Charles is going to town on Thursday; he will bring you
the hemlock. Tell mamma that there is an old woman here who
knows some wonderful cure for sore eyes. She will not tell
what the ingredients are, but it cures every one, and there is no
use in giving an oculist two guineas for telling us that reading
in bed is bad for the eyes, when we know perfectly well that
mamma will not give up doing it. If you pay Berkeley's debts,
do not forget that he owes me £3.

"Another schoolfellow of mine is staying here now, and I think that Mr Trefusis will have the pleasure of paying her bills some day. He is a great pet of Lady Brandon's. Sir Charles was angry at first because she invited him here, and we were all surprised at it. The man has a bad reputation, and headed a mob that threw down the walls of the park; and we hardly thought he would be cool enough to come after that. But he does not seem to care whether we want him or not; and he comes when he likes. As he talks cleverly, we find him a godsend in this dull place. It is really not such a paradise as you seem to think, but you need not be afraid of my returning any sooner than I can help.—Your affectionate daughter,   GERTRUDE LINDSAY."

When Gertrude had closed this letter, and torn up her father's, she thought little more about either. They might have made her unhappy had they found her happy; but as hopeless discontent was her normal state, and enjoyment but a rare accident, recriminatory passages with her father only put her into a bad humor, and did not in the least disappoint or humiliate her.

For the sake of exercise, she resolved to carry her letter to the village post office and return along the Riverside Road, whereby she had seen hemlock growing. She took care to go out unobserved, lest Agatha should volunteer to walk with her, or Jane declare her intention of driving to the post office in the afternoon, and sulk for the rest of the day unless the trip to the village were postponed until then. She took with her, as a protection against tramps, a big St Bernard dog named Max. This animal, which was young and enthusiastic, had taken a strong fancy to her, and had expressed it frankly and boisterously; and she, whose affections had been starved in her home and in society, had encouraged him with more kindness than she had ever shewn to any human being.

In the village, having posted her letter, she turned towards a lane that led to the Riverside Road. Max, unaware of her reason for choosing the longest way home, remonstrated by halting in the middle of the lane, wagging his tail rapidly, and uttering gruff barks.

"Dont be stupid, sir," said Gertrude impatiently. "I am going this way."

Max, apparently understanding, rushed after her, passed her, and disappeared in a cloud of dust raised by his effort to check himself when he had left her far enough behind. When he came back she kissed his nose, and ran a race with him until she too was panting, and had to stand still to recover her breath, whilst he bounded about, barking ferociously. She had not for many years enjoyed such a frolic, and the thought of this presently brought tears to her eyes. Rather peevishly she bade Max be quiet, walked slowly to cool herself, and put up her sunshade to avert freckles.

The sun was now at the meridian. On a slope to Gertrude's right hand, Sallust's House, with its cinnamon-colored walls and yellow frieze, gave a foreign air to the otherwise very English landscape. She passed by without remembering who lived there. Further down, on some waste land separated from the road by a dry ditch and a low mud wall, a cluster of hemlocks, nearly six feet high, poisoned the air with their odour. She crossed the ditch, took a pair of gardening gloves from her plaited straw handbasket, and busied herself with the hemlock leaves, pulling the tender ones, separating them from the stalk, and filling the basket with the web. She forgot Max until an impression of dead silence, as if the earth had stopped, caused her to look round in vague dread. Trefusis, with his hand abandoned to the dog, who was trying how much of it he could cram into his mouth, was standing within a few yards of her, watching her intently. Gertrude turned pale, and came out hastily from among the bushes. Then she had a strange sensation as if something had happened high above her head. There was a threatening growl, a commanding exclamation, and an unaccountable pause, at the expiration of which she found herself supine on the sward, with her parasol between her eyes and the sun. A sudden scoop of Max's wet warm tongue in her right ear startled her into activity. She sat up, and saw Trefusis on his knees at her side holding the parasol with an unconcerned expression, whilst Max was snuffing at her in restless anxiety opposite.

"I must go home," she said. "I must go home instantly."

"Not at all," said Trefusis soothingly. "They have just sent word to say that everything is settled satisfactorily and that you need not come."

"Have they?" she said faintly. Then she lay down again, and it seemed to her that a very long time elapsed. Suddenly recollecting that Trefusis had supported her gently with his hand to prevent her falling back too rudely, she rose again, and this time got upon her feet with his help.

"I must go home," she said again. "It is a matter of life or death."

"No, no," he said softly. "It is all right. You may depend on me."

She looked at him earnestly. He had taken her hand to steady her, for she was swaying a little. "Are you sure?" she said, grasping his arm. "Are you quite sure?"

"Absolutely certain. You know I am always right, do you not?"

"Yes, oh, yes; you have always been true to me. You—" Here her senses came back with a rush. Dropping his hand as if it had become red hot, she said sharply, "What are you talking about?"

"I dont know," he said, resuming his indifferent manner with a laugh. "Are you better? Let me drive you to the Beeches. My stable is within a stone's-throw; I can get a trap out in ten minutes."

"No, thank you," said Gertrude haughtily. "I do not wish to drive." She paused, and added in some bewilderment, "What has happened?"

"You fainted, and—"

"I did not faint," said Gertrude indignantly. "I never fainted in my life."

"Yes, you did."

"Pardon me, Mr Trefusis. I did not."

"You shall judge for yourself. I was coming through this field when I saw you gathering hemlock. Hemlock is interesting on account of Socrates, and you were interesting as a young lady gathering poison. So I stopped to look on. Presently you came out from among the bushes as if you had seen a snake there. Then you fell into my arms—which led me to suppose that you had fainted—and Max, concluding that it was all my fault, nearly sprang at my throat. You were overpowered by the scent of the water-hemlock, which you must have been inhaling for ten minutes or more."

"I did not know that there was any danger," said Gertrude, crestfallen. "I felt very tired when I came to. That was why I lay so long the second time. I really could not help it."

"You did not lie very long."

"Not when I first fell; that was only a few seconds, I know. But I must have lain there nearly ten minutes after I recovered."

"You were nearly a minute insensible when you first fell, and when you recovered you only rested for about one second. After that you raved, and I invented suitable answers until you suddenly asked me what I was talking about."

Gertrude reddened a little as the possibility of her having raved indiscreetly occurred to her. "It was very silly of me to faint," she said.

"You could not help it; you are only human. I shall walk with you to the Beeches."

"Thank you; I will not trouble you," she said quickly.

He shook his head. "I do not know how long the effect of that abominable water-weed may last," he said, "and I dare not leave you to walk alone. If you prefer it I can send you in a trap with my gardener, but I had rather accompany you myself."

"You are giving yourself a great deal of unnecessary trouble. I will walk. I am quite well again and need no assistance."

They started without another word. Gertrude had to concentrate all her energy to conceal from him that she was giddy. Numbness and lassitude crept upon her, and she was beginning to hope that she was only dreaming it all when he roused her by saying—

"Take my arm."

"No, thank you."

"Do not be so senselessly obstinate. You will have to lean on the hedge for support if you refuse my help. I am sorry I did not insist on getting the trap."

Gertrude had not been spoken to in this tone since her childhood. "I am perfectly well," she said sharply. "You are really very officious."

"You are not perfectly well, and you know it. However, if you make a brave struggle, you will probably be able to walk home without my assistance, and the effort may do you good."

"You are very rude," she said peremptorily.

"I know it," he replied calmly. "You will find three classes of men polite to you—slaves, men who think much of their manners and nothing of you, and your lovers. I am none of these, and therefore give you back your ill manners with interest. Why do you resist your good angel by suppressing those natural and sincere impulses which come to you often enough, and sometimes bring a look into your face that might tame a bear—a look which you hasten to extinguish as a thief darkens his lantern at the sound of a footstep?"

"Mr Trefusis, I am not accustomed to be lectured."

"That is why I lecture you. I felt curious to see how your good breeding, by which I think you set some store, would serve you in entirely novel circumstances—those of a man speaking his mind to you, for instance. What is the result of my experiment? Instead of rebuking me with the sweetness and dignity which I could not, in spite of my past observation, help expecting from you, you churlishly repel my offer of the assistance you need, tell me that I am very rude, very officious, and, in short, do what you can to make my position disagreeable and humiliating."

She looked at him haughtily, but his expression was void of offence or fear, and he continued, unanswered:

"I would bear all this from a working woman without remonstrance, for she would owe me no graces of manner or morals. But you are a lady. That means that many have starved and drudged in uncleanly discomfort in order that you may have white and unbroken hands, fine garments, and exquisite manners —that you may be a living fountain of those influences that soften our natures and lives. When such a costly thing as a lady breaks down at the first touch of a firm hand, I feel justified in complaining."

Gertrude walked on quickly, and said between her teeth, "I dont want to hear any of your absurd views, Mr Trefusis."

He laughed. "My unfortunate views!" he said. "Whenever I make an inconvenient remark it is always set aside as an expression of certain dangerous crazes with which I am supposed to be afflicted. When I point out to Sir Charles that one of his favorite artists has not accurately observed something before attempting to draw it, he replies, 'You know our views differ on these things, Trefusis.' When I told Miss Wylie's guardian that his emigration scheme was little better than a fraud, he said, 'You must excuse me, but I cannot enter into your peculiar views.' One of my views at present is that Miss Lindsay is more amiable under the influence of hemlock than under that of the social system which has made her so unhappy."

"Well!" exclaimed Gertrude, outraged. Then, after a pause, "I was under the impression that I had accepted the escort of a gentleman." Then, after another pause, Trefusis being quite undisturbed: "How do you know that I am unhappy?"

"By a certain defect in your countenance, which lacks the crowning beauty of happiness; and a certain defect in your voice which will never disappear until you learn to love or pity those to whom you speak."

"You are wrong," said Gertrude, with calm disdain. "You do not understand me in the least. I am particularly attached to my friends."

"Then I have never seen you in their company."

"You are still wrong."

"Then how can you speak as you do, look as you do, act as you do?"

"What do you mean? How do I look and act?"

"Like one of the railings of Belgrave Square, cursed with consciousness of itself, fears of the judgment of the other railings, and doubts of their fitness to stand in the same row with it. You are cold, mistrustful, cruel to nervous or clumsy people, and more afraid of the criticisms of those with whom you dance and dine than of your conscience. All of which prevents you from looking like an angel."

"Thank you. Do you consider paying compliments the perfection of gentlemanly behavior?"

"Have I been paying you many? That last remark of mine was not meant as one. On my honor, the angels will not disappoint me if they are no lovelier than you should be if you had that look in your face and that tone in your voice I spoke of just now. It can hardly displease you to hear that. If I were particularly handsome myself, I should like to be told so."

"I am sorry I cannot tell you so."

"Oh! Ha! ha! What a retort, Miss Lindsay! You are not sorry either; you are rather glad."

Gertrude knew it, and was angry with herself, not because her retort was false, but because she thought it unladylike. "You have no right to annoy me," she exclaimed, in spite of herself.

"None whatever," he said humbly. "If I have done so, forgive me before we part. I will go no further with you; Max will give the alarm if you faint in the avenue, which I dont think you are likely to do, as you have forgotten all about the hemlock."

"Oh, how maddening!" she cried. "I have left my basket behind."

"Never mind; I will find it and have it filled and sent to you."

"Thank you. I am sorry to trouble you."

"Not at all. I hope you do not want the hemlock to help you to get rid of the burden of life."

"Nonsense. I want it for my father, who uses it for medicine."

"I will bring it myself tomorrow. Is that soon enough?"

"Quite. I am in no hurry. Thank you, Mr Trefusis. Good-bye."

She gave him her hand, and even smiled a little, and then hurried away. He stood watching her as she passed along the avenue under the beeches. Once, when she came into a band of sunlight at a gap in the trees, she made so pretty a figure in her spring dress of violet and white that his eyes kindled as he gazed. He took out his notebook, and entered her name and the date, with a brief memorandum.

"I have thawed her," he said to himself as he put up his book. "She shall learn a lesson or two to hand on to her children before I have done with her. A trifle underbred, too, or she would not insist so much on her breeding. Henrietta used to wear a dress like that. I am so glad to see that there is no danger of her taking to me personally."

He turned away, and saw a crone passing, bending beneath a bundle of sticks. He eyed it curiously; and she scowled at him and hurried on.

"Hallo," he said.

She continued for a few steps, but her courage failed her and she stopped.

"You are Mrs Hickling, I think?"

"Yes, please your worship."

"You are the woman who carried away an old wooden gate that lay on Sir Charles Brandon's land last winter and used it for firewood. You were imprisoned for seven days for it."

"You may send me there again if you like," she retorted, in a cracked voice, as she turned at bay. "But the Lord will make me even with you some day. Cursed be them that oppress the poor and needy; it is one of the seven deadly sins."

"Those green laths on your back are the remainder of my garden gate," he said. "You took the first half last Saturday. Next time you want fuel come to the house and ask for coals, and let my gates alone. I suppose you can enjoy a fire without stealing the combustibles. Now pay me for my gate by telling me something I want to know."

"And a kind gentleman too, sir; blessings—"

"What is the hemlock good for?"

"The hemlock, kind gentleman? For the evil, sir, to be sure."

"Scrofulous ulcers!" he exclaimed, recoiling. "The father of that beautiful girl!" He turned homeward, and trudged along with his head bent, muttering, "All rotten to the bone. Oh, civilization! civilization! civilization!"

CHAPTER XIV

"What has come over Gertrude?" said Agatha one day to Lady Brandon.

"Why? Is anything the matter with her?"

"I dont know; she has not been the same since she poisoned herself. And why did she not tell about it? But for Trefusis we should never have known."

"Gertrude always made secrets of things."

"She was in a vile temper for two days after; and now she is quite changed. She falls into long reveries, and does not hear a word of what is going on around. Then she starts into life again, and begs your pardon with the greatest sweetness for not catching what you have said."

"I hate her when she is polite; it is not natural to her. As to her going to sleep, that is the effect of the hemlock. We know a man who took a spoonful of strychnine in a bath, and he never was the same afterwards."

"I think she is making up her mind to encourage Erskine," said Agatha. "When I came here he hardly dared speak to her— at least, she always snubbed him. Now she lets him talk as much as he likes, and actually sends him on messages and allows him to carry things for her."

"Yes. I never saw anybody like Gertrude in my life. In London, if men were attentive to her, she sat on them for being officious; and if they let her alone she was angry at being neglected. Erskine is quite good enough for her, *I* think."

Here Erskine appeared at the door and looked round the room.

"She's not here," said Jane.

"I am seeking Sir Charles," he said, withdrawing somewhat stiffly.

"What a lie!" said Jane, discomfited by his reception of her jest. "He was talking to Sir Charles ten minutes ago in the billiard room. Men are such conceited fools!"

Agatha had strolled to the window, and was looking discontentedly at the prospect, as she had often done at school when alone, and sometimes did now in society. The door opened again, and Sir Charles appeared. He, too, looked round, but when his roving glance reached Agatha it cast anchor; and he came in.

"Are you busy just now, Miss Wylie?" he asked.

"Yes," said Jane hastily. "She is going to write a letter for me."

"Really, Jane," he said, "I think you are old enough to write your letters without troubling Miss Wylie."

"When I do write my own letters you always find fault with them," she retorted.

"I thought perhaps you might have leisure to try over a duet with me," he said, turning to Agatha.

"Certainly," she replied, hoping to smooth matters by humoring him. "The letter will do any time before post hour."

Jane reddened, and said shortly, "I will write it myself, if you will not."

Sir Charles quite lost his temper. "How can you be so damnably rude?" he said, turning upon his wife. "What objection have you to my singing duets with Miss Wylie?"

"Nice language that!" said Jane. "I never said I objected; and you have no right to drag her away to the piano just when she is going to write a letter for me."

"I do not wish Miss Wylie to do anything except what pleases her best. It seems to me that writing letters to your tradespeople cannot be a very pleasant occupation."

"Pray dont mind me," said Agatha. "It is not the least trouble to me. I used to write all Jane's letters for her at school. Suppose I write the letter first, and then we can have the duet. You will not mind waiting five minutes?"

"I can wait as long as you please, of course. But it seems such an absurd abuse of your good nature that I cannot help protesti—"

"Oh, let it wait!" exclaimed Jane. "Such a ridiculous fuss to make about asking Agatha to write a letter, just because you happen to want her to play you your duets! I am certain she is heartily sick and tired of them."

Agatha, to escape the altercation, went to the library and wrote the letter. When she returned to the drawing room, she found no one there; but Sir Charles came in presently.

"I am so sorry, Miss Wylie," he said, as he opened the piano for her, "that you should be incommoded because my wife is silly enough to be jealous."

"Jealous!"

"Of course. Idiocy!"

"Oh, you are mistaken," said Agatha incredulously. "How could she possibly be jealous of *me?*"

"She is jealous of everybody and everything," he replied bitterly, "and she cares for nobody and for nothing. You do not know what I have to endure sometimes from her."

Agatha thought her most discreet course was to sit down immediately and begin "I would that my love." Whilst she played and sang, she thought over what Sir Charles had just let slip. She had found him a pleasant companion, light-hearted, fond of music and fun, polite and considerate, appreciative of her talents, quick-witted without being oppressively clever, and, as a married man, disinterested in his attentions. But it now occurred to her that perhaps they had been a good deal together of late.

Sir Charles had by this time wandered from his part into hers; and he now recalled her to the music by stopping to ask whether he was right. Knowing by experience what his difficulty was likely to be, she gave him his note and went on. They had not been singing long when Jane came back and sat down, expressing a hope that her presence would not disturb them. It did disturb them. Agatha suspected that she had come there to watch them, and Sir Charles knew it. Besides, Lady Brandon, even when her mind was tranquil, was habitually restless. She could not speak because of the music, and, though she held an open book in her hand, she could not read and watch simultaneously. She gaped, and leaned to one end of the sofa until, on the point of overbalancing, she recovered herself with a prodigious bounce. The floor vibrated at her every movement. At last she could keep silence no longer.

"Oh, dear!" she said, yawning audibly. "It must be five o'clock at the very earliest."

Agatha turned round upon the piano-stool, feeling that music and Lady Brandon were incompatible. Sir Charles, for his guest's sake, tried hard to restrain his exasperation.

"Probably your watch will tell you," he said.

"Thank you for nothing," said Jane. "Agatha, where is Gertrude?"

"How can Miss Wylie possibly tell you where she is, Jane? I think you have gone mad today."

"She is most likely playing billiards with Mr Erskine," said Agatha, interposing quickly to forestall a retort from Jane, with its usual sequel of a domestic squabble.

"I think it is very strange of Gertrude to pass the whole day with Chester in the billiard room," said Jane discontentedly.

"There is not the slightest impropriety in her doing so," said Sir Charles. "If our hospitality does not place Miss Lindsay above suspicion, the more shame for us. How would you feel if anyone else made such a remark?"

"Oh, stuff!" said Jane peevishly. "You are always preaching long rigmaroles about nothing at all. I did not say there was any impropriety about Gertrude. She is too proper to be pleasant, in my opinion."

Sir Charles, unable to trust himself further, frowned and left the room, Jane speeding him with a contemptuous laugh.

"Dont ever be such a fool as to get married," she said, when he was gone. She looked up as she spoke, and was alarmed to see Agatha seated on the pianoforte, with her ankles swinging in the old school fashion.

"Jane," she said, surveying her hostess coolly, "do you know what I would do if I were Sir Charles?"

Jane did not know.

"I would get a big stick, beat you black and blue, and then

lock you up on bread and water for a week."

Jane half rose, red and angry. "Wh—why?" she said, relapsing upon the sofa.

"If I were a man, I would not, for mere chivalry's sake, let a woman treat me like a troublesome dog. You want a sound thrashing."

"I'd like to see anybody thrash *me*," said Jane, rising again and displaying her formidable person erect. Then she burst into tears, and said, "I wont have such things said to me in my own house. How dare you!"

"You deserve it for being jealous of me," said Agatha.

Jane's eyes dilated angrily. "I!—I!—jealous of you!" She looked round, as if for a missile. Not finding one she sat down again, and said in a voice stifled with tears, "J—jealous of *you*, indeed!"

"You have good reason to be, for he is fonder of me than of you."

Jane opened her mouth and eyes convulsively, but only uttered a gasp, and Agatha proceeded calmly: "I am polite to him, which you never are. When he speaks to me I allow him to finish his sentence without expressing, as you do, a foregone conclusion that it is not worth attending to. I do not yawn and talk whilst he is singing. When he converses with me on art or literature, about which he knows twice as much as I do, and at least ten times as much as you" (Jane gasped again), "I do not make a silly answer and turn to my neighbor at the other side with a remark about the stables or the weather. When he is willing to be pleased, as he always is, I am willing to be pleasant. And that is why he likes me."

"He does *not* like you. He is the same to every one."

"Except his wife. He likes me so much that you, like a great goose as you are, came up here to watch us at our duets, and made yourself as disagreeable as you possibly could whilst I was making myself charming. The poor man was ashamed of you."

"He wasnt," said Jane, sobbing. "I didnt do anything. I didnt say anything. I wont bear it. I will get a divorce. I will—"

"You will mend your ways if you have any sense left," said Agatha remorselessly. "Do not make such a noise, or someone will come to see what is the matter, and I shall have to get down from the piano, where I am very comfortable."

"It is you who are jealous."

"Oh, is it, Jane? I have not allowed Sir Charles to fall in love with me yet, but I can do so very easily. What will you wager that he will not kiss me before tomorrow evening?"

"It will be very mean and nasty of you if he does. You seem to think that I can be treated like a child."

"So you are a child," said Agatha, descending from her perch and preparing to go. "An occasional slapping does you good."

"It is nothing to you whether I agree with my husband or not," said Jane, with sudden fierceness.

"Not if you quarrel with him in private, as well-bred couples do. But when it occurs in my presence it makes me uncomfortable, and I object to being made uncomfortable."

"You would not be here at all if I had not asked you."

"Just think how dull the house would be without me, Jane!"

"Indeed! It was not dull before you came. Gertrude always behaved like a lady, at least."

"I am sorry that her example was so utterly lost on you."

"I wont bear it," said Jane, with a sob and a plunge upon the sofa that made the lustres of the chandeliers rattle. "I wouldnt have asked you if I had thought you could be so hateful. I will never ask you again."

"I will make Sir Charles divorce you for incompatibility of temper and marry me. Then I shall have the place to myself."

"He cant divorce me for that, thank goodness. You dont know what youre talking about."

Agatha laughed. "Come," she said good-humoredly, "dont be an old ass, Jane. Wash your face before anyone sees it, and remember what I have told you about Sir Charles."

"It is very hard to be called an ass in one's own house."

"It is harder to be treated as one, like your husband. I am going to look for him in the billiard room."

Jane ran after her, and caught her by the sleeve. "Agatha," she pleaded, "promise me that you wont be mean. Say that you wont make love to him."

"I will consider about it," replied Agatha gravely.

Jane uttered a groan and sank into a chair, which creaked at the shock. Agatha turned on the threshold, and seeing her shaking her head, pressing her eyes, and tapping with her heel in a restrained frenzy, said quickly:

"Here are the Waltons, and the Fitzgeorges, and Mr Trefusis coming upstairs. How do you do, Mrs Walton? Lady Brandon will be *so* glad to see you. Good evening, Mr Fitzgeorge."

Jane sprang up, wiped her eyes, and, with her hands on her hair, smoothing it, rushed to a mirror. No visitors appearing, she perceived that she was, for perhaps the hundredth time in her life, the victim of an imposture devised by Agatha. She, gratified by the success of her attempt to regain her old ascendancy over Jane—she had made it with misgiving, notwithstanding her apparent confidence—went downstairs to the library, where she found Sir Charles gloomily trying to drown his domestic troubles in art criticism.

"I thought you were in the billiard room," said Agatha.

"I only peeped in," he replied; "but as I saw something particular going on, I thought it best to slip away, and I have been alone ever since."

The something particular which Sir Charles had not wished to interrupt was only a game of billiards. It was the first opportunity Erskine had ever enjoyed of speaking to Gertrude at leisure and alone. Yet their conversation had never been so commonplace. She, liking the game, played very well and chatted indifferently; he played badly, and broached trivial topics in spite of himself. After an hour-and-a-half's play, Gertrude had announced that this game must be their last. He thought desperately that if he were to miss many more strokes the game must presently end, and an opportunity which might never recur pass beyond recall. He determined to tell her without preface that he adored her, but when he opened his lips a question came forth of its own accord relating to the Persian way of playing billiards. Gertrude had never been in Persia, but had seen some Eastern billiard cues in the India museum. Were not the Hindoos wonderful people for filigree work, and carpets, and such things? Did he not think the crookedness of their carpet patterns a blemish? Some people pretend to admire them, but was not that all nonsense? Was not the modern polished floor, with a rug in the middle, much superior to the old carpet fitted into the corners of the room? Yes. Enormously superior. Immensely—

"Why, what are you thinking of today, Mr Erskine? You have played with my ball."

"I am thinking of you."

"What did you say?" said Gertrude, not catching the serious turn he had given to the conversation, and poising her cue for a stroke. "Oh! I am as bad as you; that was the worst stroke I ever made, I think. I beg your pardon; you said something just now."

"I forget. Nothing of any consequence." And he groaned at his own cowardice.

"Suppose we stop," she said. "There is no use in finishing the game if our hands are out. I am rather tired of it."

"Certainly—if you wish it."

"I will finish if you like."

"Not at all. What pleases you, pleases me."

Gertrude made him a little bow, and idly knocked the balls about with her cue. Erskine's eyes wandered, and his lips moved irresolutely. He had settled with himself that his declaration should be a frank one—heart to heart. He had pictured himself in the act of taking her hand delicately, and saying, "Gertrude, I love you. May I tell you so again?" But this scheme did not now seem practicable.

"Miss Lindsay."

Gertrude, bending over the table, looked up in alarm.

"The present is as good an opportunity as I will—as I shall— as I will—"

"Shall," said Gertrude.

188

"I beg your pardon?"

"*Shall*," repeated Gertrude. "Did you ever study the doctrine of necessity?"

"The doctrine of necessity?" he said, bewildered.

Gertrude went to the other side of the table in pursuit of a ball. She now guessed what was coming, and was willing that it should come; not because she intended to accept, but because, like other young ladies experienced in such scenes, she counted the proposals of marriage she received as a Red Indian counts the scalps he takes.

"We have had a very pleasant time of it here," he said, giving up as inexplicable the relevance of the doctrine of necessity. "At least, I have."

"Well," said Gertrude, quick to resent a fancied allusion to her private discontent, "so have I."

"I am glad of that—more so than I can convey by words."

"Is it any business of yours?" she said, following the disagreeable vein he had unconsciously struck upon, and suspecting pity in his efforts to be sympathetic.

"I wish I dared hope so. The happiness of my visit has been due to you entirely."

"Indeed," said Gertrude, wincing as all the hard things Trefusis had told her of herself came into her mind at the heels of Erskine's unfortunate allusion to her power of enjoying herself.

"I hope I am not paining you," he said earnestly.

"I dont know what you are talking about," she said, standing erect with sudden impatience. "You seem to think that it is very easy to pain me."

"No," he said timidly, puzzled by the effect he had produced. "I fear you misunderstand me. I am very awkward. Perhaps I had better say no more."

Gertrude, by turning away to put up her cue, signified that that was a point for him to consider; she not intending to trouble herself about it. When she faced him again, he was motionless and dejected, with a wistful expression like that of a dog that has proffered a caress and received a kick. Remorse, and a vague sense that there was something base in her attitude towards him, overcame her. She looked at him for an instant and left the room.

The look excited him. He did not understand it, nor attempt to understand it; but it was a look that he had never before seen in her face or in that of any other woman. It struck him as a momentary revelation of what he had written of in The Patriot Martyrs as

"The glorious mystery of a woman's heart,"

and it made him feel unfit for ordinary social intercourse. He hastened from the house, walked swiftly down the avenue to the lodge, where he kept his bicycle, left word there that he was going for an excursion and should probably not return in time for dinner, mounted, and sped away recklessly along the Riverside Road. In less than two minutes he passed the gate of Sallust's House, where he nearly ran over an old woman laden with a basket of coals, who put down her burthen to scream curses after him. Warned by this that his headlong pace was dangerous, he slackened it a little, and presently saw Trefusis lying prone on the river bank, with his cheeks propped on his elbows, reading intently. Erskine, who had presented him, a few days before, with a copy of The Patriot Martyrs and other Poems, tried to catch a glimpse of the book over which Trefusis was so serious. It was a Blue Book, full of figures. Erskine rode on in disgust, consoling himself with the recollection of Gertrude's face.

The highway now swerved inland from the river, and rose to a steep acclivity, at the brow of which he turned and looked back. The light was growing ruddy, and the shadows were lengthening. Trefusis was still prostrate in the meadow, and the old woman was in a field, gathering hemlock.

Erskine raced down the hill at full speed, and did not look behind him again until he found himself at nightfall on the skirts of a town, where he purchased some beer and a sandwich, which he ate with little appetite. Gertrude had set up a disturbance within him which made him impatient of eating.

It was now dark. He was many miles from Brandon Beeches, and not sure of the way back. Suddenly he resolved to complete his unfinished declaration that evening. He now could not ride back fast enough to satisfy his impatience. He tried a short cut, lost himself, spent nearly an hour seeking the high road, and at last came upon a railway station just in time to catch a train that brought him within a mile of his destination.

When he rose from the cushions of the railway-carriage he found himself somewhat fatigued, and he mounted the bicycle stiffly. But his resolution was as ardent as ever, and his heart beat strongly as, after leaving his bicycle at the lodge, he walked up the avenue through the deep gloom beneath the beeches. Near the house, the first notes of Crudel perche finora reached him, and he stepped softly on to the turf lest his footsteps on the gravel should rouse the dogs and make them mar the harmony by barking. A rustle made him stop and listen. Then Gertrude's voice whispered through the darkness:

"What did you mean by what you said to me within?"

An extraordinary sensation shook Erskine; confused ideas of fairyland ran through his imagination. A bitter disappointment, like that of waking from a happy dream, followed as Trefusis's voice, more finely tuned than he had ever heard it before, answered:

"Merely that the expanse of stars above us is not more illimitable than my contempt for Miss Lindsay, nor brighter than my hopes of Gertrude."

"Miss Lindsay always to you, if you please, Mr Trefusis."

"Miss Lindsay never to me, but only to those who cannot see through her to the soul within, which is Gertrude. There are a thousand Miss Lindsays in the world, formal and false. There is but one Gertrude."

"I am an unprotected girl, Mr Trefusis, and you can call me what you please."

It occurred to Erskine that this was a fit occasion to rush forward and give Trefusis, whose figure he could now dimly discern, a black eye. But he hesitated, and the opportunity passed.

"Unprotected!" said Trefusis. "Why, you are fenced round and barred in with conventions, laws, and lies that would frighten the truth from the lips of any man whose faith in Gertrude was less strong than mine. Go to Sir Charles and tell him what I have said to Miss Lindsay, and within ten minutes I shall have passed these gates with a warning never to approach them again. I am in your power; and were I in Miss Lindsay's power alone, my shrift would be short. Happily, Gertrude, though she sees as yet but darkly, feels that Miss Lindsay is her bitterest foe."

"It is ridiculous. I am not two persons; I am only one. What does it matter to me if your contempt for me is as illimitable as the stars?"

"Ah, you remember that, do you? Whenever you hear a man talking about the stars you may conclude that he is either an astronomer or a fool. But you and a fine starry night would make a fool of any man."

"I dont understand you. I try to, but I cannot; or, if I guess, I cannot tell whether you are in earnest or not."

"I am very much in earnest. Abandon at once and for ever all misgivings that I am trifling with you, or passing an idle hour as men do when they find themselves in the company of beautiful women. I mean what I say literally, and in the deepest sense. You doubt me; we have brought society to such a state that we all suspect one another. But whatever is true will command belief sooner or later from those who have wit enough to comprehend truth. Now let me recall Miss Lindsay to consciousness by remarking that we have been out for ten minutes, and that our hostess is not the woman to allow our absence to pass without comment."

"Let us go in. Thank you for reminding me."

"Thank you for forgetting."

Erskine heard their footsteps retreating, and presently saw the two enter the glow of light that shone from the open window of the billiard room, through which they went indoors. Trefusis, a man whom he had seen that day in a beautiful landscape, blind to everything except a row of figures in a Blue Book, was his successful rival, although it was plain from the very sound of his voice that he did not—could not—love Gertrude. Only a poet could do that. Trefusis was no poet, but a sordid brute unlikely to inspire interest in anything more human than a public meeting, much less in a woman, much less again in a woman so ethereal as Gertrude. She was proud, too, yet she had allowed the fellow to insult her—had forgiven him for the sake of a few broad compliments.

Erskine grew angry and cynical. The situation did not suit his poetry. Instead of being stricken to the heart with a solemn sorrow, as a Patriot Martyr would have been under similar circumstances, he felt slighted and ridiculous. He was hardly convinced of what had seemed at first the most obvious feature of the case, Trefusis's inferiority to himself.

He stood under the trees until Trefusis reappeared on his way home, making, Erskine thought, as much noise with his heels on the gravel as a regiment of delicately bred men would have done. He stopped for a moment to make inquiry at the lodge as he went out; then his footsteps died away in the distance.

Erskine, chilled, stiff, and with a sensation of a bad cold coming on, went into the house, and was relieved to find that Gertrude had retired, and that Lady Brandon, though she had been sure that he had ridden into the river in the dark, had nevertheless provided a warm supper for him.

CHAPTER XV

ERSKINE soon found plenty of themes for his newly begotten cynicism. Gertrude's manner towards him softened so much that he, believing her heart given to his rival, concluded that she was tempting him to make a proposal which she had no intention of accepting. Sir Charles, to whom he told what he had overheard in the avenue, professed sympathy, but was evidently pleased to learn that there was nothing serious in the attentions Trefusis paid to Agatha. Erskine wrote three bitter sonnets on hollow friendship and shewed them to Sir Charles, who, failing to apply them to himself, praised them highly and shewed them to Trefusis without asking the author's permission. Trefusis remarked that in a corrupt society expressions of dissatisfaction were always creditable to a writer's sensibility; but he did not say much in praise of the verse.

"Why has he taken to writing in this vein?" he said. "Has he been disappointed in any way of late? Has he proposed to Miss Lindsay and been rejected?"

"No," said Sir Charles, surprised by this blunt reference to a subject they had never before discussed. "He does not intend to propose to Miss Lindsay."

"But he did intend to."

"He certainly did, but he has given up the idea."

"Why?" said Trefusis, apparently disapproving strongly of the renunciation.

Sir Charles shrugged his shoulders and did not reply.

"I am sorry to hear it. I wish you could induce him to change his mind. He is a nice fellow, with enough to live on comfortably, whilst he is yet what is called a poor man, so that she could feel perfectly disinterested in marrying him. It will do her good to marry without making a pecuniary profit by it; she will respect herself the more afterwards, and will neither want bread and butter nor be ashamed of her husband's origin, in spite of having married for love alone. Make a match of it if you can. I take an interest in the girl; she has good instincts."

Sir Charles's suspicion that Trefusis was really paying court to Agatha returned after this conversation, which he repeated to Erskine, who, much annoyed because his poems had been shewn to a reader of Blue Books, thought it only a blind for Trefusis's design upon Gertrude. Sir Charles pooh-poohed this view, and the two friends were sharp with one another in discussing it. After dinner, when the ladies had left them, Sir Charles, repentant and cordial, urged Erskine to speak to Gertrude without troubling himself as to the sincerity of Trefusis. But Erskine, knowing himself ill able to brook a refusal, was loth to expose himself to one.

"If you had heard the tone of her voice when she asked him whether he was in earnest, you would not talk to me like this," he said despondently. "I wish he had never come here."

"Well, that, at least, was no fault of mine, my dear fellow," said Sir Charles. "He came among us against my will. And now that he appears to have been in the right—legally—about the field, it would look like spite if I cut him. Besides, he really isnt a bad man if he would only let the women alone."

"If he trifles with Miss Lindsay, I shall ask him to cross the Channel, and have a shot at him."

"I dont think he'd go," said Sir Charles dubiously. "If I were you, I would try my luck with Gertrude at once. In spite of what you heard, I dont believe she would marry a man of his origin. His money gives him an advantage, certainly, but Gertrude has sent richer men to the rightabout."

"Let the fellow have fair play," said Erskine. "I may be wrong, of course; all men are liable to err in judging themselves, but I think I could make her happier than he can."

Sir Charles was not so sure of that, but he cheerfully responded: "Certainly. He is not the man for her at all, and you are. He knows it, too."

"Hmf!" muttered Erskine, rising dejectedly. "Let's go upstairs."

"By the bye, we are to call on him to-morrow, to go through

his house, and his collection of photographs. Photographs! Ha, ha!"

"Damn his house!" said Erskine.

Next day they went together to Sallust's House. It stood in the midst of an acre of land, waste except a little kitchen garden at the rear. The lodge at the entrance was uninhabited, and the gates stood open, with dust and fallen leaves heaped up against them. Free ingress had thus been afforded to two stray ponies, a goat, and a tramp, who lay asleep in the grass. His wife sat near, watching him.

"I have a mind to turn back," said Sir Charles, looking about him in disgust. "The place is scandalously neglected. Look at that rascal asleep within full view of the windows."

"I admire his cheek," said Erskine. "Nice pair of ponies, too."

Sallust's House was square and painted cinnamon color. Beneath the cornice was a yellow freize with figures of dancing children, imitated from the works of Donatello, and very unskilfully executed. There was a meagre portico of four columns, painted red, and a plain pediment, painted yellow. The colors, meant to match those of the walls, contrasted disagreeably with them, having been applied more recently, apparently by a color-blind artist. The door beneath the portico stood open. Sir Charles rang the bell, and an elderly woman answered it; but before they could address her, Trefusis appeared, clad in a painter's jacket of white jean. Following him in, they found that the house was a hollow square, enclosing a courtyard with a bath sunk in the middle, and a fountain in the centre of the bath. The courtyard, formerly open to the sky, was now roofed in with dusty glass; the nymph that had once poured out the water of the fountain was barren and mutilated; and the bath was partly covered in with loose boards, the exposed part accommodating a heap of coals in one corner, a heap of potatoes in another, a beer barrel, some old carpets, a tarpaulin, and a broken canoe. The marble pavement extended to the outer walls of the house, and was roofed in at the sides by the upper stories, which were supported by fluted stone columns, much stained and chipped. The staircase, towards which Trefusis led his visitors, was a broad one at the end opposite the door, and gave access to a gallery leading to the upper rooms.

"This house was built in 1780 by an ancestor of my mother," said Trefusis. "He passed for a man of exquisite taste. He wished the place to be maintained for ever—he actually used that expression in his will—as the family seat, and he collected a fine library here, which I found useful, as all the books came into my hands in good condition, most of them with the leaves uncut. Some people prize uncut copies of old editions; a dealer gave me three hundred and fifty pounds for a lot of them. I came into possession of a number of family fetishes—heirlooms, as they are called. There was a sword that one of my forebears wore at Edgehill and other battles in Charles the First's time. He fought on the wrong side, of course, but the sword fetched thirty-five shillings nevertheless. You would hardly believe that I was offered one hundred and fifty pounds for a gold cup worth about twenty-five, merely because Queen Elizabeth once drank from it. This is my study. It was designed for a banqueting hall."

They entered a room as long as the wall of the house, pierced on one side by four tall windows, between which square pillars, with Corinthian capitals supporting the cornice, were half sunk in the wall. There were similar pillars on the opposite side, but between them, instead of windows, were arched niches in which stood life-size plaster statues, chipped, broken, and defaced in an extraordinary fashion. The flooring, of diagonally set narrow boards, was uncarpeted and unpolished. The ceiling was adorned with frescoes, which at once excited Sir Charles's interest, and he noted with indignation that a large portion of the painting at the northern end had been destroyed and some glass roofing inserted. In another place bolts had been driven in to support the ropes of a trapeze and a few other pieces of gymnastic apparatus. The walls were whitewashed, and at about four feet from the ground a dark band appeared, produced by pencil memoranda and little sketches scribbled on the whitewash. One end of the apartment was unfurnished, except by the gymnastic apparatus, a photographer's camera, a ladder in the corner, and a common deal table with oil cans and paint pots upon it. At the other end a comparatively luxurious show was made by a large bookcase, an elaborate combination of bureau and writing desk, a rack with a rifle, a set of foils, and an umbrella in it, several folio albums on a table, some comfortable chairs and sofas, and a thick carpet under foot. Close by, and seeming much out of place, was a carpenter's bench with the usual implements and a number of boards of various thicknesses.

"This is a sort of comfort beyond the reach of any but a rich man," said Trefusis, turning and surprising his visitors in the act of exchanging glances of astonishment at his taste. "I keep a drawing room of the usual kind for receiving strangers with whom it is necessary to be conventional, but I never enter it except on such occasions. What do you think of this for a study?"

"On my soul, Trefusis, I think you are mad," said Sir Charles. "The place looks as if it had stood a siege. How did you manage to break the statues and chip the walls so outrageously?"

Trefusis took a newspaper from the table and said, "Listen to this:

" 'In spite of the unfavorable nature of the weather, the sport of the Emperor and his guests in Styria has been successful. In three days 52 chamois and 79 stags and deer fell to 19 single-barrelled rifles, the Emperor allowing no more on this occasion.'

"I share the Emperor's delight in shooting, but I am no butcher, and do not need the royal relish of blood to my sport. And I do not share my ancestor's taste in statuary. Hence—" Here Trefusis opened a drawer, took out a pistol, and fired at the Hebe in the farthest niche.

"Well done!" said Erskine coolly, as the last fragment of Hebe's head crumbled at the touch of the bullet.

"Very fruitlessly done," said Trefusis. "I am a good shot, but of what use is it to me? None. I once met a gamekeeper who was a Methodist. He was a most eloquent speaker, but a bad shot. If he could have swapped talents with me I would have given him ten thousand pounds to boot willingly, although he would have profited as much as I by the exchange alone. I have no more desire or need to be a good shot than to be king of England, or owner of a Derby winner, or anything else equally ridiculous, and yet I never missed my aim in my life—thank blind fortune for nothing!"

"King of England!" said Erskine, with a scornful laugh, to show Trefusis that other people were as liberty-loving as he. "Is it not absurd to hear a nation boasting of its freedom and tolerating a king?"

"Oh, hang your republicanism, Chester!" said Sir Charles, who privately held a low opinion of the political side of the Patriot Martyrs.

"I wont be put down on that point," said Erskine. "I admire a man that kills a king. You will agree with me there, Trefusis, wont you?"

"Certainly not," said Trefusis. "A king nowadays is only a dummy put up to draw your fire off the real oppressors of society, and the fraction of his salary that he can spend as he likes is usually far too small for his risk, his trouble, and the condition of personal slavery to which he is reduced. What private man in England is worse off than the constitutional monarch? We deny him all privacy; he may not marry whom he chooses, consort with whom he prefers, dress according to his taste, or live where he pleases. I dont believe he may even eat or drink what he likes best; a taste for tripe and onions on his part would provoke a remonstrance from the Privy Council. We dictate everything except his thoughts and dreams, and even these he must keep to himself if they are not suitable, in our opinion, to his condition. The work we impose on him has all the hardship of mere task work; it is unfruitful, incessant, monotonous, and has to be transacted for the most part with nervous bores. We make his kingdom a treadmill to him, and drive him to and fro on the face of it. Finally, having taken everything else that men prize from him, we fall upon his character, and that of every person to whom he ventures to show favor. We impose enormous expenses on him, stint him, and then rail at his parsimony. We use him as I use those statues—stick him up in the place of honor for our greater convenience in disfiguring and abusing him. We send him forth through our crowded cities, proclaiming that he is the source of all good and evil in the nation, and he, knowing that many people believe it, knowing that it is a lie, and that he is powerless to shorten the working day by one hour, raise wages one penny, or annul the smallest criminal sentence, however unjust it may seem to him; knowing that every miner in the kingdom can manufacture dynamite, and that revolvers are sold for seven and sixpence apiece; knowing that he is not bullet proof, and that every king in Europe has been shot at in the streets; he must smile and bow and maintain an expression of gracious enjoyment whilst the mayor and corporation inflict upon him the twaddling address he has heard a thousand times before. I do not ask you to be loyal, Erskine; but I expect you, in common humanity, to sympathize with the chief figure in the pageant, who is no more accountable for the manifold evils and abominations that exist in his realm than the Lord Mayor is accountable for the thefts of the pickpockets who follow his show on the ninth of November."

Sir Charles laughed at the trouble Trefusis took to prove his case, and said soothingly, "My dear fellow, kings are used to it, and expect it, and like it."

"And probably do not see themselves as I see them, any more than common people do," assented Trefusis.

"What an exquisite face!" exclaimed Erskine suddenly, catching sight of a photograph in a rich gold and coral frame on a miniature easel draped with ruby velvet. Trefusis turned quickly, so evidently gratified that Sir Charles hastened to say, "Charming!" Then, looking at the portrait, he added, as if a little startled: "It certainly is an extraordinarily attractive face."

"Years ago," said Trefusis, "when I saw that face for the first time, I felt as you feel now."

Silence ensued, the two visitors looking at the portrait, Trefusis looking at them.

"Curious style of beauty," said Sir Charles at last, not quite so assuredly as before.

Trefusis laughed unpleasantly. "Do you recognize the artist——the enthusiastic amateur—in her?" he said, opening another drawer and taking out a bundle of drawings, which he handed to be examined.

"Very clever. Very clever indeed," said Sir Charles. "I should like to meet the lady."

"I have often been on the point of burning them," said Trefusis; "but there they are, and there they are likely to remain. The portrait has been much admired."

"Can you give us an introduction to the original, old fellow?" said Erskine.

"No, happily. She is dead."

Disagreeably shocked, they looked at him for a moment with aversion. Then Erskine, turning with pity and disappointment to the picture, said, "Poor girl! Was she married?"

"Yes. To me."

"Mrs Trefusis!" exclaimed Sir Charles. "Ah! Dear me!"

Erskine, with proof before him that it was possible for a beautiful girl to accept Trefusis, said nothing.

"I keep her portrait constantly before me to correct my natural amativeness. I fell in love with her and married her. I have fallen in love once or twice since; but a glance at my lost Hetty has cured me of the slightest inclination to marry."

Sir Charles did not reply. It occurred to him that Lady Brandon's portrait, if nothing else were left of her, might be useful in the same way.

"Come, you will marry again one of these days," said Erskine, in a forced tone of encouragement.

"It is possible. Men should marry, especially rich men. But I assure you I have no present intention of doing so."

Erskine's color deepened, and he moved away to the table where the albums lay.

"This is the collection of photographs I spoke of," said Trefusis, following him and opening one of the books. "I took many of them myself under great difficulties with regard to light —the only difficulty that money could not always remove. This is a view of my father's house—or rather one of his houses. It cost seventy-five thousand pounds."

"Very handsome indeed," said Sir Charles, secretly disgusted at being invited to admire a photograph, such as house agents exhibit, of a vulgarly designed country-house, merely because it had cost seventy-five thousand pounds. The figures were actually written beneath the picture.

"This is the drawing room, and this one of the best bedrooms. In the right-hand corner of the mount you will see a note of the cost of the furniture, fittings, napery, and so forth. They were of the most luxurious description."

"Very interesting," said Sir Charles, hardly disguising the irony of the comment.

"Here is a view—this is the first of my own attempts—of the apartment of one of the under servants. It is comfortable and spacious, and solidly furnished."

"So I perceive."

"These are the stables. Are they not handsome?"

"Palatial. Quite palatial."

"There is every luxury that a horse could desire, including plenty of valets to wait on him. You are noting the figures, I hope. There is the cost of the building and the expenditure per horse per annum."

"I see."

"Here is the exterior of a house. What do you think of it?"

"It is rather picturesque in its dilapidation."

"Picturesque! Would you like to live in it?"

"No," said Erskine. "*I* dont see anything very picturesque about it. What induced you to photograph such a wretched old rookery?"

"Here is a view of the best room in it. Photography gives you a fair idea of the broken flooring and patched windows, but you must imagine the dirt and the odour of the place. Some of the stains are weather stains, others came from smoke and filth. The landlord of the house holds it from a peer and lets it out in tenements. Three families occupied that room when I photographed it. You will see by the figures in the corner that it is more profitable to the landlord than an average house in Mayfair. Here is the cellar, let to a family for one and sixpence a week, and considered a bargain. The sun never shines there, of course. I took it by artificial light. You may add to the rent the cost of enough bad beer to make the tenant insensible to the filth of the place. Beer is the chloroform that enables the laborer to endure the severe operation of living; that is why we can always assure one another over our wine that the rascal's misery is due to his habit of drinking. We are down on him for it, because, if he could bear his life without beer, we should save his beer-money—get him for lower wages. In short, we should be richer and he soberer. Here is the yard; the arrangements are indescribable. Seven of the inhabitants of that house had worked for years in my father's mill. That is, they had created a considerable part of the vast sums of money for drawing your attention to which you were disgusted with me just now."

"Not at all," said Sir Charles faintly.

"You can see how their condition contrasts with that of my father's horses. The seven men to whom I have alluded, with three hundred others, were thrown destitute upon the streets by this." (Here he turned over a leaf and displayed a photograph of an elaborate machine.) "It enabled my father to dispense with their services, and to replace them by a handful of women and children. He had bought the patent of the machine for fifty pounds from the inventor, who was almost ruined by the expenses of his ingenuity, and would have sacrificed anything for a handful of ready money. Here is a portrait of my father in his masonic insignia. He believed that freemasons generally get on in the world, and as the main object of his life was to get on, he joined them, and wanted me to do the same. But I object to pretended secret societies and hocus pocus, and would not. You see what he was— a portly, pushing, egotistical tradesman. Mark the successful man, the merchant prince with argosies on every sea, the employer of thousands of hands, the munificent contributor to public charities, the churchwarden, the member of parliament, and the generous patron of his relatives; his self-approbation struggling with the instinctive sense of baseness in the money-hunter, the ignorant and greedy filcher of the labor of others, the seller of his own mind and manhood for luxuries and delicacies that he was too low-lived to enjoy, and for the society of people who made him feel his inferiority at every turn—"

"And the man to whom you owe everything you possess," said Erskine boldly.

"I possess very little. Everything he left me, except a few pictures, I spent long ago, and even that was made by his slaves and not by him. My wealth comes day by day fresh from the labor of the wretches who live in the dens I have just shown you, or of a few aristocrats of labor who are within ten shillings a week of being worse off. However, there is some excuse for my father. Once, at an election riot, I got into a free fight. I am a peaceful man, but as I had either to fight or be knocked down and trampled upon, I exchanged blows with men who were perhaps as peacefully disposed as I. My father, launched into a free competition (free in the sense that the fight is free: that is, lawless)—my father had to choose between being a slave himself and enslaving others. He chose the latter, and as he was applauded and made much of for succeeding, who dare blame him? Not I. Besides, he did something to destroy the anarchy that enabled him to plunder society with impunity. He furnished me, its enemy, with the powerful weapon of a large fortune. Thus our system of organizing industry sometimes hatches the eggs from which its destroyers break. Does Lady Brandon wear much lace?"

"I— No; that is— How the deuce do I know, Trefusis? What an extraordinary question!"

"This is a photograph of a lace school. It was a filthy room, twelve feet square. It was paved with brick, and the children were not allowed to wear their boots, lest the lace should get muddy. However, as there were twenty of them working there for fifteen hours a day—all girls—they did not suffer much from cold. They were pretty tightly packed—may be still, for aught I know. They brought three or four shillings a week sometimes to their fond parents; and they were very quick-fingered little creatures, and stuck intensely to their work, as the overseer always hit them when they looked up or—"

"Trefusis," said Sir Charles, turning away from the table, "I beg your pardon, but I have no appetite for horrors. You really must not ask me to go through your collection. It is no doubt very interesting, but I cant stand it. Have you nothing pleasant to entertain me with?"

"Pooh! you are squeamish. However, as you are a novice, let us put off the rest until you are seasoned. The pictures are not all horrible. Each book refers to a different country. That one contains illustrations of modern civilization in Germany, for instance. That one is France; that, British India. Here you have the United States of America, home of liberty, theatre of manhood suffrage, kingless and lordless land of Protection, Republicanism, and the realized Radical Programme, where all the black chattel slaves were turned into wage-slaves (like my father's white fellows) at a cost of 800,000 lives and wealth incalculable. You and I are paupers in comparison with the great capitalists of that country, where the laborers fight for bones with the Chinamen, like dogs. Some of these great men presented me with photographs of their yachts and palaces, not anticipating the use to which I would put them. Here are some portraits that will not harrow your feelings. This is my mother, a woman of good family, every inch a lady. Here is a Lancashire lass, the daughter of a common pitman. She has exactly the same physical characteristics as my well-born mother—the same small head, delicate features, and so forth; they might be sisters. This villainous-looking pair might be twin brothers, except that there is a trace of good humor about the one to the right. The good-humored one is a bargee on the Lyvern Canal. The other is one of the senior noblemen of the British Peerage. They illustrate the fact that Nature, even when perverted by generations of famine fever, ignores the distinctions we set up between men. This group of men and women, all tolerably intelligent and thoughtful-looking, are so-called enemies of society—Nihilists, Anarchists, Communards, members of the International, and so on. These other poor devils, worried, stiff, strumous, awkward, vapid, and rather coarse, with here and there a passably pretty woman, are European kings, queens, grand-dukes, and the like. Here are ship-captains, criminals, poets, men of science, peers, peasants, political economists, and representatives of dozens of degrees. The object of the collection is to illustrate the natural inequality of man, and the failure of our artificial inequality to correspond with it."

"It seems to me a sort of infernal collection for the upsetting of people's ideas," said Erskine. "You ought to label it A Portfolio of Paradoxes."

"In a rational state of society they would be paradoxes; but now the time gives them proof—like Hamlet's paradox. It is, however, a collection of facts; and I will give no fanciful name to it. You dislike figures, dont you?"

"Unless they are by Phidias, yes."

"Here are a few, not by Phidias. This is the balance sheet of an attempt I made some years ago to carry out the idea of an International Association of Laborers—commonly known as *The* International—or union of all workmen throughout the world in defence of the interests of labor. You see the result. Expenditure, four thousand five hundred pounds. Subscriptions received from working-men, twenty-two pounds seven and tenpence halfpenny. The British workmen showed their sense of my efforts to emancipate them by accusing me of making a good thing out of the Association for my own pocket, and by mobbing and stoning me twice. I now help them only when they shew some disposition to help themselves. I occupy myself partly in working out a scheme for the reorganization of industry, and partly in attacking my own class, women and all, as I am attacking you."

"There is little use in attacking us, I fear," said Sir Charles.

"Great use," said Trefusis confidently. "You have a very different opinion of our boasted civilization now from that which you held when I broke your wall down and invited those Land

Nationalization zealots to march across your pleasure ground. You have seen in my album something you had not seen an hour ago, and you are consequently not quite the same man you were an hour ago. My pictures stick in the mind longer than your scratchy etchings, or the leaden things in which you fancy you see tender harmonies in grey. Erskine's next drama may be about liberty, but its Patriot Martyrs will have something better to do than spout balderdash against figure-head kings who in all their lives never secretly plotted as much dastardly meanness, greed, cruelty, and tyranny as is openly voted for in London by every half-yearly meeting of dividend-consuming vermin whose miserable wage-slaves drudge sixteen hours out of the twenty-four."

"What is going to be the end of it all?" said Sir Charles, a little dazed.

"Socialism or Smash. Socialism if the race has at last evolved the faculty of co-ordinating the functions of a society too crowded and complex to be worked any longer on the old haphazard private-property system. Unless we reorganize our society socialistically—humanly a most arduous and magnificent enterprise, economically a most simple and sound one—Free Trade by itself will ruin England, and I will tell you exactly how. When my father made his fortune we had the start of all other nations in the organization of our industry and in our access to iron and coal. Other nations bought our products for less than they might have spent to raise them at home, and yet for so much more than they cost us, that profits rolled in Atlantic waves upon our capitalists. When the workers, by their trade-unions, demanded a share of the luck in the form of advanced wages, it paid better to give them the little they dared to ask than to stop gold-gathering to fight and crush them. But now our customers have set up in their own countries improved copies of our industrial organization, and have discovered places where iron and coal are even handier than they are by this time in England. They produce for themselves, or buy elsewhere, what they formerly bought from us. Our profits are vanishing, our machinery is standing idle, our workmen are locked out. It pays now to stop the mills and fight and crush the unions when the men strike, no longer for an advance, but against a reduction. Now that these unions are beaten, helpless, and drifting to bankruptcy as the proportion of unemployed men in their ranks becomes greater, they are being petted and made much of by our class; an infallible sign that they are making no further progress in their duty of destroying us. The small capitalists are left stranded by the ebb; the big ones will follow the tide across the water, and rebuild their factories where steam power, water power, labor power, and transport are now cheaper than in England, where they used to be cheapest. The workers will emigrate in pursuit of the factory, but they will multiply faster than they emigrate, and be told that their own exorbitant demand for wages is driving capital abroad, and must continue to do so whilst there is a Chinaman or a Hindoo unemployed to underbid them. As the British factories are shut up, they will be replaced by villas; the manufacturing districts will become fashionable resorts for capitalists living on the interest of foreign investments; the farms and sheep runs will be cleared for deer forests. All products that can in the nature of things be manufactured elsewhere than where they are consumed will be imported in payment of deer-forest rents from foreign sportsmen, or of dividends due to shareholders resident in England, but holding shares in companies abroad, and these imports will not be paid for by exports, because rent and interest are not paid for at all—a fact which the Free Traders do not yet see, or at any rate do not mention, although it is the key to the whole mystery of their opponents. The cry for Protection will become wild, but no one will dare resort to a demonstrably absurd measure that must raise prices before it raises wages, and that has everywhere failed to benefit the worker. There will be no employment for anyone except in doing things that must be done on the spot, such as unpacking and distributing the imports, ministering to the proprietors as domestic servants, or by acting, preaching, paving, lighting, housebuilding, and the rest; and some of these, as the capitalist comes to regard ostentation as vulgar, and to enjoy a simpler life, will employ fewer and fewer people. A vast proletariat, beginning with a nucleus of those formerly employed in export trades, with their multiplying progeny, will be out of employment permanently. They will demand access to the land and machinery to produce for themselves. They will be refused. They will break a few windows and be dispersed with a warning to their leaders. They will burn a few houses and murder a policeman or two, and then an example will be made of the warned. They will revolt, and be shot down with machine guns—emigrated—exterminated anyhow and everyhow; for the proprietary classes have no idea of any other means of dealing with the full claims of labor. You yourself, though you would give fifty pounds to Jansenius's emigration fund readily enough, would call for the police, the military, and the Riot Act, if the people came to Brandon Beeches and bade you turn out and work for your living with the rest. Well, the superfluous proletariat destroyed, there will remain a population of capitalists living on gratuitous imports and served by a disaffected retinue. One day the gratuitous imports will stop in consequence of the occurrence abroad of revolution and repudiation, fall in the rate of interest, purchase of industries by governments for lump sums, not reinvestable, or what not. Our capitalist community is then thrown on the remains of the last dividend, which it consumes long before it can rehabilitate its extinct machinery of production in order to support itself with its own hands. Horses, dogs, cats, rats, blackberries, mushrooms, and cannibalism only postpone—"

"Ha! ha! ha!" shouted Sir Charles. "On my honor, I thought you were serious at first, Trefusis. Come, confess, old chap; it's all a fad of yours. I half suspected you of being a bit of a crank." And he winked at Erskine.

"What I have described to you is the inevitable outcome of our present Free Trade policy without Socialism. The theory of Free Trade is only applicable to systems of exchange, not to systems of spoliation. Our system is one of spoliation, and if we dont abandon it, we must either return to Protection or go to smash by the road I have just mapped. Now, sooner than let the Protectionists triumph, the Cobden Club itself would blow the gaff and point out to the workers that Protection only means compelling the proprietors of England to employ slaves resident in England and therefore presumably—though by no means necessarily—Englishmen. This would open the eyes of the nation at last to the fact that England is not their property. Once let them understand that and they would soon make it so. When England is made the property of its inhabitants collectively, England becomes socialistic. Artificial inequality will vanish then before real freedom of contract; freedom of competition, or unhampered emulation, will keep us moving ahead; and Free Trade will fulfil its promises at last."

"And the idlers and loafers," said Erskine. "What of them?"

"You and I, in fact," said Trefusis, "die of starvation, I suppose, unless we choose to work, or unless they give us a little outdoor relief in consideration of our bad bringing-up."

"Do you mean that they will plunder us?" said Sir Charles.

"I mean that they will make us stop plundering them. If they hesitate to strip us naked, or to cut our throats if we offer them the smallest resistance, they will shew us more mercy than we ever shewed them. Consider what we have done to get our rents in Ireland and Scotland, and our dividends in Egypt, if you have already forgotten my photographs and their lesson in our atrocities at home. Why, man, we *murder* the great mass of these toilers with overwork and hardship; their average lifetime is not half as long as ours. Human nature is the same in them as in us. If we resist them, and succeed in restoring order, as we call it, we will punish them mercilessly for their insubordination, as we did in Paris in 1871, where, by the bye, we taught them the folly of giving their enemies quarter. If they beat us, we shall catch it, and serve us right. Far better turn honest at once and avert bloodshed. Eh, Erskine?"

Erskine was considering what reply he should make, when Trefusis disconcerted him by ringing a bell. Presently the elderly woman appeared, pushing before her an oblong table mounted on wheels, like a barrow.

"Thank you," said Trefusis, and dismissed her. "Here is some good wine, some good water, some good fruit, and some good bread. I know that you cling to wine as to a good familiar creature. As for me, I make no distinction between it and other vegetable poisons. I abstain from them all. Water for serenity, wine for excitement. I, having boiling springs of excitement within myself, am never at a loss for it, and have only to seek serenity. However" (here he drew a cork), "a generous glass of this will make you feel like gods for half an hour at least. Shall we drink to your conversion to Socialism?"

Sir Charles shook his head.

"Come, Mr Donovan Brown, the great artist, is a Socialist, and why should not you be one?"

"Donovan Brown!" exclaimed Sir Charles with interest. "Is it possible? Do you know him personally?"

"Here are several letters from him. You may read them; the mere autograph of such a man is interesting."

Sir Charles took the letters and read them earnestly, Erskine reading over his shoulder.

"I most cordially agree with everything he says here," said Sir Charles. "It is quite true, quite true."

"Of course you agree with us. Donovan Brown's eminence as an artist has gained me one recruit, and yours as a baronet will gain me some more."

"But—"

"But what?" said Trefusis, deftly opening one of the albums at a photograph of a loathsome room. "You are against that, are you not? Donovan Brown is against it, and I am against it. You may disagree with us in everything else, but there you are at one with us. Is it not so?"

"But that may be the result of drunkenness, improvidence, or—"

"My father's income was fifty times as great as that of Donovan Brown. Do you believe that Donovan Brown is fifty times as drunken and improvident as my father was?"

"Certainly not. I do not deny that there is much in what you urge. Still, you ask me to take a rather important step."

"Not a bit of it. I dont ask you to subscribe to, join, or in any way pledge yourself to any society or conspiracy whatsoever. I only want your name for private mention to cowards who think Socialism right, but will not say so because they do not think it respectable. They will not be ashamed of their convictions when they learn that a baronet shares them. Socialism offers you something already, you see; a good use for your hitherto useless title."

Sir Charles colored a little, conscious that the example of his favorite painter had influenced him more than his own conviction or the arguments of Trefusis.

"What do you think, Chester?" he said. "Will you join?"

"Erskine is already committed to the cause of liberty by his published writings," said Trefusis. "Three of the pamphlets on that shelf contain quotations from The Patriot Martyrs."

Erskine blushed, flattered by being quoted; an attention that had been shown him only once before, and then by a reviewer with the object of proving that the Patriot Martyrs were slovenly in their grammar.

"Come!" said Trefusis. "Shall I write to Donovan Brown that his letters have gained the cordial assent and sympathy of Sir Charles Brandon?"

"Certainly, certainly. That is, if my unknown name would be of the least interest to him."

"Good," said Trefusis, filling his glass with water. "Erskine, let us drink to our brother Social Democrat."

Erskine laughed loudly, but not heartily. "What an ass you are, Brandon!" he said. "You, with a large landed estate, and bags of gold invested in railways, calling yourself a Social Democrat! Are you going to sell out and distribute—to sell all that thou hast and give to the poor?"

"Not a penny," replied Trefusis for him promptly. "A man cannot be a Christian in this country. I have tried it and found it impossible both in law and in fact. I am a capitalist and a land-holder. I have railway shares, mining shares, building shares, bank shares, and stock of most kinds; and a great trouble they are to me. But these shares do not represent wealth actually in existence; they are a mortgage on the labor of unborn generations of laborers, who must work to keep me and mine in idleness and luxury. If I sold them, would the mortgage be cancelled and the unborn generations released from its thrall? No. It would only pass into the hands of some other capitalist, and the working class would be no better off for my self-sacrifice. Sir Charles cannot obey the command of Christ; I defy him to do it. Let him give his land for a public park; only the richer classes will have leisure to enjoy it. Plant it at the very doors of the poor, so that they may at least breathe its air, and it will raise the value of the neighboring houses and drive the poor away. Let him endow a school for the poor, like Eton or Christ's Hospital, and the rich will take it for their own children as they do in the two instances I have named. Sir Charles does not want to minister to poverty, but to abolish it. No matter how much you give to the poor, everything except a bare subsistence wage will be taken from them again by force. All talk of practising Christianity, or even bare justice, is at present mere waste of words. How can you justly reward the laborer when you cannot ascertain the value of what he makes, owing to the prevalent custom of stealing it? I know this by experience. I wanted to pay a just price for my wife's tomb, but I could not find out its value, and never shall. The principle on which we farm out our national industry by private marauders, who recompense themselves by blackmail, so corrupts and paralyses us that we cannot be honest even when we want to. And the reason we bear it so calmly is that very few of us really want to."

"I must study this question of value," said Sir Charles dubiously, refilling his glass. "Can you recommend me a good book on the subject?"

"Any good treatise on political economy will do," said Trefusis. "In economics all roads lead to Socialism, although in nine cases out of ten, so far, the economist doesnt recognize his destination, and incurs the malediction pronounced by Jeremiah on those who justify the wicked for reward. I will look you out a book or two. And if you will call on Donovan Brown the next time you are in London, he will be delighted, I know. He meets with very few who are capable of sympathizing with him from both his points of view—social and artistic."

Sir Charles brightened on being reminded of Donovan Brown. "I shall esteem an introduction to him a great honor," he said. "I had no idea that he was a friend of yours."

"I was a very practical young Socialist when I first met him," said Trefusis. "When Brown was an unknown and wretchedly poor man, my mother, at the petition of a friend of his, charitably bought one of his pictures for thirty pounds, which he was very glad to get. Years afterwards, when my mother was dead, and Brown famous, I was offered eight hundred pounds for this picture, which was, by the bye, a very bad one in my opinion. Now, after making the usual unjust allowance for interest on thirty pounds for twelve years or so that had elapsed, the sale of the picture would have brought me in a profit of over seven hundred and fifty pounds, an unearned increment to which I had no righteous claim. My solicitor, to whom I mentioned the matter, was of opinion that I might justifiably pocket the seven hundred and fifty pounds as reward for my mother's benevolence in buying a presumably worthless picture from an obscure painter. But he failed to convince me that I ought to be paid for my mother's virtues, though we agreed that neither I nor my mother had received any return in the shape of pleasure in contemplating the work, which had deteriorated considerably by the fading of the colors since its purchase. At last I went to Brown's studio with the picture, and told him that it was worth nothing to me, as I thought it a particularly ·bad one, and that he might have it back again for fifteen pounds, half the first price. He at once told me that I could get from any dealer more for it than he could afford to give me; but he told me too that I had no right to make a profit out of his work, and that he would give me the original price of thirty pounds. I took it, and then sent him the man who had offered me the eight hundred. To my discomfiture Brown refused to sell it on any terms, because he considered it unworthy of his reputation. The man bid up to fifteen hundred, but Brown held out; and I found that instead of putting seven hundred and seventy pounds into his pocket I had taken thirty out of it. I accordingly offered to return the thirty pieces. Brown, taking the offer as an insult, declined all further communication with me. I then insisted on the matter being submitted to arbitration, and demanded fifteen hundred pounds as the full exchange value of the picture. All the arbitrators agreed that this was monstrous, whereupon I contended that if they denied my right to the value in exchange, they must admit my right to the value in use. They assented to this after putting off their decision for a fortnight in order to read Adam Smith and discover what on earth I meant by my values in use and exchange. I now shewed that the picture had no value in use to me, as I disliked it, and that therefore I was entitled to nothing, and that Brown must take back the thirty pounds. They were glad to concede this also to me, as they were all artist friends of Brown, and wished him not to lose money by the transaction, though they of course privately thought that the picture was, as I described it, a bad one. After that Brown and I became very good friends. He tolerated my advances, at first lest it should seem that he was annoyed by my disparagement of his work. Subsequently he fell into my views much as you have done."

"That is very interesting," said Sir Charles. "What a noble thing—refusing fifteen hundred pounds! He could ill afford it, probably."

"Heroic—according to nineteenth-century notions of heroism. Voluntarily to throw away a chance of making money! that is the *ne plus ultra* of martyrdom. Brown's wife was extremely angry with him for doing it."

"It is an interesting story—or might be made so," said Erskine. "But you make my head spin with your confounded exchange values and stuff. Everything is a question of figures with you."

"That comes of my not being a poet," said Trefusis. "But we Socialists need to study the romantic side of our movement to interest women in it. If you want to make a cause grow, instruct every woman you meet in it. She is or will one day be a wife, and will contradict her husband with scraps of your arguments. A squabble will follow. The son will listen, and will be set thinking if he be capable of thought. And so the mind of the people gets leavened. I have converted many young women. Most of them know no more of the economic theory of Socialism than they know of Chaldee; but they no longer fear or condemn its name. Oh, I assure you that much can be done in that way by men who are not afraid of women, and who are not in too great a hurry to see the harvest they have sown for."

"Take care. Some of your lady proselytes may get the better of you some day. The future husband to be contradicted may be Sidney Trefusis. Ha! ha! ha!" Sir Charles had emptied a second large goblet of wine, and was a little flushed and boisterous.

"No," said Trefusis, "I have had enough of love myself, and am not likely to inspire it. Women do not care for men to whom, as Erskine says, everything is a question of figures. I used to flirt with women; now I lecture them, and abhor a man-flirt worse than I do a woman one. Some more wine? Oh, you must not waste the remainder of this bottle."

"I think we had better go, Brandon," said Erskine, his mistrust for Trefusis growing. "We promised to be back before two."

"So you shall," said Trefusis. "It is not yet a quarter past one. By the bye, I have not shewn you Donovan Brown's pet instrument for the regeneration of society. Here it is. A monster petition praying that the holding back from the laborer of any portion of the net value produced by his labor be declared a felony. That is all."

Erskine nudged Sir Charles, who said hastily: "Thank you, but I had rather not sign anything."

"A baronet sign such a petition!" exclaimed Trefusis. "I did not think of asking you. I only shew it to you as an interesting historical document, containing the autographs of a few artists and poets. There is Donovan Brown's, for example. It was he who suggested the petition, which is not likely to do much good, as the thing cannot be done in any such fashion. However, I have promised Brown to get as many signatures as I can; so you may as well sign it, Erskine. It says nothing in blank verse about the holiness of slaying a tyrant, but it is a step in the right direction. You will not stick at such a trifle—unless the reviews have frightened you. Come, your name and address."

Erskine shook his head.

"Do you then only commit yourself to revolutionary sentiments when there is a chance of winning fame as a poet by them?"

"I will not sign, simply because I do not choose to," said Erskine warmly.

"My dear fellow," said Trefusis, almost affectionately, "if a man has a conscience he can have no choice in matters of conviction. I have read somewhere in your book that the man who will not shed his blood for the liberty of his brothers is a coward and a slave. Will you not shed a drop of ink—my ink, too—for the right of your brothers to the work of their hands? I at first sight did not care to sign this petition, because I would as soon petition a tiger to share his prey with me as our rulers to relax their grip of the stolen labor they live on. But Donovan Brown said to me, 'You have no choice. Either you believe that the laborer should have the fruit of his labor or you do not. If you do, put your conviction on record, even if it should be as useless as Pilate's washing his hands.' So I signed."

"Donovan Brown was right," said Sir Charles. "*I* will sign." And he did so with a flourish.

"Brown will be delighted," said Trefusis. "I will write to him today that I have got another good signature for him."

"Two more," said Sir Charles. "You will sign, Erskine; hang me if you shant! It is only against rascals that run away without paying their men their wages."

"Or that dont pay them in full," observed Trefusis, with a curious smile. "But do not sign if you feel uncomfortable about it."

"If you dont sign after me, you are a sneak, Chester," said Sir Charles.

"I dont know what it means," said Erskine, wavering. "I dont understand petitions."

"It means what it says; you cannot be held responsible for any meaning that is not expressed in it," said Trefusis. "But never mind. You mistrust me a little, I fancy, and would rather not meddle with my petitions; but you will think better of that as you grow used to me. Meanwhile, there is no hurry. Dont sign yet."

"Nonsense! I dont doubt your good faith," said Erskine, hastily disavowing suspicions which he felt but could not account for. "Here goes!" And he signed.

"Well done!" said Trefusis. "This will make Brown happy for the rest of the month."

"It is time for us to go now," said Erskine gloomily.

"Look in upon me at any time; you shall be welcome," said Trefusis. "You need not stand upon any sort of ceremony."

Then they parted; Sir Charles assuring Trefusis that he had never spent a more interesting morning, and shaking hands with him at considerable length three times. Erskine said little until he was in the Riverside Road with his friend, when he suddenly burst out:

"What the devil do you mean by drinking two tumblers of such staggering stuff at one o'clock in the day in the house of a dangerous man like that? I am very sorry I went into the fellow's place. I had misgivings about it, and they have been fully borne out."

"How so?" said Sir Charles, taken aback.

"He has overreached us. I was a deuced fool to sign that paper, and so were you. It was for that that he invited us."

"Rubbish, my dear boy. It was not his paper, but Donovan Brown's."

"I doubt it. Most likely he talked Brown into signing it just as he talked us. I tell you his ways are all crooked, like his ideas. Did you hear how he lied about Miss Lindsay?"

"Oh, you were mistaken about that. He does not care two straws for her or for any one."

"Well, if you are satisfied, I am not. You would not be in such high spirits over it if you had taken as little wine as I."

"Pshaw! youre too ridiculous. It was capital wine. Do you mean to say I am drunk?"

"No. But you would not have signed if you had not taken that second glass. If you had not forced me—I could not get out of it after you set the example—I would have seen him d—d sooner than have had anything to do with his petition."

"I dont see what harm can come of it," said Sir Charles, braving out some secret disquietude.

"I will never go into his house again," said Erskine moodily. "We were just like two flies in a spider's web."

Meanwhile, Trefusis was fulfilling his promise to write to Donovan Brown.

"SALLUST'S HOUSE.

"Dear Brown—I have spent the forenoon angling for a couple of very young fish, and have landed them with more trouble than they are worth. One has gaudy scales: he is a baronet, and an amateur artist, save the mark. All my arguments and my little museum of photographs were lost on him; but when I mentioned your name, and promised him an introduction to you, he gorged the bait greedily. He was half drunk when he signed; and I should not have let him touch the paper if I had not convinced myself beforehand that he means well, and that my wine had only freed his natural generosity from his conventional cowardice and prejudice. We must get his name published in as many journals as possible as a signatory to the great petition; it will draw on others as your name drew him. The second novice, Chichester Erskine, is a young poet. He will not be of much use to us, though he is a devoted champion of liberty in blank verse, and dedicates his works to Mazzini, etc. He signed reluctantly. All this hesitation is the uncertainty that comes of ignorance; they have not found out the truth for themselves, and are afraid to trust me, matters having come to the pass at which no man dares trust his fellow.

"I have met a pretty young lady here who might serve you as a model for Hypatia. She is crammed with all the prejudices of the peerage, but I am effecting a cure. I have set my heart on marrying her to Erskine, who, thinking that I am making love to her on my own account, is jealous. The weather is pleasant here, and I am having a merry life of it, but I find myself too idle. Etc., etc., etc."

CHAPTER XVI

ONE sunny forenoon, as Agatha sat reading on the doorstep of the conservatory, the shadow of her parasol deepened, and she, looking up for something denser than the silk of it, saw Trefusis.

"Oh!"

She offered him no further greeting, having fallen in with his habit of dispensing, as far as possible, with salutations and ceremonies. He seemed in no hurry to speak, and so, after a pause, she began, "Sir Charles——"

"Is gone to town," he said. "Erskine is out on his bicycle. Lady Brandon and Miss Lindsay have gone to the village in the wagonette, and you have come out here to enjoy the summer sun and read rubbish. I know all your news already."

"You are very clever, and, as usual, wrong. Sir Charles has not gone to town. He has only gone to the railway station for some papers; he will be back for luncheon. How do you know so much of our affairs?"

"I was on the roof of my house with a field-glass. I saw you come out and sit down here. Then Sir Charles passed. Then Erskine. Then Lady Brandon, driving with great energy, and presenting a remarkable contrast to the disdainful repose of Gertrude."

"Gertrude! I like your cheek."

"You mean that you dislike my presumption."

"No, I think cheek a more expressive word than presumption; and I mean that I like it—that it amuses me."

"Really! What are you reading?"

"Rubbish, you said just now. A novel."

"That is, a lying story of two people who never existed, and who would have acted very differently if they had existed."

"Just so."

"Could you not imagine something just as amusing for yourself?"

"Perhaps so; but it would be too much trouble. Besides, cooking takes away one's appetite for eating. I should not relish stories

220

of my own confection."

"Which volume are you at?"

"The third."

"Then the hero and heroine are on the point of being united?"

"I really dont know. This is one of your clever novels. I wish the characters would not talk so much."

"No matter. Two of them are in love with one another, are they not?"

"Yes. It would not be a novel without that."

"Do you believe, in your secret soul, Agatha—I take the liberty of using your Christian name because I wish to be very solemn—do you really believe that any human being was ever unselfish enough to love another in the story-book fashion?"

"Of course. At least I suppose so. I have never thought much about it."

"I doubt it. My own belief is that no latter-day man has any faith in the thoroughness or permanence of his affection for his mate. Yet he does not doubt the sincerity of her professions, and he conceals the hollowness of his own from her, partly because he is ashamed of it, and partly out of pity for her. And she, on the other side, is playing exactly the same comedy."

"I believe that is what men do, but not women."

"Indeed! Pray do you remember pretending to be very much in love with me once when—"

Agatha reddened and placed her palm on the step as if about to spring up. But she checked herself and said: "Stop, Mr Trefusis. If you talk about that I shall go away. I wonder at you! Have you no taste?"

"None whatever. And as I was the aggrieved party on that—stay, dont go. I will never allude to it again. I am growing afraid of you. You used to be afraid of me."

"Yes; and you used to bully me. You have a habit of bullying women who are weak enough to fear you. You are a great deal cleverer than I, and know much more, I daresay; but I am not in the least afraid of you now."

"You have no reason to be, and never had any. Henrietta, if

she were alive, could testify that if there is a defect in my relations with women, it arises from my excessive amiability. I could not refuse a woman anything she had set her heart upon—except my hand in marriage. As long as your sex are content to stop short of that they can do as they please with me."

"How cruel! I thought you were nearly engaged to Gertrude."

"The usual interpretation of a friendship between a man and a woman! I have never thought of such a thing; and I am sure she never has. We are not half so intimate as you and Sir Charles."

"Oh, Sir Charles is married. And I advise you to get married if you wish to avoid creating misunderstandings by your friendships."

Trefusis was struck. Instead of answering, he stood, after one startled glance at her, looking intently at the knuckle of his forefinger.

"Do take pity on our poor sex," said Agatha maliciously. "You are so rich, and so very clever, and really so nice looking, that you ought to share yourself with somebody. Gertrude would be only too happy."

Trefusis grinned and shook his head, slowly but emphatically.

"I suppose *I* should have no chance," continued Agatha pathetically.

"I should be delighted, of course," he replied with simulated confusion, but with a lurking gleam in his eye that might have checked her, had she noticed it.

"Do marry me, Mr Trefusis," she pleaded, clasping her hands in a rapture of mischievous raillery. "Pray do."

"Thank you," said Trefusis determinedly; "I will."

"I am very sure you shant," said Agatha, after an incredulous pause, springing up and gathering her skirt as if to run away. "You do not suppose I was in earnest, do you?"

"Undoubtedly I do. *I* am in earnest."

Agatha hesitated, uncertain whether he might not be playing with her as she had just been playing with him. "Take care," she said. "I may change my mind and be in earnest, too; and then how will you feel, Mr. Trefusis?"

"I think, under our altered relations, you had better call me Sidney."

"I think we had better drop the joke. It was in rather bad taste, and I should not have made it, perhaps."

"It would be an execrable joke; therefore I have no intention of regarding it as one. You shall be held to your offer, Agatha. Are you in love with me?"

"Not in the least. Not the very smallest bit in the world. I do not know anybody with whom I am less in love or less likely to be in love."

"Then you must marry me. If you were in love with me, I should run away. My sainted Henrietta adored me, and I proved unworthy of adoration—though I was immensely flattered."

"Yes; exactly! The way you treated your first wife ought to be sufficient to warn any woman against becoming your second."

"Any woman who loved me, you mean. But you do not love me, and if I run away you will have the advantage of being rid of me. Our settlements can be drawn so as to secure you half my fortune in such an event."

"You will never have a chance of running away from me."

"I shall not want to. I am not so squeamish as I was. No; I do not think I shall run away from you."

"I do not think so either."

"Well, when shall we be married?"

"Never," said Agatha, and fled. But before she had gone a step he caught her.

"Dont," she said breathlessly. "Take your arm away. How dare you?"

He released her and shut the door of the conservatory. "Now," he said, "if you want to run away you will have to run in the open."

"You are very impertinent. Let me go in immediately."

"Do you want me to beg you to marry me after you have offered to do it freely?"

"But I was only joking; I dont care for you," she said, looking round for an outlet.

223

"Agatha," he said, with grim patience, "half an hour ago I had no more intention of marrying you than of making a voyage to the moon. But when you made the suggestion I felt all its force in an instant, and now nothing will satisfy me but your keeping your word. Of all the women I know, you are the only one not quite a fool."

"I should be a great fool if—"

"If you married me, you were going to say; but I dont think so. I am the only man, not quite an ass, of your acquaintance. I know my value, and yours. And I loved you long ago, when I had no right to."

Agatha frowned. "No," she said. "There is no use in saying anything more about it. It is out of the question."

"Come, dont be vindictive. I was more sincere then than you were. But that has nothing to do with the present. You have spent our renewed acquaintance on the defensive against me, retorting upon me, teasing and tempting me. Be generous for once, and say Yes with a good will."

"Oh, I *never* tempted you," cried Agatha. "I did not. It is not true." He said nothing, but offered his hand. "No; go away; I will not." He persisted, and she felt her power of resistance suddenly wane. Terror-stricken, she said hastily: "There is not the least use in bothering me; I will tell you nothing today."

"Promise me on your honor that you will say Yes tomorrow, and I will leave you in peace until then."

"I will not."

"The deuce take your sex," he said plaintively. "You know my mind now, and I have to stand here coquetting because you dont know your own. If I cared for my comfort I should remain a bachelor."

"I advise you to do so," she said, stealing backward towards the door. "You are a very interesting widower. A wife would spoil you. Consider the troubles of domesticity, too."

"I like troubles. They strengthen—Aha!" (she had snatched at the knob of the door, and he swiftly put his hand on hers and stayed her). "Not yet, if you please. Can you not speak out like a woman—like a man, I mean? You may withhold a bone from Max until he stands on his hind legs to beg for it, but you should not treat me like a dog. Say Yes frankly, and do not keep me begging."

"What in the world do you want to marry me for?"

"Because I was made to carry a house on my shoulders, and will do so. I want to do the best I can for myself, and I shall never have such a chance again. And I cannot help myself, and dont know why; that is the plain truth of the matter. You will marry some one some day." She shook her head. "Yes, you will. Why not marry me?"

Agatha bit her nether lip, looked ruefully at the ground, and, after a long pause, said reluctantly, "Very well. But mind, I think you are acting very foolishly, and if you are disappointed afterwards, you must not blame *me*."

"I take the risk of my bargain," he said, releasing her hand, and leaning against the door as he took out his pocket diary. "You will have to take the risk of yours, which I hope may not prove the worse of the two. This is the seventeenth of June. What date before the twenty-fourth of July will suit you?"

"You mean the twenty-fourth of July next year, I presume?"

"No; I mean this year. I am going abroad on that date, married or not, to attend a conference at Geneva, and I want you to come with me. I will show you a lot of places and things that you have never seen before. It is your right to name the day, but you have no serious business to provide for, and I have."

"But you dont know all the things I shall—I should have to provide. You had better wait until you come back from the continent."

"There is nothing to be provided on your part but settlements and your trousseau. The trousseau is all nonsense; and Jansenius knows me of old in the matter of settlements. I got married in six weeks before."

"Yes," said Agatha sharply, "but I am not Henrietta."

"No, thank Heaven," he assented placidly.

Agatha was struck with remorse. "That was a vile thing for me to say," she said; "and for you too."

"Whatever is true is to the purpose, vile or not. Will you come to Geneva on the twenty-fourth?"

"But— I really was not thinking when I— I did not intend to say that I would— I—"

"I know. You will come if we are married."

"Yes. *If* we are married."

"We shall be married. Do not write either to your mother or Jansenius until I ask you."

"I dont intend to. I have nothing to write about."

"Wretch that you are! And do not be jealous if you catch me making love to Lady Brandon. I always do so; she expects it."

"You may make love to whom you please. It is no concern of mine."

"Here comes the wagonette with Lady Brandon and Ger— and Miss Lindsay. I mustnt call her Gertrude now except when you are not by. Before they interrupt us, let me remind you of the three points we are agreed upon. I love you. You do not love me. We are to be married before the twenty-fourth of next month. Now I must fly to help her ladyship to alight."

He hastened to the house door, at which the wagonette had just stopped. Agatha, bewildered, and ashamed to face her friends, went in through the conservatory, and locked herself in her room.

Trefusis went into the library with Gertrude, whilst Lady Brandon loitered in the hall to take off her gloves and ask questions of the servants. When she followed, she found the two standing together at the window. Gertrude was listening to him with the patient expression she now often wore when he talked. He was smiling, but it struck Jane that he was not quite at ease.

"I was just beginning to tell Miss Lindsay," he said, "of an extraordinary thing that has happened during your absence."

"I know," exclaimed Jane, with sudden conviction. "The heater in the conservatory has cracked."

"Possibly," said Trefusis; "but, if so, I have not heard of it."

"If it hasnt cracked, it will," said Jane gloomily. Then, assuming with some effort an interest in Trefusis's news, she added: "Well, what has happened?"

"I was chatting with Miss Wylie just now, when a singular idea occurred to us. We discussed it for some time; and the upshot is that we are to be married before the end of next month."

Jane reddened and stared at him; and he looked keenly back at her. Gertrude, though unobserved, did not suffer her expression of patient happiness to change in the least; but a greenish-white color suddenly appeared in her face, and only gave place very slowly to her usual complexion.

"Do you mean to say that you are going to marry *Agatha?*" said Lady Brandon incredulously, after a pause.

"Yes. I had no intention of doing so when I last saw you, or I should have told you."

"I never heard of such a thing in my life! You fell in love with one another in five minutes, I suppose."

"Good Heavens, no! we are not in love with one another. Can you believe that I would marry for such a frivolous reason? No. The subject turned up accidentally, and the advantages of a match between us struck me forcibly. I was fortunate enough to convert her to my opinion."

"Yes; she wanted a lot of pressing, I daresay," said Jane, glancing at Gertrude, who was smiling unmeaningly.

"As you imply," said Trefusis coolly, "her reluctance may have been affected, and she only too glad to get such a charming husband. Assuming that to be the case, she dissembled remarkably well."

Gertrude took off her bonnet, and left the room without speaking.

"This is my revenge upon you for marrying Brandon," he said then, approaching Jane.

"Oh, yes," she retorted ironically. "I believe all that, of course."

"You have the same security for its truth as for that of all the foolish things I confess to you. There!" He pointed to a panel of looking glass, in which Jane's figure was reflected at full length.

"I dont see anything to admire," said Jane, looking at herself with no great favor. "There is plenty of me, if you admire that."

"It is impossible to have too much of a good thing. But I must not look any more. Though Agatha says she does not love me, I am not sure that she would be pleased if I were to look for love from any one else."

"Says she does not love you! Dont believe her; she has taken trouble enough to catch you."

"I am flattered. You caught me without any trouble, and yet you would not have me."

"It is manners to wait to be asked. I think you have treated Gertrude shamefully—I hope you wont be offended with me for saying so. I blame Agatha most. She is an awfully double-faced girl."

"How so?" said Trefusis, surprised. "What has Miss Lindsay to do with it?"

"You know very well."

"I assure you I do not. If you were speaking of yourself I could understand you."

"Oh, you can get out of it cleverly, like all men; but you cant hoodwink me. You shouldnt have pretended to like Gertrude when you were really pulling a cord with Agatha. And she, too, pretending to flirt with Sir Charles—as if he would care twopence for her!"

Trefusis seemed a little disturbed. "I hope Miss Lindsay had no such—but she could not."

"Oh, couldnt she? You will soon see whether she had or not."

"You misunderstand us, Lady Brandon; Miss Lindsay knows better. Remember, too, that this proposal of mine was quite unpremeditated. This morning I had no tender thoughts of any one —except one whom it would be improper to name."

"Oh, that is all talk. It wont do *now*."

"I will talk no more at present. I must be off to the village to telegraph to my solicitor. If I meet Erskine I will tell him the good news."

"He will be delighted. He thought, as we all did, that you were cutting him out with Gertrude."

Trefusis smiled, shook his head, and, with a glance of admiring homage to Jane's charms, went out. Jane was contemplating herself in the glass when a servant begged her to come and speak to Master Charles and Miss Fanny. She hurried upstairs to the nursery, where her boy and girl, disputing each other's prior right to torture the baby, had come to blows. They were somewhat frightened, but not at all appeased, by Jane's entrance. She scolded, coaxed, threatened, bribed, quoted Dr Watts, appealed to the nurse and then insulted her, demanded of the children whether they loved one another, whether they loved mamma, and whether they wanted a right good whipping. At last, exasperated by her own inability to restore order, she seized the baby, which had cried incessantly throughout, and, declaring that it was doing it on purpose and should have something real to cry for, gave it an exemplary smacking, and ordered the others to bed. The boy, awed by the fate of his infant brother, offered, by way of compromise, to be good if Miss Wylie would come and play with him, a proposal which provoked from his jealous mother a box on the ear that sent him howling to his cot. Then she left the room, pausing on the threshold to remark that if she heard another sound from them that day, they might expect the worst from her. On descending, heated and angry, to the drawing room, she found Agatha there alone, looking through the window as if the landscape were especially unsatisfactory this time.

"Selfish little beasts!" exclaimed Jane, making a miniature whirlwind with her skirts as she came in. "Charlie is a perfect little fiend. He spends all his time thinking how he can annoy me. Ugh! He's just like his father."

"Thank you, my dear," said Sir Charles from the doorway.

Jane laughed. "I knew you were there," she said. "Where's Gertrude?"

"She has gone out," said Sir Charles.

"Nonsense! She has only just come in from driving with me."

"I do not know what you mean by nonsense," said Sir Charles, chafing. "I saw her walking along the Riverside Road. I was in the village road, and she did not see me. She seemed in a hurry."

"I met her on the stairs and spoke to her," said Agatha, "but she didnt hear me."

229

"I hope she is not going to throw herself into the river," said Jane. Then, turning to her husband, she added: "Have you heard the news?"

"The only news I have heard is from this paper," said Sir Charles, taking out a journal and flinging it on the table. "There is a paragraph in it stating that I have joined some infernal Socialistic league, and I am told that there is an article in the Times on the spread of Socialism, in which my name is mentioned. This is all due to Trefusis; and I think he has played me a most dishonorable trick. I will tell him so, too, when next I see him."

"You had better be careful what you say of him before Agatha," said Jane. "Oh, you need not be alarmed, Agatha; I know all about it. He told us in the library. We went out this morning—Gertrude and I—and when we came back we found Mr Trefusis and Agatha talking very lovingly to one another on the conservatory steps, newly engaged."

"Indeed!" said Sir Charles, disconcerted and displeased, but trying to smile. "I may then congratulate you, Miss Wylie?"

"You need not," said Agatha, keeping her countenance as well as she could. "It was only a joke. At least it came about in a jest. He has no right to say that we are engaged."

"Stuff and nonsense," said Jane. "That wont do, Agatha. He has gone off to telegraph to his solicitor. He is quite in earnest."

"I am a great fool," said Agatha, sitting down and twisting her hands perplexedly. "I believe I said something; but I really did not intend to. He surprised me into speaking before I knew what I was saying. A pretty mess I have got myself into!"

"I am glad you have been outwitted at last," said Jane, laughing spitefully. "You never had any pity for me when I could not think of the proper thing to say at a moment's notice."

Agatha let the taunt pass unheeded. Her gaze wandered anxiously, and at last settled appealingly upon Sir Charles. "What shall I do?" she said to him.

"Well, Miss Wylie," he said gravely, "if you did not mean to marry him you should not have promised. I dont wish to be unsympathetic, and I know that it is very hard to get rid of Trefusis when he makes up his mind to get something out of you, but still—"

"Never mind her," said Jane, interrupting him. "She wants to marry him just as badly as he wants to marry her. You would be preciously disappointed if he cried off, Agatha; for all your interesting reluctance."

"That is not so, really," said Agatha earnestly. "I wish I had taken time to think about it. I suppose he has told everybody by this time."

"May we then regard it as settled?" said Sir Charles.

"Of course you may," said Jane contemptuously.

"Pray allow Miss Wylie to speak for herself, Jane. I confess I do not understand why you are still in doubt—if you have really engaged yourself to him."

"I suppose I am in for it," said Agatha. "I feel as if there were some fatal objection, if I could only remember what it is. I wish I had never seen him."

Sir Charles was puzzled. "I do not understand ladies' ways in these matters," he said. "However, as there seems to be no doubt that you and Trefusis are engaged, I shall of course say nothing that would make it unpleasant for him to visit here; but I must say that he has—to say the least—been inconsiderate to me personally. I signed a paper at his house on the implicit understanding that it was strictly private, and now he has trumpeted it forth to the whole world, and publicly associated my name not only with his own, but with those of persons of whom I know nothing except that I would rather not be connected with them in any way."

"What does it matter?" said Jane. "Nobody cares twopence."

"*I* care," said Sir Charles angrily. "No sensible person can accuse me of exaggerating my own importance because I value my reputation sufficiently to object to my approval being publicly cited in support of a cause with which I have no sympathy."

"Perhaps Mr Trefusis has had nothing to do with it," said Agatha. "The papers publish whatever they please, dont they?"

"Thats right, Agatha," said Jane maliciously. "Dont let any one speak ill of him."

"I am not speaking ill of him," said Sir Charles, before Agatha could retort. "It is a mere matter of feeling, and I should not have mentioned it had I known the altered relations between him and Miss Wylie."

"Pray dont speak of them," said Agatha. "I have a mind to run away by the next train."

Sir Charles, to change the subject, suggested a duet.

Meanwhile Erskine, returning through the village from his morning ride, had met Trefusis, and attempted to pass him with a nod. But Trefusis called to him to stop, and he dismounted reluctantly.

"Just a word to say that I am going to be married," said Trefusis.

"To—?" Erskine could not add Gertrude's name.

"To one of our friends at the Beeches. Guess to which."

"To Miss Lindsay, I presume."

"What in the fiend's name has put it into all your heads that Miss Lindsay and I are particularly attached to one another?" exclaimed Trefusis. "*You* have always appeared to me to be the man for Miss Lindsay. I am going to marry Miss Wylie."

"Really!" exclaimed Erskine, with a sensation of suddenly thawing after a bitter frost.

"Of course. And now, Erskine, you have the advantage of being a poor man. Do not let that splendid girl marry for money. If you go further you are likely to fare worse; and so is she." Then he nodded and walked away, leaving the other staring after him.

"If he has jilted her, he is a scoundrel," said Erskine. "I am sorry I didnt tell him so."

He mounted and rode slowly along the Riverside Road, partly suspecting Trefusis of some mystification, but inclining to believe in him, and, in any case, to take his advice as to Gertrude. The conversation he had overheard in the avenue still perplexed him. He could not reconcile it with Trefusis's profession of disinterestedness towards her.

His bicycle carried him noiselessly on its india-rubber tyres to the place by which the hemlock grew, and there he saw Gertrude sitting on the low earthen wall that separated the field from the road. Her straw bag, with her scissors in it, lay beside her. Her fingers were interlaced, and her hands rested, palms downwards, on her knee. Her expression was rather vacant, and so little suggestive of any serious emotion that Erskine laughed as he alighted close to her.

"Are you tired?" he said.

"No," she replied, not startled, and smiling mechanically— an unusual condescension on her part.

"Indulging in a day-dream?"

"No." She moved a little to one side and concealed the basket with her dress.

He began to fear that something was wrong. "Is it possible that you have ventured among those poisonous plants again?" he said. "Are you ill?"

"Not at all," she replied, rousing herself a little. "Your solicitude is quite thrown away. I am perfectly well."

"I beg your pardon," he said, snubbed. "I thought—Dont you think it dangerous to sit on that damp wall?"

"It is not damp. It is crumbling into dust with dryness." An unnatural laugh, with which she concluded, intensified his uneasiness.

He began a sentence, stopped, and to gain time to recover himself, placed his bicycle in the opposite ditch, a proceeding which she witnessed with impatience, as it indicated his intention to stay and talk. She, however, was the first to speak; and she did so with a callousness that shocked him.

"Have you heard the news?"

"What news?"

"About Mr Trefusis and Agatha. They are engaged."

"So Trefusis told me. I met him just now in the village. I was very glad to hear it."

"Of course."

"But I had a special reason for being glad."

"Indeed?"

"I was desperately afraid, before he told me the truth, that

233

he had other views—views that might have proved fatal to my dearest hopes."

Gertrude frowned at him, and the frown roused him to brave her. He lost his self-command, already shaken by her strange behavior. "You know that I love you, Miss Lindsay," he said. "It may not be a perfect love, but, humanly speaking, it is a true one. I almost told you so that day when we were in the billiard room together; and I did a very dishonorable thing the same evening. When you were speaking to Trefusis in the avenue I was close to you, and I listened."

"Then you heard him," cried Gertrude vehemently. "You heard him swear that he was in earnest."

"Yes," said Erskine, trembling, "and I thought he meant in earnest in loving you. You can hardly blame me for that: I was in love myself; and love is blind and jealous. I never hoped again until he told me that he was to be married to Miss Wylie. May I speak to you, now that I know I was mistaken, or that you have changed your mind?"

"Or that *he* has changed his mind," said Gertrude scornfully.

Erskine, with a new anxiety for her sake, checked himself. Her dignity was dear to him, and he saw that her disappointment had made her reckless of it. "Do not say anything to me now, Miss Lindsay, lest—"

"What have I said? What have I to say?"

"Nothing, except on my own affairs. I love you dearly."

She made an impatient movement, as if that were a very insignificant matter.

"You believe me, I hope," he said timidly.

Gertrude made an effort to recover her habitual ladylike reserve, but her energy failed before she had done more than raise her head. She relapsed into her listless attitude, and made a faint gesture of intolerance.

"You cannot be quite indifferent to being loved," he said, becoming more nervous and more urgent. "Your existence constitutes all my happiness. I offer you my services and devotion. I do not ask any reward." (He was now speaking very quickly and almost inaudibly.) "You may accept my love without returning it. I do not want—seek to make a bargain. If you need a friend you may be able to rely on me more confidently because you know I love you."

"Oh, you think so," said Gertrude, interrupting him; "but you will get over it. I am not the sort of person that men fall in love with. You will soon change your mind."

"Not the sort! Oh, how little you know!" he said, becoming eloquent. "I have had plenty of time to change, but I am as fixed as ever. If you doubt, wait and try me. But do not be rough with me. You pain me more than you can imagine when you are hasty or indifferent. I am in earnest."

"Ha, ha! That is easily said."

"Not by me. I change in my judgment of other people according to my humor, but I believe steadfastly in your goodness and beauty—as if you were an angel. I am in earnest in my love for you as I am in earnest for my own life, which can only be perfected by your aid and influence."

"You are greatly mistaken if you suppose that I am an angel."

"You are wrong to mistrust yourself; but it is what I owe to you and not what I expect from you that I try to express by speaking of you as an angel. I know that you are not an angel to yourself. But you are to me."

She sat stubbornly silent.

"I will not press you for an answer now. I am content that you know my mind at last. Shall we return together?"

She looked round slowly at the hemlock, and from that to the river. Then she took up her basket, rose, and prepared to go, as if under compulsion.

"Do you want any more hemlock?" he said. "If so, I will pluck some for you."

"I wish you would let me alone," she said, with sudden anger. She added, a little ashamed of herself, "I have a headache."

"I am very sorry," he said, crestfallen.

"It is only that I do not wish to be spoken to. It hurts my head to listen."

He meekly took his bicycle from the ditch and wheeled it along beside her to the Beeches without another word. They went in through the conservatory, and parted in the dining room. Before leaving him she said with some remorse: "I did not mean to be rude, Mr Erskine."

He flushed, murmured something, and attempted to kiss her hand. But she snatched it away and went out quickly. He was stung by this repulse, and stood mortifying himself by thinking of it until he was disturbed by the entrance of a maid-servant. Learning from her that Sir Charles was in the billiard room, he joined him there, and asked him carelessly if he had heard the news.

"About Miss Wylie?" said Sir Charles. "Yes, I should think so. I believe the whole country knows it, though they have not been engaged three hours. Have you seen these?" And he pushed a couple of newspapers across the table.

Erskine had to make several efforts before he could read. "You were a fool to sign that document," he said. "I told you so at the time."

"I relied on the fellow being a gentleman," said Sir Charles warmly. "I do not see that I was a fool. I see that he is a cad, and but for this business of Miss Wylie's I would let him know my opinion. Let me tell you, Chester, that he has played fast and loose with Miss Lindsay. There is a deuce of a row upstairs. She has just told Jane that she must go home at once; Miss Wylie declares that she will have nothing to do with Trefusis if Miss Lindsay has a prior claim to him; and Jane is annoyed at his admiring anybody except herself. It serves me right; my instinct warned me against the fellow from the first."

Just then luncheon was announced. Gertrude did not come down. Agatha was silent and moody. Jane tried to make Erskine describe his walk with Gertrude, but he baffled her curiosity by omitting from his account everything except its commonplaces.

"I think her conduct very strange," said Jane. "She insists on going to town by the four o'clock train. I consider that it's not polite to me, although she always made a point of her perfect manners. I never heard of such a thing!"

When they had risen from the table, they went together to the drawing room. They had hardly arrived there when Trefusis was announced, and he was in their presence before they had time to conceal the expression of consternation his name brought into their faces.

"I have come to say goodbye," he said. "I find that I must go to town by the four o'clock train to push my arrangements in person; the telegrams I have received breathe nothing but delay. Have you seen the Times?"

"I have indeed," said Sir Charles emphatically.

"You are in some other paper too, and will be in half a dozen more in the course of the next fortnight. Men who have committed themselves to an opinion are always in trouble with the newspapers; some because they cannot get into them, others because they cannot keep out. If you had put forward a thundering revolutionary manifesto, not a daily paper would have dared allude to it: there is no cowardice like Fleet Street cowardice! I must run off; I have much to do before I start, and it is getting on for three. Goodbye, Lady Brandon, and everybody."

He shook Jane's hand, dealt nods to the rest rapidly, making no distinction in favor of Agatha, and hurried away. They stared after him for a moment, and then Erskine ran out and went downstairs two steps at a time. Nevertheless he had to run as far as the avenue before he overtook his man.

"Trefusis," he said breathlessly, "you must not go by the four o'clock train."

"Why not?"

"Miss Lindsay is going to town by it."

"So much the better, my dear boy; so much the better. You are not jealous of me now, are you?"

"Look here, Trefusis. I dont know and I dont ask what there has been between you and Miss Lindsay, but your engagement has quite upset her, and she is running away to London in consequence. If she hears that you are going by the same train she will wait until tomorrow, and I believe the delay would be very disagreeable. Will you inflict that additional pain upon her?"

Trefusis, evidently concerned, looked doubtfully at Erskine, and pondered for a moment. "I think you are on a wrong scent about this," he said. "My relations with Miss Lindsay were not of a sentimental kind. Have you said anything to her—on your own account, I mean?"

"I have spoken to her on both accounts, and I know from her own lips that I am right."

Trefusis uttered a low whistle.

"It is not the first time I have had the evidence of my senses in the matter," said Erskine significantly. "Pray think of it seriously, Trefusis. Forgive my telling you frankly that nothing but your own utter want of feeling could excuse you for the way in which you have acted towards her."

Trefusis smiled. "Forgive me in turn for my inquisitiveness," he said. "What does she say to your suit?"

Erskine hesitated, shewing by his manner that he thought Trefusis had no right to ask the question. "She says nothing," he answered.

"Hm!" said Trefusis. "Well, you may rely on me as to the train. There is my hand upon it."

"Thank you," said Erskine fervently. They shook hands and parted, Trefusis walking away with a grin suggestive of anything but good faith.

CHAPTER XVII

GERTRUDE, unaware of the extent to which she had already betrayed her disappointment, believed that anxiety for her father's health, which she alleged as the motive of her sudden departure, was an excuse plausible enough to blind her friends to her overpowering reluctance to speak to Agatha or endure her presence; to her fierce shrinking from the sort of pity usually accorded to a jilted woman; and, above all, to her dread of meeting Trefusis. She had for some time past thought of him as an upright and perfect man deeply interested in her. Yet, comparatively liberal as her education had been, she had no idea of any interest of man in woman existing apart from a desire to marry. He had, in his serious moments, striven to make her sensible of the baseness he saw in her worldliness, flattering her by his apparent conviction—which she shared—that she was capable of a higher life. Almost in the same breath, a strain of gallantry which was incorrigible in him, and to which his humor and his tenderness to women whom he liked gave variety and charm, would supervene upon his seriousness with a rapidity which her far less flexible temperament could not follow. Hence she, thinking him still in earnest when he had swerved into florid romance, had been dangerously misled. He had no conscientious scruples in his love-making, because he was unaccustomed to consider himself as likely to inspire love in women; and Gertrude did not know that her beauty gave to an hour spent alone with her a transient charm which few men of imagination and address could resist. She, who had lived in the marriage market since she had left school, looked upon love-making as the most serious business of life. To him it was only a pleasant sort of trifling, enhanced by a dash of sadness in the reflection that it meant so little.

Of the ceremonies attending her departure, the one that cost her most was the kiss she felt bound to offer Agatha. She had been jealous of her at college, where she had esteemed herself the better bred of the two; but that opinion had hardly consoled her for Agatha's superior quickness of wit, dexterity of hand, audacity, aptness of resource, capacity for forming or following intricate associations of ideas, and consequent power to dazzle others. Her jealousy of these qualities was now barbed by the knowledge that they were much nearer akin than her own to those of Trefusis. It mattered little to her how she appeared to herself in comparison with Agatha. But it mattered the whole world (she thought) that she must appear to Trefusis so slow, stiff, cold, and studied, and that she had no means to make him understand that she was not really so. For she would not admit the justice of impressions made by what she did not intend to do, however habitually she did it. She had a theory that she was not herself, but what she would have liked to be. As to the one quality in which she had always felt superior to Agatha, and which she called "good breeding," Trefusis had so far destroyed her conceit in that, that she was beginning to doubt whether it was not her cardinal defect.

She could not bring herself to utter a word as she embraced her schoolfellow; and Agatha was tongue-tied too. But there was much remorseful tenderness in the feelings that choked them. Their silence would have been awkward but for the loquacity of Jane, who talked enough for all three. Sir Charles was without, in the trap, waiting to drive Gertrude to the station. Erskine intercepted her in the hall as she passed out, told her that he should be desolate when she was gone, and begged her to remember him, a simple petition which moved her a little, and caused her to note that his dark eyes had a pleading eloquence which she had observed before in the kangaroos at the Zoological Society's gardens.

On the way to the train Sir Charles worried the horse in order to be excused from conversation on the sore subject of his guest's sudden departure. He had made a few remarks on the skittishness of young ponies, and on the weather, and that was all until they reached the station, a pretty building standing in the open country, with a view of the river from the platform. There were two flies waiting, two porters, a bookstall, and a refreshment room with a neglected beauty pining behind the bar. Sir Charles waited in the booking office to purchase a ticket for Gertrude, who went through to the platform. The first person she saw there was Trefusis, close beside her.

"I am going to town by this train, Gertrude," he said quickly. "Let me take charge of you. I have something to say, for I fear that some mischief has been made between us which must be stopped at once. You—"

Just then Sir Charles came out, and stood amazed to see them in conversation.

"It happens that I am going by this train," said Trefusis. "I will see after Miss Lindsay."

"Miss Lindsay has her maid with her," said Sir Charles, almost stammering, and looking at Gertrude, whose expression was inscrutable.

"We can get into the Pullman car," said Trefusis. "There we shall be as private as in a corner of a crowded drawing room. I may travel with you, may I not?" he said, seeing Sir Charles's disturbed look, and turning to her for express permission.

She felt that to deny him would be to throw away her last chance of happiness. Nevertheless she resolved to do it, though she should die of grief on the way to London. As she raised her head to forbid him the more emphatically, she met his gaze, which was grave and expectant. For an instant she lost her presence of mind, and in that instant said, "Yes. I shall be very glad."

"Well, if that is the case," said Sir Charles, in the tone of one whose sympathy had been alienated by an unpardonable outrage, "there can be no use in my waiting. I leave you in the hands of Mr Trefusis. Goodbye, Miss Lindsay."

Gertrude winced. Unkindness from a man usually kind proved hard to bear at parting. She was offering him her hand in silence when Trefusis said:

"Wait and see us off. If we chance to be killed on the journey —which is always probable on an English railway—you will reproach yourself afterwards if you do not see the last of us.

Here is the train; it will not delay you a minute. Tell Erskine that you saw me here; that I have not forgotten my promise, and that he may rely on me. Get in at this end, Miss Lindsay."

"My maid," said Gertrude, hesitating; for she had not intended to travel so expensively. "She—"

"She comes with us to take care of me; I have tickets for everybody," said Trefusis, handing the woman in.

"But—"

"Take your seats, please," said the guard. "Going by the train, sir?"

"Goodbye, Sir Charles. Give my love to dear Jane, and Agatha, and the darling children; and thanks so much for a very pleasant—" Here the train moved off, and Sir Charles, melting, smiled and waved his hat until he caught sight of Trefusis looking back at him with a grin which seemed, under the circumstances, so Satanic, that he stopped as if petrified in the midst of his gesticulations, and stood with his arm out like a semaphore.

The drive home restored him somewhat, but he was still full of his surprise when he rejoined Agatha, his wife, and Erskine in the drawing room at the Beeches. The moment he entered, he said without preface: "She has gone off with Trefusis."

Erskine, who had been reading, started up, clutching his book as if about to hurl it at some one, and cried: "Was he at the train?"

"Yes, and has gone to town by it."

"Then," said Erskine, flinging the book violently on the floor, "he is a scoundrel and a liar."

"What is the matter?" said Agatha rising, whilst Jane stared open-mouthed at him.

"I beg your pardon, Miss Wylie, I forgot you. He pledged me his honor that he would not go by that train. I will—" He hurried from the room. Sir Charles rushed after him, and overtook him at the foot of the stairs.

"Where are you going? What do you want to do?"

"I will follow the train and catch it at the next station. I can do it on my bicycle."

"Nonsense! youre mad. They have thirty-five minutes start; and the train travels forty-five miles an hour."

Erskine sat down on the stairs and gazed blankly at the opposite wall.

"You must have mistaken him," said Sir Charles. "He told me to tell you that he had not forgotten his promise, and that you may rely on him."

"What *is* the matter?" said Agatha, coming down, followed by Lady Brandon.

"Miss Wylie," said Erskine, springing up, "he gave me his word that he would not go by that train when I told him Miss Lindsay was going by it. He has broken his word and seized the opportunity I was mad and credulous enough to tell him of. If I had been in your place, Brandon, I would have strangled him or thrown him under the wheels sooner than let him go. He has shown himself in this, as in everything else, a cheat, a conspirator, a man of crooked ways, shifts, tricks, lying soph-istries, heartless selfishness, cruel cynicism—" He stopped to catch his breath, and Sir Charles interposed a remonstrance.

"You are exciting yourself about nothing, Chester. They are in a Pullman, with her maid and plenty of people; and she expressly gave him leave to go with her. He asked her the question flatly before my face, and I must say I thought it a strange thing for her to consent to. However, she did consent, and of course I was not in a position to prevent him from going to London if he pleased. Dont let us have a scene, old man. It cant be helped."

"I am very sorry," said Erskine, hanging his head. "I did not mean to make a scene. I beg your pardon."

He went away to his room without another word. Sir Charles followed and attempted to console him, but Erskine caught his hand, and asked to be left to himself. So Sir Charles returned to the drawing room, where his wife, at a loss for once, hardly ventured to remark that she had never heard of such a thing in her life.

Agatha kept silence. She had long ago come unconsciously

to the conclusion that Trefusis and she were the only members of the party at the Beeches who had much common sense, and this made her slow to believe that he could be in the wrong and Erskine in the right in any misunderstanding between them. She had a slovenly way of summing up as "asses" people whose habits of thought differed from hers. Of all varieties of man, the minor poet realized her conception of the human ass most completely, and Erskine, though a very nice fellow indeed, thoroughly good and gentlemanly, in her opinion, was yet a minor poet, and therefore a pronounced ass. Trefusis, on the contrary, was the last man of her acquaintance whom she would have thought of as a very nice fellow or a virtuous gentleman; but he was not an ass, although he was obstinate in his Socialistic fads. She had indeed suspected him of weakness almost asinine with respect to Gertrude, but then all men were asses in their dealings with women, and since he had transferred his weakness to her own account it no longer seemed to need justification. And now, as her concern for Erskine, whom she pitied, wore off, she began to resent Trefusis's journey with Gertrude as an attack on her recently acquired monopoly of him. There was an air of aristocratic pride about Gertrude which Agatha had formerly envied, and which she still feared Trefusis might mistake for an index of dignity and refinement. Agatha did not believe that her resentment was the common feeling called jealousy, for she still deemed herself unique, but it gave her a sense of meanness that did not improve her spirits.

The dinner was dull. Lady Brandon spoke in an undertone, as if some one lay dead in the next room. Erskine was depressed by the consciousness of having lost his head and acted foolishly in the afternoon. Sir Charles did not pretend to ignore the suspense they were all in pending intelligence of the journey to London; he ate and drank and said nothing. Agatha, disgusted with herself and with Gertrude, and undecided whether to be disgusted with Trefusis or to trust him affectionately, followed the example of her host. After dinner she accompanied him in a series of songs by Schubert. This proved an aggravation instead of a relief. Sir

Charles, excelling in the expression of melancholy, preferred songs of that character; and as his musical ideas, like those of most Englishmen, were founded on what he had heard in church in his childhood, his style was oppressively monotonous. Agatha took the first excuse that presented itself to leave the piano. Sir Charles felt that his performance had been a failure, and remarked, after a cough or two, that he had caught a touch of cold returning from the station. Erskine sat on a sofa with his head drooping, and his palms joined and hanging downward between his knees. Agatha stood at the window, looking at the late summer afterglow. Jane yawned, and presently broke the silence.

"You look exactly as you used at school, Agatha. I could almost fancy us back again in Number Six."

Agatha shook her head.

"Do I ever look like that—like myself, as I used to be?"

"Never," said Agatha emphatically, turning and surveying the figure of which Miss Carpenter had been the unripe antecedent.

"But why?" said Jane querulously. "I dont see why I shouldnt. I am not so changed."

"You have become an exceedingly fine woman, Jane," said Agatha gravely, and then, without knowing why, turned her attentive gaze upon Sir Charles, who bore it uneasily, and left the room. A minute later he returned with two buff envelopes in his hand.

"A telegram for you, Miss Wylie, and one for Chester." Erskine started up, white with vague fears. Agatha's color went and came again with increased richness as she read:

"I have arrived safe and ridiculously happy. Read a thousand things between the lines. I will write tomorrow. Good night."

"You may read it," said Agatha, handing it to Jane.

"Very pretty," said Jane. "A shilling's worth of attention—exactly twenty words! He may well call himself an economist."

Suddenly a crowing laugh from Erskine caused them to turn and stare at him. "What nonsense!" he said, blushing. "What a fellow he is! I dont attach the slightest importance to this."

Agatha took a corner of his telegram and pulled it gently.

"No, no," he said, holding it tightly. "It is too absurd. I dont think I ought—"

Agatha gave a decisive pull, and read the message aloud. It was from Trefusis, thus:

"I forgive your thoughts since Brandon's return. Write her tonight, and follow your letter to receive an affirmative answer in person. I promised that you might rely on me. She loves you."

"I never heard of such a thing in my life," said Jane. "Never!"

"He is certainly a most unaccountable man," said Sir Charles.

"I am glad, for my own sake, that he is not so black as he is painted," said Agatha. "You may believe every word of it, Mr Erskine. Be sure to do as he tells you. He is quite certain to be right."

"Pooh!" said Erskine, crumpling the telegram and thrusting it into his pocket as if it were not worth a second thought. Presently he slipped away, and did not reappear. When they were about to retire, Sir Charles asked a servant where he was.

"In the library, Sir Charles; writing."

They looked significantly at one another and went to bed without disturbing him.

CHAPTER XVIII

WHEN Gertrude found herself beside Trefusis in the Pullman, she wondered how she came to be travelling with him against her resolution, if not against her will. In the presence of two women scrutinizing her as if they suspected her of being there with no good purpose, a male passenger admiring her a little further off, her maid reading Trefusis's newspapers just out of earshot, an uninterested country gentleman looking glumly out of window, a city man preoccupied with the Economist, and a polite lady who refrained from staring but not from observing, she felt that she must not make a scene; yet she knew he had not come there to hold an ordinary conversation. Her doubt did not last long. He began promptly, and went to the point at once.

"What do you think of this engagement of mine?"

This was more than she could bear calmly. "What is it to me?" she said indignantly. "I have nothing to do with it."

"Nothing! You are a cold friend to me, then. I thought you one of the surest I possessed."

She moved as if about to look at him, but checked herself, closed her lips, and fixed her eyes on the vacant seat before her. The reproach he deserved was beyond her power of expression.

"I cling to that conviction still, in spite of Miss Lindsay's indifference to my affairs. But I confess I hardly know how to bring you into sympathy with me in this matter. In the first place, you have never been married, I have. In the next, you are much younger than I, in more respects than that of years. Very likely half your ideas on the subject are derived from fictions in which happy results are tacked on to conditions very ill calculated to produce them—which in real life hardly ever do produce them. If our friendship were a chapter in a novel, what would be the upshot of it? Why, I should marry you, or you break your heart at my treachery."

Gertrude moved her eyes as if she had some intention of taking to flight.

"But our relations being those of real life—far sweeter, after all—I never dreamed of marrying you, having gained and enjoyed your friendship without that eye to business which our nineteenth century keeps open even whilst it sleeps. You, being equally disinterested in your regard for me, do not think of breaking your heart, but you are, I suppose, a little hurt at my apparently meditating and resolving on such a serious step as marriage with Agatha without confiding my intention to you. And you punish me by telling me that you have nothing to do with it—that it is nothing to you. But I never meditated the step, and so had nothing to conceal from you. It was conceived and executed in less than a minute. Although my first marriage was a silly love match and a failure, I have always admitted to myself that I should marry again. A bachelor is a man who shirks responsibilities and duties; I seek them, and consider it my duty, with my monstrous superfluity of means, not to let the individualists outbreed me. Still, I was in no hurry, having other things to occupy me, and being fond of my bachelor freedom, and doubtful sometimes whether I had any right to bring more idlers into the world for the workers to feed. Then came the usual difficulty about the lady. I did not want a helpmeet; I can help myself. Nor did I expect to be loved devotedly, for the race has not yet evolved a man lovable on thorough acquaintance; even my self-love is neither thorough nor constant. I wanted a genial partner for domestic business, and Agatha struck me quite suddenly as being the nearest approach to what I desired that I was likely to find in the marriage market, where it is extremely hard to suit oneself, and where the likeliest bargains are apt to be snapped up by others if one hesitates too long in the hope of finding something better. I admire Agatha's courage and capability, and believe I shall be able to make her like me, and that the attachment so begun may turn into as close a union as is either healthy or necessary between two separate individuals. I may mistake her character, for I do not know her as I know you, and have scarcely enough faith in her as yet to tell her such things as I have told you. Still, there is a consoling dash of romance in the transaction. Agatha has charm. Do you not think so?"

Gertrude's emotion was gone. She replied with cool scorn, "Very romantic indeed. She is very fortunate."

Trefusis half laughed, half sighed with relief to find her so self-possessed. "It sounds like—and indeed is—the selfish calculation of a disilluded widower. You would not value such an offer, or envy the recipient of it?"

"No," said Gertrude, with quiet contempt.

"Yet there is some calculation behind every such offer. We marry to satisfy our needs, and the more reasonable our needs are, the more likely are we to get them satisfied. I see you are disgusted with me; I feared as much. You are the sort of woman to admit no excuse for my marriage except love—pure emotional love, blindfolding reason."

"I really do not concern myself—"

"Do not say so, Gertrude. I watch every step you take with anxiety; and I do not believe you are indifferent to the worthiness of my conduct. Believe me, love is an overrated passion; it would be irremediably discredited but that young people, and the romancers who live upon their follies, have a perpetual interest in rehabilitating it. No relation involving divided duties and continual intercourse between two people can subsist permanently on love alone. Yet love is not to be despised when it comes from a fine nature. There is a man who loves you exactly as you think I ought to love Agatha—and as I dont love her."

Gertrude's emotion stirred again, and her color rose. "You have no right to say these things now," she said.

"Why may I not plead the cause of another? I speak of Erskine." Her color vanished, and he continued, "I want you to marry him. When you are married you will understand me better, and our friendship, shaken just now, will be deepened; for I dare assure you, now that you can no longer misunderstand me, that no living woman is dearer to me than you. So much for the inevitable selfish reason. Erskine is a poor man, and in his comfortable poverty —save the mark—lies your salvation from the baseness of marrying for wealth and position; a baseness of which women of your class stand in constant peril. They court it; you must shun it. The man is honorable and loves you; he is young, healthy, and suitable. What more do you think the world has to offer you?"

"Much more, I hope. Very much more."

"I fear that the names I give things are not romantic enough. He is a poet. Perhaps he would be a hero if it were possible for a man to be a hero in this nineteenth century, which will be infamous in history as a time when the greatest advances in the power of man over nature only served to sharpen his greed and make famine its avowed minister. Erskine is at least neither a gambler nor a slave-driver at first hand; if he lives upon plundered labor he can no more help himself than I. Do not say that you hope for much more; but tell me, if you can, what more you have any chance of getting? Mind, I do not ask what more you desire; we all desire unutterable things. I ask you what more you can obtain!"

"I have not found Mr Erskine such a wonderful person as you seem to think him."

"He is only a man. Do you know anybody more wonderful?"

"Besides, my family might not approve."

"They most certainly will not. If you wish to please them, you must sell yourself to some rich vampire of the factories or great landlord. If you give yourself away to a poor poet who loves you, their disgust will be unbounded. If a woman wishes to honor her father and mother to their satisfaction nowadays she must dishonor herself."

"I do not understand why you should be so anxious for me to marry someone else?"

"Someone else?" said Trefusis, puzzled.

"I do not mean someone else," said Gertrude hastily, reddening. "Why should I marry at all?"

"Why do any of us marry? Why do I marry? It is a function craving fulfilment. If you do not marry betimes from choice, you will be driven to do so later on by the importunity of your suitors and of your family, and by weariness of the suspense that precedes a definite settlement of oneself. Marry generously. Do not throw yourself away or sell yourself; give yourself away. Erskine has as much at stake as you; and yet he offers himself fearlessly."

Gertrude raised her head proudly.

"It is true," continued Trefusis, observing the gesture with some anger, "that he thinks more highly of you than you deserve; but you, on the other hand, think too lowly of him. When you marry him you must save him from a cruel disenchantment by raising yourself to the level he fancies you have attained. This will cost you an effort, and the effort will do you good, whether it fail or succeed. As for him, he will find his just level in your estimation if your thoughts reach high enough to comprehend him at that level."

Gertrude moved impatiently.

"What!" he said quickly. "Are my long-winded sacrifices to the god of reason distasteful? I believe I am involuntarily making them so because I am jealous of the fellow after all. Nevertheless I am serious; I want you to get married; though I shall always have a secret grudge against the man who marries you. Agatha will suspect me of treason if you dont. Erskine will be a disappointed man if you dont. You will be moody, wretched, and— and unmarried if you dont."

Gertrude's cheeks flushed at the word jealous, and again at his mention of Agatha. "And if I do," she said bitterly, "what then?"

"If you do, Agatha's mind will be at ease, Erskine will be happy, and you! You will have sacrificed yourself, and will have the happiness which follows that when it is worthily done."

"It is you who have sacrificed me," she said, casting away her reticence, and looking at him for the first time during the conversation.

"I know it," he said, leaning towards her and half whispering the words. "Is not renunciation the beginning and the end of wisdom? I have sacrificed you rather than profane our friendship by asking you to share my whole life with me. You are unfit for that, and I have committed myself to another union, and am begging you to follow my example, lest we should tempt one another to a step which would soon prove to you how truly I tell you that you are unfit. I have never allowed you to roam through all the chambers of my consciousness, but I keep a sanctuary there for you alone, and will keep it inviolate for you always. Not even Agatha shall have the key; she must be content with the other rooms—the drawing room, the working room, the dining room, and so forth. They would not suit you; you would not like the furniture or the guests; after a time you would not like the master. Will you be content with the sanctuary?"

Gertrude bit her lip; tears came into her eyes. She looked imploringly at him. Had they been alone, she would have thrown herself into his arms and entreated him to disregard everything except their strong cleaving to one another.

"And will you keep a corner of your heart for me?"

She slowly gave him a painful look of acquiescence.

"Will you be brave, and sacrifice yourself to the poor man who loves you? He will save you from useless solitude, or from a worldly marriage—I cannot bear to think of either as your fate."

"I do not care for Mr Erskine," she said, hardly able to control her voice; "but I will marry him if you wish it."

"I do wish it earnestly, Gertrude."

"Then, you have my promise," she said, again with some bitterness.

"But you will not forget me? Erskine will have all but that—a tender recollection—nothing."

"Can I do more than I have just promised?"

"Perhaps so; but I am too selfish to be able to conceive anything more generous. Our renunciation will bind us to one another as our union could never have done."

They exchanged a long look. Then he took out his watch, and began to speak of the length of their journey, now nearly at an end. When they arrived in London the first person they recognized on the platform was Mr Jansenius.

"Ah! you got my telegram, I see," said Trefusis. "Many thanks for coming. Wait for me whilst I put this lady into a cab."

When the cab was engaged, and Gertrude, with her maid, stowed within, he whispered to her hurriedly:

"In spite of all, I have a leaden pain here" (indicating his heart). "You have been brave, and I have been wise. Do not speak to me, but remember that we are friends always and deeply."

He touched her hand, and turned to the cabman, directing him whither to drive. Gertrude shrank back into a corner of the vehicle as it departed. Then Trefusis, expanding his chest like a man just released from some cramping drudgery, rejoined Mr Jansenius.

"There goes a true woman," he said. "I have been persuading her to take the very best step open to her. I began by talking sense, like a man of honor, and kept at it for half an hour, but she would not listen to me. Then I talked romantic nonsense of the cheapest sort for five minutes, and she consented with tears in her eyes. Let us take this hansom. Hi! Belsize Avenue. Yes; you sometimes have to answer a woman according to her womanishness, just as you have to answer a fool according to his folly. Have you ever made up your mind, Jansenius, whether I am an unusually honest man, or one of the worst products of the social organization I spend all my energies in assailing—an infernal scoundrel, in short?"

"Now pray do not be absurd," said Mr Jansenius. "I wonder at a man of your ability behaving and speaking as you sometimes do."

"I hope a little insincerity, when meant to act as chloroform—to save a woman from feeling a wound to her vanity—is excusable. By the bye, I must send a couple of telegrams from the first post office we pass. Well, sir, I am going to marry Agatha, as I sent you word. There was only one other single man and one other virgin down at Brandon Beeches, and they are as good as engaged. And so——

> " 'Jack shall have Jill,
>   Nought shall go ill,
>   The man shall have his mare again;
>   And all shall be well.' "

APPENDIX

LETTER TO THE AUTHOR FROM MR SIDNEY TREFUSIS

My Dear Sir—I find that my friends are not quite satisfied with
the account you have given of them in your clever novel entitled
An Unsocial Socialist. You already understand that I consider it
my duty to communicate my whole history, without reserve, to
whoever may desire to be guided or warned by my experience,
and that I have no sympathy whatever with the spirit in which
one of the ladies concerned recently told you that her affairs were
no business of yours or of the people who read your books. When
you asked my permission some years ago to make use of my
story, I at once said that you would be perfectly justified in giving
it the fullest publicity whether I consented or not, provided only
that you were careful not to falsify it for the sake of artistic effect.
Now, whilst cheerfully admitting that you have done your best
to fulfil that condition, I cannot help feeling that, in presenting
the facts in the guise of fiction, you have, in spite of yourself,
shewn them in a false light. Actions described in novels are
judged by a romantic system of morals as fictitious as the actions
themselves. The traditional parts of this system are, as Cervantes
tried to shew, for the chief part barbarous and obsolete: the
modern additions are largely due to the novel readers and writers
of our own century—most of them half-educated women, re-
belliously slavish, superstitious, sentimental, full of the intense
egotism fostered by their struggle for personal liberty, and, outside their families, with absolutely no social sentiment except love.
Meanwhile, man, having fought and won his fight for this personal liberty, only to find himself a more abject slave than before,
is turning with loathing from his egotist's dream of independence
to the collective interests of society, with the welfare of which he
now perceives his own happiness to be inextricably bound up.
But man in this phase (would that all had reached it!) has not yet
leisure to write or read novels. In noveldom woman still sets the
moral standard, and to her the males, who are in full revolt

254

against the acceptance of the infatuation of a pair of lovers as the highest manifestation of the social instinct, and against the restriction of the affections within the narrow circle of blood relationship, and of the political sympathies within frontiers, are to her what she calls heartless brutes. That is exactly what I have been called by readers of your novel; and that, indeed, is exactly what I am, judged by the fictitious and feminine standard of morality. Hence some critics have been able plausibly to pretend to take the book as a satire on Socialism. It may, for all I know, have been so intended by you. Whether or no, I am sorry you made a novel of my story; for the effect has been almost as if you had misrepresented me from beginning to end.

At the same time, I acknowledge that you have stated the facts, on the whole, with scrupulous fairness. You have, indeed, flattered me very strongly by representing me as constantly thinking of and for other people, whereas the rest think of themselves alone; but on the other hand you have contradictorily called me "unsocial," which is certainly the last adjective I should have expected to find in the neighborhood of my name. I deny, it is true, that what is now called "society" is society in any real sense; and my best wish for it is that it may dissolve too rapidly to make it worth the while of those who are "not in society" to facilitate its dissolution by violently pounding it into small pieces. But no reader of An Unsocial Socialist needs to be told how, by the exercise of a certain considerate tact (which on the outside, perhaps, seems the opposite of tact) I have contrived to maintain genial terms with men and women of all classes, even those whose opinions and political conduct seemed to me most dangerous.

However, I do not here propose to go fully into my own position, lest I should seem tedious, and be accused, not for the first time, of a propensity to lecture: a reproach which comes naturally enough from persons whose conceptions are never too wide to be expressed within the limits of a sixpenny telegram. I shall confine myself to correcting a few misapprehensions which have, I am told, arisen among readers who from inveterate habit cannot bring the persons and events of a novel into any relation with the actual conditions of life.

In the first place, then, I desire to say that Mrs Erskine is not dead of a broken heart. Erskine and I and our wives are very much in and out at one another's houses; and I am therefore in a position to declare that Mrs Erskine, having escaped by her marriage from the vile caste in which she was relatively poor and artificially unhappy and ill-conditioned, is now, as the pretty wife of an art-critic, relatively rich, as well as pleasant, active, and in sound health. Her chief trouble, as far as I can judge, is the impossibility of shaking off her distinguished relatives, who furtively quit their abject splendour to drop in upon her for dinner and a little genuine human society much oftener than is convenient to poor Erskine. She has taken a patronizing fancy to her father, the Admiral, who accepts her condescension gratefully as age brings more and more home to him the futility of his social position. She has also, as might have been expected, become an extreme advocate of Socialism; and indeed, being in a great hurry for the new order of things, looks on me as a lukewarm disciple because I do not propose to interfere with the slowly grinding mill of Evolution, and effect the change by one tremendous stroke from the united and awakened people (for such she—vainly, alas! —believes the proletariat already to be).

As to my own marriage, some have asked sarcastically whether I ran away again or not; others, whether it has been a success. These are foolish questions. My marriage has turned out much as I expected it would. I find that my wife's views on the subject vary with the circumstances under which they are expressed.

I have now to make one or two comments on the impressions conveyed by the style of your narrative. Sufficient prominence has not, in my opinion, been given to the extraordinary destiny of my father, the true hero of a nineteenth-century romance. I, who have seen society reluctantly accepting works of genius for nothing from men of extraordinary gifts, and at the same time helplessly paying my father millions, and submitting to monstrous mortgages of its future production, for a few directions as to the most business-like way of manufacturing and selling cotton, cannot but wonder, as I prepare my income-tax returns, whether society was mad to sacrifice thus to him and to me. He was the man with power to buy, to build, to choose, to endow, to sit on committees and adjudicate upon designs, to make his own terms for placing anything on a sound business footing. He was hated, envied, sneered at for his low origin, reproached for his ignorance; yet nothing would pay unless he liked or pretended to like it. Looking round at our buildings, our statues, our pictures, our newspapers, our domestic interiors, our books, our vehicles, our morals, our manners, our statutes, and our religion, I see his hand everywhere; for they were all made or modified to please him. Those which did not please him failed commercially: he would not buy them, nor sell them, nor countenance them; and except through him, as "master of the industrial situation," nothing could be bought, or sold, or countenanced. The landlord could do nothing with his acres except let them to him; the capitalist's hoard rotted and dwindled until it was lent to him; the worker's muscles and brain were impotent until sold to him. What king's son would not exchange with me—the son of the Great Employer—the Merchant Prince? No wonder they proposed to imprison me for treason when, by applying my inherited business talent, I put forward a plan for securing his full services to society for a few hundreds a year. But pending the adoption of my plan, do not describe him contemptuously as a vulgar tradesman. Industrial kingship, the only real kingship of our century, was his by divine right of his turn for business; and I, his son, bid you respect the crown whose revenues I inherit. If you dont, my friend, your book wont pay.

I hear, with some surprise, that the kindness of my conduct to Henrietta (my first wife, you recollect) has been called in question: why, I do not exactly know. Undoubtedly I should not have married her; but it is waste of time to criticize the judgment of a young man in love. Since I do not approve of the usual plan of neglecting and avoiding a spouse without ceasing to keep up appearances, I cannot for the life of me see what else I could have done than vanish when I found out my mistake. It is but a short-sighted policy to wait for the mending of matters that are bound to get worse. As the notion that her death was my fault is sheer unreason on the face of it, I need no exculpation on that score; but I must disclaim the credit of having borne her death like a philosopher. I ought to have done so; but the truth is that I was greatly affected at the moment, the proof being that I and Jansenius (the only other person who cared) behaved in a most unbecoming fashion, as men invariably do when they are really upset. Perfect propriety at a death is seldom achieved except by the undertaker, who has the advantage of being free from emotion.

Your rigmarole (if you will excuse the word) about the tombstone gives quite a wrong idea of my attitude on that occasion. I stayed away from the funeral for reasons which are, I should think, sufficiently obvious and natural, but which you somehow seem to have missed. Granted that my fancy for Hetty was only a cloud of illusions, still I could not, within a few days of her sudden death, go in cold blood to take part in a grotesque and heathenish mummery over her coffin. I should have broken out and strangled somebody. But on every other point I—weakly enough —sacrificed my own feelings to those of Jansenius. I let him have his funeral, though I object to funerals and to the practice of sepulture. I consented to a monument, although there is, to me, no more bitterly ridiculous outcome of human vanity than the blocks raised to tell posterity that John Smith, or Jane Jackson, late of this parish, was born, lived, and died worth enough money to pay a mason to distinguish their bones from those of the unrecorded millions. To gratify Jansenius I waived this objection, and only interfered to save him from being fleeced and fooled by an unnecessary West End middleman, who, as likely as not, would have eventually employed the very man to whom I gave the job. Even the epitaph was not mine. If I had had my way I should have written: "Henrietta Jansenius was born on such a date, married a man named Trefusis, and died on such another date; and now what does it matter whether she did or not?" The whole notion conveyed in the book that I rode roughshod over everybody in the affair, and only consulted my own feelings, is the very reverse of the truth.

As to the tomfoolery down at Brandon's, which ended in Erskine and myself marrying the young lady visitors there, I can only congratulate you on the determination with which you have striven to make something like a romance out of such very thin material. I cannot say that I remember it all exactly as you have described it: my wife declares flatly there is not a word of truth in it as far as she is concerned; and Mrs Erskine steadily refuses to read the book.

On one point I must acknowledge that you have proved yourself a master of the art of fiction. What Hetty and I said to one another that day when she came upon me in the shrubbery at Alton College was known only to us two. She never told it to anyone; and I soon forgot it. All due honor, therefore, to the ingenuity with which you have filled the hiatus, and shewn the state of affairs between us by a discourse on "surplus value," cribbed from an imperfect report of one of my public lectures, and from the pages of Karl Marx! If you were an economist I should condemn you for confusing economic with ethical considerations, and for your uncertainty as to the function which my father got his start by performing. But as you are only a novelist, I compliment you heartily on your clever little *pasticcio*, adding, however, that as an account of what actually passed between myself and Hetty, it is the wildest romance ever penned. Wickens's boy was far nearer the mark.

In conclusion, allow me to express my regret that you can find no better employment for your talent than the writing of novels. The first literary result of the foundation of our industrial system upon the profits of piracy and slave-trading was Shakespear. It is our misfortune that the sordid misery and hopeless horror of his view of man's destiny is still so appropriate to English society that we even today regard him as not for an age, but for all time. But the poetry of despair will not outlive despair itself. Your nineteenth-century novelists are only the tail of Shakespear. Dont tie yourself to it: it is fast wriggling into oblivion.—I am, dear sir, yours truly,   SIDNEY TREFUSIS.

Give them the pleasure of choosing

Book Tokens can be bought and exchanged at most bookshops in Great Britain and Ireland.